Critical A
Eileen Dre

NOTHING PERSONAL

"Dreyer clearly knows the territory and gives us some moments of fine dark humor in the wards."
—*San Francisco Examiner & Chronicle*

"Readers will certainly get their money's worth from this book. Not only is it a page turner, but its earthy portrayal of life in a large hospital stays in the mind."
—*The Drood Review of Mystery*

"[A] mesmerizing new thriller by [a] talented and irrepressible author. . . . Filled with heart-stopping suspense, ironic humor, and some hard-edged truths about the current medical system that are guaranteed to keep you on the edge of your seat to the very last page."
—*Romantic Times*

"Has everything that one could ask for—a fast-moving plot, a dandy murder mystery, and a cast of eccentric characters that are reminiscent of inmates in an asylum . . . Blends just enough romance into her psychological suspense thriller to produce a first-class reading experience."
—*The Talisman*

PLEASE TURN THE PAGE FOR
MORE RAVES FOR EILEEN DREYER

IF LOOKS COULD KILL

"A sharp and witty thriller with a twist. This one has it all, a heroine readers will cheer, crackling dialogue, and enough suspense to keep you up all night. Dreyer has a deft touch with characterization. She tells a compelling, wonderfully exciting story that readers will devour in one sitting. A great read."

—Jayne Ann Krentz

"Adroitly crafted and ingeniously plotted . . . This one is a spellbinder."

—John Lutz,
author of *Single White Female* and *Hot*

"A gritty, funny, compassionate novel about the dark side of the human psyche."

—Ann Maxwell

"For anyone who loves a taut, impossible-to-put-down thriller, this is the book for you. Eileen Dreyer once again demonstrates why she is rapidly becoming a master of the suspense genre."

—*Rave Reviews*

"Gripping . . . Generous helpings of mystery, horror, and romance blend in a delectably rich treat."

—*The Drood Review of Mystery*

A MAN TO DIE FOR

"A wicked prescription guaranteed to give you sleepless nights."

—Nora Roberts

"Eileen Dreyer creates the sort of skin-crawling suspense that will leave her readers looking with a wild and wary eye upon anyone at the other end of a stethoscope."

—Elizabeth George

"Dreyer . . . levels a roguish sense of humor at the medical establishment in this entertaining romantic thriller."

—*Publishers Weekly*

"Hold on to your hats and get ready for the scare of your life as Eileen Dreyer makes a courageous emergency room nurse the target of a fiendish serial killer. . . . In a triumph of superb writing, Ms. Dreyer keeps us in a turmoil of agonizing suspense. . . . The utterly authentic ambience of a busy emergency room is an added plus, providing biting humor and acerbic dialogue to create a bevy of unforgettable characters. All things considered, you just might want to postpone that doctor's appointment for a while."

—*Romantic Times*

Books by Eileen Dreyer

Bad Medicine
Nothing Personal
If Looks Could Kill
A Man to Die For

Available from HarperPaperbacks

Bad Medicine

EILEEN DREYER

HarperPaperbacks
A Division of HarperCollins*Publishers*

This is a work of fiction. The characters, incidents, and dialogues are products of the author's imagination and are not to be construed as real. Any resemblance to actual events or persons, living or dead, is entirely coincidental.

HarperPaperbacks *A Division of* HarperCollins*Publishers*
10 East 53rd Street, New York, N.Y. 10022

Cover illustration by Kam Mak

First printing: July 1995

Printed in the United States of America

HarperPaperbacks and colophon are trademarks of HarperCollins*Publishers*

❖ 10 9 8 7 6 5 4 3 2

ACKNOWLEDGMENTS

For help above and beyond the call. On the technical side: Dr. Mary Case and Mary Fran Ernst of the St. Louis County Medical Examiner's Office, who taught me how to be a good investigator. Lt. John Podolak and his always lovely wife Michelle, who never let me get away with faulty procedure. Dr. John Ponzillo, RPh, Pharm D., with special mention for coming up with the names for my drug. Always, of course, to the nurses out there who still share their stories (with special mention to Susan from McGurk's for crack cocaine) and fight the good fight.

Any errors in the work are mine. As to the caves beneath St. Louis: there are caves, just not where I put them.

On a professional side: A special thank-you to all the booksellers and distributors who have been out there hand-selling me when nobody knew who the heck I was, or just what it was I was doing. I couldn't have better friends in the industry. Unfortunately, I'm too big a coward to give individual names, for fear that I'm going to forget somebody. But you know who you are.

On the personal side: it's redundant, but thank you Karyn for seeing the way when I couldn't. Thank you Carolyn and Karen for the unflagging support and enthusiasm, even when we switch ball games in the sixth inning. And always, to Rick, for not only letting me fly, but dogfight. What more could a girl ask for?

He is not an honest man who has burned his tongue on the soup and does not tell the company that the soup is hot.

—Yugoslavian proverb

Tell the truth and run.

—Ibid.

✦ Prologue ✦

NOBODY NOTICED THAT there was something wrong with the mayor's press conference. It was a small thing, and the press was preoccupied with the breaking airline strike story at the airport, not to mention the ongoing investigation into morals charges against the Speaker of the House, on which most of them had sizeable bets. So they all slumped in the stifling room in the city hall waiting for Mayor Martell Williamson to announce who was finally going to be given the contract to open the casino on the St. Louis riverfront, and not one of them noticed who was missing.

The citizens of the St. Louis metropolitan area didn't notice, even though they were being dished up the news live with lunch. Most St. Louisans found politics tiresome—especially city politics. It wasn't even as if it was that important an announcement. During the two years the Board of Aldermen had carried on their public and often bitter debate over the contract, some thirty riverboats had already set up business on the nearby Missouri and Meramec rivers, which were much preferable places to park and wander than north St. Louis anyway.

Besides, it was hot out, and the people of St.

Louis were far more interested in their weather than their politics. If they were even home to watch the news, instead of lurking half-submerged in one of the neighborhood pools to escape the humidity or at the stadium watching the Cardinals warm up against the Phillies, they were busy refilling their iced tea during the press conference so they wouldn't miss Wally the Weatherman telling them just when they could expect a break from the two solid weeks of hundred degree weather.

Harry McGivers and Peg Ryan would have noticed. Unfortunately they were already seated at the Missouri Athletic Club Grille about a mile away, celebrating the news with their favorite scotch and pharmaceutical chaser as they waited for the star of the story to return from the press conference and fill them in.

That was the problem. The star of the story wasn't there. Up on Hodiamont Street where she lived with her mother, Pearl Johnson had the television turned to the news conference as she drifted off to sleep. Pearl was dressed in her best nightgown and robe, buttoned neatly to her chin, her hair brushed out, and her lipstick on. Her door was locked, and her Bible was at her side. Her pill bottles were lined up along her nightstand, and they were empty, each and every one of them.

Pearl knew what was wrong with the press conference. She was listening to her betrayal. But she wasn't really paying attention. She was too busy dying.

✦ Chapter 1 ✦

THE MANNER OF DEATH was not that unusual for St. Louis, but the tattoo certainly was.

"Incredible," the ER physician said as he considered the man laid out on his cart.

"Impressive," the respiratory therapist agreed.

A roomful of people nodded in awe.

Considering how busy the shift was running at the Grace Hospital emergency department on this hot summer night, there was quite a crowd in the trauma room, even for the extent of the injury evident along the left side of the victim's forehead. Possible gunshot wound had been the call. Definite gunshot wound was the diagnosis, as evidenced by the police report, the absence of a good portion of skin and bone from the young man's left temple, and the scattering of suspicious opaque objects visible throughout the man's skull films that were even now displayed on the viewer at the other end of the room.

But the attention at the moment was not on the method of injury or its obvious effects on the patient's cardiovascular system, which had shut down operations shortly after the introduction of a concentrated load of buckshot to his face. It was instead focused on the sight uncovered when one of the trauma nurses threw back the ambulance sheet in a vain effort to insert a Foley catheter into the patient's bladder to assist in the resuscitation efforts. The nurse, a new graduate without much experience in the real world, let out a squeal. From that moment on, the focus of the trauma team wandered from the ABCs of resuscitation to the XYs of the chromosome.

For there, tattooed along the shaft of the victim's penis, ran brilliant flames of orange, blue, and red.

"Redefines the term hot rod," one of the paramedics offered.

"Smokin' good time."

The med nurse snorted. "Probably closer to flaming dick, you ask me."

"It's better than the question mark," the emergency department physician admitted.

All nodded, having seen the question mark no more than a week earlier under similar circumstances. A simple blue tattoo etched along the shaft of another once-working penis, it had raised, if nothing else, a host of questions.

"Is it a statement?" they'd all asked upon seeing it. Maybe a gang identifier. A gay identifier. A message to the owner's date, or a prediction of his talents. That young man with the tattoo had ended up being shipped to the medical examiner's office without answering any of the questions.

This time, the crew didn't think there was any question at all about what the statement was.

"Time of death?" somebody called.

"I think," the physician answered, "the proper term would be flameout."

The nurse nodded agreeably. "Time of flameout?"

"11:02 P.M."

"Do we know what MIG managed to shoot this young flier down?"

"Enemy pilot is in custody," one of the cops obliged as he recorded the time in his notebook.

Positioned by the door so that she could watch the entire room, Molly Burke made a similar notation on the code flow sheet that recorded this action for medical and legal posterity. "Would that be *his* wife or *her* husband?" she asked.

Molly was a petite woman with short mahogany hair, restless hands, and a wealth of crow's-feet crowding the edges of sharp brown eyes. Older than almost everyone else in the room by at least a decade, she considered herself an optimist because sights like the one on the cart still surprised her.

"His wife," the cop said. "Must have suspected something, because the girlfriend says she never heard the shotgun being racked. The wife must have locked and loaded before she broke open the door."

Molly nodded absently, a forearm up to wipe damp hair off her forehead. "I like a woman who thinks ahead. Are you going to have somebody break the news to her that he didn't make it?"

The cop laughed, a dry, knowing sound. "You kiddin'? She told us. And I quote, 'Now that whore-fuckin', scum-sucking son of a bitch ain't gonna hit me no more.' "

Molly looked at the remains on the cart, imagined the scene. Nodded. "Okay."

"I don't guess he's a lawyer," somebody said hopefully. They had had two lawyers come in dead in the last week. Since everything tended to run in threes, the staff was particularly interested in making this hat trick. Even though the other two had been suicides, no one really minded murder rounding out the count. Lawyers were almost as popular in emergency departments as the man who invented managed-care insurance.

Molly considered the victim's long hair, bad teeth, and cracked, stained fingernails, and shook her head. "Not unless he went to the Wal-Mart School of Law."

"It's possible," the physician retorted. "I'm pretty sure that's where my divorce lawyer trained."

"You know how to tell a lawyer from a vulture?" Molly asked, going back to her notes. "Removable wing tips."

"Molly's ex-husband was a lawyer," the physician told the chuckling crowd.

"No," Molly demurred with feeling. "My ex-lawyer was a lawyer."

There was nothing left to do for the body on the cart except report his demise to the death investigator on duty for the city. Still, not any of the twenty or so people crowded into the littered, humid trauma room could seem to move. The intercom announced the arrival of two new patients, and outside the work lane door a security guard pounded down the hall. It wasn't enough to incite the team to action. Sasha Petrovich, on the other hand, was. Leaning her considerable blond self in the door, the evening charge nurse dispatched a withering glare on the assembled crew.

"I give up," she said. "We're posing for a commemorative stamp?"

"Look," the respiratory therapist said in explanation.

Sasha looked. Then she lifted an expressive eyebrow in comment. "If he were Russian," she said simply, "he'd have had room to include the logs and fireplace in that picture. Now, everybody come out and play."

It wasn't the order so much as the tone of voice. People began pouring out of the room like water over a dam break. The rookie nurse pulled the sheet back over the patient and the physician handed Molly the braided blue ball cap that designated him Code Captain, thereby officially ending his responsibilities. Molly set the hat on its official place on the crash cart, gathered her paperwork, and followed him out the door. She was the only one to catch Sasha grinning.

Whenever Molly thought of the ER, she thought of noise. Not sights or smells or actions. Just constant, ululating cacophony, like a rock concert. Tonight was the same. Babies wailing, kids on crack shouting, phones ringing, radios crackling, sirens worrying at the darkness outside. Half a dozen arguments raging along the hallways so the whole of it sounded like a Mozart octet on acid, everybody singing a different song at the same time, and you were supposed to figure out what was going on.

The difference was, Mozart kept it on key. And Mozart would never have written a tune for The Diver.

Molly stopped dead in her tracks at the distinctive sound. "Oh, great," she said with a scowl. "The backup band's here."

The Diver was one of their regulars, an old black man who lived in condemned housing down the road and rolled in regularly about two weeks after the welfare checks came in and his supply of Thunderbird ran out. The Diver made a constant, God-awful whooping noise, like the claxons on submarines, that never slowed, never stopped until they managed to turf him upstairs to the floor where they could snow him until they could safely get him back out the door again.

"And he's asking for you to do harmony," Sasha informed her. "We also got the call from City 235. There's a lot of popping and banging over by Terrell Street. We should be getting business anytime soon."

Molly grimaced. "Just in time for me to get the

paperwork when I change into my investigator's tights. What a happy thought."

Molly, a twenty-year veteran of the emergency wars, was also the newest part-time death investigator in the city, which meant that after a code team walked out of a room like the one in which Mr. O'Halloran still lay, they called her to figure out what to do next. Her shift tonight began thirty minutes after she escaped this circus at eleven-thirty. If she was lucky.

Sasha was not impressed. "Serves you right for trying to run with the big dogs. The big dogs have more paperwork and worse hours."

"And lousier pay," Molly agreed, spreading the paperwork she'd just collected across the nearest desk so she could finish this mess before diving into another.

"Then why do you do it?" Lorenzo demanded as he unloaded a nest of EKG strips onto the desk from the code. Lorenzo, Molly's favorite tech, was about a hundred pounds stretched over almost seven feet, ebony dark, and on his way to med school, courtesy of a fiery grandmother and a sensible set of Jesuits who had pressed him with a full scholarship. "Isn't working here hassle enough? You got to go out looking for trouble?"

Molly grinned. "I just like riding around in that big van that says MEDICAL EXAMINER'S OFFICE on it. Guys whistle at me at all the stoplights."

Rearranging name tags on the flow board over Molly's head, Sasha lowered herself to a snort. "You just like hanging around strapping young men with guns."

Molly dealt paperworks across her desk like cards. "No. If that were the case, I'd hang around with the highway patrol. Now, *they're* strapping." Especially since Molly barely topped five-one in her tennis shoes, and Missouri Highway Patrol officers seemed to have a height requirement of at least six-foot-four. Molly spent a lot of time at accident scenes looking up noses.

An X-ray tech scuttled by, arms filled with large manila brown folders. "Molly, your lady in four's back from X ray. She needs to be cleaned up again."

Molly didn't bother to look up. "I'll pay you a dollar to do it for me, Suze."

"Not if she were rich and you were famous. You goin' with us tomorrow?"

A good percentage of the evening shift had booked a ride on one of the riverboats to go gambling the next night. Molly was not one of them.

"Thanks, no, hon. I owe enough money as it is. I'll wait until they untangle all the politics downtown and build that new complex by the riverfront."

"You mean when hell freezes over," Sasha offered.

Molly tossed a chart to the surgeon and collected lab reports on two of her other patients.

"It's untangled," Suze retorted.

Molly looked up, surprised. "What do you mean? I didn't hear anything."

"This very afternoon. The mayor gave in and awarded the contract to that hotel group from Chicago. They're going to break ground for the casino in October."

Molly hadn't heard a thing. But then, Molly had been here since noon, and hiding in her backyard before that. "Call me when it's built," she told the X-ray tech.

"Spoilsport."

"I prefer the term *realist.* Who's death investigator on?" Molly yelled across to the secretary's station.

"You work there," Karla snapped back. "Don't you have the schedule?"

"I have *my* schedule, and I'm not on it till midnight."

"It's only another hour. We won't tell anybody you forgot to call."

"Karla!"

Karla made it a point to answer in a near-whisper. "Vic Fellows."

Molly groaned. Great. Mr. We Never Have Enough Paperwork himself. An ex–homicide cop with an old ax to grind, Vic spent his time making sure that he came up with one more question to ask than anyone had the answer for. Just what Molly needed right now.

"Call him!" she yelled anyway, deciding that she wasn't about to let him off the hook just because he annoyed her. The way this night was shaping up, she'd have enough forms of her own to fill out before the end of her own eight-hour shift down at the medical examiner's office.

To the right of the secretary's station, the radio sputtered to life. "Grace, this is City 235. Grace, 235 calling Code Three."

"Shit," three people snapped in unison.

More trauma. Gunshots, undoubtedly. Summer in the city.

Molly needed something for the headache she was brewing. Sasha strolled for the sputtering equipment as if answering a social call, and Suze trotted on back to X ray before anybody could ask her to help out.

From the other end of the hall, Lance Frost tossed a paper airplane that skimmed the top of Molly's hair and stuck into the corner of the PDR at her elbow.

"I'm telling you, Molly," he prodded, just as he had all evening. Just as he had for the four years Molly had known him. "It's easy money."

Dr. Lance Frost, a veteran of more ERs than Molly,

had never quite made his certification in Emergency Medicine. He didn't see the need, since his fortune would surely come from any one of the great and fantastic money-making ideas Lance was always conjuring up while lying in the call room. Considering the disproportionate relationship of his girth to his wallet, it was well-known that Lance was better at the position than the inspiration.

Lance also had the questionable distinction of being known as Chicken Soup behind his back for his distinctive brand of body odor, which was cleared up about as often as his credit rating.

"Dr. Frost's Fishy Food," he said, rubbing at his impressive belly like a free-market Buddha. "Just think of it."

"No thanks," Molly answered without looking up. "I'm doing Chinese tonight."

That was if she ever ate. If things didn't slow down out there, she'd be driving the medical examiner's van through the drive-up window at McDonald's on the way to answer a homicide call. She was hungry, she ached to her hips from running the halls, and she didn't imagine she was going to get any time off until at least dawn.

"Come on, Molly," Lance Frost wheedled, as if she'd ever given in before. "I already have the perfect formula, and fish are going to be the pets of the future. We can make a fortune. All we need is salesmanship."

"I don't want a fortune, Lance."

Lance laughed as if Molly were the funniest thing he'd ever heard. "I'm serious. Come on, you're single. You have that expendable cash and no one to spend it on but me. I mean, you're not gonna do something dumb at your age like have kids or anything, are you?"

Filling in the particulars on the ME's questionnaire,

Molly ignored him. Lance wasn't cruel, just thoughtless. A fine trait in a trauma physician. No, Molly wasn't going to have kids or anything. But that wasn't a subject she broached with anyone, especially Lance Frost.

"I thought you were investing in that new experimental drug the hospital's testing," she said without looking up. "You know, the one that will make Prozac obsolete."

Of course, every new antidepressant that hit the market was touted as the one that was going to make Prozac obsolete, but that was beside the point with Lance.

"I'm gonna be in gravy in a year," he said. "I would have preferred to be their front man. You know, the team researcher who gives the official party line to the medical masses about how wonderful the product is in exchange for only a small fortune and free travel. But I didn't get into psych fast enough. Besides, fish food is fast return on your money. And I don't have to share it with corporate bigs."

"Maybe next time, Lance."

"What's wrong with a little success, Molly?" he demanded, seriously offended by her disapproval. "Tell me that. Why shouldn't we get ours?"

"Molly doesn't have any money," Karla insisted from behind her protective barrier. "She's got all that legal stuff to pay off, Lance. You know that."

Karla, on the other hand, *was* cruel. She didn't like Molly. She didn't like nurses or doctors or anybody who gave her work or made more money than she. As always, Molly ignored her too. The lawsuit was another matter entirely.

A little more than a year ago, an emergency physician at a prestigious county hospital had decided that hiding in the bathroom would keep him from having to hear about the new patient Molly wanted him to see. It had. In the end, it hadn't mattered one bit to the jury that Molly had done everything but break down the bathroom door to get to him. The patient's family's lawyer had convinced them that it had been just as much Molly's fault as everybody else's that the patient had eventually had a stroke and died, even though she'd come in complaining of abdominal pain.

"Oh, God," Lance whispered. "That's right. The lawsuit." Said like other people said *cancer*. "Where does it stand?"

"Stand?" Molly retorted easily. "It doesn't have to stand. For that kind of money, it can sit wherever it wants."

"Vic Fellows, line four," Karla called out.

From one treat to another. Molly picked up the phone. "Hello, Vic. It's Molly."

"You couldn't have just shelved this until you came on?" was his answer. "For God's sake, it's not even an hour."

Molly ignored that too, and told him the particulars of the case. As investigator, he would take all the information, make sure the body got to the city morgue, and then coordinate the case with the medical examiner, the lab, and the police. Vic spent the time while Molly spoke making disparaging grunts and sighs. That is, until she gave him the capper.

"He has a tattoo, Vic."

Silence. Molly knew just where to get Vic. He was the tattoo collector on the team. A necessary position, a vital clue in identification of some of their less-obvious victims. Vic just enjoyed his task a little too much.

"Better than the question mark?"

Vic had taken to the question mark like Champollion to the Rosetta Stone, certain it meant something they couldn't fathom. He'd been driving everybody nuts with it.

"Easier to figure out."

"What is it?" he demanded.

Molly thought of the double take the trauma surgeon had done at the unveiling and smiled. "You'll see."

"All right, then," he said, suddenly enthusiastic.

Well, Molly figured. Everybody had to have a hobby. She would have preferred porcelain frogs, herself.

"Method of death?"

Not a question Vic should be asking at this point. Not one Molly should technically answer. The method of death, by what vehicle the victim died, was pretty obvious, although it should never go in a death investigator's report that way. When she was a nurse, Molly had a lot more leeway to say "Possible gunshot wound to the forehead." As a death investigator, she could only go so far as, "four centimeter defect to left temporal region of skull with tissue and bone loss, exposed brain matter." The city figured that since it paid those big bucks to have a forensic pathologist on staff, it should give the doctor the honor of classifying that defect as being the result of a bullet. Or pellets, as the case might be.

"Big load of buckshot to the left temporal artery," she said anyway, hoping Vic would have the sense not to make that an official statement.

The next question, the only other one of interest to the Medical Examiner's Office, was manner of death. The manner of death was defined as why that tissue and bone was missing. What—or who—put that gun to that forehead. The four basic classifications were natural, accidental, homicide, suicide. And not one should be determined before all results were in.

"Manner of death?" Vic asked, just as Molly knew he would. Another question that was not theirs to answer.

"Woman scorned in the first degree."

Woman Scorned, of course, being the subheading B to manner type three.

Vic took it like a professional. "I hate when that happens."

"Molly!"

Molly whipped around at the sharp sound of Sasha's voice.

"We need your room. Peds is bustin' out, and we gotta eight-year-old coming in. Drive-by to the neck."

"Send transport for our man," Molly told Vic, who was already sputtering in protest, not yet having heard what the victim had for lunch, or what his mother had worn to her wedding. "Gotta go."

"Stick him in holding," she informed Sasha, already on her feet, adrenaline honing the edge of the anxiety that always lived in her chest.

"I've already got The Diver in there."

"Well, he's the only one in here who won't notice that the body next to him isn't breathing. And would you ask one of the other techs to clean up my lady in twelve? I'll treat 'em to a drink later. Lorenzo!"

"On my way!" he yelled, hands already full of fluids and IV lines as he loped toward the room.

Molly was going to have to get in to see Gene soon. She just couldn't take it like this if the rest of the summer didn't slow up. She needed to sleep. It was worse this time than it had ever been. But then, there were more kids dying this summer, and that was what always set her off. At least, that was what her psychiatrist told her. And Gene hadn't been wrong about her yet.

But for now, she ran.

"Lorenzo, get us set up," she instructed, bringing her paperwork right back into the still-cluttered trauma room and pulling out more. Knowing right in her gut that she was going to be in charge of this little boy, both now and later when she changed clothes and jobs. It made her want to vomit.

She waited to do that until it was all over. Right between the time they pronounced Tyrell donor organs and the moment Molly had to assume both her position as trauma nurse and death investigator and walk into the quiet room to tell his young mother and his young grandmother that Tyrell had been sacrificed to a gang feud.

It was where Lance Frost found her. "Molly?" he called through the door to the john. "What are you doing in there?"

Molly straightened from where she'd emptied her empty stomach into the can and grabbed a couple of paper towels. "Making my editorial comment for the evening."

"Well, check your watch, because we have another gift for you out here."

Molly checked her watch. It read that she'd been on the city's payroll for some twenty minutes.

"This isn't any DOA," she said five minutes later as she stood in the doorway to trauma room six, where another small crowd had gathered. "She was DRT. LLT."

On the cart lay a large, probably middle-aged black woman in a state of almost complete rigor mortis, which meant two things. She was definitely Molly's problem, and she definitely should not have been brought into an ER. Not when she was stiff enough to have been lying in one position for at least ten hours.

So she hadn't been DOA, which meant dead on arrival. She'd been DRT. LLT. Paramedic terminology for Dead Right There. Long, Long Time.

"I really appreciate your bringing my work to me," Molly said, still drying her hands as she turned on the very nervous paramedic team. "But I prefer to see only my almost-dead bodies here. The really dead ones do better at the morgue. It's less confusing that way."

"You think I was gonna argue with that family and tell 'em I wasn't gonna bring their little girl here?" one of the paramedics demanded. "Don't you know who that is?"

The truth was that Molly hadn't even bothered to look. She'd quickly scanned the scene, taken in the body, the nightclothes, the stack of brand-new empty pill bottles that shared the Mayo stand with an empty bottle of gin, and she'd come up with an assumption of suicide.

Her first thought had been that if they had any more dead bodies in this ER tonight, they were going to have to take out a mortuary permit. Her second was that she'd rather wade through a pile of trauma victims than one suicide. She hated suicides.

"No," she admitted, tossing the paper towels in the trash and stepping in. "I don't know who it is. Who—"

Molly stopped just as fast as she'd started. Her dropping jaw must have given her away.

"Uh-huh." Her paramedic friend nodded emphatically. "Uh-*huh*."

"Oh." Molly groaned, sensing imminent disaster. "This isn't good. It isn't good at all. What's the story?"

The second paramedic, an easygoing, soft-spoken black guy named Dwayne with just about as much experience as Molly, shrugged equably. "We found her just like this, decked out in her best Come-to-Jesus clothes. Mother said she was up in her room for about twenty hours before anybody thought to look. Said she'd been a little down lately, but says her child wouldn't do this. Definitely did not want to admit that she was dead."

"It'll come to her," Lance offered.

Dwayne was right about the clothing. It looked like their victim had pulled out her best nightie. A classic sign in women. For some reason, they traditionally preferred dressing up for that last ride out.

Molly had a bad feeling about this. She really did. She decided, looking down on those half-open, staring eyes, that she should have called Gene while she'd had the chance.

"Lorenzo," she said. "Get my keys out of my purse. In my trunk is a metal case. Bring it in, will ya?"

Lorenzo knew all about that case, which held all the equipment Molly carried into a death scene to do her job. He nodded and headed back out the door.

"Who is it?" Sasha asked as she let Lorenzo by her in the doorway, not interested in entering the room far enough to get her scrubs dirty if she didn't have to.

Since she lived out in the county, which was separate from and had as little contact with the city as possible on its best days, and since she preferred watching anything rather than news, Sasha's ignorance could be excused. Sasha had never seen the protracted City Council meetings that were such a daily part of city life. She'd never watched the interviews about funding for stadiums or housing projects or juvenile rehabilitation. She had not, no matter what had been splattered all over the news, watched the details of the public fight over gambling on the St. Louis riverfront.

Molly had. Moreover, she'd attended some of those meetings, been involved in some of those arguments herself. She knew perfectly well that every one of those meetings and fights and the political influence in town would change forever, because the woman lying on her cart was named Pearl Johnson.

"Why, me?" she protested, rubbing at throbbing temples.

"You can see the meds she had there," Dwayne offered next to her. "We brought everything we found in the bedroom, even the stuff that rolled under the bed, so there wouldn't be a question."

Molly nodded absently. "Thanks. Did you . . . uh . . ."

"Try and resuscitate her?" Dwayne asked. "No. The lady wanted a little dignity, who are we to argue? We gave the folks a good show, but we really didn't touch her."

Molly nodded again. For the first time, she heard the rhythmic dip and rise of voices outside, a couple of women, maybe. A man. Praying. After all this time working in disaster zones, Molly knew the sound too well.

"Who *is* it?" Sasha repeated, her throaty voice straining to remain civil.

"Our third lawyer of the month," Molly allowed, pulling out a pair of gloves and assuming her new identity as death investigator.

"Her?" Dwayne demanded, taking another look down at his patient as if she'd lied to him. "Really?"

"Really."

Sasha tried one more time. "Who is she?"

"You know the decision they made today to let the gambling complex be built by the Chicago group over the express protests of the mayor?" Molly asked, stepping on in to do her first quick evaluation of the body on the cart.

"Yeah. So?"

"Did you know that the person who won that fight with the mayor about who was going to build the riverfront complex was the city comptroller, or that the mayor had been accusing the comptroller of taking kickbacks and the comptroller's been accusing the mayor of being shortsighted and stupid?"

"Okay, if you say so. Why?"

Molly looked up. "Sasha. Meet the comptroller."

✦ Chapter 2 ✦

SHE FOUND THE suicide note when she was checking the pockets of Pearl's robe. By then everybody else had vacated the room, leaving it just to the death investigator and her client. Molly could hear the babble of voices gather in the work lane as the word spread about who was in this room, still heard the drone of supplication out in the public hallway from those who already knew. She smelled the sour aroma of fresh death and felt the utter stillness of her subject. Taking a deep breath, she snapped on her gloves and began the search she was obliged to make of the body for any signs of violence, any needle marks. Any surprises that didn't fit the scenario.

Any note, which might have been slipped into a robe pocket to be found after it was all over.

The paramedics hadn't needed a note to make their tentative diagnosis. Just the drugs. Six empty prescription bottles for everything from Elavil to Robaxin, which was a muscle relaxant. A small baggie of leftovers, the pills and capsules looking like the beads of a broken, brightly colored necklace. Pink and green and a bright, almost neon blue Molly didn't recognize that seemed too pretty to be deadly. The only surviving evidence of the fact that Pearl must have been swallowing pills by the handsful for a good half hour.

Molly didn't want to think about it. She'd always liked Pearl, a self-made woman from the bad side of town. A pusher, a shover, in the mostly male world of St. Louis politics. Well connected, as any politician expecting lifetime employment in this neck of the woods had to be. Her uncle's best friend was the Speaker of the Missouri House, which controlled a lot of the city budget and all of its police department. Her mother's sister's brother-in-law ran the multimillion-dollar convention complex.

Her fights, though, had all been to benefit her city. Her neighborhood. Her friends, who still lived next to crack houses and feared to let their children out as far as a school bus. She'd fought for the right reasons, no matter whom she'd taken on.

At least, that was what Molly had thought until she found the note. Folded up as neatly as a love note, handwritten in a clear, calm penmanship that betrayed the quiet determination of the act.

The peacemaker made me see the light. Oh, it did, Pearl's note read. *And I can't live with it. The ends don't justify the means. Never, never, never. I slept with snakes, and his name was William T. Peterson. I got bit. I'm sorry, Mama. Forgive me.*

She had slept with snakes. Molly wasn't sure what it meant. She recognized the name William Peterson from somewhere, but she couldn't immediately place it. She had a feeling, though, that he was going to turn out to be trouble with a capital T. Otherwise, Molly couldn't imagine Pearl killing herself to make amends.

Her poor mama.

Now Molly was going to have to go and walk Pearl's mama to the quiet room, and she was going to have to tell her that yes, Pearl really was dead, and she was going to have to pick at her memories and her picture of her daughter to discover why.

Molly really, *really* hated suicides.

"Molly," Lorenzo said, sticking his head in the doorway to drop off her battered silver case. "Here's your stuff. You gonna finish Tyrell, or should somebody else do it?"

"Tyrell." Molly stared at the tech as if he were speaking in Farsi. "What . . ."

It said something for how long Molly had already been on that it took her so long to remember the job she'd left unfinished.

"Oh, shit. His mother."

She still had Tyrell's blood on the surgical gown she hadn't changed out of. Still had her goggles hanging around her neck from when she'd pulled them down in her hurry to get away from that crowded room and its lonely little occupant. She couldn't face his mother and grandmother this way.

Pearl's mother was going to have to wait.

Another mother. It seemed, sometimes, that this city only had mothers left to grieve. But that wasn't something Molly wanted to think about now, either.

"Is anybody in with them?" she asked, stripping clothing and throwing it in laundry baskets until she was left wearing her scrubs.

"Sasha was in, but you know how well she handles this stuff."

Molly's laugh was dry. Sasha did not believe in death. It was merely an inconvenience in her otherwise perfect schedule.

"Okay. Have the doc meet me in there to break the news. If anybody else needs me, tell 'em they just have to wait. Tell Beth to call down to the ME's office and transfer my calls here for now."

Molly picked up a white lab coat as she passed the last door of the work lane on her way to quiet room one. In the nurse's lounge, the new shift was setting down their stuff on the way out to wade into the high tide of trauma. The hall still ricocheted with activity. Sasha was fielding two separate radio calls on incoming patients. Outside on the streets, the bars hadn't even let out yet. There wasn't a hope in hell things would settle down until at least three.

But that wasn't Molly's problem anymore. She didn't have to save anybody else tonight. She just had to identify them when they were dead.

She had to identify them and tell their frantic, wild-eyed mothers that they weren't coming home again.

Word always got out on the street fast when there was a disaster. Word got out at record speed that morning. By the time Molly made it back from seeing Tyrell's mother out the door, the hall was awash in city bigwigs.

"Get them *outa* here," Lance Frost groused, turning surly as he approached the second half of the double shift he'd volunteered to pull.

Molly was just about to ask Lance for the same favor.

The Grace Emergency Department was set up like half a six-spoked wheel, with three halls of fifteen rooms each stretching away at equal angles from the central secretarial station. This helped centralize the paperwork and keep the hallways in contact. It also tended to collect staff around the station as if it were magnetized, since it was also where the gossip tended to hover, where the bitching could be conducted at its most concentrated. It was where the triage and the charge nurse tended to confer, so that most questions were answered there.

Especially for the benefit of staff, police, or politicians, all of whom had begun to gather like barely disguised vultures. By the time she'd made it halfway down the hallway to dispose of Tyrell's paperwork so she could pick Pearl's up again, Molly had already spotted three senior police officials, two aldermen, and the head of Catholic Charities. At least Sasha had been able to keep the press blocked out in the driveway.

"Well, if it isn't Molly Malone."

Stunned, Molly turned around. For a minute she wasn't sure whether in all the chaos she hadn't made that phone call asking for help after all. "Gene, what are you doing here?" she asked, truly pleased.

Gene Stavrakos was probably the only person in the room shorter than Molly. Round, pink-cheeked, and tonsured like a woolly monk, he looked much more like Poppin Fresh than Freud. He always smelled like pipe smoke, and his eyes sparkled with a well-being that was infectious, which, Molly decided, was a much more important requirement for a psychiatrist.

Clad in the kind of rumpled clothing that betrayed a sudden call in the middle of the night, Gene shrugged, his smile faltering. "Ettie Johnson. Pearl's mother. She called me first."

Molly thought back to the prescriptions, couldn't come up with Gene's name on any of them. "You saw her?"

He shook his head. "I see Ettie. She's been a clinic patient for years, bipolar disorder. Is she here?"

"I'll be heading in to talk to her in a minute. Wanna help?"

Gene's smile was a shade sadder. "Yeah. She's been kind of fragile lately. This isn't going to help at all. She thought Pearl had made it. Survived the city with her degree and her position and all."

"Well, I'd keep a real close eye on any lawyers

you know right now. They seem to be trying to take over as highest risk group."

"You're kidding. Suicide?"

Molly nodded. "I think you should look into it."

Gene didn't seem to know quite how to take that. But then, neither did Molly. "Me?" he said. "Why?"

"Okay, then, I will. A good thesis for my master's in nursing."

"You're not getting a master's in nursing."

"It's on my list of things to do."

"How 'bout *you*?" he asked. "Isn't it time for a twenty-thousand-mile checkup?"

Molly turned back to him. Smiled, knowing she didn't look appreciably happier than he did. "I was just thinking that very thing. We're losing more kids than we are lawyers."

"You puking again?"

"When I'm not sweating."

He nodded briskly, as if they were talking about somebody else's symptoms. Someone else's stress. "Summer's always the worst. You know that. You should have seen me weeks ago."

"You're right, I should have. I've been getting so claustrophobic lately I have to park on the top level of the parking lot every time I come in to work, and that's a bitch when it rains. Will next week do?"

"If it won't, you know where to find me."

If they hadn't been standing in the work lane, Molly would have kissed him right on the top of his shiny head. Gene had been listening to her for twenty years, long before the clinical world had caught up with them and given a name to the nightmares and depressions and addictions Molly brought home with her from Vietnam. By the time the government came up with the tag of Post Traumatic Distress Syndrome, Molly was mostly through it.

Once identified and examined, it had weakened. Once recognized, it had become less frightening. An easily described series of reactions to a year of trauma a lifetime away. Most times Molly thought of it as a snake, lying in the sun. Quickly spotted, carefully avoided. Well managed when confronted.

Except for the summers, when the children died. Except when Molly lost not only a lawsuit but her job and ended up wading around in the carnage of a city to stay afloat. Except when it was too hot and her back hurt and she didn't sleep.

Except when she stood with her hands full of shit and she heard a voice that betrayed how big that pile she held was about to get. Molly looked over Gene's shoulder and sighed.

"If you'd sit with Ettie," she told him, her attention already on her next problem, "we'll be there in a minute."

Gene followed her line of sight and damn near flinched. The ruckus at the door had focused itself into one six-foot hurricane that was headed straight Molly's way.

"Okay," he said, understanding perfectly. "See you later."

And then, with one more pat to the arm for support, he got out of the way before he could be literally run over by the next contestant to sign in on Molly's never-ending night.

"Why the *hell* didn't you call me?" her problem demanded in full mezzo-soprano rage from the other end of the hall.

A tall woman with almond-shaped eyes and skin the color of glossy deep chocolate, she had high cheekbones and corn-rowed hair that had been scraped away from her face and twisted into an impossibly elegant coiffure. Even at one in the morning in an emergency department, she swept down the hall with the kind of haughty posture that transformed the trendy, tailored khaki linen outfit she wore into model's attire.

Molly's boss.

Suddenly Molly yearned for another trip to the bathroom.

Winnie was furious. And when Winnie was furious, no one within a twelve-mile radius was safe.

Winnie's official name was Dr. Jemimah Winnifred Sweet Harrison, Chief Medical Examiner of the City of St. Louis. No one, to Molly's knowledge, however, had ever had the guts to call the Chief ME Jemimah. At least not to her face.

Having survived med school when being a woman had been even more of a detriment than being black, Winnie had the kind of personality often referred to as FDS, or Female Doc Syndrome. Aggressive, angry, and full of attitude. Those less secure also called it Friggin' Dyke Style.

Winnie had also been head of her class at Georgetown, senior surgical and pathology resident at Washington U., and was board certified in forensic pathology, neuropathology, and pediatric pathology. Not someone to screw around with on her best days. Today, Molly knew, was not going to be one of her best days. She was scything through the crowd around the desk like a fullback hitting the line of scrimmage.

"I asked you a question," Winnie snapped, eyes hard and unforgiving, posture threatening as hell.

All activity on the work lane paused in equal parts awe and discomfort. Everybody knew about Winnie. No one at the hospital had actually met her. Winnie never darkened the doors of emergency departments. She never attended death scenes. She never ventured from the antiseptic environs of her morgue for anything but the odd press conference at the medical examiner's office, attendance at any of the many criminal trials in and around town that might need her professional opinion, or the environs of city hall when funding questions were being raised.

Which was why she was here tonight. Pearl Johnson had not only been a political ally. She had been Winnie's best friend. It was the only thing that kept Molly planted squarely in Winnie's path, ready for her fury. Pearl had been the only person in Molly's experience who had made Winnie laugh.

"I had to clear the homicide of an eight-year-old first," Molly answered as quietly as she could. "I was just about to call you."

Winnie stalked right up to her. Since Winnie was wearing her three-inch heels tonight, she ended up staring straight down at Molly as if her investigator were a tardy preschooler. "And *this* case?" she snarled.

Molly never flinched. "I'm sorry, Winnie. It looks like a suicide."

If Molly had been talking about any other client in public, Winnie would have reminded her with acerbic precision that this was not a conclusion Molly was qualified to reach. In any other situation, Molly wouldn't have put it that way, at least not to Winnie. But there were more city hall hangers-on showing up by the minute just for the purpose of gloating, and Molly didn't have time to play the games.

Winnie somehow managed to raise herself another good two inches. Molly saw her nostrils flare and was probably the only person in the place who knew how hard her boss was struggling for control. "Who says?" Winnie demanded, her voice suddenly hushed. The kind of hush that made people flinch.

"Me. There's a note." Molly tried her best to walk on down the hall, hoping the ME would follow her. "Do you want to talk about it in the lounge?"

Winnie grabbed her. "No, I don't want to talk about it in the goddamn lounge! You talk to me about it here!"

"You know the difference between a lawyer and a dead skunk on the road?" somebody asked a little farther down the hall, obviously having heard that they'd made their lawyer hat trick after all. "There are skid marks in front of the skunk."

Molly hoped like hell Winnie didn't hear it. They both had bigger things to worry about. Winnie was so intent on intimidating Molly that she hadn't noticed one of her political foes sidling up behind her. Molly had, though.

Risking Winnie's wrath, she deliberately made a half turn away from her boss and smiled. The man standing by the door to Pearl's room smiled back.

"It was good of you to come out tonight, Mr. Maguire," Molly said evenly.

Winnie whipped around so fast she created eddies in the air. It was the night for nervous reactions, and Alderman Tim Maguire didn't disappoint Molly in the least. A florid, round-faced man with a halfhearted blond mustache and eyes like a Boston terrier's, he flashed the kind of smile that made Molly think of a third-rate salesman seeing his commission slide down the drain. He was also sweating like a pig.

But then, Molly couldn't really blame him. It was about a hundred degrees outside, and his greatest ally on the City Board of Aldermen was lying in that room.

"I'm so very sorry, Dr. Harrison," he greeted them, jerking to an uncertain start and approaching. "I know you two were close. Does anyone know . . . ?"

"No," Winnie answered him, her glare enough to make the top of his head steam up. "They don't. Who called you?"

"Why, the mayor himself. He wanted to make sure that everything was . . . well, you know . . . afforded the family."

He wanted to make sure the body was shoved well to the side of the road before morning.

Even so, it amused Molly that of all people, Mayor Williamson had sent out somebody he really didn't like to do his work. If it hadn't been Pearl Johnson lying in that room, Molly might not have minded at all watching how this whole thing was going to fall out.

"I'll take care of the family," Winnie assured him baldly.

Timothy Maguire was left standing in an ineffectual sweat in the middle of the hall as Winnie spun away from him and stalked toward the room in question.

Molly had no choice but to follow. She also had a few more things she needed to clear up with her boss.

"Lorenzo, transport's coming for Tyrell," she informed her tech, who was doing his best to look invisible. "Let me know the minute they get here. I'll be . . ."

She gave a vague motion toward the door that was even now shushing shut behind Winnie. Lorenzo simply nodded. Timothy Maguire shoved his hands in his pockets and meandered over to where the assistant chief of police was talking to the homicide officer who was going to end up catching both Tyrell and Pearl. It didn't take a lot of guesswork to figure out which victim was puckering up their foreheads.

Molly figured it would be a good quarter of an hour before the poor homicide guy got to her, so she spent a couple of minutes reporting off her other cases to the oncoming nurse to afford Winnie a little time, and then followed into Pearl's room.

". . . stupid, stupid," she heard her boss chant, only the raw grief in her voice giving her away. Winnie's hand was out, hovering above her friend's stiff arm as if she couldn't quite close the gap. "You dumb nigger."

Molly took up her station at the door, knowing how hard it was for Winnie to have a witness. Knowing nonetheless that her place was here.

"You want to tell me about that note?" Winnie's voice was cold now, crisp as breaking ice.

Molly didn't insult her by softening the blow. "Do you know who William T. Peterson is?" she asked.

Winnie's head came up, but she didn't look at Molly. "Why?"

"His name was mentioned in the same sentence with a reference to sleeping with snakes and getting bitten."

That got Winnie's full attention. There was fire in her eyes. "She said that?"

"I'm sorry, Winnie."

For a long moment, Winnie didn't say a word. Then, she sighed. "Yeah. Me, too. Where's her mama?"

Molly didn't hear any voices out in the hall anymore. It meant that Sasha had gotten the family out of sight safely before the bottom feeders could find them. "Quiet room two. Ettie's psychiatrist is in there with her, I think. You gonna tell her?"

Winnie laughed, but it was a bitter sound. "It's why I decided to stay here, ya know, with this system. Cause I never in my life wanted to have to be the one to tell another mama that her baby was dead. That's why I hired you, cause you're good at it." She looked down at what was left of her friend, her eyes gleaming with unshed tears. "You're good at it. I'm not."

Winnie shook her head a final time, a regal farewell from a formidable lady, and addressed her friend a final time. "I'm never forgiving you for this one, Pearlie."

And then she turned to the door.

"I need to talk to them when you're finished," Molly said simply.

Winnie nodded without turning around. "Make sure they schedule her as my first case in the morning."

Molly straightened from the wall and put her job on the line. Probably her life. "I was just about to call Terrence."

Terrence Freeman, assistant medical examiner. Winnie turned on Molly as if she'd slapped her.

"What are you saying?" she demanded, stalking right back to her. "Are you telling me you think I can't handle this? That some pimply-faced, nappy-headed, diaper-wearing choirboy's supposed to do my job for me?"

"I'm saying," Molly answered, wishing she were home, wishing she were anywhere else, "that if William T. Peterson isn't her boyfriend—and I don't think he is—the last thing you need, with that suicide note, is to be doing the autopsy on your best friend. If Pearl was involved in something political, it's not going to help her if you go down in flames with her."

For a minute Molly seriously thought Winnie was going to hit her. She wouldn't have stood a chance. Winnie had a good fifty pounds and years of boxing practice behind her. Boxing, Molly thought in no little desperation. Of all the things for a woman to do to keep herself in shape.

"Call Terrence," Winnie said, very quietly, her teeth showing in a half snarl, her nostrils wide again. She was trembling, hands clenched, posture so rigid she should have snapped in half. Molly wanted to reach out to her. She knew better.

This time, when Winnie walked out the other door, Molly did nothing to stop her. She just stayed where she was, for once preferring the silence of the room here to the chaos of the hallway outside. She stood against the wall watching Pearl's face and wondering what she saw with those half-open eyes.

On the television, they got it wrong. On TV, when people died, their eyes closed. Neat and tidy and sterile. It never worked that way. It took effort to close one's eyes, muscle groups that couldn't maintain tone in death. Eyes always stayed open. They watched the ones who were left behind, and sometimes they seemed to accuse, or ask, or beg. Molly thought maybe Pearl just looked tired.

Tired.

Molly understood that, sometimes more than others. Molly just wished she knew what it was in Pearl's eyes that betrayed lost hope. She wondered when she would see it in her own.

Molly hated suicides.

"She gone?"

Molly must have jumped a foot. She hadn't heard the door open, but right next to her, Sasha was poking her head in.

"She's been gone since noon, Sasha. Where've you been?"

Sasha's expression was guarded as she stepped into the room, her hands behind her back, her street clothes back on. Precision-pressed cotton slacks and shirt in perfect pastels, white-blond hair brushed into a smooth cap around her head. She also had yellow fingertips and a lingering aroma of cigarette smoke about her. Sasha, the ice queen, was also one of the driveway fraternity who stood shivering all winter in the snow so they could have their smokes.

"Not her," she said, then motioned in the general direction of the other door. "*Her.*"

Finally getting the chance to get out her equipment to finish the task at hand, Molly nodded. "Yeah. She went to sit with Pearl's family."

Sasha nodded once, a sharp movement that failed to reach her hair. "Good. Then she can't bitch about dinner."

"What dinner?" Molly was busy unlatching the metal case so she could get to the thermometer and Polaroid camera inside. Everything else she needed, she had at hand.

"This dinner," Sasha said, and proceeded to bring her hands forward with the panache of a magician to produce a sack of White Castles.

Molly should have smelled them. She'd been too preoccupied. She wasn't now. Her saliva glands went into immediate overtime.

In her life, Molly had picked up a bad habit or two. The worst, without question, was her addiction to junk food. When she'd lived in LA, she'd dined on hot dogs at Pink's; in Austin, tacos at Willy's Mex. In Chicago, Italian beef anywhere on Diversey; and in Little Rock, hamburgers at Doe's. But in all the world, there simply was not a treat like White Castles, little flattened balls of meatlike material smothered in onions on buns the size of credit cards. Alternately called Belly Bombers and Sliders, eaten not by unit, but by sackful. There was simply nothing to compare with the taste or the clientele met at the drive-up around three in the morning or the taste of the food with a nice dry Ripple.

It wasn't the professional thing to do, but Molly figured that Pearl would forgive her. She let the case fall closed again and pulled off her gloves. There was a dead certainty she wasn't going to get food any other way, and it was bad etiquette to eat hamburgers in formal attire.

"You know that this is the real test that sets sentient beings apart from lower life-forms," Molly was saying as she dug into the bag and came up with her first treat.

"Of course."

"Only a higher form of life would create something that tasted like this and then choose to eat it. Someday we'll elevate it to the religious form it deserves, and you will be its first saint for crossing the desert to deliver me."

"Damn right I will. I had to sneak these past half a dozen crows out there. Thompson just showed up."

Crows being Sasha's term for mucky-mucks. As in, "if he makes you nervous, picture him with a crow sitting on his head." And Thompson was a big crow. Chief operating officer of the medical center, the man who held all their professional lives in his hand.

His arrival was no surprise. His taking even this long, was. Nobody respected the politics of St. Louis more fervently than Dr. Stanley Thompson, nor profited from them better. Born with the rare talent to finesse both politicians and civilians, he always managed to get extra funding for his hospital and exemptions from his taxes. Molly toasted him with her first hamburger.

"So, you got a note, I hear?" Sasha said, leaning a sleek hip against the counter by the door.

Her full attention on the taste of old onions and mystery meat, Molly scowled. "Word travels."

Sasha checked her watch. "It's like a game of telephone out there. The first rumor I heard mentioned rejection by a boyfriend. As of two minutes ago, it's rejection by the mob. We probably wouldn't have three people out there if Pearl hadn't missed the press conference today announcing that gambling thing. Evidently nobody can imagine anybody on God's good earth passing up the chance to rub the mayor's nose in a big win."

Molly was glad she'd already dispatched the first hamburger, because the sense of déjà vu damn near took her appetite. "Gambling," she muttered to herself, the name Peterson fitting in there somewhere. "Gambling. God, I wonder if that's it. She mentioned something about sleeping with snakes."

Sasha's eyes widened. "Scandal. How droll. You still have it?"

Licking the juice off the fingers of her left hand, Molly used the right to reach into her scrub pocket. Then she dipped her wet fingers into the other pocket. All she came up with was lint and one lone rubber band.

She looked at Sasha and then at Pearl, her appetite suddenly gone.

"Oh, shit."

"Am I going to have to take your reward back?" Sasha asked.

Molly forgot the bag of hamburgers. Suddenly she couldn't remember what she'd done with that note when she'd gotten called out of the room. Dropping the wrapper in the trash, she headed toward her next best bet. Pearl herself.

"I bet I left it on her," Molly said. "Since I got called away and didn't want to just leave it out."

Suddenly, she couldn't remember, and that was the last thing she needed.

"Go find Lorenzo for me," she begged.

Sasha didn't move. Molly checked the robe, checked the gown beneath. Checked the cart and came up just as empty.

"Might as well finish your hamburgers," Sasha offered with a dry grin. "Looks like you're going laundry-diving."

Molly just stood there, trying her damnedest to remember just what she'd done right after Lorenzo had poked his head in the door.

As if in answer to her thoughts, he did it again. "Molly, the chief of police wants to talk to you. You have a note?"

"Lorenzo," she begged. "You saw the note. Didn't you? Did you see what I did with it?"

Lorenzo's handsome face wrinkled. "I saw you holding something. Didn't you stick it back in her robe?"

"Get out her scuba tank," Sasha suggested.

"Hear the one about the lawyer and the rabbi?" somebody asked just outside the doorway.

Molly *hated* suicides.

✦ Chapter 3 ✦

MOLLY NEVER DID get her sleep. She spent the night fielding phone calls and irate questions at the Grace ER, where she used her free time to wade through laundry bins and trash bags, and she spent her morning watching autopsies. By the time she made it back to her house at the north edge of the Central West End, she was feeling dirty, exhausted, and impatient. Which was not the way to run into her next-door neighbor.

Molly's neighborhood was a quietly genteel one of old houses lovingly restored. Her street had once emptied onto Euclid, the main thoroughfare for the West End. In these times of higher crime and upscale paranoia, though, iron gates kept the circling cars away. Molly's neighbors were successful gays, adventurous young families, and older urban pioneers. Molly's house, which her grandparents had owned and passed along, was a graceful three-story Federalist-style brick box with black shutters and a lawn cultivated with more care than most children in the city.

Molly had grown up in the house. She did not love it. But then, she'd never felt much more for her parents, who had communed more comfortably with their careers and acquirements than with their offspring. They had in the end had the foresight to leave what they had accumulated in an unbreakable trust that allowed Molly the use of the house with all contents during her lifetime. Afterward, it would pass to her brother and his children. Even that long ago, Molly's father had just assumed that Molly would never have anyone of her own to pass it all down to. He'd been right. It didn't make her any more grateful to him for the security.

Molly lived there anyway, among the antiques and art her parents had collected over the many years of traveling the world courtesy of Uncle Sam. She ignored the statuary and the pedigreed paintings in favor of the hostas and iris and azaleas that were her real love. People who walked by on their way to the bookstores and restaurants and antiques shops of the Central West End always told her when they saw her how lucky she was. When she was in her garden, she agreed.

She was in her garden when Sam noticed her.

"Bad night, huh?" he asked as he hobbled across the lawn, propped up with his silver-headed ebony cane.

Molly didn't bother to look up from her work. "What makes you say that?"

He laughed, a gravelly sound that made Molly want to grab the cigarette out of his mouth. "The fact that you usually use more than your bare hands to dig up the dirt."

Molly sat back on her heels and peered up at the gnarled old man who looked more like a German gnome than the corporate wizard he'd once been. "Immigration's open, Sam."

Sam just nodded. He knew Molly's theory on death and dying. Heaven, she'd long since decided, was run on a quota system, like the INS. When St. Peter was low on bodies, people dropped in the street like flies. Young people, innocent people, people who had no business succumbing to stupid illnesses and incredibly bad luck. When the numbers were met, on the other hand, you couldn't kill somebody if you beat them over the head for half an hour with a hammer.

Tyrell's autopsy had proved the point all too clearly. According to the findings, he should not have died. The gunshot had not been fatal. The shock had.

And according to the family, there should have been no reason for Pearl to have written a suicide note or taken her own life.

Immigration was open, and lawyers and small black kids were on the list. It was enough for Molly.

"I also heard on the news," the old man said, pulling out his handkerchief to wipe the perspiration from his ashen face, the cigarette bobbing at the corner of his mouth as he talked, "that there is some kind of scandal brewing in the Medical Examiner's Office. Did I hear your name mentioned?"

Molly turned her attention back to the weeds that seemed to have taken root amid the dahlias during her absence of the last few days. "You heard my name mentioned."

"Should you be talking to a lawyer?"

"You ever catch me talking to a lawyer as long as I live, Sam," she said with feeling, "and you have permission to put a gun right to my head and pull the trigger. It's easier that way."

Sam *tsk*ed and shook his head. "It was a bad thing, that lawsuit, Molly."

Molly couldn't have agreed more. "A bad thing, Sam. Especially for that ambulance chaser who started it all, if I ever get my hands on him."

Sam gazed up at the hazy August sky as if awaiting inspiration. "You know, there's an old Jewish saying."

"If you hear the sound of boots, get the hell out of Warsaw?"

Sam chuckled, an old man with emphysema and a faint East European accent. "No. That's just Sam's saying. I was thinking more along the lines of clouds and silver linings."

"The Jews came up with that?"

"Who else?"

Molly grinned up at the crinkled, gray face and sly eyes of the old man she did love. "Who else."

"We also say that a hot cup of tea will make any problem better."

"I thought that was the English."

"They stole it from the Jews."

Molly smiled, straightened, decided that she would like some tea after all. Even if she was still dressed in her scrubs and nursing shoes. Even if her back was hurting like a sore tooth. Even if she hadn't slept in over twenty-four hours and still had to complete the paperwork she'd brought home with her.

The news crews who had done their damnedest to hound her all night and morning would not know to find her at her neighbor's house, and since she was the only person on her block without an answering machine, they couldn't leave messages.

Besides, Sam's tea was not exactly a ritual the English would have recognized. Sam's tea, which he claimed cured all ills, probably killed them instead. Especially with the alcohol content involved.

"Yeah," Molly said, linking arms with him. "Tea sounds wonderful."

Molly left her nursing bag right there among the oak toe. She wasn't about to walk inside and find that maybe the phone was ringing. It was much easier to ignore that way. Much better to sip tea with Sam than sling mud with the newsmen. Sam would have his tea, and Molly would have the regulation kind.

"How's Myra?" she asked, slowing her step to match his, especially in the heat.

"She sends her best."

Myra, Sam's wife, had Alzheimer's. She hadn't made sense in five years. Sam's son and daughter took him to the nursing home to see her every day. At least once a week they begged Molly to talk their father into moving into the home himself. For his safety. Considering what a Bedouin tent the inside of Sam's house was, Molly couldn't ever imagine him surviving the sterile, tiled halls of a nursing home. She'd never told him what his children wanted.

"Somebody needs to work the soil around your bulbs," Molly chastised the old man, knowing perfectly well that she'd be the one doing it while Sam sat in his wrought-iron chair offering tips.

"Tea first," he said, patting her hand with gnarled fingers. "Then a nap. Maybe later, after dinner."

They almost made it across. Down the street a couple of kids were roller-blading along the sidewalk. Pat Breedlove was watering her lawn, and two doors up, Allen Turner was trying to get a huge gilt mirror out of the backseat of his Volvo. The only real sounds came from traffic beyond the iron fence. Voices drifting on the breeze from outdoor cafés, music from passing cars. The air was close, hot, sticky as warm donuts. Molly was just beginning to feel better.

"Excuse me, Molly? Molly Burke?"

That took care of that.

"Don't turn around," Sam suggested, holding on more tightly. "It's probably a salesman."

But Molly knew that voice. She knew that no

salesman was worse, or more persistent. She also knew she'd end up talking to him in the end. She'd just make him work for it, as was only proper.

"You haven't been taking your medicine again, have you, Sam?" she accused as he puffed his way along next to her.

"For what?" he demanded. "So the *pisher* druggist can send his son to school in a Porsche?"

"You need to breathe, Sam."

"I need to sleep. I can't with all that money going down the toilet. A hundred-thirty dollars for one month's worth of one prescription. One! I ask you, does that make sense?"

"Molly, please! A moment, that's all I need."

"You on something new?" Molly asked Sam as if she couldn't hear the slick-soled wing tips slipping over her lawn behind them like an uncoordinated angel of death trying to catch up.

"Always something new. Something that lines pockets, you ask me. Something that makes the druggist rich, the doctor rich, the company rich. The poor old men eating cat food to survive."

Molly chuckled. "Seems to me that this poor old man owns more pharmaceutical stock than Eli Lilly himself."

Sam chuckled back and patted at Molly's hand. "Something's wrong with that? Somebody besides sharks should benefit from an old man's illnesses."

"The Irish have a saying about that, you know."

"They do?"

"Yeah. Get what you can while you can. Then get out."

Sam took a last, long drag from his cigarette, until there wasn't much left but ash, and considered Molly with shrewd eyes. "It's just not time to get out," he said.

Molly couldn't answer. Not for Sam, or for her, not for Pearl. So she smiled and came to a stop so her pursuer could catch up.

"She won't even talk to me," he complained in a voice that was somehow breathier than Sam's.

Sam raised hoary, caterpillar-like eyebrows at the young man who had joined them on the cracked, weed-choked driveway that separated Sam's house from Molly's. "Maybe you should try roses."

Finally, Molly felt like laughing. She did, which made Sam frown and the newcomer blush. "Sam," she said. "I'd like to introduce you to Rhett Butler, St. Louis's newest homicide officer."

Sam squinted. Scowled. "You're going to interrupt my tea, aren't you, young man?"

"If I'm lucky," Rhett answered honestly.

Actually, his name was John. John Jason Butler. But back when he'd been a uniform, the women had started calling him Rhett, and it had stuck. Why, Molly wasn't sure. A more unlikely Rhett Butler, she'd never seen. This one was middle-sized, middle height, with thinning brown hair over a high forehead and a face that had been arrested at about age thirteen. It was said down at homicide that Rhett had an almost perfect confession rate, because even the nastiest mopes ended up trusting those guileless brown eyes. Rhett enthusiastically sported the trappings of office; ubiquitous police detective mustache, limp gray suit, and snap brim hat. None of it did squat to make him look like anything but a kid.

Sizing up the uncomfortable detective as he would have an underperforming employee, Sam finally pulled his hand free from Molly to dispose of his cigarette. It landed along with several others in a clump of dandelions. "Well, young Mr. Butler," he chastised, "we Jews have a saying."

Molly fought another smile. Jewish mothers, more likely.

"I apologize," Rhett immediately responded, obviously well acquainted with that tone of voice. "I wouldn't interrupt if it weren't important."

"Rhett here missed at least one autopsy this morning," Molly explained as if Rhett were a recalcitrant kindergartner. Technically, Rhett was not expected to sit in on the autopsy of a suicide. That didn't mean he wouldn't have questions about it, though.

"It was unavoidable," he protested.

Molly still didn't face him. "And, if I'm any judge of character—and I am—"

Sam nodded, Molly nodded, and Rhett squirmed out in the August heat in his brand-new homicide suit with half the neighborhood watching him.

"The chief medical examiner will not now return his calls about what she found on said autopsy. Correct, Detective?"

The detective looked as if he wanted to crawl in with the cigarette butts. "I tried to explain."

"You don't explain to the chief medical examiner," Molly said. "It makes her even more angry."

"So then she isn't talking to either of you," Sam concluded.

Molly nodded. "Exactly. Which is why I'm going to help this young man."

Ten minutes later Molly saw Rhett's eyes widen as he stepped into her entry hall. She caught him sizing up the original Hoppers and Rembrandt sketches, the gleaming woodwork and pristine eggshell walls and high white ceilings. She imagined what he thought and ignored it, just as she would anyone else. Instead, she walked through to the kitchen with its red tile counters and windowsills of African violets and old green bottles, and she poured them glasses of iced tea. Then she led him out to the back patio, where the catalpa trees whispered in an afternoon breeze and the goldfish circled lazily in her little pond.

Rhett didn't look any more settled on the black wrought-iron chair than he would have on the Chippendale settee in the living room.

"This is . . ."

Molly settled into the chair across from him and began picking dead buds from the hot pink impatiens and purple pansies that filled the planters. "Something else," she obliged for him.

"Nice," he corrected, yanking at his tie.

Molly knew it was unfair to make him sit out in the heat. There was no way she was going to discuss suicide inside that house, though.

"So," she said, "you caught both Tyrell and Pearl?"

Rhett's attention was all hers. "Just my lucky night. I got more press on my ass than Madonna, and not a damn thing to sing."

"Got anybody on Tyrell yet?"

He shook his head. "Looks like North Side Posse, but no IDs. How's his mother?"

Molly sighed and rubbed at her own tired eyes. "You tell me. He was the third son she's lost."

For a minute they both paused, the only tribute time afforded a little boy. Afforded a family shattered on the stones of violence. And then, dispassionately and clinically, Molly told Rhett the findings of the autopsy. She told him that Tyrell had not bled to death, had not drowned in his own blood. She told him that Tyrell had simply not had the strength to survive.

Rhett took notes, asked questions, and moved on. Just as they all did.

"What about Pearl?" he asked.

"Blood alcohol was two-fifty, so that empty gin

bottle did belong to her. The rest of the tox screen is pending. The rest of the autopsy was unremarkable."

"Did Dr. Johnson do it?"

"Terry Freeman. Winnie was there."

Rhett snorted. "Poor Freeman. You did the profile?"

Molly scowled, picked apart a wilted petal. "I did the profile."

Psychosocial profiles were done on all suicide victims. Interviews with family and friends who would be able to trace the person's final days toward disaster.

Was she drinking any more than usual, Mrs. Johnson?

Was there a problem on the job?

Pearl's mother had sat in that stuffy, impersonal little room and ripped apart tissues just like Molly picked at scarlet petals in her yard, hands trembling, eyes full, her voice tight as pain.

"You don't understand," Mrs. Johnson had kept saying, shaking her head as if that could rid her of the notion that her daughter might really be dead. "She was so happy. So . . . *strong.* Especially when she was fighting for that gambling bill. Lord, but she did love a good fight, and she hadn't had one since she left the prosecutor's office."

"When did that change, Mrs. Johnson?" Molly had asked, the questionnaire waiting in her hands for its answers. Each blank worth a point. Four points equals depression. Drinking? Not sleeping? Agitated, preoccupied? Talking about dying? Beep. You do go on to Final Jeopardy.

Molly asked the questions, filled in the blanks, and looked just about anywhere but into Ettie Johnson's eyes.

"I don't know," the woman had answered. "I don't . . . just the last few days, she been so . . . quiet. Sittin' in her room all night and not telling me why.

Just tellin' me she was sorry. What for? What should my little girl be sorry for?"

Molly thought she knew. But Molly didn't have the proof anymore, so nobody else really wanted to believe her. It didn't matter. She still had enough points for a depression, enough factors for a suicide. Molly gave Pearl's mother the numbers for Crisis Intervention, for Grieving Support Groups, for Suicide Survivors. And then Molly had gotten the hell out of Warsaw.

"Her mother has been treated for manic depression for years," Molly told Rhett, focusing her gaze over to where she could see people strolling out on Euclid through the cedar trees that isolated her. "My guess is that Pearl got her first taste and did the big dirt dive. The people at city hall said she'd been uncommunicative for the last two or three days, smelled alcohol on her breath. Anxious. Not eating. And she missed the biggest press conference of her career."

"And her alcohol level was two-fifty?"

"Yup."

Rhett nodded, understanding.

Alcohol, the great suicide toggle switch. Everyone, at one time in his life, dabbled with suicidal ideations. Maybe just a quick flirtation, an ugly temptation. A way out of weariness or pain or loss. Maybe serious courtship with the danger of death. An answer to desperation.

Most people, no matter what, walked by the lure. Laughed or cursed or simply closed their eyes. Unless there was alcohol on board.

Something about alcohol blocks up every self-preservational instinct in man. Something about alcohol makes man impatient, uncertain, unreachable.

Something about alcohol disintegrates the distance between temptation and reality.

Molly never drank in the summer. Never.

"You never did find the note?" Rhett asked.

It actually took Molly a minute to pull her thoughts back to the conversation in her backyard. Overhead, the trees creaked, and beyond a plane threaded through the dim and milky sky. Water chattered over the rocks at the edge of her pond. Life was quiet and ordered and pleasant, just as her parents had wanted to believe.

"I did everything but put on waders and dive into the trash compactors in the basement," Molly admitted. "I don't know what happened to it."

Rhett bent his attention to the notes he was scribbling. "There's a lot of talk downtown that there was no note."

Molly kept her silence long enough to force him to look at her. "Is that why you're still on it?"

Rhett was beginning to sweat. "You know who William T. Peterson is, Molly?"

"No, I don't. Do you?"

His nod was minuscule, as if his complicity could be kept at a minimum. "He used to own several casinos in Vegas. Got sent up for racketeering in 1980, and has been banned from holding a gaming license anywhere in the United States since."

Molly slumped back in her chair. "Oh, God. That's it. He must have his fingers in that American Federal bunch."

"It's the only reason I can think he'd be linked to Pearl Johnson . . . that is, if he was."

Molly gave him the kind of glare a forty-something-year-old woman could give a twenty-something-year-old kid and get away with. "I know you wouldn't question my word, Rhett," she said. "Especially after I helped you today."

He was beginning to squirm like a toddler in

church. "Molly, I have to cover all bases. You know that. I just wanted to make sure that, well, you remembered right. I mean, you know, it was a busy night and all. . . ."

"Suicide notes are tough to forget, Rhett. And tough to invent. Find somebody else to go after."

"Could it have been murder?" he asked.

She sighed, wishing for the hundredth time that she could remember what she'd done with that damn note when she'd run off to deal with Tyrell's mother. Wondering what could have happened to it in the interim.

"Everybody and his sister-in-law was in that ER last night," she said rather than answer him. "And every one of them knew about that note. Could it be as simple as somebody also involved in this Peterson business lifting the incriminating evidence?"

Rhett actually flinched. "Please don't make suggestions like that. My life's complicated enough as it is."

"Tell me about it."

All the same, the two of them stayed right where they were for quite a while, considering the implications. Of a suicide note. Of a theft. Of the possibility that nobody, in the end, was going to believe Molly that a note existed at all so that Pearl's supporters on the board could blame her death on anything but a guilty conscience.

After all, Rhett asked, why would Pearl choose the exact moment of her triumph to kill herself?

Molly knew. But then, Molly knew all about guilt. But it wasn't something Molly thought about during the summer, so she asked instead what would happen next. Unfortunately, Rhett didn't know that, either.

Molly spent the rest of her evening finishing her reports and half of Thursday giving an affadavit about the note only she had seen. She spent Thursday afternoon in the senior death investigator's office discussing implications and the early evening in her lawyer's office discussing precautions.

By that time, the media had discovered her role in the little drama and proceeded to splash her picture—and history—across the televisions of the entire metropolitan area. Half the members of the Board of Aldermen were calling for her resignation, and the other half were calling for an investigation into the murder and subsequent cover-up by the police, the Medical Examiner's Office, and the FBI, which had no idea what anybody was talking about.

"The death investigator in question," the vacuously handsome anchor of the six o'clock news reported, "has a history of problems on the job. Just over a year ago, she was part of a lawsuit against Metro Health Center alleging negligence and malpractice, which was settled out of court for a figure reported to be in the millions. Ms. Burke has worked since that time in the ER of Grace Hospital."

Which meant, of course, that Molly spent Friday morning in Gene Stavrakos's office yelling at the poor psychiatrist as if he, rather than the action news, had been the perpetrator.

"It makes me sound like a public menace!" she protested. "'Mothers, keep your children away from this woman.'"

"It's the press," Gene reminded her calmly. "They'll forget all about you in another week."

Molly stared at the same mountain photo she'd looked at every time she'd been there for the last twenty years. She'd inspected it so thoroughly she could almost swear she'd be able to find it just by landing at the Denver airport and walking west. Sharp, ragged peaks, a cool mountain river slicing through meadows of columbine and daisies. Aspen trees and blue spruce and a hawk high against the sun. Nirvana, Shangri-la, heaven.

The rest of the office didn't match as well as it used to. A little more tired-looking, the paint scratched, the carpet worn. A lot of grief and guilt scuffing it all up over the years.

"I just don't feel like going through this all over again, Gene."

"I know, Mol. That scab's a little too fresh to be picking at."

"I'll tell you the scab I'd like to pick," she retorted, boiling all over again, the pain and humiliation indeed too fresh to have it dissected in public. "Frank Patterson. That asshole's probably driving to work in the friggin' Mercedes he bought with the money he made off me."

"The lawyer?"

Molly had been seeing Gene during the trial, just so she could maintain her composure on the witness stand when she had to stare down the slick, carnivorous good looks of the opposing attorney.

"The lawyer," she snarled.

"He was just doing his job, too," Gene protested mildly. "Just like you. Just like me."

"Not like you or me," Molly protested immediately. "You and I are trying to help people, Gene. He's trying to retire to the Caymans."

Gene smiled, but for the first time Molly could see that he was tired, too. Worn-out like his carpet. "He's just trying to get by. It's what we all do, Mol."

Molly closed her eyes, fought surprise tears that betrayed just how much she was enjoying herself in the renewed notoriety. "I don't know, Gene."

"Yes, you do. You're a survivor, Mol. You're gonna make it through."

Molly sighed. Thought about the nightmares she'd been having every night, where she'd somehow found herself wearing her old fatigues as she tried to stem the flood of street kids who poured through the ER doors.

Well, they said you saw one war you saw 'em all.

"Yeah, Gene. I'll make it through."

"But you'd like some help?"

She sighed again. "I'd like some help."

Molly took the prescription in hand and hoped for the best.

She wondered what her best was going to be when she found a bottle matching hers at the site of her fourth lawyer suicide three days later.

✦ Chapter 4 ✦

"MOLLY, WHAT ARE you doing here? The sun's up."

Molly squinted up to where a uniformed cop leaned against the railing on the second floor of the Gateway Motel. "I'm an investigator, Mort. Not a vampire. Pete's on vacation."

The minute she'd driven into the parking lot of the economy motel that sat just off Highway 44 near the Zoo exit, Molly had spotted the certain signs of disaster. The motel, a two-story, U-shaped prefab kind of gray-and-tan economy motel with cracked pavement and pressboard walls, had outside entry so the guests could park beneath their rooms. Halfway down the nearly deserted parking lot, a city patrol car sat at right angles to an unmarked, their radios chattering. Alongside sat a city ambulance, the lights off, the paramedics wiping sweat off their foreheads as they finished their reports. The evidence van was next to that.

The vehicles and the open door on the second floor said that something bad had happened. The fact that nobody was moving fast said that it was already too late to help.

Mort and another uniformed cop bracketed the open door. A twentyish brunette woman in slacks and a polo shirt with a walkie-talkie stood at the head of the outside concrete steps, and a thin teen with a straggly goatee and grimy Metallica T-shirt sat about two steps down, his face in his hands. Molly bet that when he lifted his face, it would be pasty. She also bet he'd been the unfortunate winner of the "Guess what's hiding behind that locked door?" award.

The police had gotten the call at 10:30 A.M. for a possible overdose. Locked, chained motel room, no answer when the maid had called. No sounds coming through the very thin walls that might have meant the guest was showering and simply couldn't hear. All the lights on, clothing strewn over the room, nobody in sight.

Or no body in sight, as the case might be.

The cleaning crew had called maintenance to get into the room. Maintenance, Molly figured, probably now wished he was working at Burger King.

Opening the van's side door, Molly yanked out the metal case. It was showtime. Today she was dressed in death investigator attire. Khaki cotton twill slacks, peach crew neck shirt, and hopsack jacket. Striding across the parking lot, she figured she looked more like she was making a sales call than a forensic search.

It was too hot to be out today. The sun hurt her eyes, and the humidity made her hair stick to the back of her neck, and it wasn't even noon. She hadn't gotten much sleep the night before. Instead, she'd repotted all her indoor ferns and plotted out the new beds she was going to plant in the fall. About four, she'd just sat out in the backyard and listened to the night.

She was paying for it now, when all she wanted to do was lie down.

"Were you the one who found her?" she asked the teen as she stopped on the stairs next to him.

He lifted his head and she won all bets. "Yes, ma'am."

Molly laid a hand on his shoulder, knowing there wasn't much more she could do for him, feeling all the same for this kid who was just trying to make his car payments with a job at the motel.

"You okay?" she asked quietly.

He didn't look okay. His dark eyes were washy with the kind of tears men aren't supposed to allow. "Yeah, I guess."

"I need to talk to you when I finish up there. Would you mind hanging around that long?"

He just shook his head and dropped it back into his arms. Molly straightened and headed up to business, too long since past that kind of reaction to even remember having it.

Well, that wasn't exactly true. She remembered it when she wasn't careful. And on days like today, she was very careful.

By the time she got to the top of the stairs, the young woman with the radio had taken up a place next to the maintenance guy. Molly's attention was already on the room and its occupants.

"Anybody hear it?" she asked Mort.

He inclined his head downward. "A couple right below. Said they just thought it was another drunk. The Cubs're in town."

Molly nodded. When the Cubs played St. Louis, the economy motels were full and the noise level was high. "What time?"

"They're not sure. Late. After three."

"You gonna be my ranking officer, Mort?"

"It's just your lucky day," a voice answered from inside the room.

With the glare of the sun, Molly had to squint to make out the features that went with the voice.

"Well, fiddle-dee-dee, Rhett," she greeted him as she headed on in to drop her case at the door and peel off her jacket. "Is this karma, or are you just on somebody's shit list down there?"

"I guess they decided I needed another suicide to complete my merit badge," Rhett responded, already in shirtsleeves and protective gloves himself, making notes in his ubiquitous notebook. "I don't need to ask whether you're on a shit list or not."

Molly just scowled, the raw spots still healing from where Winnie had been chewing on her butt for the last few days.

"But why get anybody from homicide at all?" she asked. "Is there a question now?"

The homicide bureau in St. Louis city was so busy that they didn't answer routine suicides anymore at all. Only patrol officer, precinct sergeant, death investigator, evidence. From what Molly had heard, there hadn't been any question about this one. On any other day, they would have run everything by the numbers to prevent surprises, told the family they were sorry, and then moved on to the tough stuff like Tyrell. They wouldn't think of cluttering the homicide desks with it.

Rhett said, "The uniform who called it in's a rookie, got a little spooked. You'll see. And there's no note. I don't see a problem, so I'm about ready to head out as soon as evidence is finished."

Almost as a punctuation, there was a flash from the area of the bathroom where the evidence tech was taking full color shots of the scene.

Because the scene was contaminated enough with the people who'd already waded through it, Molly took care of her own housecleaning at the door. Shaking the wrinkles out of her jacket, she reached up and hung it over the top of the open doorway.

Then she laid her case on the little round table by the window and opened it to pull out her gloves.

"Victim's in the bathroom?" she asked, pulling them on.

"Aren't all victims in the bathroom?" Rhett demanded. "I swear, I'm gonna do a study on it some day. 'The propensity of humans to migrate to the john to die.' You think it's an instinct, like elephants, or a societal problem?"

Molly looked up from the paperwork she was pulling out. "You're really hung up on this, Rhett."

He glared—well, as much as Rhett could glare. "This is my third dead body in two days, and every damn one of them has been wedged in between a tub and a toilet. Do me a favor, Molly. If you ever answer a sudden death call and it's me, make sure I'm not in the bathroom."

Molly began cataloging the scene before she headed on into the bathroom. "I promise, Rhett," she answered. "I'll drag you out by your heels with your pants around your ankles."

"You're a pal, Burke."

The bed was unmade, the pillows bunched up as if the victim had used them to read or watch TV. There was a pair of black alligator pumps by the bed and a red Ann Taylor suit crumpled on the chair. Hose, hair-brush, handbag. This one hadn't arranged herself in bed like Juliet waiting for Romeo to come find her. This one, evidently, had gone out like a man.

"Suicides," Molly protested with a shake of her head. "What's the rush, all of a sudden? I mean, suicide season doesn't even open until the first frost. Don't these people know they can be fined?"

Rhett, still busy with his own facts and figures, grinned. "I think they've bagged more than their limit of lawyers, too."

Molly stopped and stared at him. "Another one?" she asked, really surprised.

His grin got a little too feral for that poor kid on the stairs to see. "Wanna know the difference between a lawyer and a dead skunk on the road?"

"I know it." She was doing another quick scan of the room. "I don't suppose this was a cross-dressing lawyer."

"Why? You hopin' to recognize somebody?"

Molly's smile was no prettier. "A small, select list. All of whom have flies in the front of their shorts."

"Then this one definitely doesn't meet the height requirements."

Molly nodded. "That makes it, what, then? Two men and two women?"

Four lawyers. Molly wondered if there was some ethics investigation going on. Something that would explain this more than the simple "things happen in bunches" theory. After all, as she'd said, summer wasn't suicide season. It was murder season. Then she reached the bathroom and stopped theorizing.

Molly saw her arm first. Outthrown as if trying to escape the disaster that was about to befall. She saw the gun, a heavy, large bore semiautomatic that had spatters of blood on it. She saw the silk and lace slip, the creamy bra beneath, the porcelain, pampered skin and long legs that were now stiff and soiled. She saw the mess that the poor maintenance crew was going to have to try and clean up after everybody left. Because whoever their victim was, she'd put that big gun in her mouth and pulled the trigger. And ended up wedged right between the toilet and the tub, what was left of her head against the wall.

"Jesus," Molly whispered, the smell in the close little room overwhelming. Musky and sharp, a little sweet, like old chicken left out in the trash. "She was serious."

Rhett looked in over her shoulder. "Women suicides used to be so simple. A coupla pills, a note, a little lipstick. Now, they want to be Dirty Harry. I'll tell you, Molly, if this is equality, I'm not so sure you should fight so hard."

"This ain't the equality *I'm* fighting for," she assured him, marking her outline with commensurate injuries. "We got a name? Family? All that good stuff?"

Rhett checked his notes. "Her name's Ryan, Mary Margaret. Single, no wants or warrants, address in the county."

Molly sighed, set her paperwork aside so she could bend to examine the body more closely. "Family?"

"Checkin' now."

"Transport's here!" Mort called from the door.

Molly nodded absently. "Send 'em in. I need to move her to do a complete exam."

No obvious tracks, no obvious bruising or abrasions. Molly wanted to check the victim's hands for defensive wounds, just in case. She'd wrap them in paper bags until they got the body downtown so they could check for blowback or residue that would prove the victim was the one holding the gun.

It should be a score. The injuries were commensurate with immediate-range injuries. The livor, where the blood had pooled inside her when she died, matched her present position. And her rigor panned out to be about seven or eight hours old. Molly would check the temperature to corroborate it, but it looked as if the couple downstairs was about right.

Molly could hear the clatter of the cart being dragged up the steps. She straightened to get her thermometer and Polaroid so she could get shots of the body before she moved it. Double the police shots with her own of the blood spatter pattern, the injuries, the placement of the gun just beyond the victim's right hand. When she told the family what happened, Molly would have to ask what hand the victim used. The last thing they needed was a closed suicide case where the gun was in the right hand of a left-handed woman.

Molly was at the front door checking her pictures when she heard the sudden squeal of tires out on the parking lot. A siren howled to life. Suddenly, there was a lot of running and yelling, and Mort was poised in the door like a jet on takeoff.

"Butler!" he yelled into the room. "Officer down!"

Rhett immediately lost interest in the bathroom. "Where?"

Mort could hardly stand still in the doorway. "On the move, Kingshighway southbound heading for Oakland. Myers got himself shot and taken with his own damn gun."

Rhett was almost dancing with impatience. "Shit! That's right down the block!"

Immediately, the suicide was put into perspective within the parameters of not only the justice system, but the medical one. Balance the effort given to a young woman who didn't care enough to sustain her own life against a known officer who was fighting to save his. Even Molly wanted to run help.

"Molly?" Rhett asked, turning on her, poised.

"Leave me the rookie," she said, and they ran.

The transport team took their place with the tarp on which they would lay out the victim so Molly could get a better look. Molly got out her thermometer and set it.

The uniform, a fresh-faced kid named Roscoe, turned up his walkie-talkie so they could listen. The evidence tech, now just waiting for Molly to be finished so he could take away the gun, stood with the rookie.

Molly took the victim's temperature and took more pictures, and all the while she listened to the terse chatter on the talkie Roscoe brought back up with him. She helped the transport team lift the body out of the bathroom onto the tarp so she could check the dorsal aspect for surprises, even though in her mind she was following the cars and helicopters along the side streets of the city. She cataloged injury, personal effects, prescription medications, and a small bag of white powder the evidence tech already held that Molly didn't really think was Equal, and prayed for a man who needed her prayers, because her patient had already taken her chances and lost. Molly gathered the medications to carry along to her lab and thought briefly that she was going to have to find out what that bright blue capsule was she was beginning to see everywhere, even as she watched the hooded eyes of the men who waited by the radio.

The suicide, Mary Margaret Ryan, got Molly's attention. The cop, Bill Myers, got her anxiety.

And then, it all ended.

"Oh, Jesus!" came the stunned voice over the radio, breaking every rule. "They just threw him out!"

All activity in the room stopped. All eyes focused on the radio. Everyone waited, even though that tone of voice told them everything.

"Pursuit is continuing southbound on Kingshighway. Tan late-model Olds, Missouri vanity plates David-Ivan-Victor-Edgar-Robert. Eleven hundred block of South Kingshighway is blocked off. Watch commander is requested at scene, eleven-thirty-eight."

No request for paramedics.

"Let's get her moved," Molly told her team, because they were all needed somewhere else. "I'll call Winnie and let her know."

And then she had to get to Kingshighway, because the last thing any of them needed was for Bill Myers to be lying out there too long.

"Did you know Mary Margaret had a prescription for Prozac, Mrs. Ryan?" Molly asked three hours later.

Crouched in the corner of the nubby brown and blue plaid Sears country comfort couch, Mrs. Mary Jane Ryan held on to the box of tissues in her lap as if it were the ballast that kept her from slipping into a little ball of grief. A small woman with old eyes in a middle-aged face, she stared at the butterflies that decorated the top of the cardboard container much the way Molly watched Gene's mountains.

"Stress," Mary Margaret Ryan's mother answered in a whisper. "She has a lot of . . . stress. A big case. She wouldn't . . . she . . ."

She would. She had.

Molly focused on the questions on her sheet, half filled in, her own words terse and clinical. Her hands were trembling almost as badly as Mrs. Ryan's. It was a good thing the woman couldn't tell.

Molly's mind was still on Myers. She'd done her job, the same she'd done for Mary Margaret Ryan, but she'd done it more quickly. More quietly. She'd been ringed by a dozen squad cars with flashing lights and a herd of media trucks, the newspeople jostling with angry police.

At least she hadn't had to break the news to Bill's wife. There were at least three chaplains and a dozen senior officers for that. Molly had ushered his body back to her cold little morgue, though. She'd handed him over to the attendants and a somber Winnie and then fought her way back out through the news crews to talk to Mary Margaret Ryan's mother while the city police force mobilized to track down the tan Olds that had gotten out into the county.

Molly had work to do. She had to go in to the hospital at five for her next shift. She had to find out whether they'd caught the fifteen-year-old who'd shot Myers in the head with his own gun and then dumped him onto a busy street at sixty miles an hour.

She had to do anything but tell this sad little lady that her bright and ambitious young daughter had been so selfish that she had ignored what would happen to her mother when she stuffed a gun in her mouth.

"Can you think of any reason Mary Margaret would have tried to take her own life, Mrs. Ryan?" Molly asked anyway, her own voice not much more certain than that of the woman she interviewed.

"Peg," she said, her head lifting, her eyes coming to brief life. "Her name is Peg."

"Peg. Yes, ma'am."

The room was filled with pictures. Mr. and Mrs. Ryan, a shy-looking couple caught smiling at the camera as if it were a trick. Children. Five maybe, with their growth and development charted in color across the living room wall.

One photo caught Molly's attention, the kind of shot taken to celebrate the end of boot camp. Short hair and an I-can-do-anything glare. A handsome kid in a First Cav patch. A familiar pose. Molly had a shot just like it of her in her Army Nurse Corps dress greens.

There were no pictures of this son in newer clothes or with older eyes. It seemed that Mrs. Ryan had gotten bad news before.

"Not my Peg," Mrs. Ryan begged, as if Molly could take the news away. Change her mind. "Please, not my Peg."

"Do you want to wait for someone else to get here before we go on?" Molly asked again.

Mrs. Ryan straightened, lifted a square, plump hand to push back the salt-and-pepper hair that sagged across her forehead. "No." Her voice was too quiet now, and Molly wanted to be gone. "She's had her problems. Haven't we all? But she wouldn't do this. She wouldn't do this to me."

Molly wanted to scream. She wanted to throw something heavy, just to hear it break. It had seemed such a good idea when she'd taken this job. She was good at it. She liked the people. She needed the hours and the money.

Sitting on this well-worn couch with this well-worn woman, Molly gave serious thought to standing in line behind that maintenance guy from the motel for a job at Burger King.

In the end, Peg Ryan's sister showed up. In the end, she admitted that yes, Peg had been on Prozac, that she was under a lot of stress with the new law firm. She'd been trying a huge case. She still lived with her parents here in Shrewsbury. Didn't have much of a social life to speak of because she wanted a career in law so badly. She'd suffered bouts of depression in high school and then in college, but it was something she'd gotten over.

Not Peg, her sister Maureen said, just as her mother had. Holding her mother's shaking hands. Round, freckled face drawn and disbelieving. Not Peg.

But Molly heard in their voices the same pause. As if the words *Not Peg* had been a prayer instead of a protest. In the end, she'd asked for the name of Peg's law firm, since Peg had spent the majority of her time there. And then, she got out of that stifling little house, because what she really wanted more than anything, as she stared at those two women holding each other against the truth, was a drink.

Molly didn't get her drink. She didn't get a nap, or time off for good behavior. Instead, figuring the day couldn't get much worse, she decided to breach the law offices of Marsdale, Beacon, Fletcher, and Richards. There were still a couple of questions on Mary Margaret Ryan's psychosocial history that had been left blank. Or at least incomplete. Since Molly was going to have to spend the evening at the ER again, and the next morning watching autopsies, she needed to get her paperwork cleared up.

At least, that was what she told herself.

She also believed in getting unpleasant things out of the way, like the dentist or divorce. The dentist she saw every year, the divorce court, twice, both preventative measures that prevented decay and disease.

Marsdale, et al, held sway on the twenty-first floor of One Metropolitan Plaza downtown. A handy little building for an impressive law firm. New, trendy, with its postmodern copper roof and marble façade for the paying customers, and the bankruptcy court taking up the seventh floor for the nonpaying ones. It boasted a two-story lobby with Thomas Hart Benton–like murals of the city of St. Louis, one of the premier restaurants in town, Kemoll's, in the lobby for the occasional business dinner, and enough red marble to jump-start a cathedral.

Molly wasn't impressed. She was surly. But that was about how she faced a visit to any law firm. Especially since she figured that the ones she'd had dealings with had been able to import their own share of marble to impress the clientele on the money she'd invested in them.

Then she got to the information board and realized it was computer generated. Punch the right buttons, get the right answer. Molly hated those almost as much as lawyers.

No. She hated buttons. She felt humiliated by lawyers. Every time she thought about facing one, she remembered sitting in that witness chair fighting for the words that would fairly represent that night Mrs. Wiedeman had died. She remembered that no matter what words she found, the lawyer for the plaintiff had turned them around so that she sounded as stupid as his original lawsuit had claimed her to be.

Molly was standing before the black board trying to punch up the right law firm when her beeper went off. Better and better. Next the eyewitness news crew would show up.

Since it was the office calling her, Molly decided to check in with them before breaching the lion's den. Maybe they'd tell her to come back. To forget the interview. To relax, because somebody had found a note after all and the file could be closed and put away.

No such luck.

"There are a couple of detectives who need to talk to you," the senior death investigator said.

"Rhett and who else?" Molly asked, watching a gaggle of precision-suited executives with their power ties and soft leather briefcases skim over that information board like they were playing a Wurlitzer.

"Not homicide," he said. An ex-DEA bomb and arson expert, Kevin McCaully was a savvy guy who had proved to have an incredible talent for getting the job done while staying out of Winnie's way. "Intelligence. Something about Pearl Johnson."

Molly leaned against the smooth wall and rubbed at her forehead. It was so cool inside this building, hushed, as if money were something to be revered on a par with the twelve apostles. That kind of hush didn't seem to help the headache she was brewing, though.

Great. First a lawyer and then a witch-hunt. Or, if she was feeling particularly foolhardy, she could try it the other way around. It came down to the fact that she liked the decor here better than downtown.

"I'll be finished here in a little while," she said. "But I have a shift at Grace tonight. I can talk to them there, or they can meet me at the morgue in the morning. I have two openings to sit in for. Do you know exactly what they're after?"

"Nope. My gut feeling is that your mention of this Peterson guy rolled some rocks, and they're collecting what's crawling out. You doing that lawyer right now?"

"Even as we speak. I'm finding out if she was more depressed than her mother admitted."

"Lucky you. There was a question from the lab about that blue pill you found."

Molly dragged up the memory of that cluttered bureau top and the bag she'd dropped the meds in to be analyzed. "Yeah," she said. "It was in the little aspirin tin with the Benadryl and Darvon. Neon blue cap. I've seen it around, but I didn't recognize it."

"Neither did they. They were just wondering if there wasn't a container or something."

"I would have sent them a container. Just like the Prozac and birth control pills. Wouldn't I?"

Kevin chuckled. "That's what I told them. I'm sorry you got the complicated ones, Mol. I got the first two. Slam-dunks, both of them."

Molly couldn't help but grin. "Yeah. You get the

flame tattoos and I get the question marks. Now, let me get this finished so I can do the really fun stuff, like Myers's investigation. They catch the kid yet?"

"They caught the kid."

"They beat the shit out of the kid?"

"He fell down a couple flights of stairs. Twice."

"Good. See ya later."

"Uh, Molly." There was a small pause, and Molly could imagine Kevin staring at the posters of the Hawaiian Islands he'd hung across the room. A skinny redhead with more beard than bicep, Kevin McCaully was nonetheless one of the top four Ironman contenders in the contiguous U.S. "Listen, be careful on that city hall business."

Molly really wasn't in the mood to hear that. "Okay, Kevin. I will."

Be careful how? she wondered. Don't say too much? Don't say anything at all? Don't even talk to the cops without a lawyer present? Well, maybe she'd find someone upstairs to bring along.

Upstairs. Right. Turning away from the bank of phones, Molly headed back to her original quest, her mood even worse.

By the time she stepped off the elevators onto the hush of gray carpets and recessed lighting on the twenty-first floor, Molly was almost looking forward in a perverse kind of way to putting a wrinkle in the world of Marsdale, Beacon, Fletcher, and Richards.

She was almost wondering if the news she brought them would, in fact, wrinkle anything.

"Can I help you?" the receptionist asked from behind her black Lucite desk. She was blonder, bustier, and better groomed than Molly. She also had teeth like a Derby contender.

"Yes," Molly answered in her most professional tone, feeling like the carpet cleaner in her slacks and jacket when surrounded by the kind of decor that comfortably cushioned big retainers. "I understand Mary Margaret Ryan is employed here?"

"Ms. Ryan is not in today," the blond answered, still completely neutral. "Could someone else help you?"

"One of the partners, please. It's about Ms. Ryan."

A frown, a gathering of poise, as if distancing herself. "Could I ask in what regard?"

Molly hated flashing her identification until she needed to. If a cop flashed a badge, it could be about anything. Death investigators only had one thing on their minds.

"Does she work with any one particular partner?" Molly asked. "I only need a few minutes."

The blond studied her as if trying to guess her genus. Molly sighed and reached into her purse. Five minutes later, a truly shaken receptionist was ushering Molly back along a hallway decorated in hunting prints and Brooks Brothers suits to a corner office that overlooked the river. She wasn't nearly as shaken as Molly when the occupant of that office looked up from the phone to see who was there.

"Oh, shit," Molly muttered.

His smile was a real two-hundred-watter. He flashed it on Molly like the searchlight from the police copter. "Well, well, well," he greeted her, pushing himself up from his gleaming oak desk. "If it isn't Saint Molly of the Battlefield."

Six feet two inches of black Irish good looks and the sartorial taste that comes with a big, big paycheck. Barracuda hungry and ethically challenged. The man Molly would have paid to have found in that motel room instead of Mary Margaret Ryan. The man she'd still pay to see dead in the worst possible way she could think of, and she'd thought of them all.

The man who had spent two weeks smiling just like that across a witness box from her, thirteen months, two weeks, and five days ago. The man who had taken the last of her idealism and sold it on the open market.

"Frank Patterson," Molly said, ignoring the smile, the outstretched hand, and the snakeskin charm. "Who'd you have to kill and eat to get here?"

✦ Chapter 5 ✦

HE LAUGHED. Molly wasn't in the least surprised. One thing she had to say about Frank Patterson, he had never apologized. Not for tracking down the family of Mrs. Wiedeman, not for filing a lawsuit that included Molly for something she didn't do, not for making sure that Molly paid more than her fair share along with everybody else.

Which just went to show you that the jokes were right. Metro Health Center, suddenly uncomfortable having a liability on its staff who had openly testified against the hospital in court, had methodically worked its bureaucratic magic until Molly had been forced off the payroll, ending her first real chance at tenure and security. Patterson, on the other hand, seemed to have leapt up the food chain like a salmon in spawning season. Frank's last address had been in a crackerbox place out in Ferguson sandwiched between a Chinese take-out and a video store.

"Have a seat, have a seat," he offered, that smile even brighter at her discomfort. "I bought them with money from Metro, you know."

"Thanks, no," she said. "They'd probably collapse."

"And risk a lawsuit?" he demanded, wide-eyed. "Don't be silly."

"Mr. Patterson," the receptionist ventured in a breathy whisper.

"Oh, Ms. Burke and I know each other from way back, don't we, Molly?"

"We do, Frank," Molly retorted, her attempts at professionalism evaporating. Damn it, he smelled so good. He always had, just a whiff of Lagerfeld to affect the witness's concentration. "I have a sneaking suspicion that it's my bones you used to build the ladder to climb to this exalted office."

Frank's laugh would have made angels cry. But then, they said, so would Lucifer's. "Overstating the case, Molly. Your settlement was the smallest of the bunch. I used much sturdier bones than yours."

"You might be surprised how sturdy my bones are, Frank."

"Mr. Patterson," the receptionist tried again, still hanging on to the door as if keeping herself upright.

Frank finally acknowledged her. He flashed her the smile. Not a barracuda smile, Molly realized. Admitted, actually. What he had was a pirate smile. The kind Errol Flynn was always leveling on Olivia de Havilland, equal parts charm, delight, and devilment. It was a smile that made Frank's eyes crinkle and his teeth gleam. It was a smile that made everyone around him want to smile back and join in the fun. Even Molly.

The receptionist obviously wasn't any more immune than anyone else. She smiled. Not as big as Molly was sure she would have before she found out why Molly was here. But under the assault of that Patterson charm, she did do some noticeable melting.

"Something else, Brittany?" he asked.

Brittany. Of course. Her name couldn't have been Selma.

"I'd prefer to tell him," Molly told the woman, turning to face her. Not because she needed to impress her, but because she had to compose herself a second before facing Frank again.

Brittany turned on Molly as if Molly had killed Peg Ryan herself. Then she gave a quick nod and fled.

"Don't tell me," Frank said. "*You're* suing *me*."

Molly took a breath to quell her temper and turned back to the business at hand. "Attractive as that offer is, I'm afraid not."

He laughed again. "I can't help it if you had a bad lawyer, Mol. He never should have let me get away with what I did."

"Thank you. I'll treasure that apology as long as I live. But that's not why I'm here."

Molly took a second to consider the fact that she probably should be talking to someone else. Anyone else. Brittany, for God's sake. Frank Patterson set her teeth on edge so fast she'd lose the most vital moment in the interview.

That first reaction to the news. Always the most important. The truest. *Are you surprised that your husband is dead, or relieved or disappointed? Did you know Aunt Martha was planning to down all those sleeping pills?* Given an hour and a lawyer, the truth usually disappeared. Suicides turned into accidents and murder to an alibi. But more often than not, the first contact with a law official betrayed the truth.

"It's about Mary Margaret Ryan," Molly said, gauging his reaction.

His reaction was that he offered her a seat and returned to his own. "Now, there's the lawyer you should have had—since you couldn't have me. Hire Peg to sue that two-bit hospital that wouldn't take care of your defense for you. She'll slice them up so badly they'll wish they were a car parts store."

Molly eased her way into the chair without taking her eyes from Frank Patterson. "That's not why I'm here."

Instinctively, her voice softened into her bad-news-and-disaster tone. Low and soothing and non-threatening.

It caught Frank's attention. "What's wrong? You don't have a problem with Peg. You can't. She's almost as good a lawyer as I am."

Molly reached into her purse again to pull out her proof. "I'm here in an official capacity, Frank, to talk to somebody who worked with Ms. Ryan. I'm afraid she's dead."

For a minute, Frank just sat there. Molly didn't wait. She opened her ID case and showed it to him.

"I'm working for the Medical Examiner's Office now," she said.

He looked at the card and still he didn't react. After what he'd done to her, Molly's less than altruistic instinct was to hurt him with the rest. Drop it on him, grind him a little. Just some payback for the stress ulcers and job-hunting.

She couldn't. No matter what, it wasn't a weapon she used.

"What happened?" he asked, his own voice changed. Chastened. A little hoarse, the timbre matching a sudden darkness in his expression. Clenched muscles instead of tears. Stillness instead of abrupt action. A man who knew how to control his reactions. A man who'd had to before.

"She committed suicide," Molly said, and watched the most closely of all.

Frank Patterson robbed her of her reaction by closing his eyes completely.

"You're not surprised," Molly said quietly, her ID retrieved, her hands quiet in her lap, her need to control the interview pushed aside by her instincts. Compassion. Empathy. Fear.

She wanted it to be okay. And then she wanted to be away from it.

"No," he finally said, opening his eyes again. "I guess I'm not. She's been really bad lately."

Molly didn't so much as think about going for her notebook. "Bad how?"

He picked up a Mont Blanc fountain pen with gold trim and marbleized shaft that matched the lobby downstairs. "She just lost her first big case. A real bruiser. And our Peg doesn't take losing well. She trashed her office."

"She's done that before?"

"She was intense. Headed for stardom in the courtroom if she could get herself focused. I always had a sneaking suspicion she was a manic-depressive."

"Why?"

He allowed himself a look now out to the empty air over Illinois, tracking the gleam of a river under full sun. "When she was on the case, she was so up she seemed six inches taller. Vibrant, energetic. Brilliant. She only lost because we represent the big companies and the jury wanted to give the money to the little guy."

"The big companies?"

Frank returned his attention to her and grinned with some deprecation. "Don't you remember who defended that hospital of yours when you got sued, Saint Molly?"

Molly sat up a little straighter. She hadn't remembered. She hadn't had any contact with the hospital lawyers past the moment they'd effectively said, "Do we know you?" Her own lawyer had been provided by her insurance company.

Frank was already nodding, arms spread. "How do

you think I leapfrogged up to the twenty-first floor? Old man Marsdale himself was so impressed with how I handed the heads of his law firm to my client on a platter, he offered me a job. It has been a very successful relationship."

Molly thought she was going to be sick. In the temple of the devil itself. She'd been gang-raped in that court, and the gang was all here.

"And Ms. Ryan?" she asked anyway, struggling to keep her focus, furious that she hadn't walked out of the office before she'd had the chance to find this out.

"She's . . . was . . . fairly new. Bright kid, good schooling. Great future in product liability defense. She'd already been put onto the Argon Pharmaceutical, Veldux Corporation, and HealthSys Manufacturing retainer teams."

"There were cases?"

"There are always cases. We do a lot of preventative maintenance for the companies involved. They appreciate the savings."

"And the case she was just on?"

"It's public record. She was on the team defending Veldux in a case involving allegedly bad incubators."

"Allegedly."

That smile again. Brash and bright, a little boy playing a game. "What's a little judgment among friends?"

"My thoughts exactly. You worked with her on what?"

He rearranged the call-back notes on his desk. "Veldux. This was her first court appearance, and I was helping her prepare. We got along well. Kindred spirits, you might say."

"How long since the case was decided?"

"About ten days. She's been having more and more trouble since then. I was hoping she'd pull out of it. But then when she didn't come in this morning . . ."

A frown passed across his face like a cloud skimming clear water. Evidently Frank Patterson wasn't the kind to brood too long.

"Is there anything else she might have talked to you about? Relationships, anything like that?"

Frank's smile was wry and knowing. "We talked precedents and briefs and redirects. Peg isn't the type to confide."

Molly nodded, considering. "Had she been drinking?"

He looked up at her, a little surprised, a little chagrined. "Probably. How's her family?"

"Not well."

He nodded, straightened, as if pulling himself into order. "Good."

Molly admitted surprise. "Good?"

This grin was even more fleeting then the frown. More knowing. "I need something to do. I'll go see them."

The last thing Molly wanted to see from Frank Patterson was altruism. "They're nice people, Frank."

"Are you saying I'm not?"

"Just . . . they didn't see what you did in the last few weeks. Okay?"

He nodded, his expression only gently mocking now. "Even the wolves who raised me respect grief, Saint Molly."

"Stop calling me that, Frank."

"Why? That's how I think of you."

"It's not how I am."

That got her one last smile, the brightest, most self-effacing smile Frank Patterson had in the repertory. "But you are. You're the most beautiful martyr I've ever burned at the stake."

• • •

"So the lawyer count is up to four, huh?"

Molly didn't bother to look away from the baby she was holding to acknowledge Sasha standing in the door. "Yep."

Six months old, he weighed six pounds. A pound more than he had at birth. He looked like an ad for Christian Children Services, and he'd come from St. Louis. Molly rocked him and smiled. The IV taped to his forehead resupplied fluids he hadn't been getting, and Molly's gloves and gown protected her from the lice and scabies he carried. He was too worn out to smile back. He just watched her, his eyes huge and patient, his mouth clamped around a pacifier. Molly hummed to him, something old and Irish, and he seemed to like it.

"You know what that makes, don't you?"

Molly looked up then. "What?"

Sasha's smile was as bright as Frank Patterson's. "A good beginning. You comin' outa here soon?"

Molly turned back to the baby and smiled a different smile. Dawayne Peters responded by slowing his sucking for a fraction of a second. "Oh, in a minute. It's my lunch hour."

"Your lunch fifteen minutes. All hell's breakin' loose out there."

"Let me take him up to his room and I'll be out."

For a second, she thought Sasha had left. Then she heard a sigh behind her. "You can't adopt them all," Sasha said.

Molly still hadn't lost her smile. She never did when she got to play with babies, no matter what was wrong with them. "I don't want to adopt any of them," she said, knowing quite well that she was lying through her perfectly straightened teeth. "I just want to play."

"Uh-huh. And I want the world run by HMOs. Listen to your Auntie Sasha. Buy a cat."

"Cats don't smile."

"They also don't make you mope around work for three weeks every time you have to realize that their abusive parents are getting them back. You had two perfectly good chances to have your own. Why didn't you?"

"I did," Molly told her, still facing the quizzical eyes of the tiny life in her lap. "It didn't take."

There was a silence from the doorway. Sasha wouldn't apologize. Molly wouldn't expect her to. It was the reason she'd told her the truth. Well, some of it. No one needed to hear about those four hospital visits, each more desperate than the last when Molly fought the inevitable with prayers and screaming and denial. No one needed to know how brightly it had all begun and how miserably it had all ended. With a whimper, as it were. In her case, a laparoscopy.

"Some women who've been exposed to Agent Orange shouldn't try to have kids," Molly said as if she were instructing the tiny life she held in her hands. "They should just play with other people's."

"I'm sorry," Sasha said, and stunned Molly to her toes.

Molly turned on her. "You hate kids. Why should you be sorry?"

Sasha didn't let anything show in those frosty blue eyes of hers. "Because you don't. You've got five more minutes, and then I'll give you the chance to feel better about your state by giving you the next patient."

Sasha was as good as her word. By the time Molly made it back downstairs to pick up the patients she'd had before her lunch break, she'd also inherited fourteen-year-old Elvin "Bone T" Marshall, brought to the ER by his mother when she'd found him battered and bruised in his bedroom. Bone T's mother was furious, frightened, and hovering. Bone T was embarrassed to his toes. He was also defiant.

One look in the room was enough for Molly to know what was going on. She just couldn't believe that in this day and age in the neighborhood where Bone T and his mama lived, that she hadn't figured out right away what was going on.

So the first thing she did was ask ma to have a seat outside while she examined the skinny, wired, wary boy. What she did instead was pull out an opaque plastic bag with the hospital logo on it.

"Okay, Bone T," she said quietly. No attitude. No condescension or control. "These are the rules. What you do on the street is your own business—although if you were a man, you'd tell your mama what's goin' on." She didn't wait for the glare, the uncomfortable shifting that answered her. Instead, she gestured to his clothes, all blue, from his shirt to his jeans to his cap and socks and shoes and bandanna. "This is a no-colors zone. I need your clothes off so I can check you out for your mama, and I need your colors put inside so we don't have an incident in the hall. If we have an incident in the hall, your mother could be the one shot, and I don't think you want that."

"I don' take my colors off for nobody," he insisted, trying with at least three broken ribs to look threatening.

As well he might. He'd just been initiated. Into which gang, Molly wasn't sure. There were dozens aligned with the Crips, whose colors he was wearing. All of them used what they called being "jumped in" as their initiation. The entire gang would batter at the new kid until he couldn't walk. Then they all hugged and shared, as if they'd just finished EST. The kids said it made them feel like they belonged. One had even explained that parents beat their kids when they loved them, and so did the gang. The Boy Scouts for dysfunctional lives.

"That's why I have this bag," Molly said, as if she didn't hear the sneer. "You keep 'em with you, just like you do at school. You just don't show them and start something."

"You dissin' my family," he retorted, trying so hard to be mean. Molly saw the residual spark of childhood in those old eyes and wondered how long he'd last.

"I got no reason to dis you, Bone T, or your family. I'm the one that helps when your homes are in trouble. If you respect my turf. Neutral ground, man. You don't like it, I'll go out and tell your ma I can't take care of you, and I'll tell her why."

It might have been different if every gang-banger on the street didn't know the rules at Grace. If every one of them hadn't benefited from them at one time or another. A sage and savvy medical director had parleyed with the gangs for rules everybody could agree on in his ER. It didn't mean it was safe. It meant the truce was holding. So far, they'd only had half a dozen incidents in the halls since June. Not bad, considering what was going on out in the streets and the fact that the gangsters they were making deals with were as young as fourteen.

"You want me to help?" Molly asked, dropping her voice into the definite no-challenge zone.

Bone managed to work his way off the cart. Molly gave brief thought to the fact that he could be carrying a weapon, and then dropped the bag on the cart. "I'll be back. Okay?"

She never would have left one of the older ones alone. Not till he was naked and she found out whether he'd socked away insurance against surprises. Not when his rivals might be hunting to finish their task. Not once the humanity in his eyes winked out.

Even so, Molly didn't feel the tension ease across her shoulders until she was out in the work lane with everybody else.

"Hey, Molly," Lance Frost called from where he was playing with a new cardiac stethoscope at one of the work stations. "I need to dismiss one and six." Lance handed the charts off to a tech who walked them the next five feet to Molly.

"I hear the lawyer tote board's up to four now," the tech said. "You know what that is, don't you?"

Lance didn't bother to look up. "You'd think my divorce lawyer would have the grace to add himself to that list. Especially considering what he let my wife get away with."

"We all paid him to do it," Betty Wheaton, one of the other nurses, offered on the way by.

"I figured as much."

"I'm going on my fifteen minutes now," Sasha told Molly. "You triage for me?"

Molly nodded, her attention on the charts in her hand. Reacquainting herself with who belonged to what room number. "As soon as I send these two home and check in on Mary Mother of God. . . ." Grabbing a prescription from the top chart, she waved it at Lance. "What the hell's this?"

When she didn't get an immediate answer, Molly walked as close as she dared to the periphery of Lance's body odor and leveled a glare on her ER physician of record.

"What does it look like?" Lance asked, still not looking up.

"Do you recognize this medication, Betty?" Molly asked, already knowing the answer.

Shifting the load of IV fluids in her arms so she could lift her glasses, the very round, very dark, very quick Betty glanced down at the prescription before her. "Why, no, Molly. I don't. I've never seen that drug before in my life."

"Neither have I," Molly answered, her suspicions high. The only reason Lance would take the trouble even to learn how to spell a new drug name was that a drug salesman had been by to pronounce it for him. The one thing the drug salesman wouldn't say was that this breakthrough, all-wonderful, ever-safe drug cost at least three dollars a pill. And the doctors, wavering beneath the spell of handouts, flattery, and free gifts, usually forgot to ask.

"This little old lady has been on the same meds for fifteen years," Molly told Lance. "What's so important about changing them now?"

"She had to come to the ER," Lance offered laconically.

"She had to come to the ER because she was lonely. Just like she does every other month. You know that."

Betty was smiling like a cat in the canary patch. "What do you suppose it means, especially since the drug salesman for Parker was just here to donate that bright, shiny new stethoscope to our physician yonder?"

"I don't suppose this medicine is a Parker product," Molly offered.

"It has a longer half-life than the latest bronchodilators," Lance said.

"It also costs eight times more than the other bronchodilators," Molly retorted.

Lance raised eyes that were the soul of innocence. "Don't you want that nice little old lady to breathe better?"

"Not only is she not going to breathe any better,"

Molly retorted. "She's gonna have a stroke when she sees the price tag on this. And then she's not going to be able to eat when she has to pay for it. Give her the generic, Lance."

"I can't do that, Molly. It wouldn't be right."

Molly counted to ten, the script still in her hand. This wasn't just enthusiasm for a newer, shinier model then. This went deeper. "You found your money-maker after all, didn't you?"

Lance didn't bother to answer. He just smiled and stroked his new toy. Molly didn't say anything either. She simply headed over to Mrs. Wilner's room, where she made a quick X in the box that would allow a generic substitution to be made by the pharmacy.

That was if the pharmacy wasn't also benefiting from the pharmaceutical's largesse by filling a prescription that would cost the patient three to six times what the generic did, and then getting a discreet kickback from the drug company in thanks. The things the consumer didn't know, Molly thought with a disparaging shake of the head.

"Tommy," she said to the tech, "get me Mrs. Wilner's wheelchair and get the kid's family in twelve. Then push the peds doc in to see Bone T before he runs out on us, okay? After I dismiss Mrs. Wilner, I think I deserve a blessing from Mary Mother of God."

By the time Molly finally did make it in to see her, Mary Mother of God was seated cross-legged on the cart in a short leather skirt and strategically ripped tube top. Mary came in every so often to deliver the second savior. Not that she was ever pregnant. She just figured that God was more mysterious than any of them thought. She had also decided, on or about her third visit, that childbirth as it stood was best left to the beasts of the field. Which meant that she kept waiting for Molly to notify her that the big guy had come up with something more suitable.

Mary didn't act much like the mother of you-know-who. She dressed more like the Queen of the Night than the Queen of Heaven, and had a mouth on her that had the staff wondering just which Madonna she professed to be. She also smelled as if she hadn't bathed since the last time she'd been struck by the hand of God.

"Mary?"

The patient looked up. "You don't believe me."

Mary's favorite accusation. Molly figured it was because most people would hope that a benevolent supreme being would pick someone with more teeth, less hair, and better hygiene to bear his son.

"Did I say that, Mary?"

Molly checked the chart, which betrayed no signs of a doctor's visit. She did, however, catch the lingering whiff of chicken soup in the air, which meant that Lance just wasn't charting again. There was also a slip of paper that said that Dr. Stavrakos was held up in clinic. It figured that he'd get this. Gene did so love the fun stuff.

"You should be fuckin' glad that I chose to come back here," Mary growled, finger pointing. "Especially after the treatment you all gave me the last time."

"It was a busy night."

"You wouldn't have put Herod in a cave."

"As a matter of fact, we did." The cave actually being room three. Herod came in periodically looking for the child Mary was supposed to have delivered. Molly was just glad that they usually missed each other. Also that Herod only came armed with a spear.

"What am I waiting for?" Mary demanded, scratching in places Molly didn't want to see.

Molly smiled. "Archangel Gabriel," she said. "He's held up in traffic."

Mary Mother of God stopped scratching. "Oh, good. I need to talk to him."

"I bet."

The area around the triage desk was stacked like the stage at a heavy metal concert. As she approached, Molly heard the computers, saw the three secretaries bobbing their heads in search of their organizer, and smelled the alcohol that hung in the air like a toxic cloud. Beer and Mad Dog. Eau de City Drunks. Out in the county they would at least have had the decency to swill Jack Daniels, or even Chivas. Down here it was Rosie O'Grady, Malt anything, and, occasionally, gold spray paint.

"Okay, what's the game plan?" she asked the senior secretary, a nervous, prim little thing who would have been much better suited to the administrative suites. Triage was tough duty to pull, the place where patients were first seen and assessed, their information obtained without too much screaming and shouting, and their treatment directed. Traffic control with Greek street signs, basically. And at Grace, it was always rush hour.

"Um, well, this woman here . . . you know . . . uh, she has a . . ."

Molly took a peek through the metroplex-like window that separated them from the unwashed sea of injured and diseased. There were people draped over every chair within a mile radius and others holding up the faded green walls. There were kids yelling and drunks wobbling and at least one complete family huddled in the corner watching the rest of the crowd as if they were aliens.

For a change, though, no one appeared to be

actively bleeding or blue, so it was first come first served. And standing first in line was an overweight blondish white woman in jeans and a Travis Tritt muscle shirt who had a definite look of discomfort on her doughy features and a posture that belied big trouble in her center of gravity area.

"She has a what?" Molly asked, desperately trying not to grab the chart from the secretary, who clutched it as if it were porn.

"Growth," the little woman whispered with a dip of her eyes and a twitch of her nose that reminded Molly of nothing so much as a mouse catching scent of a cat. "Down there."

"I see."

Bartholin cyst, probably. They hit women where it hurt, right in the vaginal area, and were preferable to childbirth only in that they lasted less than nine months.

Losing patience, Molly made a grab for the chart. Truth be told, she couldn't wait to see how the secretary had described the problem. This was, after all, the woman who had fainted dead away when finally convinced that a person could, indeed, contract syphilis in the throat. And why. Her attempts to gentrify descriptions of bodily functions regularly ended up in the book of fame in the back.

Molly read this one and burst out laughing.

The secretary blanched. The patient sighed. Molly apologized.

"It's not you," she said to the woman, who was certainly not happy to be there in the first place.

It was the line on the chart that said, *Chief complaint.* The place where the secretary was supposed to transcribe the complaint as the patient gave it. Molly was sure the now-blushing secretary had meant to write "Patient has a swelling in her vagina." What it came out as, though, was, *Patient states she has a swell vagina.*

Molly couldn't wait to get back to the back and show this one off.

"Yo, bitch! You dissin' me?"

A woman screamed. Half a dozen people started running. Molly looked up just in time to see a tall black youth in a blue bandanna and Raiders jacket level a MAC-10 at her head. The truce hadn't lasted as long as they'd hoped. Molly dropped like a stone, taking two of the secretaries with her just as the gun went off.

✦ Chapter 6 ✦

I SHOULDN'T HAVE LAUGHED, was Molly's only coherent thought as she hit the floor. Over her head the Plexiglas shattered, spraying her with fragments. Out in the hall, the crowd had disappeared like kids at a school bell.

"Hail Mary, full of grace," the little secretary squeaked in her ear.

Molly almost laughed again. *She's right back in the back*, she wanted to tell the distraught woman, who was curled up tighter than a hedgehog beneath her. *I'll go get her right now.*

The gunman emptied the clip into the wall over Molly's head and reloaded, walking and shouting epithets as he did. Molly finally reached up high enough to hit the toggle switch set into the wall right next to the chair. If she pushed it up, it called for security to respond. If she pulled it down, it meant for them to run like hell, and bring guns. She pulled it down. Then she yanked the cord to the mike so she could pull it onto the floor and alert the people in the back, who probably hadn't even heard the popping through the din of patients.

"Doctor Holliday to the desk stat," she announced,

hearing her breathless voice throughout the floor. "Doctor Holliday."

A code they'd once thought cute. Doc Holliday meant a gunslinger on the street. Get the women and children into the saloon. With so many Wyatt Earp movies out lately, the gang-bangers were catching on. The staff was thinking of coming up with something else. Even so, Molly heard the brief halt in noise at the back, the terrible scramble to get the patients to safety.

The gang-banger was moving around to the doorway. Molly could hear him. At least she thought she could. Her heart was hammering so hard, she wasn't sure of anything.

For just the briefest of moments, she smelled the cordite and fought a rush of old memory. Crouched beneath a window in a Quonset hut, trying her damnedest to hand off instruments during a rocket raid in the middle of the night. Heart pounding, hands sweating, breath rasping in her throat as if she'd been in a fire. Trying to stay calm when the only thing keeping her alive was luck.

But she wasn't in a Quonset hut, and the enemy wasn't half a mile away. He had just reached the door to the triage station, where Molly and the secretaries crouched beneath the protective overhang of the desk.

He was smiling. A strong, handsome kid dressed in blue and black with dead eyes and a gun as his mouthpiece. A gun he was leveling at her again.

"This gonna be fun, ho'." He gave her a big smile. And then, before Molly could even close her eyes or start praying along with her secretary, he froze. Turned. Began to topple.

Only then did Molly hear the double sounds of a pistol shot and a deep, laconic voice.

"Police. Halt."

The gang-banger hit the floor like a felled tree, his eyes still open, and the secretary beneath Molly wet her pants. Molly damn near did the same thing.

"You okay?" a voice asked over her head.

It took that to make her realize that she'd closed her eyes after all. It was all she could do to breathe, much less respond. All she could see were those eyes. Dead, hard, cold eyes in a seventeen-year-old. God, what had this country done to its children?

"Yo, ladies, you okay?"

Molly opened her eyes again to find that there were two of them, one black, one white. Both as closed-off and controlled as the youth they'd shot. Both so similar to each other in dress, grooming, and demeanor, that Molly wouldn't have needed them to announce their occupations to know. Cops the world over looked alike.

"I think so," she said, trying her best to straighten up.

She thought to check the boy on the floor. One look at the back of his head took care of that. The policeman hadn't taken a chance. Molly realized she was glad.

She got as far as her butt and stayed there. So far, not one of the secretaries seemed the least inclined to follow even that far.

"Ms. Burke?" the black cop addressed her, his expression never changing.

Molly allowed her surprise.

"Can I help you?" she asked, and realized that her voice was even less impressive than on the horn. Soon she was going to start squeaking like an asthmatic pigeon.

The white cop flipped a badge as the black cop reholstered his gun. "Detectives Martin and Jones from intelligence. We needed to talk to you."

"As soon as we take care of all this," the other one put in, bending to check out the young man he'd just brought down.

Just as he did, three security officers armed with everything from .9 mms to riot guns rounded the desk at a run. Their first reaction was to take aim at the black man bent over the black youth. Their second, upon seeing the badge the white cop flashed them, was to come to a screeching halt. Only then did Molly think to announce an all clear. She pulled the mike back into her lap and hit the switch.

"Billie Burke to the desk, please. Billie Burke."

Billie Burke being the actress who had played the Good Witch of the North in *The Wizard of Oz*. The witch who had sung to the Munchkins, "Come out, come out, wherever you are."

Who said a crisis couldn't be creative?

"You piss him off, or what?" the homicide detective asked.

Molly tried to take another drink from a cup of coffee that was sloshing like a pool in an earthquake. The crisis had caught up with her so hard she couldn't hold still.

"Not unless he was dating the lady at the front desk," she said, swallowing back the bile that kept trying to work its way loose. It had already made it three times, and she was not in the mood to make it a fourth.

They were sitting back in the lounge, a converted linen closet that held a bulletin board full of notices, secondhand furniture from the Salvation Army resale shop, and a microwave. On the back wall where nobody who shouldn't could see it, was the hand inscribed plaque left by one of the first trauma residents to make it through Grace's program. *Traumaland.* It read. *From the slime to the ridiculous.*

Molly couldn't agree more. She was sharing her shakes with the now-familiar intelligence team, a homicide guy she didn't know very well, the shooting team from the metropolitan police, and, for good measure, Kevin McCaully, who'd just happened to be the death investigator on for her big moment.

Every one of them had spent time at the front desk, where they considered, shook their heads, and told Molly how lucky she was. She hadn't argued. After about an hour of intense activity along a work lane that was still packed to the rafters, most of the rest of the gathered forces were milling around waiting for evidence to finish, while the intelligence team and homicide sat back with Molly, who was around waiting for her legs to work.

"What gang did he belong to?" she asked.

Martin looked up. "That boy was a bad fucker. Name's Mustaffa. Belongs to one of the Hoover offshoots."

Molly nodded. Wondered if she should bring Bone into this. Wondered whether this cop would ruin her uneasy alliance with a boy who still had a spark left in his eye. Cops saw gang-bangers for the crimes they committed. Molly could still, sometimes, see the children searching for a place to belong, a family to call their own. A flag they could show with pride.

She understood how the cops felt. But she understood how the kids felt, too. At least the very young ones, who still had a small chance at survival.

"It was my fault," Sasha said, walking in, her ashen face frozen into stone to prevent betraying emotion. In defiance of every hospital and city ordinance, she was working on a cigarette. As hard as she was pulling on the thing, she must have left a smoke trail halfway down the hall, which would explain why Georgia Prendergast followed her into the room at warp speed.

"This is a no-smoking area," she informed Sasha in arch tones. Georgia, a chunky little bleached blond who had her blue-shadowed eye on the administrative suite, loved nothing more than impressing the people who could promote her by ratting on the ones who couldn't.

Sasha didn't even bother to turn around to confront the interloper. "This is also a no-kill zone," she countered icily, "but we've already shot that to hell tonight. And since everybody's already here, I bet they wouldn't mind making it a deuce now rather than having to come all the way back out again."

She glared at all three policemen, who just shrugged agreeably. The homicide guy was even obliging enough to pull out a clean DD-5 form and click open his pen. Sensing that a frontal attack wasn't going to do her any good, Georgia beat a strategic retreat.

Sasha never condescended to notice. Her attention was equally divided between Molly and Phillip Morris.

"She's running right home to the nursing supervisor to tell on you," Molly warned her.

Sasha took care of the last of her cigarette and ground it out in an emesis basin. "I'll eat her liver."

The police shifted around to continue their questioning. It wasn't yet meant to be, though. From behind Sasha, another country was heard from.

"Hey, Chernobyl, was that you in the Gunfight at the O. K. Corral up there?"

Only one person had the guts to call Sasha Chernobyl. He wedged his way through the crowd at the door and grinned for everybody in the room. "We on the news," he announced. "Of course, you man

James here jus' happen to be there when the cameras showed up. The hospital now owes me time and a half for public relations."

"Of course they do," Sasha retorted.

James wasn't in the least intimidated. In fact, he broadened his grin to exhibit his two prize gold crowns. Short, black, bald, and round, James was the evening pharmacy supervisor. He was also the proud holder of the best collection of reggae in the city, which seemed to follow him long after the radio was switched off. He never stopped moving, and he always moved to the beat of invisible drums.

"We're kind of busy here," one of the cops informed him.

He didn't bother to answer. "Oh, it was you, Miss Molly."

As in, "Good Golly Miss Molly." James had a nickname for everybody he supplied.

"It was me, James."

His nod was brisk. "Fearsome. Real fearsome. You need a little help wit' you nerves? Your man James is holdin', just like always."

Everybody on the couch but Molly went right on point.

"We're police," Martin informed him so that he might have the chance to sneak back out before incriminating himself and causing them more paperwork.

"It's okay," Molly informed them both. "He's not holding what you think he is. Would you mind, James? Just put it on my tab."

James laughed and bounced a little on the balls of his feet. "James always takes care of his customers." Then he reached into his lab coat pocket and pulled out a Ding Dong. Molly caught it on the fly, which just left James with his real mission up here. "Hey, Chernobyl, where you want that stat streptokinase?"

"Medprep," Sasha told him, looking straight down at the top of his head as if he were a Munchkin who had somehow strayed into *Swan Lake.* "I'll be there in a minute."

James nodded, took another bright, assessing look at the glowering police, and bounced back out the door. As he headed down the hall, Molly could hear him singing, "Kill the white man," just loud enough for the white cops to hear.

Martin sighed, his attention drawn to Sasha, who still hadn't moved. "We have to talk to Ms. Burke—"

"You have to talk to me, too," she said, then turned to Molly for what sounded suspiciously like an apology. "He said he needed to be seen," she said in a way that made Molly think that these weren't the first cops she'd relayed the information to. "I told him to wait with everybody else." She couldn't quite say she was sorry, but Molly understood.

"No," Detective Jones said, closing his notebook. "It was his fault. You all were just there. Word's already out on the street that it was a cop shoot, so you don't have to worry about the rest of his posse comin' back on a mission to even things up. We'll have everything else cleaned up as quick as we can."

Sasha couldn't seem to break eye contact with Molly, as if waiting for her absolution but incapable of asking for it. Molly didn't know what would make Sasha feel better.

Molly did her best to smile. She could have told Sasha it hadn't been the first time she'd been shot at, but Sasha already knew that. She could have told her at least they were all alive, but Sasha knew that, too.

"Well," she said instead, "at least I'm not the investigator on. I don't think I can be very objective about this one."

Maybe she shouldn't have said that after all,

because suddenly Jones pulled his book back out and Martin edged forward on his chair.

"I'll go out and talk to the other witnesses," the homicide guy said, rising.

"We'll be right here for a while," Martin said with some meaning.

Molly almost groaned. She wasn't in the mood for this. Especially if Kevin had thought it important enough to warn her. She shot Sasha a pleading glance, but Sasha picked that moment to feel absolved and grin.

"They're coming down for Mary Mother of God. Any messages?"

Molly sighed and fought the urge to ask for her own cigarette. "Yeah. Tell 'em I want some of whatever she has."

"We all do, honey," she said, and swung on out the door.

Molly was left behind with the two intelligence guys, who had obviously never learned that a good cop begins an interrogation with a little small talk.

"You were the investigator on when Pearl Johnson came in," Detective Martin asked in his most official voice. "Correct?"

"I guess this means we're not talking about Mustaffa anymore, huh?"

"That's right," Detective Jones said.

Molly ripped open the cellophane on the Ding Dong and settled back in the couch. "In that case, buy me a drink, big boy, and I'll tell you everything I know."

Two hours later, Molly was still waiting for that drink. She was also waiting for the cops to figure out that she'd already told them everything she knew, twice, with color commentary as a bonus. She supposed she should be glad the detectives had shown up, because they'd ended up saving her life. Then they'd proceeded to screw it up, yet again.

"Could you have been mistaken about the note?" Detective Martin asked again and again, his face passive, his eyes opaque.

"No," Molly said. "I saw it. That's what it said. End of story."

"And you didn't know anything about the gambling issue when you saw the note."

"I did. I just didn't know who William T. Peterson was. Is he who I heard he was?"

"Do you invest, Ms. Burke?"

"Invest?" she responded, tired, anxious, still quivering with the aftereffects of seeing a muzzle flash five feet away. "What do you mean?"

"Well," Jones said, scratching his neck as if the question were a confusion instead of an important issue, "you know those riverboat gaming stocks have been pretty hot lately."

He could have given Columbo lessons in how to look innocent, Molly thought. *I don't know, ma'am. I just have a little problem here I need to clear up. Maybe you can help . . .*

"All you have to do is take a look at my bank statement," she retorted, not at all happy with the turn of the conversation. "It will show you just how much money I have available to invest in anything but lunchmeat and gas."

Martin's one eyebrow went up. A sure sign he smelled blood. "You needed money, did you?"

As if she'd already received it. Lots of it. As in, I fake this suicide note for you, you pay off my legal fees.

Molly laughed. "Get a real suspect, Martin. I'm just the death investigator who had the misfortune to lose a suicide note. You don't believe me, fine. But don't take me off a busy work lane just to feed me crap like that. Now, are we finished?"

The smile she got out of Jones was one of surprise. "Did we sound like we were after you? We're sorry, Ms. Burke. Really."

Molly got to her feet and smiled back. "I know you are. Now, unless you can start an IV or do a cardiac assessment, I have things I have to do."

Martin never looked up. "Did you know that there were other city employees involved in a possibly illegal connection to the gambling?"

For a minute Molly stared. Then she laughed again. "What's your point?"

That was like saying that Madonna might have had sex. Pearl had surprised Molly. Disappointed her. But Molly had lived in St. Louis too long to be amazed or disconcerted by the news that one or two of her elected officials might be realizing a financial gain from a big political move. Hell, she would have been surprised if this gambling issue had gotten through without half the state legislature turning up as the landowners, bond holders, or gambling licensees for the complex they'd taken bids on and voted for.

Martin lifted his attention to her as if he still didn't believe her. "We know you were friends with Ms. Johnson. So was the medical examiner, wasn't she?"

This time Molly couldn't even gather the breath or the coherence to answer. Winnie Harrison was many things. Arrogant, self-centered, driven, slave-driving, sarcastic. She was also completely and totally focused on her work. One had to have a passion for advancement or position or money to be seduced by graft. Winnie was interested in none of those things. She was interested in science. In forensics. In answers. She didn't even know where the money came from to fund her work. In fact, the only time she realized that her office came with its own administrator was when she didn't get equipment and he had to explain that it wasn't budgeted yet.

"Anybody else on your list?" Molly asked. "Santa Claus? St. Christopher?"

"We're just doing our job, Ms. Burke."

"Uh-huh. Read my report, guys. It's all in there. Now, I have to get back."

"One more thing, Ms. Burke."

Molly stopped one more time. "Yes."

"If Pearl Johnson's death was murder and we don't find out who was involved, there could be other incidents."

Incidents. Molly sighed. "There was a note. There was excellent reason to suspect suicide. I'm sorry it's not more interesting than that, but it isn't."

"We'll see."

And that was all she got from them. So she thanked them again for saving her life and then left them to the bad furniture and old mildew smells and lame suspicions.

✦ Chapter 7 ✦

"YOU'RE ALL RIGHT?"

Preoccupied with gathering her work gear off the front seat of her car, Molly squinted into the early morning sun. "Sam, what are you doing out this early?"

Sam had the habits of a vampire, which was one of the reasons he and Molly got along so well. The idea that he was up at sunrise made Molly nervous.

He waved a half-smoked cigarette at her from the other side of her car window. "I worry."

Molly took hold of her paraphernalia and climbed out of her '89 Celica. It had taken more wear and tear than Sam's lungs, but it was fast, handled well, and Molly had been able to afford the payments, which had ended a year earlier.

"Worry about what?" she asked, assessing the state of his health as she joined him outside.

He was a little bluer than usual, but then, Molly wasn't sure that wasn't Sam's usual color in early morning light.

"And just what is that in your hand?"

Molly actually looked down, as if she hadn't seen it before. As if she hadn't been smelling it all the way home from the drive-in window. "Breakfast."

Sam snorted and shook his head. "Some breakfast. Does it have eggs in it?"

Molly didn't bother to tell him that eggs were nothing to get at a drive-in. She thanked her stars for twenty-four-hour drive-ups. Especially the kinds with big, fat, everything-you-can-stuff-inside-them burritos. To each man his breakfast.

Sam waved a hand in front of his nose. "*Feh!* And just what is your cholesterol?"

Molly grinned. "Heart disease does not seem to be a favorite cause of death in the Burke clan," she admitted.

"What is?"

She thought about it a second. "Car accidents. Rebel uprisings. Nongenetic stuff."

"How about gang shootings?" Sam demanded, his eyes suspiciously moist.

Oh, God. It had been such a long night, one asthma patient after another, every female abdominal pain victim in the city, a couple of car accidents. Molly had damn near forgotten that the shooting had only happened twelve or so hours ago.

"Oh, Sam."

"We Jews have a saying, you know."

Molly tried to grin. "Call your mother?"

He wasn't mollified. "Something like that. I heard on the news."

She reached a hand out to the slumped, taut old shoulder. "I'm sorry. I didn't know. You can see perfectly well that I'm fine, though. It was just some excitement."

Sam wasn't convinced. "*Chas vesholem,* he was standing right at your desk. There was no glass left! I saw the pictures. Haven't they put in bulletproof glass there yet? What are they thinking?"

He'd obviously been saving up his outrage. Molly

patted his shoulder in commiseration. "Tea," she said softly. "My house. We'll talk."

Ten minutes with Sam and she sounded like Yenta.

The old man deflated a little. "Why? Was there any reason for this madness?"

"Who knows, Sam? Who knows?"

"And that poor young policeman who died yesterday," Sam continued, not quite ready to move up the walk yet. "I saw you on the news. You had to see that, too."

He clucked like a mother. Molly smiled. Sam still preferred to believe that she'd served her term in Vietnam in a bubble and come home to give bedbaths to little old ladies. It didn't do for Sam to think about what Molly had seen and done. It didn't do for Molly either on some days.

"They caught the boy who did it," she assured the old man.

"Did they beat him?"

"What?"

"That little *momzer* who shot the policeman."

Molly nodded absently. "Probably."

Sam nodded back. Definite and emphatic. "Good. We have three teeth, now."

And with that non sequitur, he began to head up Molly's walk. "Still crabby?" she asked, knowing perfectly well he was talking about his youngest granddaughter, Rebecca. Sam had four grandchildren, two of whom he saw, two who lived too far away to visit, considering his Myra's health. Molly got updates as if they were NASA shuttles in orbit.

"You ever know a teething baby who wasn't?" he demanded with a rasping laugh.

Molly didn't know why she looked over then. She wasn't sure why she spotted the car. After all, it was on the other side of the gate that kept traffic from turning off Euclid onto her street. But there it slowed, and there it stopped, a square, dark, late model sedan with two solid-looking young men in sunglasses who had decided to wait at a corner. Across from a restaurant. A restaurant that wouldn't be open for six more hours.

An unmarked car.

"See that car, Sam?" she asked.

Sam stopped and looked. Squinted. "Yeah?"

"Good. Just so I'm not hallucinating."

Sam turned his squint on her. "You might not be hallucinating. But you're not making sense, either."

"They're cops. Nobody I know, but definitely cops."

He took another considered look. "How do you know?"

Good question. Molly thought about it. "I hang around with 'em enough, I think I can smell 'em down the block. I wonder if I should go over and ask what they want."

"They want to watch," Sam said. "Or they wouldn't be sitting there."

"Well, what the hell do they want to watch?"

Sam patted. "An old man having tea with a beautiful young woman."

The morning was a pretty one, with the sun striking off the dew and birds chattering in the big oak and maples in the backyards. Molly's lawn was lush and green, its borders perfectly edged, the walks lined in white impatiens, and her porch bracketed by planters spilling over with geraniums and lobelia. A lovely sight, quiet and peaceful and comfortable. As comfortable a lie as Sam's.

But he was right. There was nothing to see, so she wasn't going to be concerned. Even though she couldn't think of a reason plainclothes anybody would want to keep an eye on her.

Unless they suspected her of something.

What a great way to start a day. No wonder she never got up this early.

"One more thing," Sam said, dropping his cigarette to her porch and grinding it beneath a battered black heel. "Later. After you've rested. My Medicare . . ."

Molly didn't say a word. She just nodded. She knew Sam hated asking her for help, but the paperwork killed him. Forms for reimbursement, forms for medical costs, for pharmaceutical costs. And then, the worst, when he got the notice on how much the government wasn't going to pay for his and Myra's treatments. He'd been a rich man in his heyday. Molly wasn't sure he was going to last through his old age intact.

"Later," she said, knowing just how both of them felt. Knowing it wouldn't do to explain to him that she wouldn't get any sleep this morning, because she was going to have to sit in on that young policeman's autopsy. "Right now," Molly said, sliding the key into her front door, "let's sit out back and decide if we like this morning business or not."

The St. Louis Medical Examiner's office and morgue sat at the corner of Clark and 14th Street, a square, unimpressive granite block building that had been put up sometime in the thirties along with the similarly designed central police station a block down. Serving first as the coroner's office and inquest court, it had, at one time, held all the paper records of every murder, suicide, and natural death in St. Louis as far back as the coroner's system went.

The system was automated now, the building inhabited by two pathologists, an administrator, secretaries, a team of investigators, the morgue attendants who watched the bodies come in and signed them back out the back door again, and the diener, who assisted in autopsies. The current staff inhabited two floors, the first holding the reception area, administrator's office, viewing room, and morgue areas. The second floor belonged to the pathologists and death investigators. The latter, with the exception of the chief investigator, shared the expansive room that had once held the inquest court. It now sported a black couch against the far wall for night shift, and as many desks, computers, and regulations books as the fire code would allow.

Recently repainted and cleaned, the building had lost some of its earlier institutional gloom to cream walls and newly washed curtains. The carpet was still seventies-era convent issue, though, which went a long way to negating the effect. Not only that, but if one walked through the front door of the building, the first thing he would see would be the viewing room to the right, which looked more like a mortician's dream than a bureaucrat's, with its rows of church pews and curtained wall into the morgue. The only thing missing was the organ and a tasteful stand for the visitors' book.

At eight o'clock in the morning, the viewing room was empty. A receptionist sat at the desk in the middle of the entryway, and a couple of homicide cops were descending the stairs from the offices after consulting with the investigator of their choice. Back in the autopsy room, the supporting cast waited for their star performer to arrive. Occupied black body bags rested on three of the gurneys that sat along the north wall. A fourth, zipped and anonymous, occupied the autopsy table. A set of skull films hung from the viewing box. Hercules Jones, the old, gnarled, almost toothless diener Winnie preferred to work with, waited alongside, aproned and still, instruments laid out and gleaming, saw tested and ready, specimen jars formalin-filled and waiting.

Arrayed across the other wall in OR gown and mask were the homicide officer of record, that being Rhett, and a severely sleep-deprived Molly.

As was custom with the St. Louis system, both homicide officer and death investigator witnessed the autopsy. The homicide officer to carry clothing and evidence that would be removed, so that the chain of evidence was as short as possible and uninterrupted; the investigator so there would be no paperwork or communications errors.

"Hey, Rhett," Molly said, leaning her head back against the tile wall. "You got any ideas why I'd have an unmarked car staking out my house this morning?"

Rhett looked over, truly surprised. "An unmarked? What kind?"

"Caprice. What else?"

"Recognize 'em?"

She shook her head. "Is there something you've forgotten to tell me? Like maybe somebody thinks I'm making money off the Pearl Johnson situation?"

Rhett snorted. "You've been talking to Martin and Jones, haven't you?"

"They should have been named Martin and Lewis, ya ask me. They got the conspiracy blues about Pearl. Want with all their hearts to believe that somebody hypnotized her into eating a hundred pills so the evil government could get her gambling contract."

"You shouldn't have shown up at work in that new Ferrari. Tips off the conspiracy cops every time."

"I know. But it was such a nice red."

The clock was creeping up to 8:00 A.M. Hercules pulled open the glove pack Winnie would use. A sense of anticipation gathered in the room. Rhett actually flipped open his notebook.

"This Ryan's gonna be a slam-dunk, isn't it?"

Molly nodded. "She scored just about every depression point I could come up with. History, attitude, availability. Alcohol."

"What about that blue pill they found? Figure out what it was?"

"Nope. Lab's still hunting that little baby down. My feeling was that she had enough other stuff, it could have been a designer of some kind. It shouldn't take 'em much longer."

At the stroke of eight, just as they knew she would, Winnie swept in. Hercules held out her gown and then her gloves, and then punched the button on the CD player in the corner. Mozart swelled into the room. Rhett came to attention. Molly just rubbed at her eyes. She never failed to enjoy Winnie's performance. It brought to mind a ballet presentation she'd once seen. The curtain had gone up to the company doing a stylized stretching exercise. Warm-ups choreographed to music, getting more and more complicated along with the music, so the audience could know just what ballet was and how impressive the talent was onstage. Stretching became recognizable moves, and then leaps and spins. And then just when the audience began to smile at the beauty onstage, they were treated to the real show. Baryshnikov, soaring onto stage, drawing a sustained gasp of wonder from the room. I showed you the world, he seemed to say. Now, I will transcend it.

It was the way Winnie ran an autopsy. Entering the stainless steel and tile room in midair and then preparing to set everyone and everything inside on figurative ears.

"I have to spend the afternoon in court," she announced, stepping up to take hold of the zipper on her first case to the sound of the overture to *The Magic Flute.* "I won't be late."

Translation: don't hold me back.

And then, dreadful silence when she saw whom she'd unearthed.

"What the hell is this?" she demanded, turning on her diener.

"Mary Margaret—"

Winnie shoved him back as if he were trying to spit in her food. "This is a woman! What the hell is she doing on my table first?"

"She was scheduled—"

Molly took an involuntary step forward. Why, she wasn't sure. She sure didn't want that wrath turned on her. It was anyway.

"Was this your idea of a joke?" Winnie demanded, swinging on her. "You think I should make this my priority today?"

"I think that the chaplain wanted to be here for Officer Myers's autopsy," Molly demurred, her recently enjoyed burrito threatening to make a return appearance.

Winnie's head shot up as if she'd heard the word pimp instead of chaplain. "The chaplain?" she retorted, her voice haughty and cold. "And is the chaplain going to sign the death certificate, too?"

"The family—"

"The medical examiner is the authority in this room, Ms. Burke," she snapped, somehow managing to look like an enraged queen of England, even in surgical gown, rubber gloves, and chocolate-colored skin. "Not the family. *Not* the chaplain. And I do not feel the need to explain to the press why I chose to put the welfare of a suicide ahead of that of a policeman. Do you? Would the chaplain, perhaps?"

That to Rhett, who had less to say than Molly.

"I shouldn't even have to waste my time on this!" Winnie continued, yanking the zipper up to cover the disaster that had been Mary Margaret Ryan's face. "I have over three hundred homicides in this city in a year, and you want me to do housecleaning!"

Molly was already moving, helping the flustered Hercules to get the offending bag from Winnie's table.

"I don't have time!" Winnie said in a snarl, the diva screaming at an ineffectual conductor. "You want me to waste it on your pet project? What about you, Detective? Now that you've decided to grace us with your illustrious presence. What do you say?"

Nobody had anything to say. Hercules pointed to the correct bag and Molly helped him move it and then heft it onto the table. Rhett changed paperwork while Hercules changed X rays while Winnie shouted about incompetence, inconsideration, and incoherence.

In fact, Winnie ranted until she reached for the zipper that would reveal Bill Myers. Then, suddenly, she too fell silent. Rhett, not fond of autopsies at any time, grew noticeably paler. Bill Myers had been in his academy class. Before he could see what Winnie was about to do to the man he'd shared more than one meal with, he sidled over to the door and looked the other way. Winnie never said a word. Winnie could be a raving maniac, but she wasn't heartless.

Bill Myers had been a handsome kid. Blond, muscular, with a strong jaw and jug ears that had incited more than one practical joke. Bill had put in ten years on the force, which meant that he'd either gained a lot of friends or a lot of enemies. Molly knew that half the combined forces in the area would be at his funeral tomorrow.

Molly was intending to go, too. Bill had yanked her to safety at a homicide scene once when the drive-by artists had decided to make another swing around the block to sign their work.

Bill had had a lousy sense of humor and a sterling sense of honor. Molly had the horrible feeling that even knowing what fifteen-year-olds were capable of in this day and age, when he'd seen how young his opponent was, Bill had hesitated. That hesitation had cost him his life.

"August 10, 8:05 A.M. Dr. Winifred Harrison performing the postmortem on case number 81094251. Subject appears to be approximately thirty-five, white male, generally well-developed . . ."

Winnie made the first cut and Rhett ran from the room.

✦ Chapter 8 ✦

"JESUS CHRIST, BURKE. Hold it still!"

"I can't! The goddamn ground's shaking!"

Just to prove it, another rocket hit, taking with it the lights. She was on her knees in the mud, in the red mud that looked more like blood than anything pumping out of these bodies, and it just didn't stop.

"Can you clamp that artery for me?"

She couldn't even see the artery. The generator was on, but the feeble light didn't help. Blood pumped so hard it hit the lights. The table was damn near on the ground, and they were on their knees so they could protect themselves from the shelling that shattered the windows and pulled the ground out from under them. Operating in flak jackets and helmets, on their goddamn knees in the goddamn dark, and she was supposed to see a blood vessel.

"Molly! Clamp it!"

"I'm clamping, damn it, but the blood won't stop!"

"Aren't you guys finished yet?" the medic screamed from the door. "We've got a full house out here, and more coming in!"

Another rocket hit, and even the generator went out.

"Flashlights!"

"Can you see it?"

"What's he doing? How's his pressure?"

"Molly!'

"I can't get it clamped! I can still feel the blood!"

"Molly!"

"Somebody get me a goddamn light so I can see this fucking artery!"

"Molly, hey!"

At first, Molly couldn't figure out why Kevin McCaully was in Pleiku. Then she couldn't figure out why he was in her bedroom. The kinks in her back should have tipped her off. No place was more uncomfortable to stretch out on than the couch in the death investigator's parlor. And Molly, who usually pulled nights in the office, had done her share of time on its cracked black Naugahyde cushions.

It was probably just that when he looked down at her, Kevin was surrounded by a nimbus of sunlight. Molly didn't equate the couch with sunlight. But then, she didn't equate Pleiku with the sun either. Only the mud. The damn mud she could still smell twenty years later.

"They've called your number down at the counter," he said with a quiet grin.

Molly yawned and did her best to hide the shakes that always followed her away from a dream. Kevin would never think to mention if she made any noise. Kevin, a survivor of more then one round of bad burnout himself, respected nightmares, no matter when they happened.

"What time is it?"

"About forty minutes before Winnie has to leave. You'd better bust butt if you still want her to do the post on your suicide."

Molly remembered now. Instead of doing Mary Margaret Ryan after Bill Myers, Winnie had insisted that her other cases took precedence. Not just

Mustaffa, but a twenty-something-year-old white kid who'd been found dead—in the bathroom—of no apparent causes. Molly wouldn't have minded so much if she hadn't needed sleep so much. If she hadn't been looking so forward to finishing her work here and taking the next two days just to herself.

Molly rolled off the couch and tested her legs. Her right one was asleep from having to be curled up to fit. She shook it a bit until she thought she could take the stairs on it without ending up on her nose. "Maybe my suicide shouldn't have been first," she griped. "But it sure as hell could have been second."

"Didn't you want the shooting board to close the case on those two nice policemen who saved your life last night?"

God bless Kevin, he even had a cup of coffee in his hand. Molly took a good slug of it and rubbed at her eyes. Allergy season in St. Louis lasted from January 1 to December 31. Summers, though, redefined the term *miserable.* They were also handy if a person wanted to hide something less acceptable, like surprise tears, behind the excuse of a pollen count.

"Those were not nice policemen," she said. "Just good shots."

"I warned you," Kevin reminded her.

Molly shot him a grin and got her butt in gear. "Thanks, Dad."

Being the newest kid on the block, Molly had the desk closest to the door and farthest away from the windows. She stopped there long enough to get her paperwork and a pocketful of licorice to see her through the postmortem, which, if she was lucky, would include nothing more than the area of injury and stomach contents to verify the assumption of suicide. Then she trotted on down the stairs before Winnie could accuse her of being late.

She could hear the saw as she rounded the corner for the back. Hercules was holding the top of the head while Winnie, ever the perfectionist, made the circular cut.

Never Molly's favorite part of an autopsy. The big cut into the chest and abdomen never really bothered her. After all, livers were just livers, spleens little bags of blood. No one ascribed poetry to intestines or debated whether the soul lived in the pancreas.

The brain was another matter entirely. It was still as cryptic as the far universe, deep thoughts as likely to reside in those gullies and folds as deep insanity. And yet, it was just gray. Just tissue, like the packets lifted from beneath the ribs and hips. Just cells and connective tissue, like every other part of the body. No magic, no mystery.

Maybe after all these years, Molly was still waiting for somebody to find a soul there after all, and all they lifted away was a sluggish, semiset Jell-O.

"Where's Rhett?" she asked.

Winnie never looked up. "I told him to go home after the Myers kid."

Her pen poised to catch any pertinent info, Molly looked up in astonishment. Compassion now. This was not like Winnie at all.

"I also told him you'd call him with these results."

"Sure. What did you find on that last kid?"

Winnie never looked away from her work as she examined the ruined remains of a once-firing system. "Bad luck. He had a big Berry's aneurysm. At least Kevin didn't have to tell his mama he'd been stuffing shit up his nose."

Berry's aneurysm. Genetic, unpredictable, deadly as a snake sleeping in the dark. A weakness in the blood vessels of the brain usually discovered when the holder of same keeled over in his bathroom.

Winnie was right. If there was good news in a dead young man, it was that he hadn't earned it.

"Ya know," Molly mused. "If you think about it, we're not just getting a run on lawyers, we're getting a run on head cases."

Winnie did look up for a millisecond, as long as it usually took her to consider anything. "Good point. Last week it was allergic reactions to front bumpers. Next week it'll be something else."

Molly just nodded. "What's Mary Margaret's final?"

"Three-fifty-seven aneurysm."

"Gets the job done."

"Waste of my time. Go ahead and release her. There's nothing here to see but bullet prints."

Molly checked her notes, found the funeral home the parents had chosen. Waited until Winnie snapped her gloves off and Hercules approached to clean up before calling and arranging for the morticians to pick the body up at their convenience. Case closed, shift ended. Molly made it home by one and finished Sam's paperwork by four and considered herself lucky.

The next morning, clad in one of her few dresses, Molly stood uphill a little from the rows of blue-uniformed officers at Resurrection cemetery. A moaning wind snaked through the trees and the sky was lowering and close. Theresa Myers stood across the casket, her dark head bare, her eyes wet and tired, each hand filled with the smaller hand of a child, all of them at perfect attention.

Molly didn't know Theresa. She did know the cops who lined up on either side of her. She saw the flag-draped casket and wondered if it had been smart to come after all. Her head was filled with old sounds, old hurts, old friends who had come home the same way. She could smell the mud again, the sharp stench of astringent and cordite, the musk of trauma. She looked at the cops lined up and thought of the kids she'd cared for two decades ago, their eyes just as distant, just as ruined.

It never changed. It had just become a different war.

At a barked command, seven rifles were lifted. Fired. Lifted. Fired. Lifted. Fired. Molly watched Theresa Myers flinch at the sound. She saw the cops stand rigid, every one of them, even Rhett in his full-dress uniform with the black electrical tape across his shield as a sign of mourning, his gloves crisp white and his eyes red. She said good-bye to Bill Myers, who had tried his best.

She heard the whine of the bagpiper, who stood alone on the hill above them as he began "Amazing Grace," and she let herself cry.

Winnie had been right. They'd had no right to try and take care of Mary Margaret Ryan first. Mary Margaret Ryan, being laid to rest somewhere on the other side of the cemetery in an hour or so, had thrown her rights away.

It would have been the last Molly thought of Mary Margaret. It would have been the last attention she'd given any of the suicides. Molly didn't like to think about suicides. She didn't want to ask the questions or demand the reasons or wonder about prevention. Nobody did, really. They only went through the motions, because suicide made them angry.

It was so hard, most days, because the fight to save lives was stacked against them. Death was capricious and nasty and clever, and always, always hungry. If law enforcement and trauma teams and everyone down the line in the system worked full-out a hundred percent of the time, they still lost. They lost children who begged and mothers who wanted just a little more time and policemen just trying to do their job. And no matter how tired or sad or empty, the good guys still fought like hell to keep just one more victim alive.

And then they were expected to fight just as hard for somebody who didn't give a crap.

Suicide made them afraid. Afraid to look in the eyes of somebody who had decided to quit, afraid to ask why, afraid that whatever the person had who had just swallowed all those pills, was contagious. Especially to someone who was so empty from burnout that they could no longer remember exactly what was worth fighting for in the first place.

So, when suicides came in, people like Molly took care of business, because that was what they were trained to do. They yelled sometimes at the ones who didn't quite get it right, and they flipped coins to see who'd have to care for them, because nobody liked doing suicides.

And as soon as they got them out of sight, they forgot them. They tried, anyway.

Molly, with more practice than most, succeeded. Which was why, when she got the call to come down to the office the next day to answer the accusations of a crazy man named Joseph Michael Ryan, she couldn't figure out why.

Molly wasn't in the mood to mollify anybody. It was supposed to be her day off, and she'd been all set to spend it up to her elbows in the dirt. She'd even been planning on sharing shoveling tips with the guys who'd shown up again at the corner to watch. One look at the man waiting for her in the foyer of the medical examiner's building assured her that at least she wouldn't be far from the dirt. It would just be on the other guy.

"Mr. Ryan?" she asked tentatively, since the receptionist wouldn't say a word. The only clues Molly got from that direction were a frantic nodding of the head toward the far end of the lobby and a very emphatic wrinkling of the nose.

Molly could hardly blame her. The man who turned was damn near unrecognizable as a human. Long, tangled hair and beard, filthy features, layers of ripped, oily clothes that had seen at least one Salvation Army bin in their lifetime, and boots that had newspaper sticking out the sides of the soles. Molly thought he was white, but she wouldn't have sworn to it.

"You're Molly Burke?" her visitor said in a raspy voice. He was bouncing on the balls of his feet as if he couldn't hold still. He didn't approach, though.

For some reason, the guy triggered a sense of unease in Molly. "Can I help you?"

Although the more she thought about it, the more she wanted to just pretend she'd never seen him.

Then he lifted his head to face her and the unease gestated sharp wings. It wasn't just the dirt or the desperation. It was something more. Something dark Molly responded to in that old, tired face and frantic smile. Something she didn't particularly want to deal with when she was this tired and stressed out.

It was his eyes. Ghostly pale, the color of ice, stark against all that grime and hair. Familiar. She thought she recognized them from somewhere. She sure as hell knew the look. The thousand-yard stare. Ancient, lost, drained out like a glass knocked over on the floor. She'd seen that look in the eyes in her nightmares. She'd seen them twenty years ago, while she'd slogged through the red dirt of Pleiku. This guy wasn't just homeless, he was Vietnam homeless. And that made it all different.

"Can I help you?" she asked again, her voice lower. Hesitant. Less a city official than a woman facing old ghosts.

She knew other guys from the Nam. Other homeless guys, balancing on the edge of reality with little cat feet. But other guys didn't make her feel crawly with dread like this guy.

"Yeah. Yeah, you can. You can help me."

This time, he moved, that same, oddly graceful gait some of the homeless guys got, as if dancing, or maybe avoiding hot spots or cold spots or filth on the sidewalks where they slept.

He smelled as if he slept in the sewer. Molly barely noticed. She was watching those eyes, those eyes that were suddenly squinting at her, as if he were the one trying to fit her face to a memory.

"Lieutenant?" he said, stopping in front of her.

Her smile was more hesitant than his voice. "Captain, actually."

His nod was jerky and stiff. He sighed. "Thought so. He said so, but now I know."

"He said so?" she asked. "Who said so?"

Her visitor crammed his hands in the pockets of his pea jacket and stared over at the receptionist. "Where, ma'am?"

"Seventy-first Evac at Pleiku," Molly said, understanding perfectly. "'70–'71. You?"

"First Cav, '68. I'd tell you where, but some days I can't remember."

First Cav. First Cav. The niggle of memory got sharper, but it couldn't work its way free just yet. Molly was still trying so hard to get over the feeling that this man could hurt her, when she could see that he was only interested in hurting himself.

"Molly," the receptionist said suddenly. "You got a message a little while ago that the police need to see you about that Johnson situation. You want me to call them?"

Interpretation: You want me to save you from this?

Molly turned to the twenty-five-year-old receptionist, who had no idea what was going on between Molly and a homeless guy, and she smiled. "No, thanks. I'll call them back. I need to talk to Mr. . . ."

Then it clicked. The picture on the wall. The I-can-do-anything glare beneath that military buzz cut. The shiny, perfectly aligned teeth that screamed orthodontics. The more mature pictures that weren't there.

Molly spun around on her guest and almost sent him running for the door. As skittish as any of the homeless guys, as desperately uncertain. A wild, frightened thing caught on the streets.

"Would you like some coffee, Mr. Ryan?" she asked gently, now even more unsettled by those shifting, startling eyes. "We could talk in the conference room upstairs if you'd like."

His nod was quick and feral. "Yes. I need . . . uh, I'd like to talk, if I could."

"We're going upstairs," Molly told the receptionist, whose eyes widened noticeably.

"Okay."

Molly knew better than to grab hold of Joseph Ryan's arm, so she just showed him the way and let him follow. He did, the secretary's outrage following the both of them up the stairs. Imagining lice dropping at every step, Molly was sure. It wouldn't be a surprise.

She got him into the small conference room at the back and produced the coffee, black for him, although he quickly pocketed a couple of packets of sugar. He smiled, too, which just showed that at one time those grimy, broken teeth had been straightened like Chiclets. Molly fought the urge to just leave. She wanted more than ever to run back and hide in her garden.

"You're Mary Margaret's brother," she said, settling into her chair across from him. "Aren't you?"

Joseph Ryan nodded. His eyes welled with silent tears as he held that coffee cup in his palms as if it were the only warmth he could get, even on a day as hot as this. He looked away, restless and afraid and grieving, and Molly was at once amazed and unnerved.

"You know?" she asked.

Another nod. "Peg," he managed, his voice sounding like a rusty hinge. "Her name is Peg."

"I'm sorry," Molly said, suddenly full of questions she didn't want answers to.

"I need help, Cap."

Molly hadn't been called that in more than twenty years. The young kids coming in from the boonies, torn up, scared, wanting to make sure their friends were okay, still delighted enough at the sight of a woman to joke. "Hey, Cap, I never kissed nobody with bars before. What'dya say?" "Hey, Cap, I'm so short I'm damn near invisible. Kiss me for luck?"

It was summer. Molly was having trouble enough with the old memories, the new traumas. She didn't need Joseph Ryan pulling her back through it all again.

"I'm not sure what I can do for you, Mr. Ryan."

He smiled again, almost a nervous tic. The window dressing of an addict. Good enough reason as any to be on the streets all these years. Molly knew better than most that even the addictions were window dressing over the real problems.

"Name's Joe, ma'am. I never made it to Mister."

It was Molly's turn to nod. "Joe. I'm Molly, okay?"

Not Cap. Don't call me Cap and put that responsibility back on my shoulders again.

"Okay, Molly. Nobody'd talk to me, but I figured you'd understand, ya know? That kid doesn't know, he doesn't . . ."

Molly waited through a pause as Joe's attention strayed out the window toward the highway. Seeing something that wasn't there. Remembering so strongly that it took over.

"He doesn't what, Joe?"

Abruptly he was back. Grinning, embarrassed. "Homicide. That guy. I talked to him, but he just knows I live in a cave, ya know?"

Molly's smile was as dark as Joe's. "Yeah. I know."

Joe leaned forward, his hands suddenly still, his eyes suddenly focused, right on Molly. "Help me find out how she died," he said.

Molly hadn't wanted to have this discussion with his mother. She certainly didn't want to have it with Joe.

"I'm sorry, Joe," she began in her best bad-news-breaking voice. He never let her finish.

"No," he said, pointing a finger. "She didn't kill herself. She did not."

Molly was already shaking her head. "I was there. I saw the autopsy. Didn't your other sister or your mother talk to you about it?"

That damn near brought him to his feet. "You can't tell them," he pleaded, eyes hurt and so young, suddenly, even in that tired, wasted face. "Please promise me. They don't know."

That one took Molly a second. "They don't know what? That you're alive? Where you live?"

"They think . . . only Peg knew where I was. She went looking for me. Mom couldn't . . ."

He looked away, the cup trembling in his hands, ashamed and alone.

"I won't say anything to them," Molly promised. "I promise." As if she could ever think of any reason to flagellate herself by revisiting that house.

He settled a little back into his chair. Patted his coat and came up with a crumpled, almost empty pack of Marlboros. "Thanks. Can I . . ."

Molly dragged over the ashtray and fought the urge to ask for one for herself. Ten years, two months, three days and counting since she'd quit that one. Vietnam had given them all some very bad habits.

"If you didn't hear from your family," Molly said, "how did you know?"

Joe paused in lighting his cigarette with an old Zippo lighter that looked as if he'd brought it home from his tour with him. "You mean how does a guy who lives in a cave and eats out of a Dumpster keep up on current affairs?"

Molly damn near blushed. Then she saw the glint of humor way at the back of those ravaged eyes. "Something like that, yeah."

"Frank told me."

He went on lighting up. Molly gaped like a landed fish.

"Frank who?"

Although she already knew. It wouldn't have all been nearly weird enough if she hadn't been right.

Joe sucked in a first lungful of smoke and slipped the lighter away in an inside pocket. "Patterson."

She couldn't help it. "You know Frank Patterson?"

That humor again, only older and a little sadder. "We went to school together."

Which, translated into St. Louis priorities, meant they went to high school together. Any other school didn't count in the small world of St. Louis friendships and accomplishments. Frank Patterson, good Catholic overachiever, had gone to St. Louis University High, *the* school for Catholic boys. That meant that Joseph Ryan had, too. From SLUH to the sewers. Via Hue, of course.

"Of course you did."

"Frank said you don't like him, but that you'd help me."

"Well, he has the first part right."

The smoke seemed to be settling Joe down a little. His smiles were a little more sustained, his sentences almost complete. Molly wasn't sure whether that was better or worse.

"Cap . . . Molly. Believe me. I knew Peg better than anybody. *Anybody.* She would never have . . . she wouldn't kill herself. No matter what anybody says they saw. Or know . . . she just . . . wouldn't."

"Did you know she was on Prozac?"

He snorted. "So's everybody. So what? She wasn't suicidal."

"She had some other things with her," Molly tried again. "Things that might have made her less . . . careful."

He was shaking his head. "You didn't try anything stupid when you were her age?"

Molly almost laughed. "Sure. I enlisted."

That quickly, they shared a smile. A memory. A private hell most of the rest of the people in this building couldn't even conjure up. And once shared, put away again.

"You talked to her the last couple of weeks?" Molly asked as gently as she could. "Frank thinks you're wrong, you know."

For a second, Molly was afraid he was going to get violent. "Frank and I disagree," was all he said.

Molly didn't know what to do. She didn't know how to make him understand. Nobody wanted to think their loved ones would put a gun in their mouths. Nobody wanted the responsibility or the legacy. Especially, Molly thought, a soul so fragile he haunted the edges of society wrapped in rags and alcoholic hazes.

"How can you be so sure?" she asked, really facing him.

He faced her right back, and suddenly Molly saw that this fragile man with his tics and addictions recognized far more about her than her old captain's bars.

"Because we're the ones who dabble with suicide, Cap," he told her. "You and me. And Peg wasn't like us at all."

✦ Chapter 9 ✦

WINNIE FOUND HER in the bathroom trying to get her hands clean.

"Scrubbing for surgery?" the medical examiner asked, eyeing the effort involved.

Molly didn't even bother to look up. "Preventing the spread of scabies," she retorted.

Leaning an elegant hip against the wall, Winnie just nodded. "Minetta said you had a visitor. He a problem?"

Molly laughed. Unfortunately her laugh sounded as sane as Joseph Ryan's. "He's a homeless vet who can't believe his sister'd kill herself. So he figures another vet would be the perfect one to help him."

"Your very self."

"My"—she shut off the water with a snap—"very self."

"What are you going to do?"

"What do you mean, what am I going to do?" Molly echoed, even though her voice sounded shrill. "I'm not going to do anything. He's a guy who's so lost he's living in a cave down by the river and he tells me he knows more than we do. You think I'm going to listen to him? Would you allow me to listen to him? *You're* the one who bitched about the fact that the Ryan autopsy was just housecleaning!"

"I did."

"Then why are you suddenly worried enough about it to ask what the hell I'm going to do?"

Winnie chose the most maddening moments to be unflappable and solemn. This seemed to be one. "I'm not worried about the victim," she said simply. "I'm worried about the investigator."

And then damn her if she didn't simply wait while Molly fell apart.

It wasn't much of a breakdown, as breakdowns went. A moment or two in the stalls, sweating and shaking and trying real hard to keep the tears at bay and her breakfast in place. Ten minutes circling the bathroom and trying to get her breath back, and all the while, Winnie simply stood by the door making sure nobody else joined in.

"Better?" the ME asked quietly when it was all over.

Molly pulled the wet paper towel from her eyes to see the quiet empathy in her boss's expression. "Yes," she said, even though she was still shaking. "Why?"

The smile grew a little wider. "When you're finished washing your hands, there's a couple gentlemen from the FBI in your office. Oh, and that intelligence team. Short on personality, aren't they?"

"Yeah, but don't piss 'em off."

"You up for it?"

Molly daubed a little more, shoved back the sudden memory of that quiet, certain statement.

We're the ones who dabble in suicide, Molly.

Son of a bitch. Where did he get off saying things like that?

Where?

"Molly?"

"Yeah." She threw the towels in the can and reached for the door handle. "What can they do to me, shave my hair short and send me to 'Nam?"

"Well, well, well," Molly greeted the team in the investigator's bull pen. "If it isn't Larry and Curly."

The two suits who'd been watching her pull weeds for two days got to their feet as she walked in the door. Jones and Martin, still verbose as ever, simply stayed on the couch. As death investigator on duty, the ever-lovely Vic Fellows tried to look unobtrusive at his desk while he listened to the police scanner and Molly's visitors at the same time. It looked like the day was going right to hell in a handbasket. And all Molly could think of was that they were all too late. She wasn't interested in gambling anymore at all.

"You recognize agents Lopez and Hickman?" Jones asked.

Molly's smile was frosty. She wanted to be home. Hell, she wanted to be on a hot air balloon over New Mexico. She did not want to spend any time with these four, who looked like they were going to be as enjoyable as hemorrhoids on a hot day.

"Yes," she said, overcoming the desire to tell them just what she thought as she settled into the straight-backed chair at her desk. "I recognize Agents Lopez and Hickman. What can I do for them? Figure out the question mark yet, Vic?" she asked, for the benefit of both audiences.

Vic didn't have the sense to be chastised. "No. Wanna ask the FBI if they have any ideas?"

"You have any ideas?" Molly asked as everybody sat down and, over by the window, Vic leaned his chair back as if he'd just turned the TV to "Oprah."

"Vic over there collects tattoos, and he had a guy who had a real interesting one. A question mark, right along the shaft of his penis. We can't figure out why."

Nobody had an answer. Molly wasn't sure why she was being so pissy, except for the fact that she could still see Joe Ryan's eyes.

"I figure it's an existential statement," she went on, digging into her drawer for her stash of extra-strength Excedrin. "A comment on man's basic insecurity. Now, the guy we had the other night who had flames tattooed on his dick—quite a lovely picture, I can tell you—I figure he knew what he wanted. The question mark, though, I think that guy wasn't so sure. Comments? Suggestions? Opinions?"

There seemed to be none. Molly swallowed the aspirin dry and followed it with licorice to a veritable chorus of grimaces from her guests and certain signs of revolt from her stomach. That was just tough. She didn't need shit from Joseph Ryan, she didn't need it from Jones or Martin or the Bobbsey Twins.

Mary Margaret wasn't like us, huh? Then why is she dead and we aren't? Tell me that, Joseph Ryan.

"Agents Lopez and Hickman are here helping us out with the gambling situation," Jones said, squirming a bit in his seat as if imagining someone approaching his own pride with a tattooing gun.

"Gambling?" Molly looked around. "You think I'm running a game out of my house?"

"No. We think you might be in some trouble."

They should have made their revelation before Joseph Ryan's. Then they might at least have had her attention.

"Look, you guys," she protested, really tired now. "I've had a bad day already. I don't need this shit, too. You got a problem with me, you stop dancing around and let me know. I told you all I know about the suicide note. I can't tell you any more; I don't care what initials you have on your badge. I'm sorry, but that's the truth."

"It's not about the note," Martin said.

Across the room, the phone rang. Vic righted his chair and pulled out paperwork. Molly watched him, thought about other things. Answered Martin anyway.

"Then what's it about?"

The four of them looked at each other, consulting with eyebrows and ESP, evidently. Finally, it was Jones who delivered the news.

"The attempt on your life."

First Molly had to figure out what Jones was saying. Then she had to remember just what the hell he meant.

Mustaffa. Oh, yeah.

"That's awfully sweet," she said. "But that was just business at the big house."

"No," Martin disagreed. "I'm afraid it isn't. Wasn't."

At that point, he pulled out a crumpled piece of what looked like wrapping paper from a hamburger and passed it across Molly's desk.

Yes, she thought, picking it up. Definitely hamburger. Steak 'n Shake, if she was any judge. A faint whiff of onions and pickles wafted up, and no matter what her stomach was telling her, her saliva glands tuned right up for Pavlov's Song.

"Ah, Tuesday," she said, lifting the paper to her nose. "It was a very good vintage."

Her audience didn't seem amused.

"Read it," Martin said.

"Read it?" Molly responded, wondering what secrets you could discern in the word *Takahomasack.*

"The other side."

The other side was, after all, another situation entirely. Molly could see that there was some scribbling along the edge. She flattened the paper between her hands so she could make it out better.

"Molly, I'm going," Vic said across the way, his chair scraping across the floor as he cradled the phone.

Molly hardly heard him. She'd just made out what the paper said. She looked up to Detectives Martin and/or Jones for an explanation.

"How did he know your name?" Jones asked instead.

"Who?" she asked. "What does this mean?"

"Molly? You listening? I've got a hot call on a cold number five."

Molly wasn't listening. Vic hovered just beyond her desk for a second anyway.

"We found it in Mustaffa's jeans when we got them to the lab," Jones said.

Molly looked back down at the white, grease-stained wrapping that blew the hell out of the theory that what had happened the other night at the hospital had just been one of those things. The man who had yelled, "Yo, bitch!" hadn't done it randomly. He'd walked into that ER with Molly's name in his pocket. Also her description and the shift she was supposed to work.

Molly was so surprised that she almost missed the fact that Vic was walking out the door on their fifth suicide.

✦ Chapter 10 ✦

"WHAT DO YOU MEAN, you have number five?" Molly yelled, leaping out of her chair and running out into the hallway.

Vic's footsteps were already echoing down the stairwell.

"Ms. Burke?" Jones asked, reaching ineffectually for the paper that fluttered in Molly's fingers as she tore by.

"Guy playing smashing pumpkins from the Wainright Building!" came Molly's answer, drifting up from below.

Molly leaned over the railing at the stairs, not even noticing that two of the four investigators had made a move to follow her into the hall. "Not Metropolitan Square?" she demanded.

Vic leaned his head back so she could see his smile. "Sorry. Wrong lawyer again."

And then he walked on out the front door.

Smashing pumpkins. A jumper. A jumper from high up. Well, as high as the Wainright went. The first skyscraper built west of the Mississippi, the Wainright had been an amazing feat of engineering when it was built in 1892. Now it was dwarfed in its nine stories by thirty- and forty-story neighbors. It was still, however, tall enough to ensure a good sidewalk splatter factor.

Another lawyer.

Molly felt a twinge of something other than annoyance.

"Ms. Burke, aren't you interested that somebody might be trying to kill you?" FBI agent Lopez demanded.

Molly turned, almost surprised to see them all still arrayed in the office like game show contestants. She was even more surprised to see that the Steak wrapper was still in her hand. She did notice, though, that whoever wrote the note had spelled her name wrong. Everybody did. Left off the E at the end of Burke. As if it were important. As if that would matter to a killer looking for a victim. *Remember now, Mustaffa. Make sure you have the right Molly Burk. The one without the E, all right?*

"Ms. Burke?"

Martin was beginning to sound long-suffering. Molly headed back into the big investigator's room, wondering what exactly she was supposed to tell them. Wondering what it meant that they had another lawyer, and what it would do to their per capita suicide stats.

"We had another lawyer commit suicide just now," Molly said, settling back into her seat. "That's five."

She looked around for reactions. Problem was, she'd said the wrong word.

"You know why they use lawyers instead of laboratory rats now?" Jones asked Martin.

"No," Martin responded, just like the good straight man he was.

"Well," Jones said as Molly stared on. "There are more lawyers than rats—"

The other three suits nodded.

"People get attached to rats—"

Another chorus of nods. Molly couldn't believe it.

Jones grinned. "And there are just some things a rat won't do."

Laughter. Out of that bunch. Well, Molly figured, it was her fault. She could have said that five clowns had died in a freak human cannonball accident and she wouldn't have gotten quite the same reaction.

"Just thought you'd like to know," she said, although she wasn't sure why.

Belatedly, their attention returned.

"What do you think?" Jones asked.

"Don't quit your day job."

If he'd had a sense of humor, he might have smiled. As it was, he just scowled and inclined his head toward the wrapper. "About the fact that you were set up."

Molly took another look at the wrapper in her hand. She fought off another urge to eat. Steakburgers for lunch. Maybe chili mac, with extra sauce, so the grease just dripped off her chin. Steak fries, thin and chewy, with extra salt. She could sit there, all alone with a book and forget everything that waited for her outside.

"Ms. Burke."

Molly looked up. Blushed. Well, it was better than thinking about lawyers. About homeless vets.

"I thought hit men ate at places called Carmine's," was all she could come up with.

"Mustaffa'd do anything for anybody," Jones let her know. "As long as he got a rush out of it. He got a rush out of hurting women."

Suddenly Molly remembered Mustaffa's eyes. Clearly. She damn near blanched. "Thanks."

No one figured apologies were necessary.

"This isn't public information yet," one of the Feds said, "but we've been in Pearl Johnson's bank accounts. She received three substantial payments in the last six months amounting to almost a quarter million dollars."

It took Molly a minute to get over that kind of amount. "Who gets it?" she asked instinctively.

Jones shifted a bit uncomfortably. "Nobody. She spent it all."

"A quarter of a million dollars?"

"Her church needed a new roof, and there are some playgrounds in the area . . ."

Spent it on her city, just like always. Poor Pearl. Hoping the ends justified the means. Finding out differently.

"Were you able to trace where the funds came from?"

"We're looking now. We're also doing some investigating on some of the other aldermen who voted for the gaming bill."

"And you found that there were no unusual deposits in any of my accounts," Molly offered for him.

Again, she got no apologies. "Nothing except the money from your trust."

"From the house's trust," she corrected him. "I'm just the caretaker."

From their expressions, they already knew that. It was also pretty obvious that they'd yet to figure it out, but Molly didn't think she needed to enlighten them.

"Somebody seems to have wanted you dead," Jones said, neatly bringing the conversation back to the subject at hand.

Molly tried to believe that. It was one thing to think of Mustaffa just randomly spraying bullets into the ER wall. After all, it had happened before. It was quite another to think that the smile he'd delivered when he'd been about to empty a full clip into her chest had been personal.

"Any ideas?" she asked, her voice suddenly very small.

"You're sure about that note?"

Molly instinctively reached to open her drawer for her Excedrin. Then she remembered that she'd just had some. She slugged down some Maalox instead. "I can't tell you any more ways."

"You're quite sure it was Pearl Johnson's handwriting on the suicide note."

For the first time since she'd seen that note, suddenly Molly wasn't so sure. "I don't . . . I'm not sure I've seen Pearl's handwriting before."

Evidently, the Feds were as prepared as Boy Scouts. Either Lopez or Hickman opened the briefcase next to his chair and pulled something out. Slid it across the desk as if it were the last card in a game of draw poker. "Familiar?"

Molly picked up the plastic-encased sheet of paper and did her best to remember the note she'd only seen once for five minutes.

What she held in her hand was a list of things to do. Laundry and shopping and stopping off for the new choir robes for the church. Molly wondered if they'd been purchased with bribe money. She wondered what the poor minister would do with his gifts once he knew.

"I can't swear to a thing," she said. "But I think the handwriting's the same."

"You think."

It was her turn to scowl. "You want to dump on me for losing that note, you're going to have to stand in line. A long line. Now, you want my opinion or what?"

It was Jones who answered. "We're just trying to get a best-case scenario here. Trying to make sure the victim wasn't . . . compromised."

"She was in her house for twenty hours by herself," Molly retorted. "Who could compromise her, aliens?"

"The mother admits to having been out for an hour or two earlier that day."

Molly sighed. "And Jack Ruby would have had plenty of time to sneak up from his hiding place in Havana to stuff drugs down Pearl's throat."

"William Peterson has had four murder charges dropped because of lack of witnesses," Jones said. "And until she died, Pearl was a witness. Now, you are."

He got Molly's attention. "Lack of witnesses, or lack of surviving witnesses?" she asked.

She just got that all-purpose cop shrug.

So Molly took another look at the hamburger wrapper. Another at the list in Pearl's handwriting. She thought about what had happened that night, played it every way she could, and still couldn't come up with anything different.

"Do you guys think Pearl was murdered?" Molly asked.

"We think it's still a real possibility."

"But all the drugs she took were prescription meds. All prescribed for her."

"You're sure."

Molly thought about it. The tox screen hadn't come back yet. She was going to have to check on that. After the Feds left. Molly's parents had taught her to be cooperative, but she'd long since learned that you took care of your hometown team first. That meant she let out her information when Winnie and Rhett said it was okay.

"As sure as I can be," she said.

"But there might have been something else in her bloodstream you hadn't counted on," Jones persisted.

Molly laughed. "She wouldn't have needed anything else. She had enough on that nightstand to drop Godzilla in full charge."

"Still . . ."

Still, she didn't have the tox screen. She would have heard if the tox lab hadn't found any of the expected drugs in Pearl's blood, but they wouldn't have known to look for any surprises.

"And you think that this Peterson guy wants me dead, too," she said, amazed that she sounded so matter-of-fact. "Why?"

Molly got another silence that stretched into discomfort.

"I told you. Because you saw the note," Jones finally said, as if she should know better. "Because you have Peterson's name."

"And?"

"And what?"

Molly was losing patience. "And now *you* have it."

"You say you saw the name on the note connecting Pearl with Peterson. That's hearsay evidence. Not admissible unless you're present to testify, shaky even with a deposition. So, even if Pearl did commit suicide and that was her final will and testament you saw, it still points the finger right where Peterson doesn't want it. Remember, there's something like forty million dollars involved here. His chance to be a player again."

"Did it occur to you that Mustaffa might just have been pissed off because one of his posse died in my ER?" Molly demanded.

"It did. We discounted it."

"Also, if Pearl was murdered to protect Peterson, what the hell was the note all about?"

"Peterson's people might not have known the note was there," one of the Feds responded evenly. "Just because a note says somebody's sorry doesn't mean it's a suicide announcement."

"But if it was, and she did commit suicide, that means Peterson managed to get somebody down to my ER pretty damn quick to get rid of it," Molly retorted. "That's just a little too much conspiracy theory, even for me."

All the same, they were making her think. Well, not think, really. React. Worry. Too much had happened today for her to have anything in her head but white noise. They were sure planting some sharp-nosed little moles in her stomach, though.

Molly couldn't think of anything to say. No disclaimer, no protest, no suggestions.

"So, assuming you're right," she said. "Now what?"

This was definitely not an inspired group.

"Now, we wait," one of the Feds said.

Molly wished she'd been paying closer attention when they'd been introduced. She'd never gotten which was Lopez and which was Hickman. She figured it probably wasn't politically correct, but she was going to decide that the guy with darker hair was Lopez, and the blond was Hickman. At least she had statistical advantage on her side.

"We wait for what?"

"For the investigation into the rest of the Board of Aldermen," Lopez said. "For some kind of concrete link between Peterson and this new gambling casino."

"For them to actually kill me so I can write out a name in blood before I die."

Molly was expecting at least a small protest. What she got was stony silence. That was exactly what they were waiting for.

"Peterson's an awfully long name to spell when your blood pressure's bottoming out," Molly protested faintly.

"We're keeping an eye on you," one of them said.

"Are you tapping my phones?"

"That would be illegal."

Molly was the one who laughed this time. "Silly me. I know you haven't been in my file, either."

Her FBI file she'd amassed in school when Richard Nixon was more afraid of students who didn't believe in his war than he was of the communists. Molly hadn't believed in his war, but she'd gone anyway. She bet the FBI guys were still shaking their heads over that one.

"We're not allowed to hold someone's youthful indiscretions against them anymore," Hickman said, and damned if Molly didn't think there was a hint of a grin somewhere behind those eyes.

"Anyway," Jones said, standing, "if there's anything you can think of to change the equation, let us know."

"I will," she said like a good girl. "I promise."

Then she waited for them to make it outside before dialing up the tox lab.

"No surprises here," the tox lab said. "We found a real smorgasbord of lethal pharmacopoeia in her blood. Everything from Valium to Lithium to birth control pills. There's a match with every prescription bottle you brought us. There were some mystery extras in the baggie you brought that we have calls out on, but I doubt they'd make much difference."

"You don't have that info, yet?"

"We've been a little busy over here, ya know?"

"Busy?" Molly retorted, figuring that the death of a city official possibly on the take would hold some precedence. "With what?"

"Haven't you read the papers?" the supervisor asked. "This is going to be a record year for homicides. Not only that, but the narcs pulled in a huge haul of dust and crack yesterday. In the great scheme of things, suicide gets bottom billing."

Until that morning when she'd spent her off-hours

with a homeless vet and people telling her that somebody was trying to kill her because of a suicide, Molly would have understood completely.

"It's getting really important," she hedged. "If you could scoot on it, I wouldn't have to tell Winnie you still weren't finished."

Molly knew the tech well enough to not be offended when the answer she got was, "Bitch."

"And I speak so well of you," she answered with a grin and was relieved to hear a chuckle in return.

Molly had been waiting to get back home all morning. For some reason, she didn't go right there. She drove, instead, across to Locust Street, where the Wainright building sat in rehabbed splendor, a neat square redbrick building with elegant terra-cotta friezes around the roof, all tucked neatly away amid all the glass and steel like a well-mannered aunt among the rowdier children.

Along the sidewalk at the base, police tape still held back the curious. A couple of units shared the street with the medical examiner's van and the transport vehicle, a dark blue van with no identification. It had once been labeled METS, for Medical Examiner's Transport Service. Unfortunately, the baseball fans in town had mistaken it for a vehicle belonging to the New York Mets, and regularly egged and spray painted it with colorful opinions of the team and its players. Since that didn't look appropriate on the ten o'clock news, the acronym had been painted over into anonymity.

Vic was standing there with a couple of uniforms, his clipboard and measuring tape in hand, his thick black hair stuck to his forehead from the heat and humidity. At his feet lay an untidy bundle hidden by a dark tarp. The tarp couldn't cover all the blood, though. It had been a mess.

"What are you doing here?" he asked as Molly walked up.

Hands in pants pockets, she shrugged. "I had to come by this way. Thought I'd check and see how you were doing."

Vic went back to his work. "Sorry, no politicians, sports figures, or actors. Just a lawyer in the middle of a divorce and a bad year at the stocks."

Molly couldn't seem to take her eyes off the lumpy tarp. "No questions?"

"Only the ones about why a successful lawyer would have such bad taste in clothes. But hell, that could have depressed him, too."

Molly looked up, saw the open window nine floors up. Saw the shadows of curious observers just inside. Probably wondering what it would take to open a window and step out into air. Wondering maybe if they saw a little of themselves in this man who worked in their offices every day.

"Molly?"

Startled, she looked up to see Vic frowning at her. She gave him a quick grin. "I was just thinking that I'm going to rip up that law school application I've been working on."

Vic snorted unkindly and went back to writing. "Oh, don't do that. If this keeps up, just think of all the open positions to be filled."

Vic never noticed that she left.

A cold front was hovering just west of the city, pushing thunderheads inexorably before it. Molly climbed back into her car with an eye to the thick, dark clouds that were boiling up to the southwest. The wind was kicking up, spinning paper and leaves in little eddies along the streets and pushing up the skirts of women scuttling to lunch. The humidity climbed, as if it had been squeezed between the clouds and the river, so that the air, even though it was moving, seemed stifling. There was a change in the wind, as the weatherman said.

Molly turned her car back down toward the morgue and the highway entrance that rose alongside it. She had her windows open and her sunroof up so the wind could batter at her. She was gearing down so she could get a decent acceleration on the entrance ramp. She checked left so no one would cut her off.

And there she saw him.

Bent, shuffling, anonymous. An upright pile of rags holding a plastic bag full of aluminum cans. Standing there alongside the morgue parking lot as if waiting for something. Wondering about something. All but invisible to the rest of the city, to her on any other day she might have flown by him in a fast sports car. Today, though, she saw him. Like a sign. A warning. A memory and a promise.

Molly turned deliberately away, her hand clamped to the gearshift as if it were the magic wand that would carry her safely away from his eyes. His voice. She shifted down until her car screamed. Then she swept onto the entrance ramp and left him behind, where he belonged.

It didn't work. By the time Molly reached home, it was that lost, lonely man who stayed with her, even after the wind had pulled everything else away. It was the formless lump on the sidewalk she saw instead of the trees that bent and writhed along the street.

The rain was coming, which meant Molly couldn't sit outside. She wouldn't watch her fish or listen to the birds argue in the trees, or wonder what the people were talking about in the patios of the restaurants down the block.

Molly parked her car in front of her house and headed up the walk. She slid her key in the lock and opened the front door. She stood there in the high, echoing entranceway, watching the shadows climb the walls of the living room and run over the furniture like dark water.

She couldn't stay here. Not when she was trying to sort out everything she'd learned today. Not when she had to think about death and suicide and hopelessness. When she stood in this house, she heard her parents' voices. She heard disapproval and dismissal and disinterest. She heard the years of polite denial pile up around her like trash on the pristine gray carpet.

"I suppose I'm not surprised you want to be a nurse, Melinda Ann," her mother had said, composed on the Chippendale settee like a ruler weary of her less disciplined subjects. "A career of subservience. You can spend the rest of your life without having to excel or take responsibility. Disappointing, but then I've come to expect that from you."

Her brother Martin Francis had not disappointed. A foreign consul by the time he was twenty-six, he was now undersecretary of something or other. A real Burke. An achiever, a brilliant star in the right universe who had made his parents proud in the years before their mostly untimely demise in a foreign post. Married, father of the two heirs apparent to the Burke name and legacy, the real owner of the house with its treasures and heritage.

Molly, the also-ran, the child who was born to disappoint, had none of these things. Just as her mother predicted, she'd failed at it all until she faced her forties alone, childless, and caught between a career she'd once found challenging and a lawsuit that threatened to bleed her dry.

She needed to talk to somebody. Run what she'd heard past understanding ears and get feedback. Reassurance. Logic.

The problem was, Molly had no one to talk to. No one who'd lasted through the years with her, no one she'd ever let close enough to burden with that kind of turmoil.

Burkes never discussed their problems. That was because they never admitted them. Problems were messy and distasteful and unpleasant. Above all, Burkes believed in the myth that all of life should be quiet and well-mannered and private. Which was why perfect Martin Francis had a great job, a host of stress-related health problems, a wife who drank herself into oblivion, and two sons who were doing their best to earn their places in the Young Psychopaths Hall of Fame. Which was why Molly stood in this empty house hearing echoes of misery instead of seeking out friends.

We're the ones who dabble in suicide, Molly. You and me.

Not anymore, Joseph Ryan, she thought, squeezing her eyes shut against the fear. That was a long time ago. A long, long time ago.

Even so, she wanted a drink. She wanted it so badly she could actually taste the smoke of good Irish whiskey at the back of her throat. It would slide down so easily. So effortlessly.

And it would be safe, because Joseph Ryan was wrong.

Even so, Molly spun around and slammed back out of the house.

She walked it off. Around her the trees shook and danced. The sky split with early lightning, turning the clouds the sickly green that made St. Louisans look up and worry. The rain came down, first a splattering, then a torrent. Big, fat drops that drenched in seconds and swirled along the street so cars could splash them back up again. Molly turned out onto Euclid and dodged people trying their best to get in out of a thunderstorm that crackled and boomed overhead. Molly barely noticed.

It just wasn't the time for all of this. It was summer, and Gene was right. Molly should have been a teacher so she could outrun her demons during the summer. She should have been a consul in a distant country where the most important thing on her schedule was arranging tables at a state function.

Instead, she was here. Up to her elbows in trauma, up to her armpits in suicides, and the summer wasn't over yet.

Suicides. It couldn't have been something simple. An epidemic. A serial killer or two. Anything but the sight of lifeless eyes and deliberate self-destruction. Anything but the suspicion that it was, after all, much easier just to give in.

And now, not only did the FBI want her to reexamine how someone would have committed suicide, Joseph Ryan wanted her to go back in and reexamine why.

Why should she listen to a guy who ate lunch behind McDonald's instead of in it? Why would his word count for more than that of a mother who sat on a Sears couch in the county?

He'd been so sure. So clear, for that solitary moment, as if it were the only thing he truly understood anymore. As if his years on the street could be distilled into that one truth. Joseph Ryan was an expert, and the area of his expertise was despair.

Before Joseph had spoken to her, Molly had managed to slip all those damn suicides neatly into an envelope marked Closed and shove them away.

Now, she was afraid she was going to have to go back and reexamine at least one.

That was if Joseph Ryan was right.

Molly walked faster. She didn't want him to be right. She didn't want him to make her look at the pictures of that room again, talk to his sister and his mother. She didn't want to wonder enough to rake back through Pearl's desperation or the futility of the life of the lawyer who had decided that the Wainright building was the door out of his life.

Molly needed to talk to somebody about this. Somebody who understood.

Nobody understood.

No, that wasn't true. The crowd at work understood. They might not have stumbled out from the disaster of Vietnam, but they slogged through the desperation that was late twentieth century urban America.

But no one in the ER would talk about this. They would talk about rage and anger, yes. Frustration, indecision, fury. They would talk about exhaustion and they would talk about rebellion. They would not talk about despair. They wouldn't admit it because they were more afraid of it than anything.

It was why none of them would deal with suicides. It was why they would never sit down and listen to Molly tell them why Joseph Ryan frightened her so much. It was why she would never think to tell them.

And that left her only outsiders. People who would need the problem explained, the loyalties defended. And Molly simply wasn't up to it. She wasn't even strong enough to have to define it all for Gene, who understood better than most. She just needed someone who would instinctively know. Someone who spoke in code, so she could shorthand past what she was too afraid to say.

Besides, even though he'd empathize, Gene would do it for a hundred-twenty an hour, and Molly simply couldn't afford it.

Alongside her, a Caprice slowed to a crawl in the downpour. Molly saw the passenger's face turn her way, a faint, pale globe of suspicion beyond the rain-fogged window. She was being watched. Being followed. More FBI agents, she thought.

She hoped.

She walked faster, ignoring them. Ignoring the new disquiet that settled on her shoulders when she considered that they could be there for some reason other than to protect her.

For whatever reason, they didn't follow. They just watched, which was just fine with Molly. She had enough on her plate.

She had to talk to someone who knew Joseph. Who knew Mary Margaret. Who shared the common bond of Vietnam so she wouldn't have to explain or excuse.

Unfortunately, there was one person who fit that bill all too neatly. Even the Vietnam part.

Molly remembered when she'd found out. It had been while Molly had been giving her deposition. When she'd outlined her nursing experience as the introduction to the questioning about how she might have let an old woman die.

"Why don't you mention the year you spent in Vietnam?" he'd asked.

Uncomfortable in her brand-new red suit and high heels, Molly had shrugged. "I never think to," she said, because she didn't. Too much effort, too many questions and assumptions. Too much to deal with on too little stamina.

"But Vietnam has cachet now," he'd said, standing so he could lean over the table toward her. So he could impress her with his crocodile smile and

Armani suit. "Everybody wants it on their résumé. Even people who haven't served."

"You have it on yours?" she'd retorted.

His smile had grown. "First line. 'I served in Vietnam. Oh, I also graduated top of my class in law school.'"

"Served where?"

That smile again, taunting, knowing. "The real war. Adjutant general's office. Saigon. I did everything I could think of to stay away, especially since I'd earned my law degree on ROTC. I mean, I figured that a top lawyer like me would take Washington by storm."

"Only you took Saigon by storm instead."

"And Bangkok on weekends."

Still, he'd been there. He'd served in a war unlike any other war, where there hadn't been rear lines, where there hadn't been a real demarcation between friend and foe. Where your friends were alive one minute and dust particles the next. He'd known Joseph Ryan before the war had ruined him, and known Mary Margaret Ryan before her case had shattered her.

He was an asshole. A user. A despoiler of hard-working people everywhere. He lived in a fancy office now, used Vietnam as punctuation in a résumé.

He was still the only one who would be able to tell Molly whether or not she should listen to Joseph Ryan.

Molly kept walking. She walked for an hour, ever mindful of the silent, watchful men who followed her; and then, when she gave up, when the storm gave up, she trudged alone back to the silent, watchful house and took a shower. She might as well. After she cleaned herself up, she was going to have to wallow back in the grime. She was going to have to call and ask a favor of Frank Patterson.

✦ Chapter 11 ✦

"CAN I HELP YOU, SIR?"

Molly had triage this morning. For a change, it was pretty quiet, which had just given her ulcer more of a chance to seize up over the decision she'd made the afternoon before.

It was a stupid idea.

It was the only one she could come up with that might let her finally get on with the summer.

Five o'clock would be fine, his secretary had said. Five o'clock it is, Molly had answered, as if she were making an appointment to get her hair done.

The way her stomach was cramping up, she wasn't going to make it to five o'clock anyway. What difference did it make? Why should she want to know any more about suicides than she did? She had enough on her hands. Enough to do at work—at both works—to keep her busy until the day she dropped dead. Which, if she continued to feel the way she did, should be anytime in the next twenty-four hours.

"I want to see a doctor."

Almost with a start, Molly returned her attention to the conversation she'd begun with the man who'd stepped up to her desk. It was a measure of how distracted she was that she hadn't heard the secretary alongside clearing her throat. It was a betrayal of how very preoccupied she was that she hadn't even noticed just why the secretary was clearing her throat in the first place.

Molly gave the man a smile.

He didn't smile back. Molly could only imagine why. On an August morning when the temperature and humidity both were hovering around the hundred mark, her mystery guest was standing in front of her in a full-length, buttoned-down, winter raincoat. He was also standing as if he were very, very uncomfortable. Oh hallelujah, Molly thought with ill-disguised glee. A distraction.

"Can you tell me what seems to be wrong?" she asked with a perfectly straight face.

Her guest glared. "I *need*," he said carefully, not moving, "to *see* a *doctor*."

No fool she, Molly grabbed a clipboard with a form and motioned him back to the work lane with her. The secretary, already blushing furiously at what she'd probably have to write down on the patient complaint line, didn't even bother to watch.

Molly opened the door into the treatment room and showed the man through. She waited only until the door was completely closed, though, before dropping the good behavior.

"All right," she demanded, hands on hips. "What's going on?"

Her patient, a youngish, smallish, baldish man with an unshaven chin and a moist upper lip, didn't answer. He just reached down to unbutton his coat.

Molly prided herself on her professionalism. She had never, ever laughed in a patient's face.

Until that moment.

She'd been expecting to hear what her patient had

inserted. After all, the ER had a virtual Foreign Body Hall of Fame, a testament to the imagination with which humans approached the idea of self-fulfillment. Everything from animal to vegetable to mineral had been pulled out of one tract or another.

This morning, when Molly needed it the most, her patient topped them all.

He opened his raincoat to reveal that beneath his best London Fog and shiny black wing tips, he was stark, staring naked. He was not, however, alone. There, hanging from the end of his penis by its bill, was a live, full-grown, white duck.

Molly burst out laughing.

"What the hell is that?" she demanded instinctively.

The man looked down, as if he had to reacquaint himself with the problem at hand. As it were.

"My friend. Albert."

Molly started laughing again. Then she clamped her hand over her mouth, as if that would help. "I'm sorry . . . really . . ."

The patient darkened all the way to his sock line.

"What do you want us to do?" she asked. "Mr. . . ."

"Betelman. Allan Betelman," he said. "Couldn't you make him let go?"

This time it was Molly who darkened. She was trying so hard, but she couldn't take her eyes off ground zero. Maybe, she thought in some distress herself, there really wasn't anything to those suicides after all. Maybe it had just been one of those group things. Like the head wounds. And penises. She'd seen an awful lot of strangely decorated penises lately. It was just too bad Vic couldn't add this one to his tattoo file.

"Sir," she said, trying her best to look him in the eye even as her voice hit two distinct notes. "We don't do ducks here."

"You have to do *something*," he protested. "I'm in agony."

"How did this . . . how did this happen?" she managed to ask.

Mr. Betelman didn't seem in the least hesitant about sharing his problems. "Well, I trained him to do it," he told her. "With duct tape. I mean . . . well, you probably wouldn't understand."

"I seldom do, sir."

"He's supposed to let go, though. When I'm . . . when we're . . . finished."

Now her shoulders were shaking. The pitch of her voice rose alarmingly. "And?"

"And—" Mr. Betelman went on. "He wouldn't. I tried everything, but I just can't make him let go."

Molly had to leave before she burst her diaphragm. What she wanted to ask was whether he'd tried offering it a cigarette.

"How long have you . . . uh, been . . . joined?"

His face crumpled a little into distress. "Almost five hours."

"What about . . . well, killing it?"

Mr. Betelman slammed his coat closed and opened his eyes so wide Molly thought they'd fall out on the floor. "How dare you?" he demanded. "This is my friend!"

Molly couldn't think of anything more productive to do than just spin around and get the hell out of the room.

It was Sasha who found her sitting on the floor with her head in her hands.

"What's the matter with you?" she demanded.

Molly just shook her head. She just laughed and wiped at her eyes. So Sasha stepped over her and shoved the door open. One minute and thirteen seconds later, Sasha stepped back out.

"We should just kill that thing and put it out of its misery," she announced dryly.

"The duck?"

"No. The dweeb wearing it."

An hour later, the problem of Allen and Albert was still, literally, at hand. The rest of the ER had jump-started with a house fire involving two adults and three children that was taking up a good part of the staff's effort and all the exhaust fans the hospital could provide. The hall hung heavy with the smell of burned tissue and the sound of raspy cries. Molly, positioned outside The Menagerie, as they'd labeled room four, had been left to deal with the now very depressed and uninsured Allan.

"How was I supposed to know the duck couldn't take Valium?" Lance Frost defended himself.

Molly was trying her best to peek through the blinds to see if Allan had figured out yet that his duck wasn't just very relaxed. "What are we going to do?"

On the other side of Lance stood a slick, button-down pharmaceutical salesman with a full bag of goodies. Molly had caught the two of them in conference when she'd pulled Lance in to address the duck issue. She'd conveniently ignored the brand-new otoscope Lance was playing with and the preprinted prescription pads the salesman had been slipping in Lance's pocket in return. She'd already gotten the call on the burns and figured that the least harm Lance could do on the hall that day was to deal with a recalcitrant duck. Go figure he'd kill the damn thing.

"Actually," the drug salesman said in his most velvet tones of persuasion, "this would be the perfect application for the new personality enhancer we're testing right now. Transcend. It's showing great results in obsessive-compulsive disorders."

"I don't know if I'd call this obsessive-compulsive," Lance answered.

"Then what?"

Molly was still watching as Allan, seated in a chair, stroked a very flaccid Albert. "Creatively deranged?"

"I think we should give it to the duck," Lorenzo said in passing, obviously not having been informed that the duck didn't need anything anymore but a nice orange sauce. "Think how depressed *he* must be."

"I think you guys are close-minded," Betty Wheatlon offered from farther down the hall, where she was struggling with an IV line. "It's nobody's business what goes on in a consensual relationship between a man and his waterfowl."

"How do you know it was consensual?" Lorenzo demanded. "That duck hasn't answered a single question."

Nor was he likely to.

"Allan said that he's been severely depressed," Molly offered. "His mother died recently, and he has no other family to speak of. I think there's a high risk of self-abuse here."

"You don't call that self-abuse in there?" Lance demanded.

"Nah," Lorenzo retorted, his arms full of equipment to distribute among the burn rooms. "A duck is bad taste. A lawyer would be self-abuse."

"Transcend is the newest generation of serotonin-uptake inhibitors," the salesman went on, pulling out readily available literature. "It seems to target problem areas even better than Prozac."

"Speaking of lawyers," Lance threw in. "Aren't there five now?"

"Five?" Betty demanded. "No shit? You heard about

the Jew, the Hindu, and the lawyer who stopped overnight at the farmhouse, didn't you?"

"Maybe we should call one for the duck."

"A lawyer or a Hindu?" a surgical resident quipped.

"Well, that's the point," Betty insisted. "See, one of them had to sleep in the barn, and so the Jew offers . . ."

The salesman didn't even draw breath. "Amazing, really. Depressed? It gives you hope. Frightened? Cojones. Unsure? A will of iron. I've seen it work miracles."

"It's still in testing," Molly reminded him, automatically pocketing the brochure as she tried to hear the rest of the lawyer joke. "And we need to get Allan some immediate help. Which we can't since he doesn't have insurance and can't be admitted anyplace but State San, which won't take you unless you get caught on eyewitness news mass-murdering a busful of nuns."

"But that's another benefit of Transcend," the salesman insisted. "It is the quickest-acting drug available today. ER applications are going to be one of its greatest benefits. It's fast, safe, and easily controlled. I'm telling you, this drug takes us so far beyond Prozac that it will define psychiatry in the twenty-first century."

"Let's just deal with today," Molly suggested, even as she was paged back to triage and one of the other nurses dropped off a request to check on transferring the burn patients.

"Easy," the salesman offered enthusiastically. "Since you're testing it here, we could simply call the clinic and have them do a quick evaluation. Wham, bam, thank you ma'am, and Allan can leave Albert behind."

". . . So the doorbell rings, and there standing on the doorstep are the pig and the cow."

Laughter drifted up from that end of the hall. Molly was thinking that she wished she'd heard the rest. Lance, meanwhile, was still watching for signs of life from Albert. "Fuckin' gold mine." He chortled.

Molly looked over at him. "The duck, the Hindu, or the cow?"

"Transcend. *That's* the drug I've been telling you about, Molly. The one I invested in. I'm tellin' you, that Argon stock is gonna make me a millionaire within the first year."

Molly nodded, understanding perfectly. "Good thing it's such a benefit for mankind."

His face perfectly sincere, the drug salesman nodded.

"Albert?" they heard from inside the room. "Albert, are you all right?"

"We're running out of time," Molly offered.

"I'll call the psych clinic," Lance told her. "Bartender, make it a round of Transcend for the house on me."

Which was how Gene ended up arriving back in the ER again, along with half the house staff, psychiatric or otherwise, to witness the latest in ER Follies.

"What are you still doing here at this hour?" Molly asked him.

"It's summer, Molly. I have new residents who still don't know a psychopath from a garden path."

"You also have staff to handle them. Haven't you figured out yet that the whole point of being the Chief of Division is that nobody can find you when there are problems? Call's for the guys practicing to get your job."

His smile was almost as tired as hers. "Not since HMOs and controlled care. Between that and Prozac, it's a whole different world now for us high and mighty."

So they all stood in a clump at one end of the hall,

as far away from the smells and sights in the trauma rooms as they could, eyes and attitudes avid. All except Gene, who was nodding in response to Lance's request.

"Not my study," he said, taking a quick peek in himself to judge the increasingly distraught Allan, "but I think it's a good call, Frost. The figures are excellent. They're in final stages of trials now. There's a good chance it could help."

"Not as good a chance as a few days in a controlled environment would make it," Molly groused.

Gene just shook his head. "Don't bet on it. Even if he did have insurance, the managed health would only allow him three meals and a couple electroshock treatments before kicking him out again."

Molly caught the tension in his voice she hadn't heard before. When she looked over, Gene noticed and offered her a wry grin. "Psychiatry just isn't as much fun as it used to be."

"Somebody should go in and tell Allan that Albert's a dead duck," one of the residents said.

"Good idea," Gene agreed. "Go right in."

That wasn't what the young Kildare had in mind, but one look at the boss changed his mind. Exchanging his smirk for an air of concern, he pushed the door open and made his introductions. The last thing Molly heard as the door swished shut was Allan's quiet voice.

"He was my friend . . ."

"Molly!" the secretary yelled. "Two-sixty-five just went out on an accident with multiples!"

Just a beautiful day in the neighborhood . . .

Gene was still standing by the room, unlit pipe in his mouth as he watched through the window, when

Molly stopped by on her way back from seeing to the second of the five burn transfers. Most of the rest of the residents had long since returned to Wonderland East. The ER had received its multiple victims in from the auto accident: six kids and three adults from one car, and a belligerent cab driver and his even more belligerent fare, who now wasn't going to make his flight home. All were complaining of the smell and the wait to be seen for their necks, backs, and hyperventilations. All were making more noise than the burn victims.

Given the choice between that, the gathering throng at triage, and a duck, Molly chose the duck. So she stopped by to check on Allan.

Watching her for a minute, Gene pulled out the pipe. "What's wrong?"

They were the only two left at that end of the hall. Molly saw the triage secretary searching for her, but she didn't look desperate. Molly ignored her. She thought of that quiet, sad little man sitting in there cradling the only unconditional love he'd ever known.

"He's a lonely little man," she said, her attention on his bowed head and the aggressively empathetic posture of the resident, who was still interviewing him.

"That's one of the reasons you shouldn't keep working here," Gene said softly. "You never get to see the progress. I promise you, given a couple of weeks and a clinic visit or two, he'll be a changed man."

"Either that or he'll work his way up to ponies."

"Nah," he said. "Ponies have teeth."

Just then, the third burn transfer patient was wheeled by, a tiny girl, unconscious and intubated, with oxygen being forced into her ruined lungs with an ambubag and the raw red of her burned chest and arms covered in sterile sheets. Three years old, and already human wreckage because her mother had fallen asleep smoking after a long double shift trying to scrape together a living for her family. The mother who was now completely sedated so she wouldn't have to deal just yet with what had become of her babies in those few minutes.

"No," Molly said without looking away. "It's exactly why I work here. I don't have to know that most of the Allans don't get better. I much prefer just to leave 'em at that door and go home alone."

"You think maybe you might need some of this magic stuff, too?" Gene asked quietly.

"Nah," she said. "It's just summer. This year I've had to investigate a lot of suicides, and you know how I love that."

"And?"

"And one victim's brother is insisting that something is fishy. He's after me like a dog on rabbits." Not really, but close enough. "So I think I have to look back into all those goddamn suicides just to shut him up."

"And there's nobody else to do it?"

"Have you seen our homicide stats this year?"

"Point taken."

"Besides, I also just found out that the O.K. Corral incident the other day wasn't random. Guy had my name in his pocket. The FBI wants to know why."

Gene stared at her as if her hair was on fire. "What do you mean he had your name?"

"I mean either somebody was really pissed at the way I triage, or I seem to possess some knowledge that makes somebody out there nervous. The Feds think it's Pearl's suicide note."

The door to Allan's room opened and the resident

appeared with the duck in his arms. Gene didn't seem to notice.

"What should I do with this?" the frustrated resident demanded.

"Pearl's note?" Gene asked Molly. "What do you mean?"

"The gambling situation. There seems to be a heavy-breather who might not like his name mentioned in public. I did that."

"And now?"

"Sir," the resident tried again.

Molly shrugged. "Now, they try and find some other way to nail this guy before he nails me. I guess."

That got the resident's attention. "You don't seem to be very upset," he said.

Molly just loved the way psychiatry guys felt it their inborn right to horn in on somebody else's conversation. "Gimme a couple of days. I have other things on my mind." She turned back to Gene. "We also got in our fifth lawyer. Ain't that something?"

"You heard the one about the lawyer in hell?" the resident immediately asked.

Both Gene and Molly stared him down. He blushed, lifted the duck. "What should I do with him?"

"Try a little stuffing," Molly suggested. "A four-hundred-degree oven for an hour."

From the slime to the ridiculous, Molly read on the wall as she sat down to use the phone in the lounge. Or in her case today, the reverse. Allan had been put into a taxi for home, Albert accompanying him in a plastic hospital bag. Lance had strongly suggested that it was unhygienic for the duck to depart the premises, but Molly had overruled him.

The burn patients had been transferred to burn centers, and the fans still ran at high to clear out a smell that clung to everyone's hair and clothing. The post–lunch hour rush was starting up, all the night crawlers just beginning to notice the sunshine, and with it, their infected tracks and gonorrhea.

Molly sat down to eat a quick lunch. She thought about calling Frank Patterson then and there so she didn't have to walk into his office. She spent a long, long time wondering why she just couldn't issue an order that Joseph Ryan not be allowed into the front door of the medical examiner's office.

Yeah, like keeping the ghost of Marley away from Ebenezer Scrooge.

It was only about two in the afternoon, and Molly was already too tired to deal with that shit. She didn't hold out any hope that she was going to feel immensely better by five. She sure as hell wasn't going to be any more patient.

She picked up the phone. Took a breath. Found herself dialing Winnie's number instead.

"I need to run something by you."

"Run fast," her boss said. "I have court in a few."

She always had court. Molly wondered how the ME got anything but testifying done these days. But that wasn't the matter at hand. The matter at hand was to complicate all their lives unspeakably.

"Did you pull that new suicide?"

"What about it?"

Molly closed her eyes, wondering why the hell she was getting even more involved. Wondering why she was asking about somebody Joseph Ryan didn't even know. "What do you think? Isn't it a little weird?"

"I tell you weird," Winnie retorted. "I got a guy today died facedown in a toilet, his feet stickin' straight up. They had to bring in the whole goddamn bowl. *That's* weird. I got another call, a lady, she swears to God that voices been telling her to make sure her neighbor's dog doesn't bark at her, cause that's just the devil trying to snatch her soul. She slits the dog's throat. But before she's finished, the dog, who just happens to be a pit bull, which might have validated her theory, gets a big chomp on her neck. He doesn't let go, so they both straighten things out with God together. You want more weird?"

"*Five* lawyers commit suicide in three damn weeks, Winnie?"

"Once in Chicago I saw four butchers die in separate ice-skating accidents."

Molly rubbed at her face. She pulled out the Maalox single-dose pack she kept in her pocket and swilled it on the spot.

"All right then, try this one on for size. Did you talk to all those nice young men who were waiting for me yesterday?"

Winnie grunted. Molly could hear the scratch of her pen across some paper or another, an infrequent keystroke of a computer. Doing three things at once, just as usual.

"What did you think of them?"

"Assholes."

"Besides that."

Silence. Molly knew what it would mean for Winnie to admit that her best friend was dirty. She knew that it would have been a stone shock to Winnie, because Winnie was incorruptible herself.

"I'm late for court, girl," she said. Which meant, I'm not going to discuss this. Now. Ever. Amen.

"I almost got shot, Winnie," Molly said. "Seriously shot. By a guy who was looking just for me. And now I've got people following me everywhere I go. Not only that, I got a psycho homeless guy following right behind them. I need to get some answers, and I don't know who else to talk to."

Yes, she did. She just didn't want to do it.

"I think you're forgetting something here," Winnie shot back, her diction suddenly a little sloppy. "*You* are working for *me*, not the other way around. When I say jump, you don't even have to ask how high. You just hope it's high enough. You *pray* you know which direction, because I'm gonna whip your white-wearin' pill-pushin' butt if it's the wrong one. And then you thank God you're jumpin' for *me* instead of some hacksaw champ with a degree from the god-damn Caribbean, you understand me?"

Molly leaned back in the couch and tried to ignore the spring that gouged her leg. For just a second, she considered distracting Winnie with the story of Allan and Albert, even though she knew it wouldn't do anything but make her madder when she finally got back around to Pearl.

"I hope you're bitin' my ass because it's safer than biting the mayor's," Molly said instead.

She heard it then. A funny, odd sound she'd never heard from Winnie in her life. She could have sworn it was a sob, and it unnerved her.

"I think Pearl killed herself," Winnie said, sounding suddenly so much like Mary Margaret Ryan's mother sitting there on her Early American country print couch. "Just like you said."

And then, before Molly could ask anything else, she hung up.

After that, it was easy for Molly to punch out Frank Patterson's number. Then she just told the lovely Brittany that she wouldn't be arriving at Frank's office at five after all, and hung up the phone.

It took her another hour and a half and two more Maalox packs to call Brittany back. This time she just rescheduled for the next day and did her best to forget about it, which, considering the fact that they ended up with a rare daylight drive-by with multiple victims, wasn't as tough as she thought.

Three hours later Molly had to admit that she'd had the right idea. She wasn't in the mood to face anybody this evening. She was so tired, so jagged. All she wanted to do was dig in the dirt.

As she troweled around her cannas and hibiscus, she noticed that the car was back. Or another one, she wasn't sure. She wasn't sure she really wanted to notice. It just elevated her blood pressure. Like watching the vultures that waited in the trees for some unlucky settler to piss off the Indians and make their day.

Molly concentrated instead on the loamy smell of the fresh earth, the sound of her new wind chimes, heavy cast brass bells that tumbled from one of the catalpas. She focused on her yard and the flowers she could always make grow, even when nothing else seemed to work for her, and finally the whisper of Joseph Ryan's voice faded away with the distant keening of that mother who had fought with her bare hands to save her children.

Molly could smell the food from one of the nearby restaurants. Garlic and basil and, undoubtedly in this neck of the woods, balsamic vinegar. She heard the faint tinny notes of old Jimmy Dorsey from Sam's house and felt the warmth from the fading sun across the back of her neck. And, just like always in her garden, she courted the quiet.

She heard the front bell first. It didn't occur to her to answer it. After all, she'd been waiting for the press to descend since the cops had informed her about Mustaffa. Her attention firmly on weeds and roots, she never even turned around.

Not even when she heard the wrought-iron gate squeak behind her.

"Go away before I call the cops," she said, jabbing at an unfortunate dandelion as if it had a press pass. "I don't have anything quotable to say."

"Even to me?"

Molly swung around so fast she landed on her butt in the dirt. Her first reaction was absolute shock. Then outrage, then fury. It was the fury that brought her charging to her feet.

"What the hell are you doing here?" she demanded, breathless with rage.

She should have felt him coming, like the devil walking on her grave. She should have at least smelled him, that stupid cologne that seemed to precede him.

Frank smiled at her, that same damn pirate smile that was so infectious, and he dug a pink plastic spoon into his cup of Ted Drewe's frozen custard. "I figured if I gave you the chance you'd cancel the appointment tomorrow, too, Saint Molly. And I know you need to ask me about Joe. Don't you?"

There in her backyard. Breaching her sanctuary. Tempting her with the sight of Ted Drewe's. Molly didn't know whether to laugh or to scream. She damn near did both.

"Frank," she said instead, her voice admirably calm, "why is it that just when I think things can't possibly get worse, you show up?"

✦ Chapter 12 ✦

ONCE AGAIN, Frank had the upper hand. He was cool and collected and decked out in his best gray pinstripe and monogrammed shirt. Molly had mulch on her knees and rose dust in her hair.

Frank was too busy sucking on the spoon and sizing up the property value to notice. "So this is what I missed out on," he said, walking on into the yard, his head on a constant swivel. "It really screwed up the size of the settlement, ya know."

Stopping five feet away, he leaned over to check out the fish pond.

"Don't do that, Frank," Molly warned. "Koi startle easily."

She was incredibly proud of herself that she didn't just push him in and make a grab for the concrete as he went over.

He straightened and grinned. "Ever the gracious hostess."

Goddamn him for being so good-looking. Standing there in the slanting sunlight, he looked like a screen image, all angles and shadows and smashing blue eyes. He smelled like a thousand fantasies.

Molly spent an unforgivable moment fighting the

feeling of inadequacy she'd carried away from the witness stand with her. She'd had trouble enough battling Frank Patterson in the sterility of his office. Here was above and beyond the call of duty. She couldn't allow him to intimidate her the minute he walked into her yard, but she couldn't think of any alternative but calling the Feds for help.

Not only that, but he was taunting her with one of the greatest sins in life. Ted Drewe's frozen custard. Heart attack in a cup, a St. Louis tradition more cherished than the Cardinals and bad weather. It was not unheard of to see the medical examiner's van parked right alongside one of the big fire department pumpers next to the stand on Chippewa, while the city employees stood in line waiting for their fix with every ball player and prom attendee in town.

Molly knew damn well that somehow Frank knew how much he was torturing her. She wanted to hurt him for it.

Then she saw the avarice in his eyes. Remembered his question, and his frustration at one particular point in the settlement hearing. The idea was so perfectly delicious a light bulb should have appeared over her head.

"Would you like to see it?" she asked.

He damn near did a double take. Molly smiled right back and dropped her trowel. For a change, she was going to break out the good furniture. She couldn't think of anything she'd like more at this moment than rubbing Frank's nose in the hunk of the settlement that got away.

"It's all in an unbreakable trust," she reminded him, leading the way back in through the kitchen door. "But, you know that. You cracked every one of your knuckles trying to get into it."

"Kept me out of the Shyster Hall of Fame," he

allowed, following into the still hush of the Burke family shrine.

Molly came to a halt just shy of the doorway into the jackpot. "You can't take that in here," she said.

Still grinning, Frank lifted the cardboard cup. "Want some?"

Molly had seen sexual innuendo before. Frank went right to the head of the class.

"You can leave it in the freezer," she said, which made him laugh.

He had no idea what it cost her to say that. Not because she wanted sex—at least not with him—but because she wanted that damn custard. Hawaiian special, if she was any judge. Pineapple, macadamia nuts, chocolate, and butterscotch. Pure bliss in a cup. And she couldn't so much as ask for a taste. Story of her life.

Just for that, Molly took Frank along the scenic route. Into the dining room where he had to pass the Chippendale table and chairs and bowfront commode he hadn't managed to get in the trial settlement, the Waterford chandelier, the eighteenth century Coney silver service and Sèvres serving pieces, the Stubbs paintings on the wall, and the Persian rug on the glossy hardwood floor.

From there, the music room, with its Steinway grand and matching Georgian settees, the rosewood inlaid secretary and gilded mirrors. Frank took a moment to acknowledge the Rembrandt sketch alongside the piano before sighing and moving on.

Molly led him through the hallway with the pair of Mings and Japanese watercolors. Into the sitting room with its fifteenth century Japanese seasonal screen, the Qua Yen ink and color over the sofa, Hopper seascape over the Adam mantel and the Queen Anne corner cabinet filled with her father's priceless jade collection. Molly actually thought she heard Frank whimper.

"Tea?" she asked, for the first time in her life enjoying what her parents had not bestowed on her.

Frank could hardly form words. "Do you have anything stronger?"

Then she really smiled. "No."

He actually looked as if he were in pain. "Tea, then."

When Molly returned with clean knees and two glasses of iced tea, Frank was studying the small Feininger behind the brace of Chippendale chairs in the corner. "I thought there was a Picasso."

Molly handed off the tea, feeling better than she had in a while. "Over the TV in the family room. Mums and Dad considered Picasso too vulgar for the good furniture."

Frank started to laugh. He stopped when he realized Molly was dead serious. By then, though, she'd ensconced herself on the sofa.

"Doesn't it piss you off?" he asked suddenly.

Molly had heard the sentiment before. "Not at all. If it hadn't been for you, I'd be living in another state altogether and renting this out to Washington U. or something. Although I admit I'd at least take the Homer with me."

"The Homer?"

She smiled. "In my bedroom."

She could see he was itching to see what was up there, and this time there was no sexual innuendo at all. True to form, when cornered, Frank struck back. "Don't give me that 'if it hadn't been for you' crap. You had liability insurance."

Molly felt the color rise in her neck. "With a cap you guys paid no attention to. Which has absolutely nothing to do with the fact that I was neither faulty nor negligent. But then, that's all behind us, isn't it?"

"I thought you were appealing."

"I considered it until my insurance company informed me that I'd pay the lawyer fees out of my own, already-depleted pocket. Which is why I don't have insurance anymore, either. So don't come after me again, cause this time all you'll get is my eight-year-old car and an empty bottle of Maalox."

"I didn't clean you out."

Molly lifted her eyebrows. "You didn't? Then why am I working two jobs?"

Frank's smile this time was knowing, taunting. "Because you need the work, Saint Molly. Not the money."

Molly opened her mouth to say something scathing. She shut it again, because she didn't have the energy to even start that particular argument.

"Any time you'd like a taste of my job, just let me know," she said instead. "After that, you might not be so quick to litigate."

"Not a problem anymore," he retorted, hand to heart. "Remember? I'm on the side of the angels now."

"You're on the side of the biggest fees. Just like always."

His eyes positively gleamed with delight. "Precisely."

Molly knew the concentration couldn't last. Even as he was answering her, he was back on his feet, drawn to the exquisite jade carvings hidden carefully behind special glass. Three shelves of them, pillaged and plundered from some of the finest ancient artists in the Orient.

"My God," he breathed, truly awed. "You really mean to tell me that you don't enjoy any of this?"

Molly looked around, brought away the memories that came unbidden with the works of art Frank saw. "I guess I just didn't get that all-important acquisition gene."

He didn't manage to answer her. For a minute, Molly thought he'd forgotten she was there as he sipped at his tea and tried to get a good look at the intricate carvings. When he did speak, he surprised her.

"Did you know there are cops watching your house?"

"Uh-huh."

That got his eyes around to her. "Okay. Does it have something to do with why you wanted to talk to me about Joey?"

Joey. A boy's name. A buddy's name, a big brother. *Hey, Joey! Can you come out and play? Yo, Joey, let's do some hoops!*

Molly wondered if it occurred to Frank that there wasn't a Joey anymore.

"I don't know. There's been a lot going on lately. Why did you send him to me?"

"Who better to send Joey to than Saint Molly of the Battlefield?"

"Cut out the crap, Frank. Why?"

For the first time since she'd known him, Frank Patterson seemed uncomfortable. Instead of joining her back on the couch, he picked one of the Chippendale chairs and eased into it as if afraid it would break. "Because he needed the official word," he said simply, the glass of tea held between his knees as if he were a young man balancing punch at a cotillion. "He needed certainty. He didn't see her dead, he couldn't very well go to the funeral—"

"*Does* his family know he's alive?"

"I don't know. It's not something I ever discussed with them."

"Don't you think you should?"

"That's up to Joey."

Molly sighed. "Joey. That means you've known him a long time."

"Fifth grade. Saint Gabriel's."

There it was again, the school association. Molly had gone to Cathedral Parish, Visitation Academy for high school. Where the "better" young Catholic women trained. Molly had fit in about as well as a rapper at the opera.

"Saint Gabe's, huh?"

Which would have put his upbringing in the near south side. Solid middle-class neighborhoods, close associations, fierce loyalties.

"Yeah."

"Why didn't you tell me before that you knew Mary Margaret from way back?"

"Peg," he said, just as they all had. "Her name was Peg."

Molly nodded acquiescence. "Peg, then. Why?"

For just a second, Frank's certain gaze faltered. "I didn't see that it would make any difference."

"Do you still think she committed suicide?"

"Yes. Don't you?"

It was Molly's turn to feel uncomfortable. "I think you wouldn't have sent Joe Ryan to me if all you wanted was for him to feel better."

Frank was up again, pacing the room, fingering the furniture as if he couldn't quite let go of the idea that it was forever out of his reach. "I owe him."

"Do you think . . . ?"

When Frank came to a halt, he did it right in front of her. Molly came close to backing away, because where there had only been challenge and humor in Frank's eyes, now there was something else. Something dark, like sin or death.

"Yes," was all he said.

All he needed to say. Molly hadn't been able to ask him, and he hadn't needed her to. Was Joe to be believed? Was he as perceptive as he seemed?

Was there something living beneath all that awful isolation?

Suddenly, Frank smiled. A terrible smile of dawning understanding. "He told you, too, didn't he?"

Too? What the hell was he talking about? How would Frank know? How would he understand?

"Told me what?"

This time, Frank laughed. He laughed out loud as if Molly were the funniest person on earth. "Don't try and squirm out of it, Saint Molly. You know he did."

"Did what?" she demanded, on her feet, too.

Frank's expression grew enigmatic. "You know, my mom used to tell us kids the story of this spooky old lady who lived near her when she was growing up. Mrs. Donatelli. Mrs. Donatelli saw her baby die in a fire. Couldn't get in to help save her. She was never the same after that. But she also started to be able to just kind of know things, ya know? She had the sight, they called it back then. Well, Joey's kind of like that. Maybe he doesn't have the sight, but he sure as hell sees things other people don't."

"What do you mean, he told me, *too*?"

Frank wagged a finger at her. Then he just took hold of her hand and sat his glass into it. "Nope, this one's all yours. Just do me a favor. Go over the case once more for Joey. Give him the facts. Let him have a little peace."

Molly followed Frank as he headed toward the front door. "What do you mean, Frank?"

"Will you do it?"

"Yes, I'll do it. Will you help me if I need it?"

He stopped by the front door, his attention once again straying, this time to the bronze pot that stood in the corner of the foyer. "That's Tang Dynasty," he protested, his hand out.

"Frank!"

"I can't do anything to compromise my clients," he told her, reaching for the front door. "But you'd probably like to know that all Peg's personal effects have been sent to her parents." Then he flashed her a completely unrepentant smile. "Help Saint Molly of the Battlefield? How can I resist an offer like that?"

"Did Peg know Pearl Johnson?" she asked quickly before he got away.

"Hell if I know."

"Did you know that four other lawyers have committed suicide?"

"Are you kidding? That's all people are talking about down at the Lawyer's Club and the MAC. We're losing members fast."

The Missouri Athletic Club. The postschool place to belong, if you wanted to follow the Right Path in St. Louis.

"Have you heard anything that might sound odd?"

This time Frank looked dumbstruck. "Don't you think five lawyers committing suicide is strange?"

"On my less-charitable days, I think it's a gift to the city."

True to form, Frank laughed. "And me not doing the gentlemanly thing and adding myself to the list."

Molly could afford a smile this time. "My thoughts exactly. Will you keep an ear out down there? There's some question about Pearl's contacts. Maybe . . . would Peg have been interested in something a little shady?"

"Like I told you. She was driven. Worked hard, played hard. Who knows?"

He did get the door open this time. Molly put a hand on his arm. "What did you mean?" she tried once more.

He didn't even answer. He just grinned and walked out.

"Hey!" she yelled as he walked down the lawn. "You forgot your Ted Drewe's!"

"Think of me when you lick the spoon!" he called over his shoulder.

It just figured that he'd be walking down to a Mercedes sports coupe. Molly would have probably felt a lot worse if she'd taken the time to actually watch him walk all the way to the curb and get in. As it was, by the time she heard the throaty roar of his engine, she was scraping the bottom of the ice cream cup to get the very last of that pineapple and custard.

The next morning found Molly back in her office going over Peg Ryan's file. She would have loved to say she found something spectacular, something that jumped out at her and told Joe Ryan that his little sister had been immune to the whispers of a quick exit.

There was nothing new. Nothing that looked any different than it had before. Peg Ryan had been mercurial, a little unpredictable, demanding on others and even harder on herself. Which, Molly thought in passing, sounded an awful lot like Winnie. Peg Ryan had lost a big case and hadn't been able to handle it. Peg Ryan had an older brother she'd been protecting who hadn't been able to handle anything for about a quarter of a century.

An older brother she was protecting. An older brother whose own family didn't even admit he was alive.

That was Molly's first niggle. Joey. The big brother Peg had been protecting. Seeing on the sly without the knowledge of her family. The big brother who needed her to stay just where she was.

If she'd been that conscientious about Joe, why would she just desert him like that?

Peg was also an up-and-coming member of the Barracuda Brigade, an aspiring partner in a company that specialized in protecting the big fish from the little fish. Not exactly a position one would imagine compatible for an idealist. Not the record one would think belonged to Mother Teresa.

None of the technical findings had changed. There was still the .357 Magnum Peg had bought six months earlier, permit included, in anticipation of a move into the city that had never materialized. The forensics still matched the scenario. The alcohol and tox screen said she'd been drunk and she'd been on prescription medication and just a little extra.

The question mark they'd had on some of the pills had been filled in. A little cornucopia of diet pills, water pills, and something that bore the generic labeling of synapsapine, which the lab tech noted was another antidepressant.

The written verification had also come in from Peg's private doctor that he'd been seeing Peg for stress symptoms and prescribed accordingly. No questions, no alerts.

Molly sat where she was for a long time watching out the window over Vic Fellows's desk and thinking.

He told you, too, didn't he?

What the hell had Frank Patterson meant? How could he possibly know what Joseph Ryan saw with those Chaldean eyes of his?

"I thought I saw your car in the lot," she heard from behind her. "What are you doing here?"

Molly spun around to see Winnie standing dead center in the doorway, a stack of mail in her hands and her hair twisted into some kind of elaborate figure eight with what looked like decorative chopsticks through it. Only Winnie could wear it and get away with it. Besides the hair, she was dressed to the nines in what could only be described as a tailored dashiki and Ferragamos.

"Hi, Winnie. You look great. Going out?"

The ME straightened as if she'd been mortally insulted. "I ask you about your private business?"

"All the time," Molly retorted with a grin. "Does he know what he's in for?"

For a second there was silence. Then, grudgingly, Winnie grinned. "We were in med school together. I haven't seen him in five years."

"And Phillip?"

Phillip LaGrange, Winnie's lover and the father of her eight-year-old son.

"Phillip is in Antigua on business," the boss said acerbically. "Now, what are you doing here?"

Molly had no problems switching gears. "Oh, I gave in and decided to just go over my stuff on this Peg Ryan case."

"Peg . . ."

"Mary Margaret. Family calls her Peg."

Winnie's expression tightened a little. Closed off. "And what did you find?"

"Nothing. But maybe if I tell her brother that I looked again, he'll feel better. I'm gonna go to the house for one more look at her private stuff, and then I'll take a walk down by the river and let him know."

"And while you're doing all this running around, do you have all the forensics reports back on Rhett's friend the cop? We're going to prelims for his shooter this week."

"Bill Myers?" Molly answered, knowing perfectly well that Winnie wasn't struggling with her memory. Winnie knew the name of every one of her cases. She just didn't believe in bandying them about, kind of a medical examiner's version of the Navajo belief that the dead can infect you by speaking of them.

"Results should all be on the file," Molly said. "Tox lab even got us a quick screen for alcohol and toxins, just to prevent any defense grandstanding. All negative."

Winnie snorted in outrage. "Of course it was. Good thought, though. They get ballistics info back to you?"

"In the file."

The ME nodded, looked out the same window Molly had. "Good. I don't want to be caught unprepared."

"It's a slam-dunk, Winnie."

A slam-dunk. No sweat. A skate, a zippo, a slider. A sure win without work. No questions, no problems. The ultimate goal in police work, the ultimate prize. Case closed with no mess, no fuss, no questions.

Just like the suicides Kevin had handled. Like Pearl.

"Winnie?"

"Yeah."

"Did you catch that latest lawyer suicide?"

"The one who did the Greg Louganis from the Wainright?"

"That's him. What was his name?"

The ME squinted at her. "You gonna bring me problems?"

"No. I promise." If Winnie bought that, Molly also had some land under the Arch to sell her.

"McGivers, Harold. Why?"

"I don't know. I still think it's a little funny. Too much of a good thing, ya know?"

"Well, don't. I don't have time for it."

Even so, right after Winnie left, Molly went looking in the computer files for the names of those other two slam-dunks. She'd heard them once, but since they hadn't been her cases, she'd shoved them aside for more important things.

VanAck, Peter, thirty-five years old.

Goldman, Aaron, fifty-four years old.

Those added to Harold McGivers, Pearl Johnson, and Peg Ryan. Molly wasn't sure why she wanted to take those names along with her. Maybe she was just getting superstitious. More superstitious. As in, five lawyers becoming suddenly overwhelmed by the guilt of screwing the general population seeming to be too good to be true. As in, why should she be the only one to have people questioning her suicides?

Molly wondered whether Peter VanAck's family had protested when Kevin had told them. She wondered whether they believed him yet that Peter had decided to die.

Not her problem, though. Not today. Today she had to go back and repaint herself with the grief of a family that still didn't know how bad it was.

That was if she got out the damn door.

Molly was just reaching into her purse for her car keys when she heard a scruffling sound in the doorway. She looked up to find that she had another visitor.

"You looking for somebody, Mr. McGuire?" she asked.

Molly hadn't seen the councilman since the night of Pearl's death. Even so, he looked no different. Suited and tied this time, for sure. But still florid and unhealthy-looking, the top of his head suspiciously moist, and his eyes unable to settle in one direction at a time.

"Oh," he said, sounding unaccountably surprised. "You're early."

"For what?"

"Uh, well, isn't your shift midnights? I mean, I thought . . . uh, Kevin was on now."

"Kevin's office is down the hall," she said meaningfully.

McGuire still seemed to be searching for something behind Molly. "Oh, yes. Of course. Everything going all right, Molly?"

Considering how surreal the conversation was getting, Molly wasn't quite sure how she wanted to answer. "Just fine," she said anyway. "You?"

That seemed to startle him. "Oh, I guess it's going all right. City hall is trying its best to recover from losing Pearl, of course."

"Of course. Has the mayor named a new comptroller yet?"

"Well, just temporarily, of course. Till elections."

"Of course. Who?"

"Me."

Molly was sure her jaw dropped. Mayor Williamson, while a savvy political player, had never been known for holding out the olive branch to his enemies, or appointing them to potentially dangerous positions.

But then, it was only Tim McGuire. How dangerous could he be?

"Congratulations. Want me to show you Kevin's office?"

"Yes. Yes, please."

When Molly dropped Tim off at the appropriate door, she had the distinct feeling he had absolutely nothing of importance to say to the senior death investigator. It didn't keep her there to find out why, though. She had a lot to do before she went to work at eleven.

If only the heat would break. If only the afternoon rains that slammed through every day at five with the predictability of freight trains would suck some of the humidity from the air. Molly drove with the windows down and the sun roof open, because her air conditioner hadn't worked since the day some kids had tried to break into her car with a rock and only succeeded in crippling her dashboard. She had sunglasses on to cut the flat, metallic glare of the sun as it sagged past its zenith, and she had the radio on rather than listen to the whine and squeal of traffic around her.

She was heading out Highway 40 toward Richmond Heights with its tidy, rolling streets of redbud and pin oak, its brick track housing and mixing population. One of the older bedroom communities, Richmond Heights straddled the highway like a lopsided saddle, all the money at one end and all the hard work at the other. Older neighborhoods in flux, loyalties bound by Little Flower parish and St. Mary's Health Center and now split by the very upscale Galleria shopping mall, Richmond Heights boasted the very ritzy community of Ladue at its one end and apologized for the very struggling streets of Maplewood at the other.

The Ryans lived somewhere in the middle, just off Big Bend Boulevard. Their house was small, tidy, and brick, just like its neighbors, with a big front porch nobody thought to use anymore and a detached one-car garage that would keep the price down. A comfortable home in a friendly neighborhood with slow streets and the kind of curtains that lifted when strangers pulled up to driveways.

Molly cut her engine in the Ryans' driveway and built up her courage to go in. She imagined Mrs. Ryan, still sitting on that couch, the progression of pictures featuring Mary Margaret abruptly ending alongside Joseph's on that wall of memories.

Suddenly Molly couldn't think for the life of her what she was doing here. Did she really want to torture these people again just so she could appease a ghost? Did she want to torture herself by stepping back into that steam bath of grief?

She didn't have a choice. She hadn't since Joseph Ryan had leveled his accusation on her.

Mrs. Ryan answered the door, a little more stooped, a little older. Molly wanted to step back, afraid of being contaminated.

"Mrs. Ryan, I'm Molly Burke from the Medical Examiner's Office, remember? I wondered if I could have a few more words with you about Mar . . . Peg."

It took Mrs. Ryan a second to react. Molly just waited.

"You have more questions? Is there a problem?"

"No, ma'am. We're just doing some . . . uh, follow-ups."

The little woman stepped back, her hand still on the door, to let Molly through.

The first thing she noticed was the smell. Before it had been briskly clean. Air freshener and Pine-Sol and coffee. Today it seemed stale, old food and new mold and dust. As if the life had been drained out of it with Peg's death.

Without turning around, Mrs. Ryan led the way back to the couch. Back to that wall of photos. Without meaning to, Molly looked back at Joseph. At Joey. Fierce and hard and proud. That hurt worse than Peg, because Molly hadn't known Peg. She hadn't known what Peg had been through. She knew just what road Joey Ryan had taken to those caves of his.

"What is it you need?" Mrs. Ryan asked.

And Molly told her. Not the truth, not really. A version of it, which Mrs. Ryan accepted without comment. Molly revisited all the questions on the suicide poll and added a few more. Questions about friends, family, connections. But Mrs. Ryan didn't really know any of Peg's friends, except, of course, Frankie Patterson, who had known her son Joey.

She understood that Peg's effects from the office had been returned home, Molly said to the little woman, her own hands carefully in her lap, her posture comforting and close. Would Mrs. Ryan still have them?

Mrs. Ryan would. She wouldn't even mind if Molly went through them.

The cardboard box was still sitting unopened on top of the girl's vanity in Peg's room. Molly took a second to take in the room, with the Anne Klein and Ann Taylor suits in the closet and the stuffed teddy bears on the old white bed. A PC and a bookcase full of original Nancy Drews. Jelly beans on the nightstand and birth control pills in the drawer.

The contents of the box were easier to figure out. Diplomas from St. Louis University, undergraduate and law school. Law degree and certificate. A clutch of family pictures and a paperweight awarded by the Professional Women's Association. A scaled-down replica of a Calder sculpture and two framed and matted stick drawings signed *To Aunt Peg, love forever Cissie.*

Molly hated this. She wanted to get the hell out of here before she couldn't. She wanted to get out into the yard and suck in some air. Instead, she reached into the bottom of the box and drew out Peg Ryan's personal daykeeper. There must, she figured, be something to go on in here, whether positive or not.

When she unzipped the leather cover, the book automatically fell open to the most current month, August. Molly scanned the notations in its tidy squares and caught her breath.

She'd struck gold on the first page.

✦ Chapter 13 ✦

AUGUST 2ND Pearl and Harry dinner MAC.

Molly's heart suddenly started hammering. She began flipping through the book, looking for names, addresses, times, anything. The first thing she noticed was that Peg had indeed been a busy girl. Client meetings, workout schedule, court dates, even a regular meeting with a masseuse. And something referred to as the Shitkicker's Club, which met regularly at lunch. No mention of where, what for, or who was involved.

Then she got lucky again.

August 5th. Funeral St. Clements. Peter.

Peter, Harry, Pearl. Molly was probably jumping to a conclusion or two. After all, she only had first names. Peg could have been referring to Pearl Smith, Harry Jones, and Peter Browne. All the same, the coincidence seemed too strong. And if there was one thing Molly had lost faith in over the years, it was coincidence. Molly felt sure Peg had known at least three of the other suicides.

Not a huge surprise in this town. After all, Peg belonged to the Lawyer's Club and the MAC, as did any other self-respecting attorney in this town. Even so, every instinct Molly had sent her heart into overdrive.

"Is this helping?" Mrs. Ryan asked from the doorway.

Molly looked up and did her best to keep her smile calm. "It might, Mrs. Ryan. Do you remember Peg mentioning anybody named Harry McGivers, or Pearl Johnson?"

"I know the name Pearl Johnson," she answered, pushing ineffectually at her bangs, which seemed grayer than ever. "But isn't she somebody . . . I don't know . . ."

"The city comptroller."

Mrs. Ryan nodded, her eyes unfocused. "Yes, that's it. I think . . . I don't know. I can't remember her saying anything."

"Peter VanAck?" Molly asked, walking closer, trying hard to keep the connection.

Mrs. Ryan shook her head, but it seemed more to clear it than to answer. "She knew so many people. She worked so hard, you know. Frankie said she was going to be a star."

"Yes, ma'am. I know. Did Peg mention a . . . well, a group of people she met with regularly for lunch?"

Mrs. Ryan laid her hand against the doorjamb, as if to stabilize herself, and sighed. Deep and long, deflating.

"She might. I don't know."

Molly knew she'd passed her optimum time with the poor woman. There was nothing left in there to offer but regrets, so it was time to go.

"May I ask a favor, Mrs. Ryan?" she asked, lifting the leather-bound book for the woman to see. "Could I borrow this for a few days? I promise I'll give it back."

The watery brown eyes couldn't quite come to life. "Anything," she said vaguely. "Anything for my Peg."

"Did she . . . do you know if she kept a diary?"

Molly got a small smile. "She used to. When she was a girl."

"Thank you, Mrs. Ryan."

There weren't any first-class junk food stands near the Ryans' house, so Molly grabbed some take-out Chinese and carried lunch and the daykeeper along to Tilles Park, where she could settle by the pond.

It wasn't any cooler outside, but at least in the shade there was a suspicion of a breeze. Nestled between Brentwood and Ladue, Tilles was a small urban surprise, rolling lawns, mature trees, and at least three baseball diamonds. Along the wandering pathways, young mothers pushed strollers and retirees marched in pairs, arms swinging like British field officers on parade. One of the volunteer gardeners was watering a patch of chrysanthemums and begonias. Traffic droned along McKnight Road, and somewhere someone was cutting a lawn with a mower that needed a tune-up. Molly settled herself on a bench where she could see the kids and the swans and the quiet water, and she set to work.

She wasn't sure what she expected to find. A confession, a connection, a cry for help. She knew damn well that what she wanted was to find that Peg hadn't committed suicide after all. She wanted a conspiracy or a serial killer or a case of massive mercury poisoning in the lunches at the MAC. Somehow that would make all this a little easier. Distance the evil from the act, like secondhand smoke, that could relieve Peg of responsibility for her death and relieve Molly of the task of telling her brother he'd been wrong.

The lo mein was only so-so, but the book was fascinating, its pages filled with Peg Ryan's personal shorthand in a strong, spiky script, its covers jammed with receipts from restaurants and one three-and-a-half-inch computer disc labeled *Veldux Notes.* Sum total of the first eight months of Peg Ryan's year. Days filled to brimming with the accumulation of success and power. Deadlines met and appointments set up already well into October, including a week-long cruise in the Aegean. The schedule petered out well into December, where the quick scrawl of *Mom and Dad's anniversary* was left as a sad coda on the Ryan family.

Not the calendar of a woman tying up loose ends.

"I don't suppose you want to tell us what you were doing at the Ryan house."

Molly damn near fell straight into the pond. She hadn't even been paying attention to the people on the path alongside her, and suddenly she looked up to find the Feds standing there, watching her like well-mannered crows in suits and regulation Ray-Bans. They'd evidently traded the pair of intelligence guys in for another interchangeable cop suit with dandruff problems and piggy eyes.

"What are you doing here?" she demanded, to cover for the guilty feeling that she was doing something wrong.

"We're Feds," the darker agent said with a smile. "We can go anywhere."

Molly's smile was just about as hospitable. "Doing what?" she demanded. "Protecting me from swans?"

"Trying to find out why you're still diddling in a closed case."

Instead of answering, Molly turned her attention on the newest member of the team, who at that moment was mopping his forehead.

"Thurmon Prentice," the dark guy said. "Gaming Commission."

"Ah. Has he found anything?"

Still the FBI guy answered as if Prentice had had his tongue cut out by gangsters or something. "This isn't exactly television. Most of these investigations take months, if not years, to complete."

"Uh-huh. Well then, you won't mind if I finish my lunch."

"What about Mary Margaret Ryan?"

Molly turned a page and kept looking. "Her brother is having a lot of trouble believing she'd kill herself. I'm taking another look just to make sure. And how did you know about Mary Margaret Ryan anyway? That's not your case."

"We were following you. We thought it would be a good idea to find out what you were up to in there. You're not removing evidence, are you?"

Molly looked up. "Evidence? For what?"

"I don't know," he answered, still evidently staring straight at her. With the shades on, it was hard to tell. "You wanna tell me?"

"All right," she said. "What do you think of this? Peg Ryan knew at least three of the other lawyers who committed suicide, one of whom was Pearl, whom you are investigating."

"And?"

"And don't you think that means something?"

He shrugged, the other two guys still standing rock solid behind him like the Pips waiting for Gladys to show up. "They're lawyers. Figures they'd know each other."

"Did you know Ricky Ricardo?" Molly retorted, hoping like hell he really was Lopez.

"What?"

"Well, you're Hispanic. Didn't you know Ricky Ricardo?"

For the first time since she'd met him, he smiled. Just a little. "Point taken. We'll look into it."

Molly nodded and went back to poring through the date book. When she looked back up ten minutes later, the Feds were gone and the park was once again in the hands of preschool terrorists.

When Molly got back to her house, her first instinct was to call Frank Patterson. But Frank didn't have the information she needed right then, so she called Brittany instead.

"Ms. Ryan's secretary?" the blonde whispered as if divulging state secrets. "Well, yes, but she works for somebody else now."

Molly bit back the urge to say that she figured as much, since legal secretaries weren't obliged to sit shiva, and just asked to speak to the woman.

"The Shitkickers?" came the answer in raspy, nicotine-sanded tones a few minutes later. "Yeah, sure. I used to make her reservations. MAC Grille, twelve-thirty the first Tuesday of the month. She'd rather miss final argument than one of those meetings."

"Who were they?" Molly asked, leaning over her kitchen counter to take notes.

"The Shitkickers? Well, I'm not really sure. Peg just talked about them as a whole, a unit, ya know?"

"What about Pearl Johnson or Harry McGivers or Peter VanAck?"

"I'm not sure. Peter maybe. She was really upset when he died. She knew Pearl, too, because I think that was the last . . . well, the last . . ."

Even that strong, certain voice faltered over that one.

"I know," Molly said simply. "Can you tell me what the Shitkickers was all about?"

"The joys of trial law, basically. Whoever was in the group did trial law. Loved it. Peg said they were thinking of calling it the Testosterone Club, because they found out there was a study that showed trial lawyers of both sexes had an inordinate amount of testosterone in their systems. From what I could gather, they kind of considered themselves the Top Guns, if you know what I mean."

"Yes. Do you think Peg Ryan committed suicide?"

For this Molly got a sigh. "Peg wasn't one to let anybody get close enough to ask questions like that. I have to say I was really surprised. But I was even more surprised when I realized that after working with her for over a year, I didn't really know her at all."

"Could I call you if I have any other questions?"

"Sure, but I thought things were all settled."

"So did I."

Molly had no sooner hung up the phone than it rang again. Against her better judgment, she picked up. "Speak."

"You're just dying to come down here and talk to me."

Molly's stomach sank. Right after she recognized Kevin McCaully's voice, she caught the undercurrent. Something was not right in the world of the senior death investigator. "I am?"

"Yes. As soon as possible."

"Is it good news or bad news?"

"I'll see you in twenty minutes."

Click.

Molly did not want to go in. If she did, she'd have to tell Kevin what she had. She'd have to give up Peg's book before she got all the way through it. It didn't occur to her that no more than twelve hours earlier, the last thing in the world she'd wanted was to look more closely into Peg Ryan's death.

There was a good chance now that Peg hadn't

committed suicide after all. It made all the difference in the world.

Molly went on down to the office. First, though, she called Rhett Butler. Unfortunately, Rhett wasn't as impressed as Molly with her information.

"She was a lawyer," he said. "Of course she knew the others."

Molly bit back an oath. She didn't think she'd get away with another Ricky Ricardo allusion. "But I think they were all in a club of some kind together."

"Oh, great. Does that mean they were Satan worshipers or something?"

"Rhett," she chided, "you're awfully churlish about this. I can't help it if I think there might be foul play involved."

"Tell you what," he said, his voice softening a little. "You come down here and coordinate the double homicide I'm working, I'll go interview suicide survivors."

"Double homicide," she scoffed. "Hell, son, you can do that in your sleep."

"Not when they're an eighty-year-old preacher and his wife, and we're down a couple of men to Major Case Squad."

"Major Case Squad?" The special crimes unit comprised of detectives from squads all over the bistate area, called together for homicides in areas without sufficient staff to solve them. Usually high-profile stuff.

"You didn't hear. They found a nine-year-old girl this morning out in Gumbo. Has all the markings of a sadistic sexual offender."

"Oh, Jesus."

"Yeah. Oh, Jesus. I'm sorry, Molly. If you get anything concrete, let me know."

"Yeah. Well, I did let the FBI know. Maybe that'll help."

"Good. Let them carry it till I'm free. Maybe by then you'll find the suicide pact note."

The news wasn't any better down at the ME's office, where Kevin's idea of waiting involved pacing the halls.

"I know you wouldn't be this stupid," Kevin greeted her.

"It's lovely to see you, too, Kevin," Molly said, leaning against the wall by his office until he made the circuit around to her again. He got there and stopped, his forehead tight with worry, his skin pale against that pirate beard of his.

"Tell me you didn't take Pearl Johnson's file out with you this morning."

"I didn't take Pearl Johnson's file out with me this morning. Why?"

That didn't seem to make him feel any better. In fact, it sent him straight to rubbing at his face with his hands. "Because it isn't here."

And here Molly had been meaning to make Kevin's day brighter by telling him that all the suicides they'd cleared and closed might actually be homicides after all. All she could come up with was a rather pathetic "Oh, boy."

"Yeah. Oh, boy."

"I didn't lose it, Kevin. Not this one."

"You're sure?"

Molly gave Kevin some latitude for being upset. Otherwise she might have decked him. "Yes," she said. "I'm sure. I don't take files out. I don't know what to tell you."

He nodded, his eyes closed. "I found out it was missing when the Feds called me asking about it. They got a sudden hair up their butts that there's some kind of conspiracy involved in her death that has to do with their gambling case. They say they found out Pearl knew the other suicide victims, think it's important."

"I know," Molly admitted. "I told them."

Kevin's hands came down and his eyes came open. "What?"

"I was looking into Peg Ryan, for the family."

"For the homeless headcase?"

"For the homeless headcase." Molly quickly explained what she'd found out. "I was gonna go down to the MAC and see if anybody there can give me a definite idea."

Kevin was even less enthused about the news than Rhett. "You're not going to tell me on top of all my other problems you're going to get those files reopened."

"I don't know. But if there's some connection to what the FBI is investigating down at city hall, we may have something more nefarious than suicidal depression on our hands."

"Besides the missing file, you mean."

"Yeah. That, too. Want me to help look?"

Molly helped look. They all looked. They even forayed down into the old catacombs where the paper records of over a hundred years worth of deaths had once shared space with cockroaches the size of Winnebagos. Only the cockroaches were left. Those, a few boxes, and the artificial Christmas tree that sat atop the filing cabinets all winter.

No file. No reprieve. After she caught herself checking under the microwave in the lunchroom for the fifth time, Molly decided that since she obviously wasn't getting anywhere, departure would be the better part of valor. Especially since Winnie was due back from court and had to be told of the latest catastrophe.

It didn't matter. Molly could have sworn she heard

Winnie's shrieks on the wind as she stepped out of her car ten blocks away at the MAC.

Molly could never walk into the lobby of the MAC without thinking of it as it had been in her childhood. The bastion of male power, white exclusion, old money. Richly paneled walls, overstuffed furniture, original artwork that all seemed to portray the sweeping male majesty of America. Beyond that, the handsome staircases and forbidden places that all smelled faintly of cigar smoke, fine liqueur, and power.

In those days, women were only allowed on certain floors, men swam in the nude, and blacks bowed and smiled at any of the subservient positions that required obedience and alacrity and little else. The term for power in St. Louis was "steam," because all the real deals went down in the sauna. At any time half a dozen white-haired heads rested in peaceful oblivion in the lobby's leather armchairs.

As a child, Molly had thought that all those men were dead. Her father had damn near had a stroke when his five-year-old progeny had stopped by the chair of one particularly wizened character and held the mirror from her purse under his nose, just like she'd seen in an Agatha Christie movie. The man had bolted upright, her father had scooped her away, and she had been exiled from family dinners in the club's dining room for six months. It had been the first time Molly remembered actively enjoying a moment of rebellion.

All the memories assailed her as she stepped inside. Some of the paintings had changed, the carpet had been redone, and everything modernized. Women were members, and members were required to respect the sensibilities of the ladies by donning swimming attire in the pool. The men and women walking about the lobby were younger, and there didn't seem to be as many priests in attendance. But Molly still smelled it. Old cigar smoke, old liquor, old power. She felt the overwhelming urge to pull out a mirror, just for old time's sake. Instead, she did something else considered unthinkable in her youth. She walked on back to the Grille.

The good thing about the MAC was that it retained the old club mentality. Members were recognized, courted, remembered, flattered. If Molly could talk to the hostess in the Grille, she could very well find out who comprised the Shitkickers themselves.

"May I help you?"

Molly had no trouble recognizing the look. The woman behind the desk was the soul of courtesy, but she still exuded the unmistakable impression that she not only knew that Molly didn't belong in that room, she didn't belong in the club at all.

So Molly smiled. "A moment, please. Are you always in charge during lunch?"

The answering smile on her pleasantly soft, sagging middle-aged features was patient. It said if you belonged here, you wouldn't have to ask that question. "Yes, I am. What can I—"

Molly already had her ID out. "I'm trying to help the family of Peg Ryan," she said, and saw the thaw. Just as she'd hoped. The other abiding impression she carried of the club was how they'd treated her Uncle Henry, who, as a widower with a weakness for scotch and a dearth of surviving friends, had all but lived there. He hadn't been a client or a member, but family.

The hostess looked around to make sure everything was running smoothly, patted once at her tightly permed brown hair, and gestured toward a table in the corner where she could still watch her desk.

"The Shitkickers," she said with a smile, like a

mother talking about the neighborhood kids. Her name tag said Helen. Molly bet she was a great mother, probably a neat grandma, too. "Sure. Unbelievable, when you think of it. All gone like that."

This time Molly's heart almost stopped. "All?"

Helen had been stirring her coffee, the spoon clinking like little wind chimes. Molly's question brought her to a stop. "You said you knew about them."

"I know about them through Peg. She didn't mention individuals. How many were there?"

"Oh, it varied. Mr. VanAck started it, kind of as a joke. A celebration after he'd won a big case. It kind of stuck. Peter VanAck, Harry McGivers, Pearl Johnson, Ms. Ryan. And Mr. Goldman. That was the core group, I guess."

Molly fought to pull up a first name. "Goldman. Aaron?"

Helen nodded. "It was just a tension reliever, ya know? They never did business."

"Did you ever hear what they did talk about?"

"Cases. Judges, other lawyers. I don't know, investing, that kind of thing. The normal kind of conversation for a place like this. They always had Theresa serve them, but she's not here today. Do you want me to ask her when she comes in tomorrow?"

"Yes, please. That would be helpful. I appreciate the fact that you have to protect your members, but anything you or Theresa could tell us might make a difference in the investigations."

Helen's eyes flickered. She looked down at her coffee a minute, as if reading it for answers. "I got the feeling they enjoyed . . . the good life."

The good life. What kind of code was that? Helen looked up, an almost pleading look in her eyes. Molly, knowing perfectly well what it could do to an employee at a club like this one, where secrets had to be sacrosanct, if she knew something that might jeopardize a reputation or two.

Then Molly remembered the cocaine she'd found in Peg Ryan's room, and a lot made sense. "Did you ever see any . . . illegal activity?"

Helen's eyes gave her away. "No. Not here. Never. I just think that some of them had the capacity to push some limits."

Some of them. Well, that made sense.

"Their suicides," Molly said as gently as she knew how. "Were you surprised?"

Helen sighed before she answered. "I'm not surprised by anything anymore."

Well, that was the difference between them, then. Molly was. She was surprised that nobody else had thought to ask this nice woman a simple question. Why five friends who had eaten lunch every first Tuesday of the month for the last eighteen months would now all be dead, allegedly by their own hands.

Molly stayed for a bit longer and asked a few more questions, but Helen had no more to give. So she exchanged phone numbers and promises to call and headed back outside, where a smiling, energetic young man in a green vest swung her old battered car around and slid her into it as if it were a Maserati and she were a princess. That was also something she'd never quite minded at the club. Just a little mercenary at heart, she decided, driving away.

Molly tried phoning Frank to let him know what was going on, but Frank was at some fund-raiser or another. Just the up-and-coming social butterfly, she decided. She tried to call Rhett back, but he was canvassing a neighborhood. She thought about heading back into the office to sit down with the other four files, but remembered that Winnie had found her way back there. No, tonight was not the night to screw around with Winnie.

Which left her with exciting news and nobody to take it to.

Molly was driving west on Market when it hit her. There was somebody she could share this with. Somebody who probably needed it.

It had been a long time since Molly had given in to instinct. Unforgivably, she gave in to it now. The sun was sliding below the high-rises to the west, and she was going to have to be in to the hospital by eleven to pick up a late swing shift. She was driving toward an area of town where a lone white woman in a little red sports car shouldn't go. She didn't have any news that would change the direction of any current investigation except her own. But she did have somebody out there who wanted to hear it, so she turned the car around and headed toward the river.

Since rush hour downtown was basically over, Molly cruised the streets in peace for a half hour or so, just on the chance she might catch Joe still working his area. She hit the places the men tended to congregate, by Saint Patrick's on North Ninth and along Washington Avenue near the Salvation Army shelter. She saw plenty of the ER's repeat customers, including The Diver, who seemed to be quite steady and clear-eyed as he slouched against the shelter wall watching traffic go by. She did not see Joe.

Molly checked with a couple of guys she recognized. One, Tehran, an emaciated black guy with milky blind eyes and an equally emaciated mutt for his seeing-eye dog, said he thought Joe was usually back home by now.

Home. The caves.

Situated in an area rich in limestone, St. Louis was an area that boasted an elaborate network of caves. Not just on the outskirts of the metropolitan area, like Meramec Caverns, which advertised the famous hiding place of Jesse James on barn roofs across the Midwest. Directly beneath the downtown area. Spread out beneath old houses and newer subdivisions.

Once used for everything from sewers to storehouses for the many breweries that had sprung up in the area, most of the caves were now closed off or filled in. Only a handful of people knew how to get into the ones that were still accessible downtown. Even fewer knew about the caves down by the riverfront that held some of the luckier homeless population.

Molly knew. She'd found out from one of her regulars, who was waiting for a vacancy. Perfect setup, he'd told her. Constant temperatures, protection from the elements, no worry about gang-bangers showing up to collect the rent or police toeing you off the warm spots. So well hidden only a few homeless guys knew where they were, so well disguised that they were considered as prime a property value as an estate in Ladue. They currently boasted a population of five, with a waiting list.

Molly pulled her car off into the vacant lot north of Laclede's Landing and locked it. She wished she'd stopped to get her jeans and T-shirt, camouflage for this neck of the woods, but she hadn't wanted to get here when it was any darker. In this neighborhood, the gardens consisted of thistle and skunkweed, and the paintings were done with spray cans. Traffic trundled overhead, and deserted railroad tracks sported the latest in cigarette butts, newspapers, and an old tire or two. There weren't any aluminum cans or bottles. Nothing that could be recycled for money.

A little farther along, the river gleamed with a

mauve reflection of the evening sky. Lights flickered from the riverfront and a steady column of black smoke rose from one of the many tire fires across the river.

Molly opened her trunk and pulled out her tennis shoes and the camouflage jacket she kept there for chilly nights outside. Cams were good because they didn't get you into any trouble when you were on the street in one of the 'hoods investigating a gang shooting. Cams were never the wrong color to a fourteen-year-old with an AK-47 and something to prove.

Cams were also her introduction to the men in the caves.

Molly also pocketed her stun gun and pepper gas, just in case. She had had a bellyful of guns, so she refused to carry one. She did not refuse to protect herself, however.

A dog started barking over by the trees. Molly could smell Sterno and old grease, the thick musk of wet trash, and the fishy smell of the river. Even so, it seemed unnaturally peaceful here, a place set apart from the rest of the city.

Behind the cottonwoods, the guy had said. The cottonwoods that seemed to just stand there in front of the overpass and next to the chainlink fence around the yard of one of the industrial plants.

Molly negotiated her way across the wasteland by the water and stood right in front of the trees. "Joe Ryan," she called gently, eyes swiveling from trees to underpass, beyond which the shadows had begun to assume shapes with feet.

Molly's hackles rose. She slipped a hand into her jacket pocket and thumbed the safety off her stun gun. She shouldn't have come down here. Not alone. Not even her.

"Joe, it's me," she said. "The Cap."

It took a second, but there was a rustling in the underbrush before her. A fresh smell, unwashed human. A fresh surge of fear. An even more unsettling shiver of dread.

"Cap?" His voice was quiet, tentative, more nervous than hers.

"Really," she said, forcing a smile to settle him. It takes a lot of energy when you have to spend your time differentiating the real voices from the phantoms. In a place like this, Molly had a feeling the work was harder than ever.

Suddenly, he was just there, a disembodied face behind the leaves of his personal privacy fence.

"I need to talk to you, Joey," Molly said, deliberately pulling her hands free in a show of passivity. "I'm alone."

Joe did his own looking around, his eyes much more suspicious than hers. "How did you know where I was?"

"I knew where the caves were," she said. "Harmon told me. I haven't told anybody else."

He gave the area another look, his eyes squinted so tight, Molly almost couldn't see his irises. "Okay."

Then he disappeared again, which Molly figured meant she was supposed to follow. She took a breath and did just that.

Actually, she figured it could have been worse. Once she'd negotiated the waist-high entrance and the sloping floor that led to the main room, she could stand up fairly easily.

The cave itself was a small one, soot-stained and fetid and littered in castoffs. Kind of like the nurses' lounge in the ER. Just about as clean. Darker, though, in ways that had nothing to do with electricity. The cave smelled of waste and loss and futility, and Molly didn't think she wanted to spend much time there.

By the back lay a black-and-white Australian shepherd-mix mutt with a red bandanna around his neck. Regulation homeless vet dog. He got to his feet when she walked in, stretched, wagged his tail, and settled silently at his master's feet. Joe motioned for Molly to take the red, white, and blue lawn chair with the trailing nylon strips, and he settled on an old dinette version covered in ripped, livid yellow Naugahyde. Beside it was a table stacked with cans and packages and half-empty bottles. In the corner was a pile of moldy paperbacks, and closer, a pile of trash can saves. Light was provided by a lone bulb that seemed to have been strung off a pole at the corner of the lot, and cooking was done on a Bunsen burner. All the comforts of home with none of the tax base.

Even so, Molly didn't like it here. She shouldn't have come. She'd been so caught up in playing detective, she'd forgotten the underscoring to this particular tune, and it was crawling up her neck like fingers on a silent piano.

Molly gingerly eased herself onto the listing chair. "It's about Peg," she said quietly.

Joe's attention was caught. His head came up and he smiled. Just a flicker, as if the real thing were too heavy. Wrapped together in his lap, his fingers scratched at each other as if they were separate entities entirely. "I miss her."

"I know. I wanted to tell you that you might have been right, Joe. There may be more to Peg's death than suicide."

Again he struggled to focus on her. He smelled sour, and his eyes were red and watery. Molly wondered if she was doing any good. In the morning, he probably wouldn't even remember she had been down here. She should just go home. Leave him to his burrow. She should get back into the air.

"I know. I told . . ."

"Me. You told me. And Frankie."

A nod. "I warned her about it, but she wouldn't listen."

Molly had been focusing on breathing, on getting out of the cave before she embarrassed herself. All of a sudden, she heard what it was Joe said.

"You warned her?" Molly asked, trying so hard to keep her voice level and nonthreatening. "About what?"

Joe wouldn't look at her now. He watched his hands, as if they were communicating with him. "You remember how you were at that . . . at that age, Cap. Fearless. Immortal. She was immortal. She told me."

Molly held her breath. Held her silence waiting for him to work through his thoughts.

"None of them was, though," he said and stopped.

"None of whom, Joe?"

His attention flickered a little, lit on her again like a frantic insect. "Her friends. She told me. She told me because she knew I wouldn't tell anybody. Because I'm her brother."

"What did they do, Joe? What was wrong? You didn't tell me before."

"I know." That smile again, dark enough to drain the light. "I wasn't . . . allowed."

"What did they do?"

"They dabbled, Cap. In this, in that. Where they shouldn't have. Got bitten, ya know?"

Bitten. Molly's skin was crawling again. That's what Pearl's note had said. *I slept with the snakes and I got bitten.* This was all getting beyond her, and she couldn't sort it out in the dark. In Joey's dark.

"Did Peg tell you what, Joe?" she asked, her voice taut with the effort to keep herself in place.

Joe's attention skipped away. His head came up

even before his dog's, both of them looking uncannily alike as they listened for outside noises.

Then Molly heard it, too.

"You okay in there, Sarge?" Low and strained and hesitant. The kind of voice that goes with sweats and shakes.

The dog let his head rest. Joe nodded to himself. "Number one, Baker. Night."

"Night, Sarge. Safe home." There was a faint rustling, and then nothing. Molly looked down to see that her own hands were twisted together and pulled them apart.

"Joe?" Molly tried again. "Did Peg tell you what they dabbled in?"

"Inside information. Now you have to go, Cap. This firebase isn't secured. VC everywhere."

It was the first time Molly had heard him really wander. She wanted to wait. Wanted to take him with her somewhere where it was safe and warm and always dry. It wasn't what Joey wanted, though. It wasn't what he could handle. She'd been hearing about the guys in the caves for a while. The folks at the various Vietnam vet counseling centers had been trying to get them to a halfway house or homeless shelter for as long as there had been counseling centers. The guys always found their way back to the caves.

Molly climbed to her feet, suddenly feeling tired. "Thanks, Joe. Come by the office any time, okay?"

He got up with her, as did his dog. Both followed her to the door. "I'll accompany the officer, ma'am," Joe said, his head and eyes always on the move out into the darkness. "Bad fuckers out there."

Molly popped out of the cave entrance right behind Joe like an air-starved second twin. She took a second to suck some in. It smelled great. Clean.

Then Joe crept away toward Molly's car and she realized she could hardly see him. It had grown dark out here.

To the south the lights of the city sapped the black out of the sky, but the shadows beneath that viaduct were about as dark as they got. And either the wind or something that breathed was rustling through the grass. It was nighttime, and it was true. Bad fuckers were out there.

Molly put her hand back in her pocket. Joe went into a half crouch, the long-remembered position of defense from another war a lifetime ago. The dog prowled ahead, sniffing for trouble. Sensing eyes out in that darkness, Molly followed along, wondering what could have possibly possessed her to wander down to the edge of the river at sunset.

The funny thing was, she was perfectly safe. Joe saw her to her car and waited there with his dog while she unlocked her door and got in. By the time she started the engine and pulled away, he, too, had retreated into the shadows.

Still shaking as if she'd just escaped within an inch of her life, Molly locked the doors and reached into her pocket to put the safety back on her stun gun. Which was where it was two hours later when she was attacked in the parking lot at work.

✦ Chapter 14 ✦

MOLLY'S FIRST THOUGHT WAS, "Damn it, when is the hospital going to do something about this?"

The Grace Hospital parking garage was also locally known as Rapist's Row and Mugger's Delight. Squeezed between about four other buildings, the five-story affair had lights that were forever shorting out and stairs that reeked of urine and semen. Just as she'd been doing for the last three or four weeks, Molly bypassed all the open slots and headed straight for the roof, where she could see the sky until the minute she walked into work.

Tonight, she swung her car in between a van and a Jeep and flipped off the lights. Clouds had settled in over the city, glowing a soft orange in reflected light, and whatever breeze they'd had had died. It was hot and sticky and empty up there. Molly took a minute to just watch the sky so she could carry it into work with her. Then she grabbed her nursing bag and purse and pushed open the door.

That quickly, a hand reached in and clamped around her arm. Which was when she realized that she'd left her stun gun in the camouflage jacket out of reach in the backseat.

Molly drew breath to scream. Another hand

slammed her head against the side of the door, igniting a shower of sparks in her vision and effectively shutting out cognitive thought. Molly could feel herself being pulled from the car, bag and all. She couldn't seem to stop it.

Damn it, damn it, damn it, was all she could seem to think. Her vision was shifting like a fun house mirror and the side of her head was on fire. Her shoes were scraping against metal and concrete as she fought against the pull of that pair of big hands.

Ski masks. How original. Two of them, black knit on white faces. Molly wasn't sure why she was so certain. Her attackers were covered head to toe. They were silent and strong and deadly, and she was suddenly terrified she was going off this roof via air express.

This time she did scream. A good one, all the way from her toes. She twisted her wrists in the man's grip, trying desperately to pull against his thumbs. She slammed her foot down on his instep and wished for the first time in her life she wore heels to work. Six-inch spike heels. Nursing shoes just didn't make the same impact.

Molly opened her mouth again, but assailant number two stepped in and simply dropped a bag over her head. A sweet-smelling bag. A sickly sweet . . .

Oh, goddamn it. Ether. When she woke up again, she was gonna puke.

If she woke up again.

If she didn't wake up raped and dismembered.

It was the last thing she remembered, except that even with a hood soaked in ether over her head, she managed to bite one guy until he howled.

He was still swearing about it when she heard him again. At least, Molly figured it was him she heard.

She was still blind, even though the ether smell was mostly gone. She was horizontal and cramped and unable to move anywhere. Whatever she was laying in, however, was moving. Fast.

"What's going on?" Molly demanded in a voice that didn't sound nearly terrified enough for what was going on inside her chest.

"Shut up."

Even though she was blindfolded, she shut her eyes. It didn't help. She was sick to death, sweating like a pig, and fighting the headache of the century. And she was being hauled somewhere in the back of a van. All she could seem to remember were all those safety videos they'd shown at the hospital instead of hiring more security to walk the nurses out to their cars that warned against ever getting into a van with a strange man. Women who get into vans never got out alive.

"This look good to you?" a voice in front of her asked.

Molly figured she wasn't the one he was asking.

"Yeah. I think so," another higher voice answered. Still a man, but somebody who didn't sound quite so masculine. Molly thought maybe it was the taller of the two men.

Two white guys, she'd say when the police asked for a description. One tall and big and the other medium and big. One of them has my teeth impressions on his forearm. Right through the black cotton of his turtleneck.

And one of them . . . she could swear she smelled something. Something familiar, even past the ether that still lingered.

The van slowed to a stop and Molly began to sweat even worse. She didn't hear any traffic. She didn't hear anything. Not only that, she had no idea how long she'd been in the damn van. A while, if the fact that she was now hog-tied and tape-wrapped was any indication. Probably out on the kind of lonely road where UFOs and decomposed bodies were always being sighted.

Except she didn't hear crickets, either.

Where the hell was she?

Why was she there?

A door opened and shut. The side door slid open and Molly felt the van list with the weight of somebody climbing in the side. Her entire body spasmed in self-defense. She fought hard not to make any noise. She would not degrade herself by pleading or whimpering.

"You're a pain in the ass, ya know it?" came the voice right by her left ear.

Molly whipped her head around, but he was too fast for her. Two hands clamped either side of her head and held it still. If she could have drawn breath, Molly probably could have smelled the cigarettes and beer on him.

"Relax," he said, his voice a sexual weapon. Laughing, controlling, taunting. Still Molly made no sound. Didn't move, even though she could feel the heat of his body through her scrubs.

Then the entire picture changed.

"This is just a warning, honey."

Molly instinctively blinked. "A what?"

Did rapists give out warnings, too? *You were caught in a lonely dark place without adequate protective measures. We're letting you off light this time, Ms. Burke. Next time you won't be so lucky.*

"Maybe reminder is a better word," he said, his mouth even closer to her, his lips brushing against her ear and sending shivers down her back. "You're a nurse. Not a cop. Not a fuckin' detective. So be a nurse and leave everything else to the pros."

"Who are you guys?" she asked, even though her heart was pounding worse than her head. "The police union or something?"

"We're reminders. You got closed suicides in a summer with a lot of open homicides. Don't give anybody any more work."

For a second, Molly battled the insane urge to laugh. They had to be kidding. This was about Pearl? These guys were the local muscle telling her to stay on her own turf? Jesus, she wasn't doing an episode of "Magnum" here.

"You understand?"

She nodded and almost broke his nose. "Sure. I understand."

"You'll behave?"

"Oh, yeah. I'll behave."

She'd get out of here and find out where the hell the damn FBI was when they'd been tailing her for the last ten days. The one damn night she needed them and they were off watching reruns of "The Untouchables" or something.

And then she was going to pore through every one of those damn files until she found out just what it was that had these guys so worried.

"Good, because if you don't, we know where you live. We know what shifts you work and where you get your junk food fixes. So remember that after we let you go."

"Let me go . . ."

The van started with a jolt. Molly felt the quick slice of a knife at the backs of her hands, another by her ankles. Before she could so much as brace herself, she felt herself hefted by two sets of hands and tossed out the side door at thirty miles an hour like a stack of papers on a delivery route. Two sets of hands. Which meant . . .

Then she hit her head a second time that night and forgot what it was that was supposed to mean.

Molly still couldn't see. She could feel. She could feel the accumulated trauma of ether, two smacks on the head, and a tumble across a trash can–littered sidewalk into a brick wall. For what seemed like forever, Molly couldn't manage much more than breathing. She wanted to cry, but the tears backed up behind whatever was covering her eyes. She wanted to get to her feet, but they didn't seem to be working. Nothing did. She just lay like a lump of ectoplasm in a cushion of trash bags. She battled the urge to throw up and lost, damn near aspirating because she couldn't seem to turn her head around quickly enough for her stomach's convenience.

At least she wasn't on a deserted country road. She was downtown. Once she managed to coordinate herself enough to get the blindfold off, she realized she'd been tossed into the street a few blocks north of the convention center. From where she lay she could see past the jagged destruction of deserted buildings to where the pristine twin steeples of St. Joseph's Shrine on Biddle stabbed into the night. A beautiful church. Old and well loved and renovated in the seventies to protect the site of the only verified miracle in North America.

Actually, she wasn't far from where she'd started the evening in the first place. A few blocks south was the MAC, and a few blocks east were the caves.

That made her want to cry, too. So did the fact that she hurt everywhere. She must have slammed against the rim of a trash can, because the ribs on her left side were fighting every breath she took. She'd scraped arms and twisted legs and knew she was bleeding from something above her eyes, because it kept gumming up her eyelids.

She was alone, hurting, and without wheels or protection in north St. Louis at eleven o'clock at night. Things couldn't get much worse.

By now, she should have known better than to even court thoughts like that. The minute she did, those clouds she'd been noticing earlier opened up.

Molly had felt miserable in her life. She'd been scared and sore and tired and pitiful. She'd never felt quite like she did lying there drenched and aching and nauseous in stuff that smelled like rotting vegetables and diapers.

That was when she heard the rustle.

God, not more. As bad as she felt, Molly figured she was just fair game. Whatever was coming, was just going to have to get her. The rain spattered down on her, and down the street, the lights blinked yellow, the color splashing across the oil-slicked streets like paint. A plane flew overhead, but that wasn't going to help her. Unless there was a ball game, downtown was one of the emptiest places in the world at this time of night.

Scrape, rustle, sniff.

Sniff?

Molly got her head up and wished that she hadn't. The world tilted and righted itself and unsettled her stomach all over again. She saw the trash moving, though. It looked like a mole was tunneling through it. A mole, great.

Or a rat.

That got her up. At least to her butt, which hurt, too. She was gasping for air to calm her stomach down and trying to keep her eyes open when she kept seeing stars and fading colors. She was trying very hard to pull together enough sense to fight off an attack of rats.

"Get out of here," Molly commanded, sounding a lot like the homeless guys over by the bridge. "Go on!"

She shoved her feet and waved her hands, which produced results. Only not a rat. A puppy.

A bedraggled, mangy, starving, big-eyed puppy. Instead of being scared off, he walked right up and licked her on the nose.

That, after everything that had happened, was what made Molly cry.

"You have a concussion."

Molly managed to lift her face out of the barf bucket. "No shit."

The surgical resident grinned unabashedly at her. "Nurses make lousy patients. You know that?"

"Of course I do. Now, go away."

Alongside the resident, a razor-pressed, fresh-faced rookie uniform made another note in his pad. "You say two white men."

It took Molly a minute to answer. It was well after two, she was still as stable as a rowboat in a hurricane, and she wanted to go home to bed. Even so, she finally began to feel safe. She had since she'd seen that sincere young face of Officer Rowdy Parker peering down at her as she sat in the trash petting the puppy and crying.

"One tall and big," she told him again, just as she'd promised herself. "One medium and big."

She knew she was forgetting something, but she couldn't work up the energy to figure out what.

"With teeth marks on his arm. Uh-huh."

"You heard from the Feds?"

That had been her first demand. Find me the goddamn FBI agents who were supposed to have been following me around. Molly could well imagine just what poor young Officer Rowdy thought of that one. Even so, he'd been patient and kind and understanding, even when Molly had decorated his spit-shined shoes as they'd waited for the city ambulance to show up to cart her in to work.

Except she wasn't going to be working tonight. She had a headache. She had a broken rib and enough road rash to qualify her for membership in the Unlucky Motorcyclists Club. She had five new stitches just above her hairline and a new pet in the corner.

"How are you getting home?" the resident asked.

Molly glared at him again. It wasn't his fault really. He wasn't even a bad surgical resident. "My car is in the parking lot, Abrams."

He gave her another bright grin. "Oh, yeah. You can't drive it though. Not when you can't stop puking long enough to drive."

"I'm puking because of the ether. Not my head."

"Even so . . ."

"I'll drive you," Officer Rowdy offered.

Molly nodded, eyes closed to ward off another wave of trouble. "Thank you. That's the second time you've come to my rescue tonight."

"Just my job, ma'am."

Molly opened her eyes to see the other four people in the room all turn around, too, just to make sure they'd actually heard him say that. They had. Officer Rowdy was even blushing. Molly kept herself from giggling.

"Even so, if you hadn't seen me there . . ."

"I didn't have to," he said. "We got a call."

There was a five-second delay switch in Molly's brain from all the trauma. Once it was tripped, Molly's head snapped up so fast she almost decorated Officer Rowdy's shoes a second time.

"What do you mean you got a call?" she asked. "From whom?"

The very young policeman looked bemused. "He didn't leave his name. Just said he'd driven by and seen something on the sidewalk. Thought it might have been someone injured. I responded."

"And you got there right away?"

"Within a few minutes."

Molly tried hard to remember the chain of events. Her brain was still pretty mushy, which meant accuracy might suffer, but she was pretty damn sure she remembered one thing for certain.

"Nobody drove by," she said, looking back at her savior. "Nobody saw me."

He looked a little less bemused. A little more interested. "You think your kidnappers called?"

"Pretty considerate kidnappers," Abrams said as he finished making notations on Molly's chart.

"They did say they just wanted to warn you," Officer Rowdy said.

"And then they dumped me in the trash on North Ninth Street at night."

"Something to think about," Officer Rowdy decided with a nod and a scribble in his notebook. "After you get a good night's sleep."

Molly waited, but he didn't say *things'll look better in the morning.* She was glad. She was already past her cliché quota for the night.

Molly glared at no one in particular. "In that case, let's go."

She slid off the cart, bucket in hand, a new set of scrubs replacing the old. Nestled in a plastic instrument tub in the corner, her new friend, Magnum, lifted his head and whimpered. Molly knew just how he felt.

"You *are* taking him with you?" the resident asked.

"No, Abrams. I figured the ER should have a mascot.

Of course I'm taking him with me." After all, he was the first life-form in almost ten years who had comforted her when she'd felt bad. Molly owed him something. Besides, there was just something about imagining a creature as ugly and scrawny as Magnum wandering around the pristine rooms of Château Burke, that pleased her immensely.

"I'll write you an excuse slip for the next four days," Abrams promised, scratching under his yarmulke with his pen.

Molly pulled out a new puke bucket from the nurse server and crouched down to pick up Magnum. Then she just dropped him in the bucket, where he promptly curled up and fell asleep.

"What breed do you think he is?" Abrams asked.

Molly considered the emaciated body, the lank, dirty fur, the big brown eyes. "Something . . . red. Or brown."

"With big feet," Officer Rowdy offered.

Molly hadn't considered that. A big, ugly dog in the house. Her smile grew. She couldn't imagine she'd never come up with that one before.

Officer Rowdy led the way out, with Molly and Abrams following. For a nanosecond, Molly felt bad. The hallway was in full riot, with a couple of auto accidents, the usual quota of barroom fights, and a homeless woman in full and vocal labor. Even so, more than one of the staff paused to pat Molly on the shoulder as she headed down the hall. A warrior in the fight. A victim of Mugger's Delight. The night supervisor even ran back to the lounge to get Molly's lab coat for extra cover, then held Magnum while Molly slipped it on. Considering that just that little bit of activity had her worn out and nauseous again, Molly decided that she really wasn't in shape to do the Night Shift Marathon anyway.

Her purse wasn't at her car, of course. Just her nursing bag—sans fifty-dollar stethoscope—and the litter from a few fast-food meals. Since nobody had had the bad sense to steal it before, Molly figured the car wasn't worth locking now. After grabbing her stun gun and pepper spray, she closed it and climbed into the front seat of Officer Rowdy's unit, where he was already calling for a locksmith to meet her at her house to change locks.

He was also nice enough to stop off for dog food and then carry it to the house for Molly.

She was so tired and sick by the time she got there that instinct pushed her hand right into her lab coat pocket for her house keys. All she came up with was five Band-aids, a tourniquet, and a handful of alcohol swabs.

"I don't suppose you can pick locks," she asked Officer Rowdy, stuffing everything away again.

"No, ma'am. Could you have given a spare key to a neighbor?"

Sure. She'd given one to Sam. But Molly wasn't about to wake him at three in the morning to the sight of her face. So she shook her head.

"In that case," Rowdy said, dropping the dog food, "we'll just wait for the locksmith."

And he did. He even waited until the disheveled, garlic-and–Old Spice-scented man had broken into Molly's house. When Molly saw how quickly the locksmith made it past what she thought were high-security locks, she let him replace them with the newest pickless variety instead.

After seeing the locks taken care of and taking care of Magnum herself in between visits to the porcelain god to purge the evil kidnap spirits, Molly tried her best to fall asleep in her bed fully clothed. She couldn't seem to do it. Someone had kidnapped her tonight. Someone who had been watching her, who could still be watching her. Someone who twice had threatened her with men who seemed to enjoy hurting women just for the fun of it. And there was only one person connected with this investigation so far who merited the word *snake*. As in, "I slept with the snakes, Mama."

In the morning when her brain was in working order again, Molly was going to sit down and find the connection between William T. Peterson and the rest of these suicides. She was going to pay him back for terrorizing her like this.

In the morning.

During the long, dark hours of the night, though, all she could think of was what an easy target she seemed to be. A woman who traveled alone. Who worked in a marginal area. Who lived by herself in a big house near a high-crime area.

Molly knew it wasn't rational. They'd already delivered their message tonight. She was in a house with new locks and a state-of-the-art alarm system she'd for once been very careful about setting. Even so, she spent the rest of the night curled up on the bathroom floor with Magnum and her stun gun, listening for intruders.

She must have fallen asleep at some time, because the phone woke her. It woke her again when it kept ringing. Molly didn't bother with it. She didn't move until the sun was well up, Magnum started whining, and the doorbell joined in the chorus.

Molly hurt everywhere, she still felt mostly like barfing, and she was having residuals from one of her 'Nam dreams that must have crept in when she'd nodded off. Even so, she slowly uncurled herself and went on down in the same scrubs and lab coat she'd fallen asleep in, a wriggling oily lump of fur in her arms.

And of all the things to find on her front porch, there

was Frank Patterson. Dressed in chinos and a chambray shirt, he looked and smelled like an ad for cologne. He was also holding a wriggling burden of his own.

"What the hell is that?" he demanded, looking at her dog.

"What the hell is *that?"* Molly demanded right back.

"I asked you first."

"This is my new friend Magnum," she said, never once taking her eyes from the solemn brown pair watching her next to Frank's. "He saved my life last night."

Frank considered her appearance. "Not a moment too soon, it appears. I've been trying to return your call from yesterday. I finally tried you at your hospital and somebody named Sasha told me what happened. In detail. She asked if I'd like to help you sue the hospital over something called Mugger's Delight. Are you all right?"

"I'm not sure," she replied. "Is that a child in your arms?"

Frank smiled. "Molly, I'd like you to meet Abigail."

She was a beautiful little girl, with thick dark hair, huge dark eyes, and a sweet bow mouth. Clad in a sweet green-and-white-striped pinafore with matching hair bows and Mary Janes that gleamed as brightly as Officer Rowdy's uniform shoes, this kid was the poster child for innocence.

"Abigail," Frank said, "say hello to Miss Burke."

"Hello, Miss Burke," the little girl responded obediently in a soft, breathy little voice.

"Hello, Abigail," Molly responded, then turned to the man holding her. "So, what'd you do, Patterson? Hire her to give you that all-important family look when you're defending an allegedly negligent daycare center?"

Frank didn't look the least perturbed. "See what I mean about those head injuries, Ab?" he asked gently of the little girl in his arms.

She nodded. "Yes, Daddy."

"You'll wear your bike helmet all the time like Grams asks now, won't you?"

"Yes, Daddy."

Daddy. Daddy?

"You're kidding," Molly whispered, truly stunned.

"*Are* you okay?" Frank asked, stepping on in as if he'd known all along that Molly meant to offer the invitation. Then he scowled, as if she'd asked him in to mop the floors. "You look like hell."

Molly never moved. "Is this really your daddy, honey?" she asked.

She really didn't have to. There was just something about the way the little girl rested her hand against Frank's cheek that spoke of the connection. Even so, Abigail nodded, still watching Molly as if unsure just what Molly was going to do. Molly didn't really blame her. Molly wasn't so sure either.

"You have breakfast yet?" Frank asked, walking on by toward the kitchen.

"What do you mean?" Molly asked, belatedly remembering to close the door.

"My wife always said that tea made anything feel better. But then she was English, wasn't she, Abs? You got tea, Burke?"

Molly was breathless with sudden distress. "Patterson, don't do this to me!" she protested.

Frank turned around just as he got to the door of the kitchen. "What?"

Molly waved in the direction of the kitchen, which just made Magnum squirm all over again. "Don't take care of me."

Frank's eyebrow went up. "How dare you, Burke?

You know what an act like that would do to my reputation?"

And then he walked right into the kitchen, set Abigail down in a chair, and put the teakettle on the stove.

"You *had* a wife?" Molly asked quietly behind him.

Without turning around, he lifted a finger in exception. "That, Saint Molly, is a discussion that we have over dinner and drinks. Not tea and concussions. By the way, have you seen your eye? You look like you went ten rounds with Tyson. And your dog needs a bath."

"Do you have any other surprises for me?" Molly demanded, completely overwhelmed.

Frank never turned around. "You mean, like the twins?"

Molly stood at a complete loss in her own kitchen. All she could think to do, finally, was crouch down next to Abigail's chair so she was eye level with the little girl, who couldn't quite decide whether she wanted to watch Molly or the intriguing package in her arms.

"Do you have twins in your family?" she asked.

"Yes, ma'am."

"Is your daddy always like this?"

Abigail nodded again. "Yes, ma'am."

They never did get around to that discussion. They did get the dog bathed, uncovering the startling discovery that whatever they had, at least had the auburn red coat of an Irish setter. They shared tea and toast and information on what Molly had found at the MAC and the caves. They let Abigail take the puppy into the backyard when the FBI guys showed up, because Molly said she didn't think it was wise for a three-year-old to be exposed to violence.

"We aren't on the job to protect you," Lopez said evenly. "We were watching to see what you'd do."

"I got tossed out a van," Molly retorted.

"We heard. And you think that the Shitkicker's Club was involved in something illegal?"

"Something ill-advised, anyway. The name William Peterson did come up, if you remember."

A round of nods. "We'll look into it. It probably has something to do with the investigation we've already instituted on Pearl."

"Well then, why didn't they throw *you* out of a van into a trash bag?" she demanded.

The FBI guy smiled. "Because we're the FBI. We'd get them back."

"That's what I'm asking you to do now," Molly told them.

They both stood up together, as if on silent cue. "We'll talk to Officer . . . uh, Parker about this. Coordinate with him. You understand, though, that simple assault isn't really under our jurisdiction. Unless you were black or Jewish, of course."

"Gee, thanks."

"Any time."

"Frank," Molly said as the two of them watched the FBI agents climb into their regulation sedan at the curb, "I think I said something important."

Frank closed the door and turned her back toward the kitchen where more tea awaited. "What's that?"

Molly was busy rubbing at her head, which was throbbing even worse. "They've been investigating Pearl, right?"

"Uh-huh."

"Everybody knows that."

"Uh-huh."

"Then why was it me those guys warned? Why *didn't* they warn the FBI?"

Frank stopped just shy of picking up the teakettle. For the first time since Molly thought she'd known him, he wasn't smiling, or at least grinning. He looked downright unhappy.

"You think it's Peg?"

Molly escaped over to the sink. "Her brother thinks she was involved in something. Her friends all committed suicide within weeks of her. Could she be the one at the head of this thing instead of Pearl? Shouldn't somebody at least have asked?"

"You think she was involved in the gambling too, then."

For just a second, Molly's attention was caught by the sight of a little girl chasing a littler dog around the yard. She could hear the squeals of delight from both of them, saw Sam wander over toward the fence to investigate. She thought, just briefly, that that was what she'd fenced in the yard for, and it broke her heart all over again.

So she closed her eyes. And remembered something she hadn't told Officer Rowdy. "There were three of them," she said suddenly.

This time, Frank wasn't laughing at all. "What?"

Molly opened her eyes wide. Faced Frank and fought an odd clutch of claustrophobia. "That's what was wrong. The van was moving when I was tossed out. And I was tossed out by two men. So there had to be three of them, only I never saw the other one. What does that mean, Frank?"

"It means you've pissed off more than two people, Saint Molly," he retorted, putting the teakettle back unused. "You're sure?"

"Yeah."

There was still something else, something she'd wanted to remember. She couldn't, though. For some reason, it made her more afraid.

Frank was nodding, his own attention caught by his daughter and the old man who leaned over the fence to smile at her.

"I think it's time to quit," he said.

"I could use a nap," Molly agreed.

"Not that quit," he said, turning to her with eyes more serious than she'd ever seen them. "The big quit. I think we've managed to step far too near the quicksand."

He'd done such a quick U-turn Molly was dizzy with trying to keep up. "What?"

He looked outside again. "Give it back to the police where it belongs."

"The police don't want it."

"They will."

Molly's head was beginning to hurt so badly she was seeing stars. Even so, she grabbed Patterson by the arm and swung him back around to face her. "What the hell are you talking about?" she demanded. "You're the one who got me into this and now you want me to just walk away?"

"Well, don't *you*?"

"Yes! No! Damn it, Frank, I can't just ignore it."

"Sure we can. We were just doing a friend a favor anyway. I don't remember ever saying anything about taking a bullet for him."

"You can't mean that."

"You really want to go back down into those caves?"

He really knew how to hit below the belt. Molly was breathless with fury. "Just about as much as you do," she challenged.

"Okay, then."

Frank flashed her the smile. Molly simply couldn't keep up with him. "Time for me to get home, Saint Molly. The twins have soccer. You gonna be okay alone?"

Molly snorted. "I've been okay alone most of my life, Patterson. Why should now be different?"

He seemed to see something on her face she didn't know was there. It made him shake his head. "No wonder you were so easy to persecute, Saint Molly. You're so damn pure."

"Shut up, Frank."

"I mean it. Give it back to the police and cut yourself some slack for a change. It won't kill you." Reaching up, he gently tapped her forehead where Molly knew he could see the brand-new bruising and scrapes. "These guys, on the other hand, just might."

Molly locked all the doors behind Frank, and she fended Sam off to a mere phone call. She called the intelligence team down at police headquarters, but they couldn't be found. She called Rhett, who could be found in conference with the Major Case Squad on the dead little girl, who, they'd found, had lived in the city. She called her credit card companies, found a substitute purse, fed her puppy, and erected elaborate barricades to keep him in the back of the house so she could try again to sleep.

She ended up wide-awake in her bed, thinking about Frank Patterson and his three children. Thinking about Joseph Ryan and the caves where he hid. Thinking about people who were trying to kill her because she didn't want to deal with suicides.

She ended up not getting much sleep that night, either.

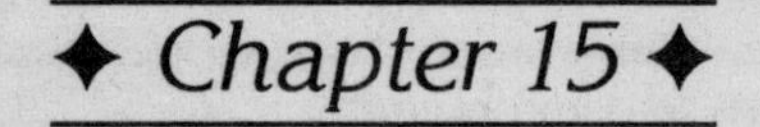

"IT'S NOT OUR INVESTIGATION ANYMORE," the intelligence guy informed her bright and early the next morning on the phone. "Hasn't the FBI told you?"

Molly had been on her hands and knees scrubbing the latest surprise Magnum had left on her kitchen floor. "No. The FBI doesn't seem to feel the need to tell me anything."

"In that case, I wouldn't worry about it."

"You wouldn't, huh? In that case, I'll tell these guys who hit me over the head to come get you instead next time."

An hour later, Rhett called.

"It's not my case anymore."

This time Molly was sitting outside on her patio where she'd talked to Rhett before, only this time she was alone, it was cooler, and she was much more unhappy. "What do you mean it isn't your case anymore?"

"No homicide, no case."

"What's going on, Rhett?" she demanded. "I've been threatened within an inch of my life, and nobody's on the case but the FBI, who can't be on the case because they don't really do simple assaults, and a prepubescent Boy Scout named Rowdy. Something's going on, damn it."

"Don't go away," he said shortly. "I'll call you back."

Molly didn't go away. She sat watching Magnum mark every one of the flower beds with great enthusiasm and thought maybe she should have *him* communicate with these guys. He probably understood how they all thought. The phone rang within ten minutes.

"Bond here," she said in very surly tones. "James Bond."

"It isn't funny, Mol."

She laughed, but that hurt. "You're not telling me a thing, Rhett. What's going on?"

"I'm in the lobby on a pay phone," he told her. "So this is going to be quick. Your suicides are the hottest potato in this town since Prohibition."

"Why?"

"This is off the record, Molly."

"I got that message when you mentioned the pay phone, Rhett."

It still took him a minute. When he finally came out with it, he sounded as if he were watching over his shoulder as he talked. "Guess whose name has come up in the gambling investigation?"

Molly had no intentions of guessing. "Not mine," she assured him.

"The mayor's."

Molly closed her eyes in frustration. Rhett was right. This was going to blow the lid off the city. She could just imagine what the city police department looked like with everybody there scrambling for cover. St. Louis was still a city of old-time politics, which meant that no matter how good a job a cop did, he still relied on influence to get him his promotions. And the man with the mojo was whatever mayor was in office. The minute he went down, anybody connected with him found himself beating flames off his ass, too.

Molly bet the central station looked like a bunker. There wasn't a policeman in the state who wanted his fingerprints on this investigation.

"Oh, shit," was all she could come up with.

"So we're really busy on this possible serial killer," Rhett said. Actually, he whined. "Okay?"

"Okay."

So Molly gathered together all her strength, faced Sam head-on so that she could ask him to keep half an eye on Magnum, and called a taxi to take her to the hospital, where she could retrieve her car and her driver's license. It was time to go into the ME's office and get some answers.

"You look like hell," Vic Fellows greeted her.

"I've been staying up nights trying to decide what the question mark means," Molly retorted, already tired of hearing how colorful her face was.

"Did you come up with anything?"

"I think it's a call to rethink masculinity as we know it."

That was quite enough to discourage Vic from further conversation. Kevin showed up, still trying to find Pearl's records anywhere in the city system, and Winnie dropped by to scowl and pat and threaten Molly that if she got sick in her building, she'd have to clean it up. Molly had known Winnie long enough to correctly interpret that as, "You really worry me. You should be home in bed. Don't take chances."

Molly didn't think poring through files would be taking any chances. Besides, she was inside a protected building, right down the block from the central police station. If things stayed slow, she might even get in a nap. She sure wasn't sleeping worth a damn at home.

"Why are you here?" Winnie demanded.

"To look through those suicides again."

"They were suicides."

"That's what I thought. But those men in the van are making me wonder."

"Wonder what? We cleared them." Considering the fact that Winnie was glaring, Molly knew a threat when she heard one.

"I'm just gonna look. That's all."

She looked. Winnie slammed around the building as if Molly had questioned her morals and Kevin kept popping up to poke through loose papers on Molly's desk. Vic, on call, just sat with his feet on his desk, drawing question marks on his notebook and watching "Oprah" on his little TV in the corner.

Molly fortified herself with more tea and Excedrin, sat her own feet on her own desk and rubbed at the fresh stitches in her scalp while she read from the accumulated data on the three dead people she hadn't handled. She went through them in order, just in case that would make more sense.

Peter VanAck, thirty-five years old. White male, six feet, one-ninety. Black hair, brown eyes, glasses, and a small scar on his upper lip from years playing football for Mizzou. Trial lawyer for a firm that specialized in criminal court stuff. Rising young hotshot who had managed to get an acquittal for the woman who had shot her wealthy husband over alimony. Married, two children, three degrees, and an eight handicap on the links. Cause of death, another gun, this one a 30–aught to the chest. Shoes off so he could pull the trigger with his toe while he sat in his favorite chair in the den. Handwritten suicide note, with samples included to verify victim's handwriting, just saying he was sorry and for his wife Judith to take care of the children. Alcohol level up, no barbiturates or opiates or cocaine by-products found on tox screen. Recent history of stress. Problems with cash flow and a rumor of possible abuse of controlled substances. Rescue squad forced to break into room with fire axes to retrieve.

Aaron Goldman, fifty-four. White male, five-eight, one-sixty. Graying, thinning hair, mustache, runner. Found hanging from rafters in barn on weekend farm. Trial lawyer specializing in malpractice. Married to second wife, three children by first. No alcohol, but a long, rambling, mostly incoherent letter to wife claiming infidelity on his part, no need to forgive on hers. Also verified with samples of handwriting. Tox screen showed antidepressants and a couple of items not on any pharmacy list, nothing in the toxic range. Medications included Xanax and synapsapine, the latter starred and noted as an antidepressant.

Harold McGivers, forty. Another white male, five-ten, two-ten. Brown hair and eyes, incipient coronary candidate with questionable taste in clothing. High dive off a short building. In the process of divorce from heiress wife. Three children, one prenuptial agreement. Hardworking public defender with an impressive track record and few friends. Enough alcohol on board to stun a moose, bad form on landing. Note, verbalized suicide ideations, recent appointment with family doc for symptoms of depression.

Molly read through each file once, then went back and picked them apart every way she could think of. She added Peg's file to them and looked again, going through the histories, the forensics reports, the tox reports, the police DD-5s, the pathology reports.

She spent the entire morning in that chair looking for something that would connect each and every one of the victims, and then tie them to a gambling syndicate. She looked for something suspicious. Some question unanswered.

As hard as she looked, there didn't seem to be any. Unless they were dealing with the same guys who had been on the grassy knoll in '63, there was just no way anybody could have murdered every one of these people and fooled everybody involved.

There seemed to have been no poisoned lunches at the MAC. No serial murderer with a fancy for suicide recreations. It just looked like these people had killed themselves.

Molly had sat down to her task so sure she'd find something. There didn't seem to be anything to find.

Maybe it was just something the FBI was going to have to clear up. A connection with William T. Peterson. An investment in the gambling operation that happened to come to light when Pearl had decided her conscience couldn't allow her to cheat, even for a good cause.

Maybe Molly could sleep in peace tonight, because she could say in all honesty that there was nothing more for her to see in these files than honest-to-god suicide.

Except that she really hated coincidence. Especially the kind of coincidence that had an entire lunch group drinking the proverbial Kool-Aid without the help of Jim Jones.

Molly was plagued by the idea that there was something there she just wasn't seeing. Something that would make all the difference.

Something that would explain the fact that somebody was going to all this trouble to stop her from looking.

After working with Winnie for so long, Molly ignored most commotions in the office. That was probably why she didn't realize what was going on until somebody switched on the lights damn near in her face.

"Get out of this office before I toss that camera down the steps!" Winnie was shrilling.

Vic was scrambling to his feet, and Kevin was backing up in Molly's direction, as if fending off the Visigoths from the gates of Rome.

"We just wanted to ask a few questions," a feminine voice suggested in honeyed tones inches from Kevin's chest.

Which was how Molly came to be on the five o'clock news in her jeans and *The one who dies with the most toys still dies* T-shirt.

"Were you in charge of the missing file, too?" the reporter asked, doing an end run on Kevin to shove the mike in Molly's face.

Molly scrambled to her feet, blinded by the light and stunned to passivity by the attack. She knew the reporter. No talent or style, just the Geraldo Rivera school of relentless intimidation.

"The Pearl Johnson file," the reporter insisted, her face intense and interested. "We've gotten word that it has been . . . misplaced. Was that your fault, too, Ms. Burke? Did you lose it before or after the police picked you up off the street at two in the morning?"

Out by the intersection of Clarkson Road and Clayton lay a planned community named Woodlawn Lakes, where houses started at the mid three hundred thousands and building sites were sold by the quarter acre. It was where Peter VanAck had lived. Where his wife Judy and his children still resided now that he was gone.

After the disastrous round with the Channel 12 news, Molly had decided that it was time to get back out of the office. She hadn't gotten her answers from the files, so she decided to try a little live question and answer to really make her day.

At least the day was a nice one, not too hot for a change, with traffic that was still fairly manageable and a westerly breeze that ruffled Molly's hair. Molly had changed, of course. One does not approach a suicide survivor in a "The one who dies . . ." T-shirt. There wasn't anything she could do about her car, of course. In comparison with the cash on the tire she passed along Miller Pond Lane, her Celica had the look of a refugee craft. But then, in the mood Molly was in, she didn't really care.

Molly really wished she could have been surprised by the VanAck house. It was her parents' fault, of course. They might not have had personalities, but they had had exquisite taste. They had demanded no less from those with whom they associated. They would never have been caught dead in this pretentious hunk of brick.

Crouching on its postage-stamp lot like an elephant on a card table, the house evidently couldn't figure out just which architectural style it wished to emulate. Therefore, there were pillars and bay windows and even a rose window in what was probably the bathroom, all topped off with a Dutch roof, which made the overall affect heavy and unwieldy. There was also a lawn with the kind of brutally precise landscaping that made Molly think of hemorrhoids.

Molly wished she could have at least been surprised by Judith VanAck, the bereaved widow. Even if Molly hadn't known the woman, she would have known the type. Basically unchanged since the days she went to Vis or Mary Institute, pageboy blond hair, lots of kilt skirts and gold jewelry, perky breasts, and downturned mouth. A clique girl, a *sochе*, they'd called them in Molly's day. Today Mrs. VanAck was wearing a tailored cotton shirt with Peter Pan collar, Pendleton slacks, and Pappagallos shoes. Two tennis bracelets, a diamond set that could take somebody's eye out, and small stud earrings. Vapid blue eyes that looked just a tad rheumy for this early in the afternoon.

She was perfectly cordial until Molly explained her mission.

"Medical Examiner's Office?" she echoed, her voice becoming breathy and distressed, her hand to her chest. "What do you want from me now? Haven't I been put through enough?"

"A few questions," Molly said, noticing that the inside of the house was just as unimaginative as its owner. Southwestern decor, designer-perfect. Of course. Next year it would be something new.

"I've been through so much," Judith VanAck repeated, eyes wet, hair perfect.

"I know, and I appreciate your help. If we could . . ."

Judith sighed and invited Molly on back into the sunroom, an uninspiring expanse of wicker and glass. There were oils of the children on the wall that made them look like Walt Disney had put them together from a diagram, and tables scattered with *Town & Country*, *M*, and *Architectural Digest*.

"Mrs. VanAck," Molly said as she sat on fern-printed cushions, "I'm sorry to be blunt, but the truth is, we've found out that several of Mr. VanAck's acquaintances have also . . . taken their lives. I was wondering if you knew anything about it."

A hand went to her heart. "You can't think I had anything to do with it."

"No, ma'am. Of course not."

"I didn't . . . I've had so much to do, you know, with the children and Peter's estate and my job, and I just don't have the strength for this. I haven't even been able to work."

"Does the name the Shitkicker's Club mean anything to you?"

"God, no. Peter didn't belong to anything but the MAC, the Lawyer's Club, and Bellerive Country Club. He wasn't a joiner. I'm the joiner. I dragged him everywhere."

"Yes, ma'am. If I could give you some names . . ."

"We only saw business friends from the office. Were they from the office?"

"No. No, they weren't. They were other lawyers."

Judith VanAck was looking even more distressed. "I see. I know it's silly, but I never remembered names. And our social circle is out here. The neighborhood, our old high school group, you know."

Molly fought the urge to rub at her head. Maybe this hadn't been a good idea after all. All she could come up with from this was if she'd been Peter VanAck, she would have done anything to get away from this woman, too.

"Do you know anything about his investments, Mrs. VanAck? I know it's an odd question, but did he talk to you recently about anything special he saw as a good risk?"

"Just what he did with that investment group he belonged to."

Molly did her best to remain neutral. "Investment group?"

"Yes. They, uh, met over lunch, he said. An informal setup that produced excellent results. Our CPA said that we'll be well taken care of."

An investment group that met over lunch. Insider information. Jesus, Molly thought. Could she be this lucky?

"You don't remember who else might have been in this . . . group?"

"No. It was something that didn't interest me."

Molly nodded, made a show of taking notes, considering, as if she were trying to find her way. "Uh, did he mention anything specific that intrigued him, investment-wise? Peter, I mean."

"Oh, I guess. I never pay attention to that kind of thing, of course. Peter would go on and on about it, but frankly, that sort of thing bored me to tears. I didn't want to know drug prices and cost-and-whatever ratios and gambling legislation."

"Gambling legislation?"

A sigh, as the bereaved widow remembered how her husband had bored her with his attempts to establish her financial windfalls. "Oh, yes. He was so excited about that one. Said he got it all straight from the horse's mouth. We'd make a killing on it. There were several investments he'd found like that through the group."

Molly just bet. "You wouldn't have the list of stocks, would you?"

"God, no. I left that to the experts. It confuses me too much."

"And your husband didn't keep any kind of personal record? Just for himself, to see how he was doing?"

"In his den. He told me all about this spreadsheet program he bought just to handle that."

"Could I see his den, ma'am?"

Mrs. VanAck looked vaguely around, as if waiting for help. "You expect me to go up there?"

"I can go in alone, if you don't mind."

Molly ended up doing just that. Peter VanAck had built his den over the attached three-car garage, an efficiency decorated along the woodwork-and-wing-back-chair look, although enlivened with a surprise pair of Vega prints. Sterile and silent and empty now. Needing the same kind of pickless locks Molly now had to get in, and wired to the house alarm. Molly stepped back outside to catch the lovely widow surreptitiously checking her hair in one of the windows.

"Would it be okay if I looked at his computer, Mrs. VanAck?"

Judy jumped. "Oh, yes, I suppose, except that I don't think you'll find anything. It seems that he wiped it off before . . ."

"How did you find out?"

"I couldn't go up, you know. I mean, how could I face something like that? But the children can always use an extra computer, so I had Austin check and see if it still worked. He said that the entire thing had been . . . um, cleaned off."

"Austin?"

"My son. He's in school now."

And by the looks of the pictures, about ten. Nice gal. Sending her ten-year-old up to where his father had blown himself to hell rather than face it herself. Molly wondered if old Judith had made Austin clean up the mess, too.

Hopes now high, Molly went from Chesterfield to Ladue to see the heiress. She sat down to coffee with the dowdy brunette, Sidney St. John McGivers, on the patio of her house on Log Cabin Lane, and found herself liking the sharp-eyed, quiet woman very much.

Until she broke Molly's heart.

"No," she said most definitely. "Harry didn't do any of the investing. He wasn't interested in it at all."

"You're sure. I mean, you were . . ."

"Getting divorced." Sidney nodded. "Yes, we were. It turns out that Harry and I were much better parents when we lived in different places. But we did talk over everything we did for the children, and investments were certainly a part of that. Investing was my talent, not Harry's."

"He met with a group for lunch, though."

Mrs. McGivers nodded, her attention on the coffee she held in her hand. "Yes, I know. He didn't really join them for that, though. The companionship, I think. Harry wasn't . . . a comfortable person to be around. He was delighted to find a group that included him."

"He never suggested investing in the new gambling casino? Anything like that the group might have suggested?"

Another definite shake of the head. "Never. It just didn't interest him. Believe it or not, money was never Harry's motivator. Belonging was." She paused a moment, still watching the liquid in her cup, her heavy-lidded eyes a bit distant. "I guess that's why we're left with this mess. He said he wanted the divorce, but I think he didn't mean it. The last few weeks, he even started that if-I-can't-have-you-no-one-can business."

"Did he become violent?"

Molly knew she'd surprised the woman. Mrs. McGivers looked up, blushed a little. She seemed more surprised by her tears than her answer. "Yes."

Molly went from Ladue to University City to see the third wife. She went back up to north St. Louis to talk to Pearl's mama again. In the end all she came away with was a crushing headache and a front seat full of fast-food wrappers.

She simply couldn't find a conspiracy. Nothing that

connected the five of them beyond those lunches. Nothing about the name William T. Peterson that rang bells among surviving family.

Even the investment itself hadn't panned out. In the end, it seemed that of the five, only Pearl and Peter had even invested in the company. There were no surprises, no families demanding more answers, no reason Molly could find that somebody would want her to stop looking into these deaths.

There was no reason to believe that they weren't what they appeared. The five members of the Shitkicker's Club had committed suicide. Each for a different reason, by a different method, without prior notice, but not without, in hindsight, fair warning.

Molly did a thorough and exemplary investigation into every aspect she could of each case, and still couldn't come up with a reason to call Rhett back and demand his time. She couldn't go back to the caves just to tell Joseph Ryan that she'd been wrong. So she went home feeling, for the first time, that she had absolutely no idea what it was she was doing that was so pissing people off.

Her new locks seemed to be working just fine. There wasn't a painting or piece of furniture out of place when she walked in. The same, unfortunately, couldn't be said about the kitchen.

"Been waiting long?" she asked the guilty party.

He hadn't actually waited. More like chewed and destroyed. Molly was glad she'd thought to erect the barricade, or one of the Hoppers might be the latest in doggy chews. As it was, many of Molly's mother's gourmet cookbooks were now hamster cage stuffing. Magnum, deliriously happy, greeted her on his back with all fours spread in anticipation of a good rub.

Molly didn't know whether to laugh or to cry. Until she'd walked in to find that mess in her kitchen, she hadn't realized how God awful exhausted she was.

"Screw it, Thomas," she said to the mutt. "Let's just leave it."

Molly opened the door and was about to follow the puppy outside, when the phone rang. Even though she saw Sam working his way across to her yard, she picked up.

"Speak."

"Then you're okay."

Molly forgot Sam for a moment. "It's lovely to hear from you too, Frank. What's up?"

"Do you still have Peg Ryan's daykeeper?" he asked, his voice unusually businesslike.

Molly leaned around so she could see the coffee table in the family room where the large black leather binder rested. "What's it to ya?"

"The Ryans just called. Their house was broken into. Along with the TV, the stereo, and the VCR, Peg's stuff is missing."

Molly lowered herself into her chair. Oh yeah, she thought, wearily. This is definitely the way I want to end my day. "Are they all right?"

Frank sighed. "I guess. Her mom wanted to know if they could have the daykeeper back. They need addresses for flower thank-yous, and the only other place they had them was on Peg's computer, which was—"

"Stolen," Molly agreed. "Yeah. Let me go through it once more. You don't think this could be another uncanny coincidence, do you, Frank?"

"I hate that word, Burke. Whatever it is, though, we're finished. File it closed, and let's just go our merry way."

"Don't want to find out the truth?"

"Don't want to jeopardize this cushy life I have, Saint Molly. I worked hard for it, and I ain't givin' it back."

"Oh, thank God. And here I thought you were worried for my welfare."

"You can take care of yourself. My bank balance can't."

"Did Peg invest in the gambling operation?"

"I told you I'm not asking questions like that anymore."

"It has to be something," she insisted, waving Sam inside. "I can't find anything else at all."

"Go back to nursing, Saint Molly. And be careful."

Sam actually backed in the door. "You know that beast of yours is trying to reach your goldfish?"

Feeling even worse than she had a minute ago, Molly hung up the phone and climbed wearily to her feet. "I hope he has better luck catching them than I have. It'll serve him right for massacring Mother's cookbooks. Tea, Sam?"

Sam turned around, squinted at her through a trail of cigarette smoke. "You look like you could use it."

She handed him the soup can she kept for an ashtray. "No Jewish proverbs, please. I'm not in the mood."

He settled himself into one of the plain oak kitchen chairs and tsked instead. "Did you give that office of yours my number?"

"A long time ago. Why?"

"Because when they couldn't find you, they found me instead. They want you to call."

Molly just waved a hand at him. Magnum was crouched flat on his belly out on the lawn, watching the fish circle. Molly figured that if his tail was wagging, the fish were safe. "I have a puzzle for you, Sam," she said as she started the tea, her gaze on the puppy, who was now yipping in frustration.

"What?"

"Why would five friends all commit suicide within a few weeks of each other?"

"Are you sure it was suicide?"

Molly laughed. "That's the only thing I am sure of. I've spent the day wading around in the detritus, and I can guarantee you that what we have is mass suicide. Or serial suicide, I guess. Mass events all happen at once. Serial events happen with time elapsing in between each event. That's what I have, a serial suicidist."

"You're tired."

"I don't understand it. There wasn't any kind of note to connect the acts, any indication to families. Most of the families didn't even know that these folks met regularly for lunch. Why are they all dead?"

Sam lit a second cigarette with the first. "Who knows? Maybe they all studied Sylvia Plath over lunch."

Molly laughed again. This time she meant it. "You want your tea or mine?"

"Don't be absurd. You should nap."

"I should get my laundry done and my kitchen cleaned up. My new houseguest turned it into excelsior while I was gone."

Taking a second to sweep up the majority of the ticker tape from her floor, Molly crouched in the far corner of the kitchen and opened the liquor cabinet. It was usually dusty during the summer. Molly pulled out a bottle of Stoli and closed the door again. "How's Myra?"

"She sends her love. We walked to the sunroom yesterday. Who was that nice young man here yesterday?"

Molly poured out the tea and harrumphed. "That was *not* a nice man. You remember the lawyer who sued me?"

"Him? With that beautiful little girl with the big eyes and good manners?"

"I know. Who'd believe it? I guess the wolves who raised him respected manners, too."

When she uncapped the bottle to sweeten Sam's tea, Molly caught a whiff of the alcohol. A whisper. A temptation. She was so tired and sore, and it was such a good muscle relaxant. She wanted to be a good hostess. It wouldn't be that much, and Sam would be here.

With deliberate motions, she recapped the bottle, put it away, and served Sam his tea. Then, instead of giving herself a chance to sit and rethink her actions, she scooped up the basket of clothes that had been waiting for the wash.

"Sit," Sam commanded. "And tell me why this *gonif* lawyer would dare darken your doorstep."

Molly smiled on her way by to the washroom. "I have to work tomorrow, and my lab coat is full of dog hair and Betadine. And there's nothing to tell about the lawyer. He knew one of the victims. That's all."

"Are you going to call your work?"

"Nah. Let 'em call me again."

She was tossing clothes in the washer, rummaging through pockets to clean them out so she didn't resterilize needles and melt rubber tourniquets. Whatever she found she tossed in a basket on the dryer, which she then brought back to the communal basket at work where all supplies inadvertently carried home in lab coat pockets were collected.

"I wanted it to be something other than suicide," she said, almost to herself as the old man sipped from her mother's good Sèvres china in her kitchen.

"Another way's better?" he asked. "Dead is dead."

Molly smiled to herself as she tossed a handful of

Band-Aids into the pile. "The guilt's easier to carry when it's not suicide."

She pulled out a glossy pamphlet and tossed it on top of the rest of the stuff until she could lob it into the trash.

"I'm sure there's a wonderful saying for this," Sam said to no one in particular. "But I've been forbidden. Your dog is now being terrorized by a squirrel."

"It'll teach him to be humble."

Molly's eyes kept drifting back to the cover of the glossy pamphlet. To the bright, pretty blue pills the nurse was holding in her palm, to the perfectly pressed and smiling patient who graced the cover beneath the scrolled lettering proclaiming the newest innovation in medicine.

Bright blue pills.

Pretty blue.

Why did that trigger something at the back of her memory?

The other day, she thought. Allan and his duck, both in need of a little relief. The drug salesman from Argon had passed out pamphlets with his promises.

No, it was something else. Molly wouldn't forget, because those pills were such an unusual color, even for the paint box of colors pills came in these days. She'd held them herself, and it hadn't been to give to Allan, because he'd been handed off to psych for evaluation before treatment.

Blue. Blue.

Molly forgot the lab coat. She forgot to put the soap into the water before she closed the lid. Her eyes were on the pamphlet she'd been carrying around for days, and the pills she kept seeing someplace besides on paper.

Oh, shit. Of course. She'd seen them scattered on a dresser like bright beads from a broken necklace.

She'd scooped them up in her hand along with the other, more easily recognizable meds, to take away for analysis.

She'd held them in a plastic bag and wondered what they were.

Now she knew. They were Transcend. Generic name, synapsapine.

They were an experimental drug that was in limited trial.

Something was wrong about that. Something that said an experimental personality enhancer didn't mix with a casual lunch group.

Jesus, Molly thought, not breathing. Could this mean something?

"Molly? Are you deaf now, too?"

Molly startled at the impatience in Sam's voice. Then she realized why. The phone must have been ringing, because he was holding it out to her, his expression at once concerned and irritated.

Molly jumped to get it. "Yes."

"Molly, it's Kevin. Can you come down?"

"I was there all morning, and it's now my dinnertime. Listen, Kevin, I think I may have something."

There was a sigh. "I need to talk to you, Molly."

"So, talk. But first, I have to tell you something. I want to go back through the files again—"

"You can't."

"What do you mean I can't?"

"As of three o'clock this afternoon, you're not working here anymore."

✦ Chapter 16 ✦

"YOU SHOULDN'T BE down here," Kevin protested.

"You told me to come down," Molly retorted, leaning over his desk. "Right before you told me I'd been fired."

Kevin had some trouble facing her with the answer. "The official term is unpaid leave. And I said we'd discuss it later."

Molly made a show of checking her watch. "It is later. Now, talk. I have some tox levels I need to check."

For the first time since she'd known him, Kevin pulled rank. Getting to his considerable feet, he leaned right back over her. "No. Not today. After this has all blown over."

Molly glared at him. "After *what* has blown over?"

He sighed and straightened. "Then you didn't see the five o'clock news."

Molly felt that old familiar tug of impending disaster. "I was in rush hour traffic. Why?"

"City hall's a little nervous right now."

"I can imagine."

"They don't feel they can stand any bad press."

Which meant that the mayor had caught wind of

the scope of the gambling investigation. "I make a lousy sacrificial goat, Kevin," she warned her supervisor. "I never stay quiet. Besides, all I have to do is go to Winnie."

Kevin was beginning to look really uncomfortable. "Winnie was the one who told me. You're on unpaid leave as of now until we can clear up the missing file situation, and . . . uh, the press settles down a little about what happened the other night."

Molly was almost breathless with fury. "I was mugged," she said very quietly.

Kevin couldn't even look at her this time. "There seems to be a question about whether there was alcohol on your breath."

That did it. Molly straightened with whatever dignity she had left. "I see," she said, struggling to keep her voice even. "I can't tell you how much I appreciate the support of this office, Kevin. I really can't."

Before she thought about what she was doing to the rest of her part-time career, she swung out of the office and marched over to Winnie's.

"Molly, this is just temporary . . ." She heard behind her. She ignored that, too.

Winnie's door was closed, but then Winnie's door was always closed. Molly didn't bother to knock. She just pushed her way in, figuring she had nothing left to lose.

Winnie wasn't home.

"Where is she?" Molly yelled without turning around.

"Finishing up at court. Go home! We'll talk later."

Molly ignored him again. She was not leaving this office without having her say. If Winnie didn't have the courage to face her, Molly guessed she'd just get a note instead.

Molly hadn't spent much time in Winnie's office.

Nobody had. The rule was inviolate. Winnie didn't even bother to lock her door, so sure was she that nobody would break the rule that her space was off-limits.

The room itself reflected her. Sparsely decorated with no-comfort furniture and a wall full of very fierce-looking African masks that all seemed to face the visitor's chair across the desk from Winnie's. Winnie wasn't into African art. She just used the masks to keep problems at a physical distance. It worked. Molly's abiding memory of being dressed down was the image of grotesque expressions and sinister gaping voids where eyes should have been.

Winnie's desk was functional and spotless, not a file out of place, not even a notepad visible anywhere convenient. Figuring she didn't have a whole lot to lose, Molly went for the drawers, breaking inviolate rule number two. Nobody went in Winnie's desk.

Molly found out why on her second drawer.

She'd just been looking for paper. Just something to leave a furious note on to the effect that if Winnie didn't have the balls to protect one of her staff, maybe she didn't deserve the job after all. Molly was that upset.

She passed upset at a gallop when she saw what was in the left-hand drawer of Winnie's desk.

"Oh, no."

White typewriter paper, as carefully folded as a love letter. As carefully printed. Tucked beneath a couple of pressed carnations right on top of the stationery and writing supplies that filled the rest of the drawer in neat, tidy compartments.

Pearl's suicide note.

"You shouldn't be in there!" Kevin yelled from across the hall. "You know that!"

Molly knew that now. She felt numb. Betrayed all over again. Deserted. She didn't know what to do or what to think. Could somebody have planted this here? Could Winnie really have had it here all this time while Molly was being pummelled by the press and city hall? Had she had it hidden away in that drawer when she'd been screaming at Molly about responsibility and accountability?

Molly scooped out the letter. She found a piece of paper beneath it and wrote two words. *Call Me.* Then she arranged it on the pressboard desktop right in front of Winnie's chair with the carnations on top. The letter, she took with her.

"Here," she said to Kevin as she handed it over. "I found this after all. It's Pearl's. You can't ask any questions about it because I don't work here anymore. Keep it someplace safe."

Kevin hadn't even begun to react before Molly was out the door and down the stairs. He reacted then, pounding after her.

"What the hell's this all about?" he demanded from the top of the stairs.

"I told you," she said. "I don't work here anymore."

"You won't if you don't answer me!" he yelled.

Molly turned at the bottom of the stairs, suddenly so tired she could hardly stand up. "Okay," she said, leaning against the banister so she could see him better. "I'll give you this for free. I found out the mayor's being investigated in the gambling contract, which is why we're getting this heat. I also found out that at least two of those suicide victims had a drug in them that isn't even on the market yet, so we may have something else tying those five suicides together. Whether you like it or not, I'm going to find out what's going on."

"What about this?" he asked, lifting the square of paper Molly knew by heart.

"That," she said, turning away again, "I'll explain when I'm ready."

"Why?" he demanded. "Why are you doing this to me?"

That stopped her all over again. "Because I want to know why Peg Ryan died, and not you or Winnie or the fucking state police are going to keep me from doing it."

It was a lovely speech. Molly knew just what kind of good it would do, so she ended it by walking out the front door.

Originally she'd wanted to go in and check a couple of things on the files she had. She couldn't now. She couldn't walk back into that building at all until she heard from Winnie. So she got in her car, set it on autopilot, and ran.

For a long time, Molly just drove. She hit Highway 40 and went west, skating along Forest Park and past the Gold Coast of suburbs that housed St. Louis's rich and famous. Clayton, Ladue, Town and Country. She passed the massive hospital complexes that crouched at Grand and at Kingshighway, at Ballas and at Woods Mill Road, high-tech temples to the gods of medicine and corporate cupidity.

She swept out past the newest communities created by white flight all the way to the Missouri River and past, out toward the country, where darkness finally ruled, where the wind battered at her and the blues on her radio competed with the traffic. For a long time, she just drove, outdistancing her problems and her questions and just relishing the feeling of flight. Just challenging herself by sweeping off the highway onto back roads that twisted along among the hills beyond the river.

Molly wasn't sure how long she drove. She really didn't pay close attention to clocks anymore, unless she was at work. She just knew that she finally had no idea where she was, and that it was completely black out, the night stars hazy with humidity and the moon a thick yellow crescent over the hills in the distance. She just knew that it was pretty quiet, except for the insects in the trees and the lazy birdcall and the hum of traffic on the highways.

Molly pulled off the road in the parking lot of a roadside vegetable stand at the top of a hill and turned off the car.

She was getting too old for this stuff. It was just too damn exhausting to keep fighting against the tide.

Maybe she should just let them have their way this time. Just ignore the case and the people and the medical examiner Molly had trusted. Maybe it didn't matter after all. It wasn't as if Molly still believed in justice, or thought she was making the streets safer or cleaner or healthier. Just like anybody else in the system, she knew perfectly well that on a good day she did no more than stick her finger in the dike.

Who really cared, in the end, why five lawyers committed suicide? Who would benefit from her continued persistence, anyway? Joseph Ryan? Hell, he'd forget within a week he'd ever met Molly. Pearl's mother? Molly was sure Mrs. Johnson would be soothed by the realization that her daughter had had a reason to kill herself after all. Molly? Not when she'd have to stay wading in the pool of suicide for another few weeks of summer.

God, she wanted to quit. She wanted to drive back home in peace and sit in her backyard and listen to the sound of water chuckling over stones in her garden. She wanted to feel safe and untroubled and content to putter in her garden.

She couldn't. She'd told Kevin the truth. After forty-something years, she didn't have much to speak for her. What she did have was the knowledge that she didn't quit, at least when it meant something to somebody else. She couldn't now.

In the end, she started the car and headed back to the city. She went home, took care of her dog, and sat down at her kitchen table with her working notebook, the glossy pamphlet she'd received from the Argon sales rep, and a large cup of coffee. Because the more she thought about those bright, pretty blue pills, the more uncomfortable she became. And the more uncomfortable she became, the more she wanted answers. She just had to figure how to go about getting them.

"You're not official anymore," the tech at the tox lab informed Molly the next morning when she called.

"I know," Molly assured her. "A small matter of paranoia in the mayor's office. It wouldn't stop you from checking a couple of things for me, though, would it?"

Silence. Molly almost held her breath.

"Like what?"

"One drug, that's all I ask. Nothing hard. And only on three of the victims. I found out for sure that two of the others had it. Please?"

"What drug?"

"Synapsapine. It's an experimental antidepressant."

"Oh, yeah. I remember. We damn near had to walk to the FDA to find out what it was. You think all of those suicidal lawyers were on it?"

Magnum started chewing on Molly's running shoe while her foot was still in it. She didn't even notice. "Maybe."

Another silence, this one shorter. "It's sure something to think about, isn't it?"

Molly struggled hard to stay calm. Without this information, she had nothing. With a negative answer, she was back at square one. She had such a feeling about this, though. Such a terrible hope that she was right, just because she wasn't sure she could leave it back at simple suicide. "What do you say?"

"What's that noise?" the tech asked instead, hearing what Molly had been listening to since she'd stumbled back downstairs earlier. "You having construction done?"

"Ignore it," Molly suggested. "I am."

Actually, she'd been trying to train Magnum to respond to it by growling. So far, he'd only managed to roll on his back and wag his tail.

"What is it?" the tech asked.

Molly sighed. "The doorbell. Voices. Pounding on my door. The vultures have begun to circle."

"You have lawyers surrounding your house?"

Molly actually laughed. "Worse. Newspeople. Magnum," she commanded. "Sic. Sic."

Magnum growled at her shoe and fell over. Molly had also been telling him that if a tall black woman in cornrows showed up at the door, to pee on her shoes. She figured she wouldn't have better luck with that, either.

"So," she said again. "What do you say?"

"I'm intrigued. Which ones are verified as having taken it?"

"Pearl Johnson and Mary Margaret Ryan."

"And Peter VanAck," the tech said, her voice coming to life. "I remember that, because I was the one who looked it up when we found it."

Molly looked out to where the breeze was skittering through a wind chime. "Really."

"Yeah, really." Even the tech was beginning to sound excited. "Tell you what. How 'bout I think about it over a particle spectrograph and call you back?"

"I'll name my firstborn after you."

"I won't hold my breath."

By two o'clock, Molly had received more answers that led to more questions. She had reached all five families again and two of the private doctors, who had made it a point to inform Molly that as they were on the staffs of several of the prominent county hospitals, they would never have deigned to send their patients to a city facility like Grace for any treatment, experimental or otherwise. Especially to the psych unit of Grace, which was renowned for taking in the indigent and chronic abusers.

Molly had also found out that in the entire metro area, Grace was the only hospital involved in Transcend trials. Not only that, but where only two of the lawyers had invested in gambling, at least four of the five had invested in Argon.

Not a slam-dunk, by any means, but inconsistency upon inconsistency, with the two big questions still to be answered. If they hadn't received the medication from official sources, how had they? And if they did all have the medication on board, what relationship did that have to the fact that they'd all committed suicide?

Molly needed to talk this out with somebody. Put her facts in some kind of order and weigh their logic. After all, the way Molly usually did detective work was with a stethoscope and a percussion hammer. Even when she was in charge at a crime scene, the only thing she was responsible for was making sure nothing disappeared or changed en route to the morgue. She wasn't supposed to solve the damn thing.

She'd planned to head in to work early to talk to the people in charge of the study, which meant she didn't have much more time to talk. She had possibilities skating around in her head and answers that seemed just out of reach. And she had Peg Ryan's daykeeper to go back through again after she got home tonight. She had an aching head, ribs, and shins, and company at the front door who wouldn't let her out as far as Sam's. She did the only other thing she could think of.

"I didn't mean for this to get to be a habit, Saint Molly."

Molly closed her eyes and leaned her head on her hand. "You're the only one I can talk to about this, Frank."

"Why does that make me nervous?"

"Shut up and listen." Resettling the phone, she dragged over the pad of paper she'd been filling up since last night. "What if we were right after all? What if it isn't Pearl's gambling contacts that's the issue here?"

"I don't think we said that at all. I think *you* said that. *I* said I quit, but you didn't seem to hear me."

"Just bear with me a minute. I need to talk out what I found."

"And you're talking it out with me because nobody will listen to you down at the ME's office."

"Yes."

"Because they put you on leave."

"You could say that."

"Which means you shouldn't be doing this."

Molly deliberately turned toward her backyard, where her flowers spread like an impressionist painting in the bright sunlight. A couple of finches were dipping at her feeder, and the waterfall was sparkling. Molly could almost imagine she could hear it over the sporadic banging and ringing at the other end of the house.

She could do this. She had to do this. She didn't know how to stop anymore.

"I was out on the road all yesterday afternoon and on the phone all morning," she told Frank. "And I found a few things out."

"Which you're going to tell me whether I want to know or not."

"I asked everyone, Frank," she said. "Each family, people the victims worked with, anybody I could think of. The only two people who talked at all about the riverboat gambling situation were Pearl and Peter VanAck. Now, if the other three didn't know anything about it, why would a crooked gambler want them dead?"

"Maybe they knew about it but didn't tell their families."

"I thought of that. But there's one guy, Harry McGivers, who evidently told everybody every bit of good news he ever got. He couldn't keep his mouth shut. He never said a word."

"So you think it's something else."

"Well, I looked for something else to link them all together. I mean, I don't think the MAC is systematically killing off its members for abusing lunch rules or anything, and not one of the suicide notes mentioned any kind of pact among the five. And that was all we had."

"Until now."

"Stop patronizing me, Frank. I've shared two very

memorable evenings with men who like to hurt women. That means something."

"It means you're really pissed off."

It took Molly a second to answer. "Yes," she admitted. "I guess it does."

"What did you find out?"

"Transcend."

"What?"

"Transcend, generic name synapsapine. It's the newest, brightest rising star in the world of psychopharmaceuticals. Still on trial, which means nobody outside the program should have it."

Molly couldn't have sworn, but she thought Frank's voice might have begun to sound just a little more chastened. "And somebody did?"

"At least three somebodies. Pearl, Peg, and Peter. I have the tox lab checking on the other two, just in case. I also found out that at least four of the group invested in the company that makes the drug."

"The tox lab over whom you hold no authority anymore."

"The tox lab who hates an unanswered question even more than I do. Are you listening to me?"

"How long will the toxicology screen take?"

"Depends on their work load. I'm going to go into work at the hospital today so I can talk to the people running the trial program." She'd tried to call Gene as a way to shortcut the situation, but he was just getting back from some out-of-town conference, and wasn't expected until later.

"So you've made the quantum leap from gambling to pharmaceuticals as cause of death?"

"It makes sense, don't you think?"

"No. You said Peg had a lot of weird stuff in her system that night. And I'm still not convinced your Mr. McGivers would have shared information that's this explosive. I think your logic leap leaves a lot to be desired, Saint Molly."

"It's not a logic leap, Frank. It's a . . . feeling."

"A feeling." He sounded as if she'd said a message from aliens.

She sighed, knowing that she wouldn't have needed to explain her feelings to Sasha or Lorenzo or even Lance Frost. Wishing there were some way she didn't have to explain them to Frank. "I'm a hell of a trauma nurse, Frank."

"A good self-opinion is healthy, Mol."

"A good trauma nurse learns to trust her instincts. Usually, that's all you have time for. By the time you get the real story about why a patient's shown up at your door, he's been dead ten minutes. After all this time, I can smell when something's wrong before it actually goes wrong."

"And you think Transcend smells wrong."

"That's the best way I can put it. It's like the cops are always telling me. Look for what *doesn't* belong at a scene. Those pills didn't belong with any of those victims. At least I don't think so."

"And what do you think this means?"

This was the crux of the phone call. The crux of everything she'd been doing for the last twenty-four hours. "I don't know," she admitted. "There's just so much going on. I mean, first I have to find out how they got hold of the medicine. Was somebody in the program and decided to share the wealth? Was this the free gift Peg's dealer was handing out with cocaine? Did one of them roll a drug salesman? And what the hell does it have to do with their suicides?"

"You do think it was suicide."

"I do think it was suicide. At least one of them was on Prozac. We could have an old-fashioned drug interaction situation on our hands, especially if these five were taking medicine they weren't supposed to."

"Then why the threats?"

"I don't know that either. But I'm going to find out."

"Why?"

Molly ignored another round of ringing. She even ignored the fact that Magnum finally seemed to have had enough and started barking at the noise. She couldn't believe what Frank had just said.

"What?"

"Why go to all this trouble, Molly? It was suicide. Leave it at that."

"When was the last time you were threatened and thrown out of a speeding van into the trash, Frank?"

"Probably the last divorce case I handled. Pardon me for sounding thick, but isn't that all the more reason to see things their way?"

"I'll tell you something, Frank," she admitted. "I'm tired. I've been called a liar and a thief, I'm held captive in a house I hate by people I don't respect, and I've lost some of the income I needed to get by since I was raped by a certain lawyer I know in full view of a civil courts judge. I just want to do my job and go home. This is my job."

"You're a nurse," he said. "Not a detective."

Molly felt an odd chill at his choice of words. The words her kidnappers had used. "Well, I don't have a hell of a lot of choice, now, do I? The detectives are busy protecting their own asses."

For a second, all she heard from Frank's end was silence. Her end was full with the hum of outdoor gatherings. Magnum was growling again.

"Molly," he finally said, his voice for once dead serious, "I don't know how many ways to tell you this. Remember that cute little kid I brought with me the other day? I'm attached to her. I don't want to hurt her. I especially don't want her going through having another parent die. And I don't want her to go through that simply because you're trying to redeem yourself for fucking up in the Wiedeman case. Take a nap, Molly. Adopt a pagan baby. Leave this mess alone before it burns the both of us."

Molly had been ambushed so many times by now, she felt like a wagon train in Kansas. Still, this one hurt. It hurt like hell.

"Oh, Frank," she said, her voice so low even the puppy lifted his head. "And here I was actually beginning to believe you might be human."

"Never jump to conclusions, Saint Molly."

She knew she shouldn't say it. She shouldn't have to. She couldn't help it. "I did not fuck up the Wiedeman case."

"Of course you did. Otherwise, I wouldn't have gone after you."

"You son of a bitch," she hissed. "What do you know? What the hell do you know about what happened that night?"

Molly thought she couldn't have been more angry. She could. She found that out when, of all things, Frank laughed. "The way I figure it, Mol, you were just trying to get through your shift that night. Trying to get by. You had a doctor on who was an ass and a patient who came in every three weeks for one complaint after another, each one of them more trouble than the last. You didn't take her seriously, so you didn't do a full-court press to get her treated, because you had to live with the doc after she left."

"I broke the skin on my knuckles trying to get him out of that door."

"All the same," he said. "You could have done

something. You could have called his supervisor or one of the other doctors on. You could really have started the tests yourself. You know it, and that's what makes you so mad at me. 'Cause I know it, too."

Molly struggled to keep her voice even. "I guess I wasted my time, Frank. Forget I called."

"Molly—"

"Just one thing, though. So I'm covered. I found Pearl's suicide note, the one that started this whole thing. It was in the office of the medical examiner."

"Why are you telling me?"

"I don't know. Just in case. I haven't said anything to anybody else until I hear from her about it."

"And you haven't heard."

"No."

He sighed, and Molly wondered why the hell his voice sounded so much like a parent's. "Oh, Saint Molly," he said mournfully. "I was right the first time. You shouldn't be let loose alone."

Molly hung up the phone and walked out her back door. Two newsmen tried to scramble over her fence. She closed the door and stood in her kitchen, in the house she hated so much. She was cornered. Furious and exhausted and alone. There was no one to call and scream at, no way to vent her anger. No friend she could ask for help.

In the end, all she had were the rest of her mother's cookbooks. Heavy, elaborate works culled straight from the great chefs of Europe. Leather-bound and gilt-lettered and rare. Molly picked one up and heaved it. She heaved another one. She didn't even notice her dog cower under the table behind her as she threw and threw again.

She kept heaving the books until there was a pile and Magnum crouched beneath the table whimpering, and each time she threw, she told herself that

Frank Patterson couldn't possibly have understood how Mrs. Wiedeman had died. She threw and she sobbed and she swore, because she'd almost begun to trust Frank and he'd betrayed her. He'd told her the truth.

✦ Chapter 17 ✦

"ARE YOU CRAZY?"

Molly looked up from where she was reading her mail to find Sasha glaring at her from the doorway of the nurses' lounge. "It's been suggested at one time or another. What's the matter this time?"

"What's the matter?" Sasha echoed in high dudgeon as she swept the rest of the way into the lounge. "What's the *matter?* Are you actually telling me that you had two sick days left, and you failed to take them? Do you realize that that is an offense punishable by hanging?"

Molly went back to her mail. "Go right ahead. I probably wouldn't notice."

The halls outside the lounge had patients stacked in them like cordwood. Gunshots, accidents, high fevers, DTs. Tattoos and body odor, foul language, and at least three concealed weapons. At one end of the hall, a pregnant woman was in four-point restraints so she wouldn't rip through her stomach with her bare hands to get at the baby inside she insisted was Satan. Full moon fever at its finest.

All Molly had been able to think about upon catching her first assessing glance was that there was enough murder and mayhem on these halls to last her a lifetime. She could keep busy, fill up her eight- and ten-and twelve-hour shifts each and every day with the detritus of humanity that walked, crawled, and slithered through the doors into triage and get her paycheck without once ever again putting in extra time or extra effort or extra tears. After all these years of working at it, it seemed stupid she hadn't figured that out yet.

She hadn't. Not even after what she'd put up with today.

She'd spent the hours until work praying that the press would leave her alone. For the president to declare war on some third world country or a rock star to be caught committing murder so the hard light of attention would focus itself somewhere else. But there had been no hard news. Nothing more interesting than the possible scandal in the city government and the woman the mayor was now calling a "rogue" in a trusted position.

She'd answered the phone every time it rang just in case she'd find Winnie on the other end, only to find more press. She'd cleaned the broken books off her kitchen floor and reminded herself that the last person on this earth she should trust was a lawyer.

Just like the good old days. Fighting her way through a pack of cameras just to get to her car, isolated and vilified and branded with the word *alleged.* "Just what was your relationship with the comptroller?" they'd asked. "We understand you have priceless artwork and antiques in that house, Ms. Burke. Exactly how do you afford that on a nurse's salary?"

Unanswerable questions from an uninterested press. Silence from the employers who should have supported her and attacks from people who didn't really know her. Raised eyebrows and quick assumptions in a circus atmosphere. Nothing new under the sun.

And now, Sasha was standing over her like the lord high executioner demanding more answers she didn't have. "Does this have something to do with that other job problem?"

Molly actually laughed. "What a nice way of putting it. No, it has to do with the fact that I'd rather be here than trapped inside that house listening to reporters make up my life. Besides, I found out something interesting in those five suicides, and I want to find out what it means. Is Chicken Soup on tonight?"

"Frost?" Sasha asked. "Yeah. He's due in soon. What suicides?" The minute she said it, she realized what it meant. "The lawyers?"

Molly nodded, folding away the letter she'd just scanned and placing it with its three identical mates in her bag.

"And?"

Molly looked up. "And what?"

Sasha looked truly confused. "What's the point? We are talking lawyers, aren't we?"

"I know I'm disappointing you," Molly said. "Hell. I'm disappointing myself. Especially after I opened my mail. Do you know that it has been about seventy-two hours since I got scooped off the parking lot, and I had four letters in my mail today—four—from lawyers who are salivating over the prospect of suing the hospital for me for only a thirty-three percent fee? And Frank wonders why lawyers have such a bad reputation."

"And you want to help them."

"It's my tragic flaw. I can't leave well enough alone."

"Well, that's the God's honest truth. You look like hell, ya know."

She knew. She felt like it. "Thanks for the vote of confidence."

Sasha reached into her lab coat for her illegal pack of cigarettes. "I just don't want you dropping over one of the patients in the middle of a code."

Molly picked up the phone and dialed psychiatry.

The unit answered, a vague-sounding woman who wanted to know what she could do for Molly.

"Is Ms. Harlow on this afternoon?" Molly asked, and then ignored the expression on Sasha's face. Haldol Harlow, as the psych supervisor was fondly referred to, was a nursing recruiter's worst nightmare. Petty, surly, protective, and unforgiving, she looked more like a two-hundred-pound sack of cement than a legendary screen star, unless it was the great white in *Jaws*. Nonetheless, Ms. Harlow was the one with the skinny on what was going on in her unit. Ms. Harlow was the first person Molly had to talk to.

"I'm sorry," Ms. Harlow said twenty minutes later as Molly sat before her desk in an office decorated in dozens of Precious Moments posters. "I can't give you that information."

"General information," Molly nudged with what she hoped was a bright smile. "We had a patient downstairs Dr. Stavrakos put on Transcend, and I wanted to know what his prognosis was."

"A patient . . ."

"Allan Betelman. The duckman."

Ms. Harlow did everything but get red. But then, Ms. Harlow was the classic example of the staff needing the treatment more than the patients. Ms. Harlow had been married three times, two of them to patients. She'd also been through a gross of twelve steps. Probably not a bad candidate for Transcend herself.

"Nobody ever tells us anything," Molly all but whined. "We treat people and then we never know what the long-term prognosis is. From what I hear about this Transcend, we're going to be handing it out like aspirin inside three months' time, and I wanted to be prepared for once."

"Not even that long," Ms. Harlow informed her as if Molly had given a wrong answer in Pharmacology 101. "The study is wrapping up now."

"Really. How many patients?"

"Thirty-three."

Molly admitted surprise. "Only thirty-three?"

"That's not unusual for a drug. We've tested quite a few here, you know."

"Of course. I guess . . . I don't know. I never paid much attention to this stage of the process. I thought trials involved hundreds. At least."

"No. Just a good cross section at each stage of the process."

"And we've had that."

"Of course. I'm sure if you were more familiar with the process, you'd understand how it works."

Molly kept a straight face with effort. "Of course. Have you seen any . . . uh, side effects? Any kind of contraindications, like drug interactions?"

"Why do you ask?"

"So I'm prepared."

"Then, no. None at all. It's a wonderfully safe drug. Easily administered, monitored, and controlled. The results are incredible. I don't think I've ever worked with a more exciting drug in my fifteen years here."

"And you think we can safely give it in the ER."

For the first time since Molly had sat down, Ms. Harlow smiled. "If it's prescribed correctly, my unit will be out of business in six months."

"And you can't tell me—besides Mr. Betelman, of course—who else is taking part in the program."

"Of course not."

• • •

"I have no idea what's going on in the trial," Gene said.

Molly couldn't believe her luck. Just as she'd been heading back to the ER to try some other tack, she'd stepped into the elevator to find Gene standing there before her, bright-eyed, smiling. Molly had spent the elevator ride asking about the conference—tolerable—and the island of Grand Cayman, where it had been held—incredible. Gene had asked how Molly's injuries were, and she had lied and told him they were more colorful than sore. By the time they'd reached the main lobby level, she'd managed to work her way around to the real question on her mind.

"But you're in charge of it, aren't you?"

Gene got that impish grin of his and steered Molly to one side so they could talk. "God, no. I've got the residents, the curriculum, and the budget, which I'm up to my ears in right now. Not to mention Mary Mother of God, who just tried to bite the ears off one of the techs. Bart Banerjee's the one you want to talk to. Why? What did you need to know?"

"We put the duckman on it, remember?"

"Sure I do. You want to find out how he's doing?"

Molly shrugged, matched Gene's stance with hands in lab coat pockets. "Yeah. I also think I may have had a suicide victim who might have gotten hold of some. I'm trying to figure out how."

Gene's smile died into surprise. "Not from here," he assured her. "I'll guarantee it. Bart's tighter than a fifty-year-old virgin about that stuff. You sure it was synapsapine?"

"I think so."

"Okay, then. Let me talk to Bart. Have him call you with any info. If there's anybody on earth I trust to be discreet about this stuff, it's you, Molly Malone."

When Gene smiled, Molly smiled back. "Thanks, Gene."

The problem was, Molly didn't know Bart Banerjee well enough to know if she trusted *him*. So the minute she hit the ER, she hedged her bets.

"So, what I needed to know," she said on the phone to the pharmacy supervisor, "is whether he's in this drug trial."

"You say he came in OD'd," the man said.

"Out like a light." Well, it was true, if you took things literally. "His name's VanAck. Peter."

Since a direct request for information hadn't worked on Ms. Harlow, Molly decided to try and pull a scam she'd learned from watching "The Rockford Files." Give the pharmacy supervisor a sort of close resemblance to the truth that would make it easier for him to release her info. She was also doing this one over the phone. Given the right tone of urgency to the call, people in hospitals tended to give information over the phone they wouldn't in person. Help out a little more, assume that the request was an official one.

"No," the supervisor said, coming back on the line. "There's no VanAck here. Are you sure he had Transcend on him?"

"That's what the psych resident says. Real pretty blue stuff. How do you think he got it if he isn't in the study?"

"Well, he shouldn't be able to. This kind of thing is all very strictly controlled."

"Well, that's what I thought. Who could have given it to him without letting you know?"

"No one. I'm the only person in the pharmacy with the authority to release Transcend while it's under testing. I receive the written orders and the parameters, deliver the medication to either the floor or the clinic, and collect the follow-up data from them for the drug company and the FDA. I have to account for every pill I get from the company, every order given, and every patient who takes it. Dosages, treatments, results, side effects, possible contraindications. It's all in my records."

Gene had forgotten to mention that the pharmacologist was even tighter than Banerjee. "No kidding. You had many suicides on this stuff?"

"None. Not one. The test group has shown wonderful response."

"Problems interacting with other drugs, maybe."

"Absolutely not. Transcend is amazingly benign for a major antidepressant group like that."

"Really? This is the first time I've set eyes on it. It's really that good?"

"Better. Look, I still can't imagine that this could really be Transcend. Why don't you send me down a sample?"

"Oh, I don't think you want me to," Molly quickly demurred. "I mean, we're talking stomach contents here."

So she knew that at least one of the victims had never been on the program. She knew that Transcend was looking like the greatest medical breakthrough since antibiotics, and that nobody, but nobody, committed suicide on Transcend.

Now she had to find out just which of those statements was false.

By the time Molly's shift officially started, the tides of insanity were at full flood. There was a screamer in room three, two howlers in cubicles one and five, and about half a dozen criers down in the kiddy lane. The Bedlam Concerto in E-Flat. Molly winced at what the sound did to her head at the same time she thought how much better it sounded than the cries of "Ms. Burke! Just one question, Ms. Burke!" She enjoyed it as long as it took to get report from day shift and realize she'd inherited both howlers and an incoming biter.

Chicken Soup was, indeed, working the shift. Molly could see his unkempt figure at the other end of the hallway, where three nurses and a tech circled him like agitated satellites trying to affect his much-slower orbit. She wanted to talk to him, too, but there was time for that. Right now she had howlers to quiet.

She caught up with Lance about the same time the cops turfed in a John Doe with DTs. A probable street guy from the looks of his clothes, the patient was simply tagged Mr. E for being the fifth unidentified person of the day, scooped up by a passing patrol car for throwing himself spread-eagled on top of moving cars and demanding compensation for going on his way. The cops had shown great humor about the whole thing until their subject had decorated the back of their unit with various bodily fluids while demanding Demerol for his back pain. For that, they had decided a round of punitive emergency medicine was the best course. At which point, the John Doe had become Molly's problem.

"I gotta get away from them!" he was screaming at the top of his lungs as Molly and Lorenzo struggled to get him undressed while Lance Frost stood at the counter writing notes. Even tied down, Mr. E managed an impressive range of motion. "They gonna eat my eyes, man, can't you see? I gotta get away before they get me like her. She got no eyes, she got no eyes!"

Lorenzo took a considered look at the still-technicolor aspect of Molly's face and grinned. "Nah," he demurred in a calm voice as he pushed the drunk back onto the cart with alacrity. "Hers was the last eyes they wanted. Tasted so bad, they decided now they's goin' for balls."

That damn near propelled the patient right off the cart, which cost Molly some seconds when he bumped into her sore side. "Thanks, Lorenzo."

Lorenzo just gave her a grin. "Hey, my man, hey, your stuff is safe. We got the protection in the walls."

"Thank you, brother," Mr. E answered, rolling over into a fetal position as if he'd just located his grate. "Lord bless you for protectin' me."

"So, Lance," Molly said in continuation of the talk they'd been having. "You're sold on Argon as an investment."

"Sold?" he countered with a big shit-eating grin. "Are you kidding? The stock price has gone up four points this week alone on the leaks about how good this new stuff is going to be. It's going to pull Argon's ass out of the fire."

Molly yanked up on sleeves and held her nose. "Why was its ass in the fire?"

Finishing his work with a scrawled signature, Lance replaced his pen. "Usual stuff. Health care reform, earlier drugs going out of patent protection, that kind of thing. Transcend isn't just gonna save the ranch, it's gonna turn it into a spa. And this little piggy has his toes right in the whirlpool."

"Transcend is that good."

"Honey, it's going to be the number one–prescribed medication. Just like Prozac before it and Valium before that. Palliatives for the masses is good business, and this is the best. I mean, shit. Prozac's probably an $800 million a year industry, and this stuff is going to make it obsolete."

Molly tried her best not to react. Eight hundred million on one drug. Quite a healthy number. Certainly enough to make a company worry if something went wrong.

"You want to invest, you'd better do it before that stuff hits the market," Lance said. "I can introduce you to the person I use, if you want."

"Oh, thanks. I have somebody."

At his end of the patient, Lorenzo was having trouble getting soggy pants over soggier hips. "A little help here?" he asked. "Now that 'Wall Street Week' is wrapping up?"

Still glowing over the fortune he was intending to make, Lance delayed peeling his gloves long enough to add a pair of hands to the effort. "Hey there, son!" he yelled in Mr. E's ear. "What's your name?"

Mr. E mumbled something unintelligible and rolled into a tighter ball.

Lance scowled mightily. He yanked and Lorenzo tugged, and like a stuck shade, all three layers of pants suddenly came loose.

Just as that happened with an odd sucking sound, a surprise popped out from between the patient's saggy cheeks. The pants slid south and a baggie flew west. The minute it hit the floor, Molly saw that it contained a couple of chunks of dirty-looking rock. She looked up to find both of the men looking down at the same sight. All three looked back at the soundly sleeping visage of Mr. E, who seemed totally unaware that he'd hatched anything important.

Lorenzo started laughing, then Lance, then Molly. Lorenzo pointed to the evidence on the floor.

"I always wondered where crack cocaine came from," he said.

Molly laughed harder, grabbing her side.

"Molly," one of the techs said, leaning in the door. "Call on line two."

Bent over double from where her rib was protesting the laughter, Molly waved the tech back out. "Damn it, Lorenzo, warn me when you're going to do that."

"No wonder he drinks," Lance agreed. "He smoked that stuff after hidin' it there, the smell alone'd stone kill him."

Molly headed for the door, wiping at her eyes and thinking that it was a nice change to be tearing up from laughter. "I wonder how long it's been there."

"Actually," Lorenzo was saying as Molly headed outside, "I don't think it's rock at all. I think it was plain coke that just petrified."

Molly picked up the phone still chuckling. "This is Burke."

"Why didn't you say something to Kevin?"

Molly's breath whooshed out of her lungs like a bellow, and she sat hard on a chair. "Winnie?"

"You didn't say anything. Why?"

Molly closed her eyes. Closed out the rest of the ER so she could concentrate on one trauma at a time. She was too tired for this. Too tired for anything but laughing at the ridiculous things that could go on in an ER. She was past caring, she was certain of it. And yet, she couldn't quite hang up the phone and just walk away.

Molly never figured Winnie for a coward. Even so, the medical examiner had waited until Molly was in the ER to get hold of her. She'd waited for Molly to be in a place where she couldn't react, couldn't assimilate. She hadn't had the balls to face her.

Molly sucked the air back into her lungs and tried to make some sense. "I wanted the chance for you and me to talk first."

"So, talk."

"I think you have this backward," Molly suggested, her voice dry with disappointment. "I'm not the one with anything to say."

For a long moment, there was just silence on the other end. Molly wondered what was in Winnie's eyes as she looked back to the night her best friend had died.

"I didn't think about it," Winnie finally said, her voice as hushed as her office. "I just picked it up. I couldn't bear the sight of the thing. I couldn't give it away to strangers who didn't even know her so they could make judgments."

Molly understood. She empathized. She knew just how hard it was for Winnie to admit her own mistake. She knew what Winnie had probably gone through every day she'd opened that drawer to find that letter in there, what she must have felt the first day she'd found it gone.

Molly even tried to forgive her for allowing Molly to take the fall for it. She couldn't quite make it to verbalization, though.

"And you just held on to it."

"I was sure Kevin would find it when he went looking for the file."

"Do you have that, too, Winnie?"

This time, there was life in the voice at the other end of the line. "How dare you? Of course I didn't take that file."

Molly tried so hard not to judge. She was too human, though. "I never thought you'd stake me out as a sacrificial goat, either."

Winnie had no answer for that. The silence stretched across the line like cooling glass, and Molly knew she couldn't stay here much longer.

"I really have to go, Winnie."

"I told Kevin."

"Thank you. I mean it. If you're going to be in tomorrow, I found something out that might make a difference in Pearl's death."

"Not tomorrow," Winnie said. "Not until city hall's calmed down."

"Then I can expect the press on my lawn again tomorrow?"

"I'm trying, Molly."

Just that admission reflected what this was doing to Winnie. Molly rubbed at her head where the pain never seemed to go away anymore. "Well, let me know when it's safe to come out again. I'll bring all the information I have about those five suicides with me, and we can figure out where to go next."

"I told you before," Winnie said, finally sounding like the old Winnie once more. "Be careful."

"Okay."

Molly was still sitting in that chair trying her best to move on to the assessment she'd been about to do on Mr. E when she heard herself paged.

"Molly Burke, line one. Molly Burke, line one."

Molly picked up the phone. "This is Burke."

"You don't listen well, do you?"

Molly forgot Winnie. She forgot the patient she'd left in room twelve, and Lorenzo, who was probably getting real tired of being blessed. She knew the voice on the phone. She knew it so well that just the sibilance of its whisper made her want to vomit. She could almost feel that hot, stale breath against her cheek.

"Listen," she said before she had a chance to think about it. "I'm real busy right now, and I'm sure you have a long list of people you still have to threaten tonight, so why don't we just consider me warned and be on our way?"

"Smart little bitch like you, I thought for sure you'd learn a lesson when it was given."

Molly found herself fighting against just saying the word *Transcend* and seeing what happened. "And don't think I didn't. I'll never park in that lot again as long as I live."

"Last time I was nice. I think that was a mistake, wasn't it?"

"Uh-huh. Well, thanks very much. Bye now."

"Don't blow me off, bitch. You don't want your next lesson."

Molly didn't even bother to answer.

By the time she hung up, Molly was actually clammy with sweat. The funny thing was, she wasn't afraid. She was furious. She was tired of the threats, all the threats. At least these guys had had the decency to threaten her outright. Other people had couched their coercion in solicitude, when Molly knew damn well where their concern had lain. And then there were all the people standing in line to throw her to the wolves, just because it was easier that way.

"Molly? You okay?"

Molly looked up to see Lorenzo at the door. She smiled for him. "Just fine," she said. "It was just a follow-up call from the guys who hauled me downtown, to see how I was recovering."

Lorenzo came right to alert. "What do you mean?" He looked down at the phone as if he could see them through it. "They *called* you here?"

Molly shrugged, as if it didn't matter. "Better than showing up."

Lorenzo was not amused. "I'm calling the police."

"Don't bother," Molly said. "I'll do it. But don't be hugely surprised if they don't run right over. Is Lance finished in there?"

Lorenzo handed her the chart. "He left the room right after you did."

Molly nodded. She should think about that phone call. Somebody knew she was back out asking questions. Somebody was upset enough about this to offer another warning, and Molly was beginning to believe she knew just who it was.

When she got up tomorrow, she was going to have to fend off the press long enough to ask Sam how he thought a company would react if somebody threatened the survival of the product that was going to save it.

The problem was, Molly had the feeling she'd already found out.

Eventually she got back to work. She didn't see any police, at least not unless they were accompanying assault victims. She wasn't surprised. In the morning she'd call Rhett and Rowdy, which sounded like she was going to notify a team of strippers. She'd do a lot in the morning. All she wanted to do when she got home was sit outside and listen to her garden.

When Molly first saw it she thought she must be mistaken. The night was overcast, with the lights of the West End reflecting back off the bellies of the clouds. Molly caught the shudder of multicolored strobes when she turned off Maryland and figured it was just neon reflecting from the streets.

She didn't notice the van. It was late, and she was driving on autopilot, her attention on getting home, on the possibility that finally, at two in the morning, she'd have the chance to sit out in her yard and enjoy her flowers and her pond without having somebody drop in over her fence to ask questions. So she didn't see the van's headlights flash on. She didn't notice the clatter of an engine turning over. But as she passed, the van swerved a little toward her, and Molly looked up.

It was a plain dirty white, the kind a business would use rather than a family. She saw that it drove more slowly through a residential street than it had to. She saw the dark figures inside and suddenly recognized it.

"Oh, my God . . ."

Molly slammed on the brakes. The van lurched into gear and sped past her. Molly didn't know what to do. It was the guys who'd kidnapped her, the big guy and the medium guy. She was sure. Molly could see that at least the guy on the passenger side was wearing a ski mask. And that he was smiling. She would have sworn to it. The van skidded around the corner onto Taylor and disappeared. They'd been waiting for her, Molly realized. Sitting along the side of her street until she showed up. Sitting on *her* street.

That was when she realized that it hadn't been neon she'd seen after all. A block and a half down there were emergency vehicles clogging up the street.

"Oh, Jesus," she breathed, slamming her car back into gear.

Two cop cars, an ambulance, a fire engine, right in front of her house. Clots of people in uniform, a couple knots of neighbors standing cross-armed in their bathrobes on nearby lawns.

Molly didn't see smoke. She didn't see anyone near the front of the house. They seemed to be walking up the driveway that separated her house from Sam's. Molly skidded to a stop behind one of the units and tumbled out of her car. She didn't even notice the neighbors who were watching her. She had eyes only for the figures she could see farther back toward her yard.

"What's going on?" she demanded.

There were a couple of shrugs, and one of the cops turned toward her.

"You can't . . ."

Molly saw the untidy group of people in her backyard and shoved right past him. "It's my house."

God, please, she thought. Don't let it be Sam. Don't let something have happened to Sam.

She could see cop hats and flashlights, the lighter blue shirts of paramedics. Something lay on the ground. Somebody. Molly ran harder.

She slammed through the gate, startling a couple of the cops. Inside the house Magnum was barking like a wild thing. Molly tried hard to see who was on the lawn, but the paramedics were in the way, their synchronized movements half a turn from frantic in the weak, flickering light. Molly remembered, suddenly, that not four hours ago a man had told her she wouldn't want her next lesson.

"Sam?" she called, frantic. "God, Sam!"

A figure separated itself from the shadows. Reached out to her. "It's all right, *bubeleh*. I'm here."

Molly grabbed the old man by the shoulders and damn near shook him for scaring her. "What happened?" she asked, her voice too shrill and her hands shaking too hard. She'd thought he was dead. God, she thought they'd used this old man for her lesson.

"I don't know," he said, half turning back to where the paramedics were crouched over the bundle on the grass.

The cops were directing flashlights to where IVs were being started on limp arms and oxygen was being administered by portable tank. Molly saw dark stains on surgical gloves that meant there was a lot of blood somewhere.

"You live here?" one of the cops asked.

Molly tried to catch her breath. "Yes. I do. What happened?"

"The dog has been barking," Sam was trying to tell her. "I came out to look. This is what I found."

"Do you know this man?" the cop asked, and redirected the light.

Molly leaned past the crouched paramedic to get a look. She saw the blood and the clothes and the pasty features the flashlight illuminated. She felt Sam grab hold of her when she almost ended up on her knees. "Oh, God," she moaned. "Oh God, no."

The message the men in the ski masks had left on her lawn was Joey Ryan.

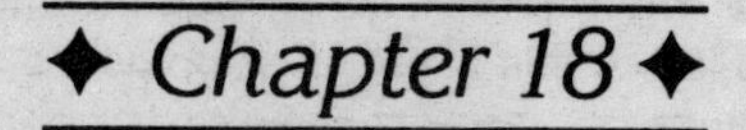

✦ Chapter 18 ✦

"THEY WERE SMILING at me," she kept saying, as if that would help her make sense out of it. "Smiling! I could see their teeth."

Leaning against the far wall, Frank didn't bother to answer. They were in the hallway by surgery where the trauma team was trying to stem the damage done by a twelve-inch fishing knife and a set of expert knuckles. Joseph had been typed in as Mr. M, just another bit of flotsam in the night's stream of wounded. Molly could have told them what his real name was. She should have. By the time she reached the hospital, though, he'd already been on his way down to OR. When she'd called Frank to tell him what happened, he'd begged her not to let anybody else know.

So she'd followed the circus down toward surgery and waited outside, where she wouldn't get in the way. Frank had found her there no more than five minutes earlier.

"Smiling," Molly said again, shaking her head. "I can't believe it."

"I'm not really wild about it either," Frank admitted.

Molly didn't even bother to look over at him. Pulled from a sound sleep at three in the morning, he still looked as if he were headed to the tennis club for brunch, all chinos and polo shirt and tasseled loafers. The only thing that betrayed how fast he'd put himself together was the windblown look of his unbrushed hair. And damn it if it didn't make him look all the more appealing. No fewer than three of the night crew had escorted him back to where Molly was waiting.

And then the son of a bitch had done the unforgivable. He'd walked up to Molly without a word and just put his arms around her.

"You okay?" he'd asked, sounding as if he'd really meant it.

Molly went rigid. "I'm not the one with the stab wound."

Frank had pulled back as if he hadn't noticed how uncomfortable she was. "Yeah, but if I know you, you're taking it harder than Joey."

He hadn't come near her since. Molly was relieved as hell. Besides, he hadn't pulled the I-told-you-so routine yet, and Molly knew it was coming. Worse, she knew she deserved it.

"Do the police know?" he asked as she went by again.

Molly kept her attention on the passing squares of terrazo. "I told them everything. They said they were going to call Rhett anyway, since this might very well end up a homicide."

She walked faster, back and forth, until it finally dawned on her that it wasn't doing any good. That left her against the wall, right alongside Frank, her gaze on the closed doors to the surgical suite, her hands in her pockets.

"We have to tell his family."

Frank never bothered to look over. "No we don't. Joey's been stabbed before. I know how to handle this without them. He wouldn't be able to deal with it if they knew."

"But Frank, they have a right—"

"No, Molly. He's the one with the rights. And now that his sister's decamped, I'm the only one around to make sure they're protected."

"Why?" she asked. "What makes you his official guardian?"

Frank didn't seem in the least perturbed by the question. "He's my friend."

"He's a ghost, Frank. A responsibility. Something you'd have to go out of your way for."

An eyebrow crooked. "And you don't think I'm capable of that?"

"Not even good wolves perform works of charity, Patterson."

Frank looked away then, toward the surgical doors, and Molly could have sworn he seemed introspective. "I told you. He's my friend."

Molly saw it then. The hint of disquiet at the back of his eyes, the quick shudder of revulsion that she knew too well.

"Oh, no," she accused quietly. "It's more than that. You see what you might have become in him."

Frank actually chuckled. "Not what I might have become, Saint Molly. What I did become."

Molly wanted so badly to laugh in his face. "A stressed-out lawyer from the adjutant general's office who went off the deep end?"

The urge died when Frank leveled those wry blue eyes on her and she knew he wasn't kidding. "A lawyer with three young children who'd just lost his wife."

Molly wanted to look away. Hell, she wanted to run away. She hadn't signed on for this. She didn't want to know.

"Didn't you ever wonder why I was in that tacky office in north county at my age?" he asked, that humor of his returning with a vengeance, as if all of life should be this amusing. "Molly, I was in the corporate suites at Monsanto by the time I was twenty-five."

"How did she die?"

Frank waggled a finger at her. "'Ah ha', she's thinking. 'Now I understand why he went after malpractice cases.' Sorry to disappoint you. It was leukemia. She had the choice between treatment and Abigail, and she chose Abigail. I wasn't quite as sanguine about the whole thing at the time."

"I'm sorry, Frank."

Frank peered at her. "You really are, aren't you? Boy, I think I need a tape of this."

Molly damn near smiled at him. "Cherish the moment. It won't happen again."

"Nor would I want it to. Goodwill from you is unsettling."

Molly turned on her heel and resumed her pacing. She tried to think of what she had to do next, but she couldn't quite get past the picture of Frank wandering along the edges of despair with no company but grief. Molly hated that. She hated hurting all over again. She especially hated hurting for him.

She just wanted to go home. She wanted to have someone who would open the door for her and pat her hands and murmur soothing words. She wanted someone to hold her and tell her it was going to be all right, and she'd never had that in her life, considering the fact that what she was looking for was a mother.

Behind her, the doors shushed open and Molly heard tired footsteps. She whirled around again to find the trauma doc untying mask strings and scratching his chest where the cotton scrubs tended to itch and the sweat collected.

"You a relative?" he asked Frank. He already knew Molly.

"His attorney."

That brought the trauma doc to a dead stop. "You're kidding."

Frank smiled. "No kidding. He's a rich eccentric. What can you tell me about him?"

"I can tell you that he's gonna be a sick son of a bitch for a while, but he should pull through okay. I can also tell you that he looks like he's been this route before, but I think you know that already. Can you get him off the streets?"

"Nope."

A quick nod. "You know if he's HIV positive or not?"

"He's not. His choice of oblivion is alcohol, not needles."

Another nod, this one more considered. "Go on home. He's gonna be on life-support for another ten hours or so. You sure he has the money for this?"

"I'm sure."

The surgeon grinned, a tired smile on a tired man with the hands of Paganini. "In that case, we'll pull out all the stops."

Molly felt herself deflating with every word. The adrenaline of crisis died, and she was left feeling like a lump of inert material.

"How 'bout I take you home, Molly?" Frank asked.

That was when Molly noticed that the trauma doc had disappeared back in the direction of the ER without her ever saying thank-you. She'd have a chance to catch him later. Right now, she couldn't think past the fact that Joseph Ryan was still alive, no thanks to her.

"What?"

Frank had the nerve to walk up and take hold of her arm. "I'm not real sure I trust you driving right now."

Molly looked up at him, suddenly weary to death. "I quit, Frank," she said. "I thought you should be the first to know."

Damn him if he didn't smile at her. "Quit what, Molly?"

She pulled away from him and started walking on her own back toward the ER and home. "You were right. You have every reason to say 'I told you so.' So I'm doing it for you."

"Oh, that quit," he said in very patient tones as he followed amiably along. "I'll believe it when I see it."

Molly stopped. "I mean it."

"I know you do. I just don't think this is a promise you're going to keep."

For some reason Molly couldn't quite fathom, he looked regretful about it.

"They tried to kill an innocent man," she said, as if he didn't know. "They did it so I'd stop. Well, I stop."

Frank was studying her face as if waiting for something. Molly wasn't sure what it was, so she looked away. Down the long corridor, she could see the back doors to ER. The place she understood, with rules she abided by. Actions and reactions that made sense.

"What kind of people would do this, Frank?" she couldn't help but ask.

Molly knew what kind of people. She saw them every day. She'd just never been responsible, even indirectly.

"Somebody with a lot at stake, I imagine," Frank answered as if Molly had really wanted to know.

Molly thought about that. She had all the answers. Almost all the answers anyway. She just didn't know what to do with them anymore. She didn't know whom to trust with them.

"How does 800 million a year hit you?" she asked without looking at him. "That's a big enough stake?"

Frank nodded in consideration. "Yeah, I bet that'd do it for some people."

Molly sighed. The men in the van hadn't done it for 800 million. They'd done it for fun. But they'd been sent by very serious men in very serious trouble, and Molly was pretty certain she knew what it was. "In that case," she said softly, "I think it might be Argon Pharmaceutical."

Molly wasn't sure what kind of reaction she'd wanted from Frank. She was very sure, however, that she didn't want laughter. Which was probably the sole reason Frank Patterson laughed.

Molly spun around to see something very close to sadness in his eyes as he shook his head at her. "See what I mean?" he said. "You keep at it, Saint Molly of the Battlefield, no matter what anybody else says."

"What's so funny?"

"A few vital facts are becoming clear to me. You figuring on telling anybody but me?"

"I don't know. Why?"

He was standing there, his weight on one hip, arms crossed, waiting for her to figure something out. When she didn't, he just shook his head again. "I guess you haven't gotten back to that part of your notes yet. Which means you don't remember one of the companies Peg was on retainer for."

The minute he said it, she remembered. "Argon?"

Frank nodded.

"That's where it starts then," Molly said, not sure yet whether the information made her feel better or worse. "We were right. It wasn't with Pearl. It was with Peg. It was something she got from Argon. My God, Frank, do you know what this means?"

"It means that I'm officially out of your loop. Three days ago, the firm put me on the Argon account."

"So?"

"So, I am barred by attorney-client privilege from revealing anything I know that would jeopardize the company in any way. I can't do anything to help."

That one damn near stopped Molly in her tracks. "Do you know what's going on? Is that what you're trying to tell me?"

"I'm telling you that even if I did, I couldn't reveal it to you. It's a felony offense, Molly. You should know that. Didn't you read *The Firm* like everybody else in America?"

"You did that knowing that I thought Transcend was the problem?"

"I did that before I ever heard the word *Transcend.* I still haven't seen anything on the company, just the notice about my new responsibilities. I'm sorry, Molly. Whatever you do, I can't help anymore. Not in any way."

Now Molly did know how she felt. She felt furious.

"Do you want me to tell you exactly what they did to Joey, Frank?"

"It doesn't matter, Molly."

Damn him for looking more sincere than she'd ever seen him. Damn him for doing this to her.

"They put you on the case for that specific reason, you know."

"That doesn't matter either."

Molly tried to find some kind of reprieve in Frank's expression. Those spectacular blue eyes were closed off, though. Decided. Finished. Molly shouldn't have been surprised. She was, though, damn it. She was disappointed.

"So I guess I was right in the first place," she said. "I quit. You can let them know that for me when you see them."

Then she just turned and walked away.

"Molly!"

Molly didn't stop. It figured, Frank followed as if she just hadn't heard him.

"She wasn't worth it."

That got her. Molly stopped dead on a heel and spun around to find Frank standing four square behind her.

"I don't know about the other lawyers," he said. "I didn't know them. But you're wasting your time on Peg. She played too hard and skirted too many corners. She probably deserved what she got."

Molly was stunned to her toes with the fury she felt. He looked so bland and harmless standing there, as if he really couldn't have said what he just did. "She took care of her brother."

Frank shrugged. "Everybody needs to be redeemed, Saint Molly. It's what gets all the real work done in this world. Joey was her redemption."

"Remind me to say the same for you when you turn up dead."

"I wouldn't expect any less. Although, in my case the password to my diary would read Elizabeth, not Joey."

"Elizabeth?"

He grinned. "The woman who chose Abigail over me."

Molly couldn't help it. She had to hurt him. "Wise choice."

"Yeah," he said, perfectly sincere and making her hate him. "It was. Just took me a while to find out. Remember Peg by Joey, not by the rest."

"It sounds like you're the one who can't figure out how to remember her, not me."

By the time Molly got home, the sun was struggling up through a haze of humidity and pollution. The grass sparkled pink and crystal with the dew, and a thousand birds greeted her from the trees as she pulled up.

She didn't notice. She could barely put one foot in front of the other as she walked up to the door and let herself in. She didn't realize that Magnum had behaved, or that he refused to leave the house until he'd licked her face, those huge, sad eyes of his watching her all the while. She didn't listen to the pond in the back or smell her roses that bloomed in the corner or feel how cool and damp the morning air was against her skin. She walked back into the kitchen to make herself some tea, only this time, when she thought about putting vodka in it, she didn't stop.

By the time Sam showed up two hours later, a quarter of the bottle was gone and Molly had made it as far as the family room.

"I came to ask how that poor boy was," he said, peering down at her where she sat curled up in her favorite armchair, the tea long gone and the vodka being drunk straight out of the mug. "I think I should ask the same of you."

"Want some tea, Sam?" she asked, not bothering to face him.

With a groan like metal stressing, Sam lowered himself onto the couch. In the corner the TV was turned to the "Today Show," but the sound was off, so that Willard Scott simply looked like his pants were too hot. "No. Not this morning. He died, that boy?"

Molly took another sip from her almost-empty tea cup. "No. He didn't die."

Sam nodded. "*Gottenyu*, this is good. It would have been a terrible thing. And you? How are you doing?"

Molly didn't bother to lift her head off the back of the chair. "I'm tired, Sam."

Sam gave her one of those peculiarly Jewish nods that seemed to carry entire trains of thought and opinion. "You knew him, then?"

Molly sighed. "I know him. He's hurt because I've been trying to be a hero."

This seemed to deserve a clucking sound. "Nonsense. He was hurt because there are evil men out there."

Molly took another sip of her vodka and thought about how much she'd missed that feeling of fire in her throat, the cold, sweet hit of numbness.

"Well, I'll tell you what. The evil men sure took this round."

For a minute Sam just peered at her. Then, yanking his cigarettes out of his pocket, he hauled himself to his feet and toward the kitchen. "Maybe I'll have tea after all."

Molly just nodded.

"It's this suicide business, *nu*?" he asked as he clattered around at her stove, the cigarette already lit and producing toxic clouds.

Molly went right on sipping. On the screen, Katie Couric was leaning toward some silicone-inflated blond who looked as if she'd run mouth-first into a wasp's nest. Obviously the latest in the thinking man's women.

"It's the suicides."

"And you still think they're not right?"

Molly wanted to laugh. "I think they're not right."

He appeared back in the doorway, a shriveled, squat old man who looked like an intruding gnome in the elegance of the Burke household. Molly liked the image. As if he were a household god from ancient times come to reacquaint the present with its baser beginnings.

"Did those five people commit suicide?"

"Yes."

He carried his mug over to the chair and carefully bent to pick up her vodka bottle. For a second, Molly thought he was going to take it away. He only wanted his share, though.

"And does this thing that isn't right affect more people than just these five unfortunates?"

"Yeah, Sam. I think it does. I think it might affect a lot of people."

"Why?"

"I think there's something wrong with a drug that's being tested and the company doesn't want anybody to find out."

"Like what?"

"Well, you invest in pharmaceuticals. What do you think would happen if a company found a drug that could put them right at the top of a very big heap. They develop it, spend a fortune publicizing it as the new, revolutionary drug that would undoubtedly take over as the number one–prescribed medication in the world, bringing in revenues probably well in excess of a billion dollars a year. And all the while they realize that there's something wrong with it."

"I think that if I were the head of the company, I'd try and keep that news to myself for as long as I could."

Molly opened her eyes, surprised. What she found was the man Sam used to be sitting on her couch, the corporate chief with a razor intelligence and carnivorous ambition.

"But people would be at risk."

Sam placidly sipped at his tea. "You're talking about a worldwide company, *nu?* Big investments, big lay-outs. If they could hold on for six months with the drug doing the business they thought it would, they'd still be rich and they could still pull out."

Molly couldn't manage to close her mouth. "Six months."

"Of course. After that time, all they have to say is that the side effects didn't show up in their trials. Then they can forestall the inevitable for as long as possible by promising studies and investigations. Presto, another fortune until the drug eventually just disappears from the market."

"You're not a virgin at this, Sam."

He grinned. "Hardly. The other popular thing, of course, is a simple warning about rare side effects on the medicine bottle. Have you read one of those things lately?"

"Oh yeah, that'd work," Molly retorted. "They're marketing this stuff to general physicians. If this thing has contraindications, how soon do you think the docs are going to find out?"

Sam's hoary eyebrows raised like humored question marks. "You mean these doctors don't learn about a drug before they give it?"

Molly did laugh then. "Are you kidding? With all the new drugs out there and all the drug companies pushing them like fast-food, all most doctors get is a quick sell, a free gift, and the drug company's own write-up in the *Physician's Desk Reference* on drugs that tells them that side effects are minimal. It's an old song, but a popular verse."

Sam started clucking again, this time amused. "Such a cynic, you are."

"You're the one who can't afford your own medicine."

"I'm also the one who gets steady income from the conglomerates who make them. Could I ask, by the way, which company I maybe shouldn't be investing in?"

"Argon."

Sam seemed to have been waiting for that. *"Gevalt!"* He sighed, sucking down the rest of his tea.

Molly didn't necessarily know Yiddish, but she knew that tone of voice. "A brand name you obviously didn't want to hear."

Sam was watching Katie Couric himself now. "Did you know the stock went up four points this week?"

"I know."

Sam considered the empty condition of his mug. "I've watched that stock for a year waiting for this time. This new drug is going to help me keep Myra and myself in our nice homes."

Molly didn't have anything to say. So she picked up the vodka bottle and just poured another dose for both herself and Sam. "Well, don't worry about it yet. I seem to have been cut off at the pass, Sam."

For a second, silence, as Sam worked through the problem. "Just what seems to be wrong with this drug?"

"I don't know. Enough to send five people to their deaths in a matter of a month, though."

The phone began to ring. Molly had no intentions of answering it. Unfortunately, it was Sam who was sitting next to it.

"You had a call out to someone at a tox lab?" he asked, handing over the receiver.

Molly stared at the phone as if it could bite. She was sure she'd wanted this news yesterday. Maybe the day before. She sure as hell didn't want it now, because now she was sure what it was going to be.

"You want me to tell her you're under the weather?" Sam asked.

"No." Molly took the phone and prepared herself for the worst.

"You win," the tech told her.

"A matter of opinion," Molly had to answer. "I was right then?"

"I got the final results just now. At least qualitatively. All five suicides were on synapsapine."

Obviously the tech was waiting for some kind of excitement. Molly just closed her eyes.

"So, what do we do now, Molly?"

Nothing. We sit here in the corner until this all passes over. Until some other schmuck finds out that synapsapine can be dangerous and takes the company to trial. After the drug's been on the market six months and Sam and Myra's future is safe and no more of Molly's acquaintances are hurt.

"I'll get back to you."

"You want me to find out more?"

"No. Keep it under your hat for now. Just send me a copy of the results, okay?"

"Okay."

For a long time Molly sat with the phone in her lap, her attention drawn from the TV to the Picasso on the far wall. All jagged edges, open mouths, and huge, naillike tears. Painted during one of his more violent divorces, all hard line and muscle and raw emotion. Bought as an investment, hidden away where the Burkes wouldn't have to see it, since none of the other Burkes had ever really made use of a family room or violent emotions.

"So?" Sam said. "What do we do?"

Molly looked over at him plumped on the edge of her couch like a lumpy cat. She thought about how the vodka she'd already had seemed to weight her to her chair. It was so seductively easy. Just sit here until everybody forgot where she was. Just keep her eyes on the television, because nothing really happened on the television anyway. She could hypnotize herself with vodka and sitcoms until she grew moss.

"I have to call Rhett," she said.

"Rhett?" Sam echoed. "That police detective who looks like Andy Hardy?"

"Yeah."

Sam nodded. He, too, looked over toward the Picasso. He seemed to study it as if it were entrails predicting the future. "I think," he said softly, "I'm going to have to sell my stock."

Molly didn't know how she'd come to her decision. She just knew that Sam was right, and she'd do anything in the world to keep from putting that old man in peril.

"I haven't really decided anything, Sam," she lied. "I'm just going to check with him."

With a harrumph and an odd sighing sound, Sam pushed himself to his feet. Before he left, though, he walked over and bent down to pick up Molly's hands. He held them in his own, patting them like a parent and smiling for her. "You've decided. Get these *chozzerim.* Just don't let them get you."

Molly couldn't move. "I'm sorry, Sam."

He just waved off her apology and headed for the back door. "Don't be silly. You think I haven't come back before? Now, you call Mr. Hardy and I'll call my broker. It's a beautiful day out, *nu?*"

Molly called Rhett, but he wasn't in. She called the FBI, but they weren't interested in her anymore. Yes, they said, they knew that a friend of hers had been attacked. But the men they were following had all been under surveillance and therefore incapable of committing the crime. So, they said, take it up with the police.

Molly was getting set to call Gene when the phone rang. The raspy, smoky voice on the other end was easily recognized.

"Ms. Burke, this is Peg Ryan's secretary, Marsha Trenton."

"Yes, I remember. How are you doing?"

"Oh, I'm okay, I guess. Look, I'm not sure why I'm doing this, but Frank Patterson asked me to give you a call."

Molly didn't know whether to be interested or angry. She was doing her best to negate the effects of early morning alcohol with a couple of protein-loaded sandwiches and raw soda, and she still wasn't really sure whether she was still trying to figure out what was going on or just tying up loose ends. Even so, Molly had always been taught to be polite.

"Of course. What can I do for you?"

"Well, it's Peg's family. They called in asking about her daykeeper. The house was robbed, evidently, and all Peg's other personal items were missing. It seems this is all they have left, and they, uh, were wondering if you were finished yet."

"Oh, yes." Molly looked into the playroom where she'd left the big black leather binder on her end table. "Sure. I can . . ."

She'd been through it twice and found nothing more interesting than *a meeting*. Since it finally dawned her that that had meant Argon meeting, she had nothing else to go on but that damn computer disk full of case notations about defective incubators.

"I can come by and pick it up if you want," the woman said in a tone that betrayed just how anxious she was to do that.

"No, that's okay. I know where they live. Listen, Marsha, I was wondering. You were Peg's secretary. Do you know if she kept a personal journal or anything?"

"Oh, sure. She was always entering notes to herself. I imagine that's gone, now, though. We gave that stuff to her parents."

Gone. As in wiped clean. "Um, could you tell me if her computer at work suffered any . . . um, did you lose any of her files?"

"Funny you should say that. All her personal stuff was gone. I went to look right after she died."

Just like Peter VanAck's personal computer at home where he kept his personal notes. So she'd been right. It hadn't been just a terrible coincidence after all. Molly wondered how many of the victims had lost their files or had their computers accessed and wiped clean. She wondered what kind of organization was that big, that powerful, and that paranoid that they would consider going to those kind of lengths.

Peg had kept a diary. And then it had been stolen.

"That's too bad," Molly admitted. "Do you know what it looked like?"

"What?"

"Her diary."

"It didn't look like anything. She kept it on disk."

"Then it's gone for sure. I didn't see anything like it in her things that first day I was there."

"Oh, it isn't labeled 'my diary' or anything. She had it mislabeled so nobody'd peek into her stuff."

"Mislabeled?"

"Yep. I saw her do it myself. Put 'Veldux Notes' on the front because she said it was so boring nobody'd think to look at it."

Her personal notes. Something that might track her psychological decline. Something that might identify where she got the Transcend, why she took it, what it had done to her.

Under the label "Veldux Notes."

"Hold on a second."

Molly dropped the phone and ran for that black binder. She almost hoped she'd find it empty, just like she'd found Peter VanAck's computer. It would have been easier. It would have been safer.

It was there, tucked into the back leather cover, just as it had always been. The ticking bomb somebody had been trying to pull out before it was found.

Molly returned to the phone. "Marsha, if you talk to Peg's family before I get there, tell them I'll be by as soon as I can, okay?"

"Yeah, sure."

Molly forgot the protein. She slammed down some antacid instead and headed upstairs to change for work.

"What are you doing on my computer?" Sasha demanded. "Come to think of it, what the hell are you doing here at all? You're not scheduled tonight."

Molly didn't bother to look up from the screen. "I don't have a computer at home. I'll be just a minute. I swear."

"As long as you tell me what's going on."

"Maybe an answer to what's been going on around here. Maybe nothing."

Molly slid in the disk and punched in the command to read drive B. With just a flutter of sound, the screen scrolled up a menu that was nearly forty items long. The first item on the list was Argon Notes. The last was, ingenuously enough, My Diary.

"Son of a bitch," Molly muttered, too afraid to go on.

Sasha peered over her shoulder. "What is it?"

"It might be the answer to why people keep getting hurt around me."

Molly flipped a mental coin and chose the diary first. The computer chuckled a little and then fed her a line.

Password.

"Password?" Molly blinked, her fragile enthusiasm threatening to crash. "I need a password?"

"Welcome to the twentieth century, hon," Sasha said to her dryly as she pulled out a cigarette and switched on the small smoke filter on her desk at the same time. "This is called protection."

Molly punched up Argon Notes, then Veldux Notes. Each denied her access with a simple request: *Password.*

"Shit," she snapped, smacking the keyboard. "There's got to be some way. Somebody must know . . ."

Password. Password. She'd just heard something like that. Something about the password on my diary . . .

Molly sat up straighter. She tried very hard not to hope, because she remembered. *The password on my diary would read Elizabeth, not Joey.*

It hadn't connected at the time what a strange thing that had been to say. It connected now. Her hands trembling, Molly typed in Joey and waited.

The computer hummed and clicked. Lights blinked and senseless code scrolled down the screen. And suddenly, like a gift from a genie, there it was. Peg's diary. And there, right on the opening page, was the proof Molly had found that she'd been right all along.

✦ Chapter 19 ✦

WHAT MOLLY FOUND was Peg Ryan's suicide note.

Peg had left it right on the first page of the diary, a personal apology to her mother she evidently hoped the people who found her would never discover. Or maybe, that even she hoped her mother would never find.

Mom. I thought that this was where I'd say I'm sorry, since you know how fond I've always been of diaries. This is my last entry. I'm sorry. I've done stupid things in my life, but nothing this stupid. Some of my friends are already gone, and I can't think of anything to do but join them. I can't stop and I can't go on. I always thought I'd have time to correct my mistakes, but Transcend doesn't give you any time. It takes everything, and I'm the one who found it. I'm the one who gave it to my friends. I'm the one who made them all die.

Try and understand. Peg.

Molly had had it all along. Now that she saw it, she still couldn't quite believe it.

"Jesus, Mary, and Joseph," Sasha murmured over Molly's shoulder. "Is this on the level?"

Molly turned on her charge nurse. "Don't tell anybody. Not till I know what to do about this."

Sasha actually looked a little dazed. "This is very hot stuff. The crows are going to want it."

"Especially the crows at Argon. I wonder how long they've known."

Sasha took another look at the notes on the screen and shook her head. "Don't be stupid. They've known all along."

Molly was looking the same way. "But if the stuff is this deadly, how can the testing be so benign?"

"Ask the pharmacy."

"I asked. I got a great company line. Transcend is the way of the future. Transcend will change our lives."

"I'm not talking real pharmacy, which gets a good deal of its funding from running tests just like this one. I'm talking James."

For the first time in at least twenty-four hours, Molly smiled. James. Of course. The evening supervisor with the taste for reggae and simple carbohydrates. If anybody would tell Molly the truth, it would be James.

She checked her watch. "He won't be here for another couple of hours. I have to finish reading this."

"Not here you don't. Borrow my portable and hide."

Molly looked up and thought about how open this room was. How she didn't want Sasha to suffer for helping. As quickly as the hospital grapevine worked, it would be all the way to the administrative offices in an hour that Molly was using Sasha's hospital computer to sabotage a very valuable drug test. And who knew, these days, just who else might be listening in on the hospital grapevine?

"I don't suppose you have any spare disks on you," Molly asked.

"Not a one."

Molly sighed. "I make a hell of a spy. I don't even come prepared."

Itching to find out what else was on Peg's disk, Molly grabbed Sasha's computer and locked herself back in the last doctor's call room, where she had access to the equipment she needed and the security of knowing that nobody would think to look there for a nurse. First she pulled up the diary. After that, once she'd talked to James, she would go through the notes on Argon. Who knew what Peg had put in there for somebody to find? Who knew whether she'd deliberately thought of a way to bring the company down after her death?

The first entries were innocuous. Musings on the firm, on success, financial gain, and the lure of dark clubs and fast men. It was along about spring that Molly found her first surprise.

Peg Ryan had not been assigned to the Argon account. Peg Ryan had brought the Argon account to the firm. And the person who had introduced her to the Argon brass had been none other than City Councilman Tim McGuire.

Sweaty, ineffectual Tim has a purpose in life after all. After putting up with him at Shitkickers for almost four months, he came through yesterday by introducing me to a couple of his classmates from Country Day who just happen to be heirs to the Argon fortune. Chemistry is good. I like their connections, they like my aggression. Tim says the Argon stock is going to be the investment of the century. Maybe. I'm more interested in the company retainer and the heir's ass.

Tim McGuire. Who could have guessed?

Tim McGuire, who always seemed to be around when something went wrong with the office. Tim McGuire, who had shown up at the building with no visible pretext, right about the time Pearl's file had disappeared.

Molly stopped dead in her tracks. This was stupid. She might as well just put herself up for the Oliver Stone Conspiracy Theory Award. After all, she'd just made her second giant leap back across the chasm.

But what if Tim were involved? Who better to throw up a convenient smoke screen by slipping out with an important file and then pointing fingers at the one person in the office who was going to cause trouble? And not to the gambling consortium. They were already under fairly well-known scrutiny by federal officers without humor. To the people involved with Transcend.

It was ridiculous.

It was just as plausible as anything else that had happened.

Molly needed a little more proof to take to Kevin. She needed some kind of smoking gun with Tim McGuire's fingerprints on it. She bent back to her reading to see if she could find it.

Molly was sure she'd only meant to skim Peg's diary. After all, what she really needed to see was the notes on the Argon transactions. Before she knew it, though, she'd been reading for two hours as Peg Ryan took her through the classic course of an addiction, the more unnerving description of the peculiarly intense Transcend reaction. From April to August the notes changed, following discovery, intoxication, addiction, and death. From exhilaration to megalomania to despair.

Several people had remarked to Molly that the suicide victims had seemed like developing manic-depressives. Intense highs and then intense lows. Maybe they had been, although these wild swings seemed to originate with the drug, like a longer, higher, headier hit of crack that came down even harder.

As Molly read Peg's journal, she also got her first real feel for the woman she'd found on the bathroom floor. Peg had been a risk-taker, a thrill-seeker. The youngest in a family of caregivers, the one who had been given all the care, Peg had never learned consequence. She'd worked her cases like video games and considered her parents almost laughably out of touch, only living with them because she hadn't yet learned how to move beyond immediate gratification. So when she'd found this new, potent high unlike any other she'd dabbled with, she'd embraced it like Babe Ruth had embraced baseball.

Is this a great job or what? Molly read from a June entry. *Not only do I get the company perks but the private ones as well. I owe Randy for slipping me the pills. I've never felt so high in my life, and I've done high in all kinds of different languages.*

So Frank Patterson had been right.

But there were also notes about Joe. About finding him after thinking all those years that he was dead. About visiting him, coordinating with Frank for his care, listening to his terrors and gentling his nightmares. Peg had honored his wish not to tell her parents about him even as she'd vilified those same parents for deserting the son they were supposed to have loved without condition.

I went looking for his military records today to try and get him benefits. He had the Silver Star and two Purple Hearts. They never said anything about that. Never. Like the life he's living negates what he's been. I guess the same goes for being their son, too. I wonder how he can forgive them. I can't.

So Frank Patterson had been wrong, too.

For the first time, Molly felt as if she knew the face

of one of her suicide victims. Molly walked alongside this phantom as she took inexorable steps to her own doom. First the challenge, then the thrill, then the confusion, finally the inevitability.

God, what's going on? How could Pearlie have done that to us? We were waiting for her, so we could share the triumph, and she was dying. Just like Peter. Just like Aaron. I can't believe it. I just can't believe it anymore.

In the end, not only had Transcend been a lie, it had been a lie Peg Ryan hadn't been able to escape.

The perfect drug for the nineties. This would make Argon the new Colombian cartel.

Molly knew that this journal alone might well scuttle the drug's future. All she had to do was print it out and give it to the press.

That made her smile. The same snapping dogs who wouldn't give her a moment's rest, would now be put to good use. Let them go after Argon instead.

But first, she had to get the rest of her information. Molly checked her watch and realized that James was due on his shift. Visiting hours were also on in the units. She'd take a break. Visit Joey and visit James. And then she'd get back to Argon Pharmaceutical.

Good thing she'd moved into the call room. Molly spent ten minutes figuring out how to work the equipment and another five using it to save the files. Then, closing the computer, she got up, grabbed her purse, and slipped on the lab coat that was her hospital camouflage. Taking one last look around to make sure she hadn't left anything behind, Molly slid the disk into her pocket and unlocked the door.

Joey was asleep when Molly saw him. Sedated and restrained so he couldn't hurt himself, a desiccated husk wound in tubes and tape. One look at him negated any lingering high the discovery of Peg's journal had produced.

"He okay?" Molly asked the nurse who was caring for him.

"Him? Oh yeah, sure. It's against the rules of trauma for homeless guys to die from stab wounds. Only young mothers and priests do that."

Molly didn't bother to lecture the nurse about Joe being a human. She'd made the same kind of off-the-cuff assessments herself, especially after a long shift when it seemed that only the hopeless got better and the good people sank like rocks.

"His name is Joey," she said instead. "You'll probably get better response from him if you try it."

The nurse looked up. "He's listed as a John Doe. You know him?"

"He comes in downstairs sometimes. He's a really nice guy. Harmless."

That the nurse responded to. "He does apologize when he's spitting on us," she admitted as she pulled a roll of two-inch surgical tape from her pocket.

Pulling out a marker, she wrote J-O-E-Y in big letters across the tape to be put on the headboard where everybody could see it.

"You might also try Sarge. That's what the other guys call him."

"Thanks."

Molly nodded, not sure what she'd accomplished, not even sure anymore what she'd wanted here. She was walking out of the unit when she saw Frank getting off the elevators.

"Out performing your corporal works of mercy, I see," he greeted her.

From anybody else, that line would have been

offensive. When Frank said it, though, he smiled that outrageous smile that sapped all insult.

For the first time since Molly had known him, he looked tired. Molly knew the feeling. Cocking her head to consider this new Frank Patterson, she shoved her hands in her pockets so she could feel the disk safe in her fingers. "Corporal works of mercy are my job, Frank. You're the one out of your environment."

"I was here last night."

"Yes," Molly answered. "You were. I remember because you said something that didn't make much sense at the time. Funny how that all changes."

Oddly enough, that seemed to take even more out of Frank. "You found it, then."

"I found it. Wanna know what it says?"

He raised a hand. "No. Not in my lifetime. I also have a feeling that this is a personal effect you won't want to share with Peg's mother."

"We may not have a choice."

A dull flush crept up Frank's neck. "You're not going to hurt those people again."

Molly raised an eyebrow. "Really? You think Mrs. Ryan would prefer to risk a lot of lives than find out that her daughter wasn't what she thought? But then, she's already sacrificed her son for the same reason, hasn't she?"

Now it was Frank who shoved hands in pockets, into the slacks of his Armani suit. Some things, it seemed, never changed. "There's very little in this world I respect, Saint Molly . . ."

"That I'll swear to."

He shifted on his feet, changed tack. "You could at least wait a while."

"Those tests are just about finished, Frank, which means the drug's about ready to go out onto the market. Exactly what would you like me to wait for?"

That was when she got the smile. "I know it's something we can work out, Saint Molly."

Molly's expression was dust dry. "So, you're telling me once again that you've asked me to do something you really didn't want me to do in the first place."

One hand came out of a pocket to be leveled at her as if she were a hostile witness. "I did *not* ask you to do anything," he informed her quite clearly, even though the edges of his mouth were suspiciously crooked. "Am I clear about this?"

Molly crooked her lips right back at him. "You didn't give me the answer to a riddle last night?"

"Not under any circumstance. That kind of behavior might violate my attorney-client relationship, of which I'm very fond."

"And you want me to wait before I don't do anything about this riddle you didn't give me that has to do with a request you know nothing about."

He beamed like a teacher who'd just found the one child who really understands algebra. "Exactly."

Molly nodded to herself. What a frustrating, obtuse, obstinate . . . frustrating man. How the hell could he keep making her smile, just so he could ambush her all over again? How the hell could she keep letting him get away with it?

"Tell you what, Frank," she finally said, not having the guts to look him in the face for fear of wanting to smile again. "I have someone to see right now. I think it's going to be a long appointment. Then I have some . . . reading to do, which will probably last until tomorrow, after which I have to pull a late shift. I still have some people to call for proof to back up my . . . reading. Only then will I be able to let you know when I'm going to do what you didn't ask me to do."

"You're going to be home tonight?"

Molly's head shot up. The topic of conversation had just made a major shift. "What's that got to do with anything?"

Molly could tell just by the look on Frank's face what it had to do with, and she was definitely not in the mood for that. Even if she'd been interested. Which she wasn't. Not as long as he had been the Wiedemans' lawyer. Not as long as he was Frank Patterson.

"We can talk about it then," he offered.

"Sure, Frank. Just remember that I carry my stun gun with me at all times to ward off people I don't want in my house. Go visit your friend. Then go home and figure out what you're going to do about your attorney-client relationship."

"Do?" he retorted with delight. "Don't be ridiculous, Saint Molly. I'm not going to do anything. Do you realize what kind of legal fees we're going to start amassing the minute you put on your Joan of Arc outfit? I'll invite you to the weekend home on the coast."

And then, before she could react, he turned for the intensive care unit. "Oh, Saint Molly," he called over his shoulder, "exactly when was it that you were going to quit?"

Molly didn't deign to answer him. She had a pharmacist to see.

The main hospital pharmacy was located as far away from the front door as possible, the idea being that impulsive gang-bangers couldn't accidently trip over it and cause mayhem trying to get what was inside. The hospital had done such a good job of hiding it, however, that new staff took an average of four months to be able to find it when they did need it.

Molly got off in the sub-subbasement level and passed the morgue, purchasing, a now-defunct laundry, and the boiler room. She knew she was nearing home when she heard the infectious rhythm of Bob Marley and smelled the coffee. The pharmacy was also far enough out of the way that supervisors wouldn't be inclined to visit and crack down on rule violations.

"James," she called into the little metallic speaker set into the wall that reminded her of the one at Jack-in-the-Box. "Can I talk to you?"

"What's the password, babe?"

Suddenly there were passwords everywhere, Molly thought. "The password is, 'I, James, would like to know that I will be cared for if I'm ever unfortunate enough to need emergency care in this hospital.'"

The door buzzed and Molly walked in.

James grinned, exposing his prize gold crown. "Oh, it's you, Miss Molly. Whatchyou need?"

"James." She greeted him with the best smile she could come up with. "I need some real skinny."

James grinned and danced back to where he'd been working with three other techs to fill stat orders. "You come to the right place. You got my askin' price?"

Without a word, Molly handed over three Ding Dongs and a Hostess Cupcake. James smiled and nodded and bounced to the beat. "I'm all yours, Miss Molly. What can I do?"

"Transcend," she said and waited for the moment of truth.

James laughed so hard she thought he was going to fall over. The other techs, protected from his music by earphones of their own, briefly looked up, then back to their work.

"You want some?" James asked.

"Can you get it for me?"

"Can I? Yes. Will I? No."

"Why not?"

"You don't need that shit, Miss Molly. You want a real buzz, you do Ding Dongs like you friend James."

"I'm not even up to Ding Dongs these days," she admitted, perching herself on a stool alongside his. "Tell me, though. If this stuff is on such a tight trial, how can you get it?"

"Not from here. From there."

"The company?"

"Sure. I hear it's some of the Argons theyselves."

Molly rubbed at her head. The sons and heirs, one of whom, evidently, was named Randy. She wanted to hurt the little bastards.

"What do you know about it, James?" she asked. "I want to know what the literature isn't telling me."

"You want to know that," he said, "call the FDA. They got all the reports of side effects."

"So do you."

James didn't even look up from where he was doling out Lasix ampules into packets that could be tubed up to the units. "Why you wanna know?" he asked.

"Because I think people are dying on this stuff, and if somebody doesn't do something, it's going to be the biggest seller on the market. Which means there are gonna be a lotta dead people."

James was nodding now, still counting and checking. "You know how trials are really run, Miss Molly?"

"Tell me."

"Well, first they screen patients for the healthiest sick people they can find to put on this stuff so they results look good. You seen the ads on TV for people needin' free medicine. That's you trial base. Okay, so they start testing. What they do is, if they come up with side effects in a preliminary trial, they just make sure they don't give the drug to anybody who might respond bad after that. Say, they got a heart medicine spikes blood pressures. Well, they make sure they don't give it after that in they trials to nobody with high blood pressure. Whammo! This stuff gets safer and safer until it's like givin' sugar water."

"And what are the restrictions on Transcend?"

James laughed again. Then he simply got off his stool and walked over to where the regulation binders were kept on the shelving by the wall. "Here," he said. "You read it yourself."

Molly received the trial instructions and began to read the list of contraindications for patient participation. In addition to the usual age, pregnancy, and heart and preexisting medical conditions, the following were included:

Manic-depressive disorder.

Aggressive pathology.

Hormone-related pathology

Organic Brain Syndrome with violent behavior

"Aggression," Molly murmured. "Why aggression?"

James shrugged. "Who am I to ask?"

"I'm pretty sure there were five basically healthy people who killed themselves on this stuff. We got a whole series of trials where I hear that nothing like that ever happened. What was the difference?"

"Could be that healthy part. Like Haldol, you know. You give Haldol to a crazy and they get better. You give it to a healthy person, they see flying monkeys."

Molly nodded, even though she knew there had to be more. Because if there weren't more, there wouldn't be people attacking her.

"Of course," he said all on his own, "you gotta understand that drug studies are real good at finding preexisting conditions to blame stuff on. Like, Oh, did this poor man try and shoot up a post office on our antidepressant? Well, he had some alcohol on board. The alcohol done turned him bad. Or, this guy on the antihypertensive drug suddenly drops dead of an arrhythmia, well, he had a history of smoking. Probably that instead o' the medicine, and that's how it's put in the literature."

"I get the message."

"We also doin' a study on the new Alzheimer's prevention. Wan' me to tell you 'bout that one?"

Molly sighed. "No. I think I've had more than enough."

"One other thing you should know. This hospital ain' gonna sing you praises you get Argon in trouble. Those drug trials bring lots of money, ya know."

"I know. Thanks, James."

She was all set to head back upstairs.

"Not to mention everybody who's invested in the stock."

She paused. "Everybody?"

James bit into a Ding Dong and nodded. "Sure. It common knowledge this gonna be the windfall of the century. Lotsa people involved in the study goin' through Dr. Frost to get some stock. Ha'n't he asked you yet?"

"You're kidding. Who's invested?"

James wagged a half-eaten lunch treat at her. "You kiddin'? Pharmacy supervisor, psych supervisor—"

"Haldol Harlow?"

"Same same. Yours truly, Dr. Banerjee—he runnin' the study, ya know. I think he sank a big chunk in. Couple of the residents, Chernobyl up in you ER. Only one I heard for sure turned it down is old Clean Gene."

"What?" Molly was stunned. "Sasha invested in this?"

James was still on his earlier train of thought. "Folks think he a little too Robin Hood for this place, ya know? Don' seem to find a need to share in the profit. Happy enough bein' the boss, I guess."

"James," Molly persisted. "You said that Sasha Petrovich is investing with Lance Frost?"

James blinked as if coming up from underwater. "Tha's what I said, i'n't it?"

Molly opened her mouth to say something. She found she had nothing to say.

Sasha. She'd never said a word. Never even hinted at the fact that she might have a hell of a financial stake in this herself.

And not just Sasha. All kinds of people investing with Lance. Another whole layer of big business Molly hadn't even suspected. No wonder she'd spent all these years as a floor nurse. She just didn't have the Machiavellian bent to anticipate stuff like this. And if she couldn't do that, chances are, she never would have made a supervisor.

"They's still time to get in," James said. "Just ask Dr. Frost."

Molly hopped off her stool and reached across to steal a dose pack of antacid. "My advice, James? Invest in computers."

James finished off the second Ding Dong and tossed two more dose packs at Molly for her trouble. "I can get out anytime," he told her. "I already made a sweet five thousand on that gain this week. Thanks for the warning, though."

By the time she reached the ER, Molly felt as if she'd been caught in an undertow. A couple of weeks ago she'd started with a simple question. Why would lawyers be dying at such a fast rate? Suddenly she was considering the notion that everybody but her was involved in this thing. She was beginning to feel like the guy who tried to take a swallow out of a spittoon.

She wanted to get back to the disk. She wanted the answers she was sure Peg Ryan had kept. There was just too big a discrepancy between what was showing up on those drug trials and what she'd read in Peg Ryan's journal. There was a question about why the trials had excluded any condition associated with aggression. And then there was the question of how the same people who ran those trials figured that this drug was going to be the Prozac of the twenty-first century if they wouldn't be able to give it to anybody who was violent.

Or did they plan on letting that information out?

Tomorrow she'd call the FDA. She'd call Rhett, and she'd call the FBI. But right now, she had to get home. She had to get away from this place.

Molly found Sasha rearranging the flow board for evening shift.

"Would you mind if I borrowed your portable?" she asked.

Sasha turned to consider her, eyes sharp. "You realize that you're going through more mood swings than a pregnant teenager?"

Molly did her best to straighten back up, as if she really felt well. "It's been an up-and-down couple of days," she said.

Sasha rested a hand on her hip. "Then you found something in the rest of that disk."

"I found out a lot of things. You wouldn't have thought to mention to me that you'd invested in this stuff, would you?"

Sasha was unconcerned. "And you tell me where all your investments are?"

Molly laughed. "I have no investments."

Just to the left of the flow board, the door to room

eleven opened and Lance Frost stepped out. "I thought that was you I saw. Got a minute?"

Molly was still faced off with Sasha, who evidently didn't feel the need to react.

"What do you want, Lance?"

"Well," he said, rubbing again at that belly that strained every button on his faded madras shirt, "I just thought I'd let you know. You're running out of time if you want to get in on the deal of the century. You said you were interested, ya know."

"I know. Can I get back to you?"

"I guess. By the way, wasn't that Frank Patterson I saw you with last night?"

Molly answered before she considered. "Yeah."

She was already turning around when Lance hit her with the kicker. "Would you tell him to give me a call? The broker's waiting on his check."

Molly completely stopped breathing. "What?"

"His check. For more shares." Lance laughed, and Molly saw tiny shreds of lunch still caught in his teeth. "I'm telling you, this hospital's gonna own a majority share in Argon before this is all over. Not counting the lawyers, of course."

But Molly was once again caught on the pertinent question. "You know Frank Patterson?"

"Sure. From the MAC. Didn't he tell you?"

"Why's he investing with you?" Molly asked. "Doesn't a big shot like him have his own investment guys?"

"I guess. He said he just thought it would be easier to do this through me. Since I have the connections."

And since Frank was on the legal team. Molly's head felt as if it were going to explode. Why the hell would Frank lower himself to deal with Lance the Loser? Why would he hide that information from her?

"What are you getting out of all this?" she asked Lance.

"Part of the commission. Finder's fee, ya know?" Lance's eyes gleamed with the prospects. Molly just bet he was envisioning the future of medicine, where the drugs were tested and the stocks sold from the same window. His.

She had to get out of here.

"Sasha?"

Sasha dropped the wipe cloth and turned for her office. "Come on."

Ripping open the last of the dose packs and tossing the antacid back like a shot of rye, Molly followed. "It's the last time," she swore. "I don't want to know anything else ever as long as I live."

Sasha shot her a glance. "Promise?"

Molly's hand went up in the air. "I don't care if drug lords are selling crack from the back of the city ambulance in the driveway. I do my eight and go home."

"Probably not a bad idea." Unlocking the door, Sasha reached behind her desk and lifted out the computer. "And just so you know," she said. "I sold my investment an hour ago."

Molly took the computer from her colleague, who was watching her with a calm, untroubled expression. It occurred to Molly, then, that she wouldn't ever have been able to tell if Sasha were telling her a lie.

Three hours later, Molly came to the realization that Sasha wasn't the only one out there who could tell a straight-faced lie. Molly had thought she had such great instincts. Such savvy, after twenty years working with and around people. The truth seemed to be that she didn't know shit.

Just as she'd hoped, the Argon file was pure gold. The proof was all there that Argon execs knew perfectly well that something was wrong with their drug, and that they planned to do nothing about it. Well, not exactly nothing. They had evidently worked very hard to misdirect the truth. And Peg Ryan, the bright, hungry young capitalist who would have been much happier in the eighties when the words *hostile takeover* had still carried some cachet, had been all too eager to help.

Molly sat down at her kitchen table with a cup of Sam's tea and read through each and every note that delineated the complicity of Peg's law firm—Frank's law firm—in the defrauding of Argon Pharmaceutical's clients. Most of the file read like a standard reflection of one person's work on a case. Communications, official correspondence, legal briefs. But salted away among perfectly obtuse legalese, Molly found the seeds of the truth.

And then, at the bottom of the file, the coup de grace. Peg had evidently copied what looked like ongoing E-mail communications between Argon and Marsdale, et al, real "60 Minutes" stuff that would have had Molly laughing if it weren't her own disaster she was watching unfold.

There were notes about damage control:

N.B. to Randy: Not distancing self enough from possible problems. Create intermediary positions to handle flak, so company's name and capital remain intact.

There were notes about acceptable risks: *in light of possible worldwide sale in billions, can easily assume cost of $10 to 20 million settlement. Remember to find ship's captain to go down with product just in case. Arnman appraised*

Arnman was the family name of the major stockholders in Argon Industries.

There were references to various players not only in the pharmaceutical company, but the law firm. References to earlier drug trials at major university hospitals that had produced questionable results, and questions about how to proceed with the next stage of trials so that the problems were not repeated. Bulletins from the company on how they planned to promote the drug, where their weak spots were in the corporate defense, and predictions of problems. Molly could have summed up the entire transaction in the one note:

Marsdale, et al: We know what the risks are at our end. We pay you to minimize any fallout from defective product. R. A.

And then, close to the end, the first hint of trouble from the Shitkicker's Club:

Check allegation by Ryan that suicide of three friends connected to product.

Only half a page later, the communications stopped with one final cryptic message: *Have received question regarding problems with him. Will have to*

No more.

Problems with whom? Molly wondered. In reference to what? And what was it they were planning on doing?

Molly scrutinized the entire file to make sure there wasn't a misplaced bit anywhere. She checked the Veldux files and the files in other cases that were contained on the disk, just in case the notes might have ended up somewhere else.

Nothing.

Molly leaned back in her chair, trying to decide how she felt.

Well, she had half an answer, anyway. Not exactly why Transcend was a problem, but at least the proof that the drug company knew. She had the link that finally connected all five lawyer suicides, and she had information on a deliberate conspiracy to endanger human lives for a profit.

Well, she thought dismally. There was certainly nothing new under the sun.

Molly sat there in her kitchen trying to figure out what to do next. Magnum was curled up at her feet and the wind was tuning up for a late evening storm. Without even realizing it, Molly reached over and poured herself another slug of vodka.

She should call Frank and demand to know what his connection was with Lance. She should get up and hide the disk somewhere no one would find it until she could get help from somebody.

Somebody who? Rhett was working homicide, and he was still busy with that little girl. The FBI was hip deep in surveillance equipment out behind city hall. The Medical Examiner's Office had already had its questions answered. Method of death, various. Manner, suicide. Cases closed, just as Winnie had asked.

Molly decided to put them all off. She wanted to read the rest of the disk. That meant Joey's file. With another dollop of vodka in her cup to assist her, she called up the file and walked in. And immediately wished she hadn't.

It was where Peg had hidden the real gold. The real tragedy. The real farce. Molly read over the notes Peg had hidden away for some reason and knew that the young lawyer had exacted her revenge after all. She read the last note, a special note about where the real proof was, where Peg had stashed one special piece of evidence that would cause the most damage, and she knew the case was made. Molly could go to anybody in the country with this and shut down

Argon Pharmeceutical tomorrow. The day after, she could shut down Marsdale, Beacon, Fletcher, and Richards, and the day after that deal a fairly mortal blow to Grace Hospital.

Molly looked at the last line of Peg Ryan's notes and wanted to cry. It was the name of the person Argon had picked to be their fall guy. She should have suspected. She should have at least wondered. But she hadn't. It had been easier that way. It had been safer.

It was the same reason, she thought, that she'd forgotten the most important part of her van ride. Not the two white guys, one large and one medium. Not the type or color of the vehicle. The smell.

Molly remembered it now. She remembered thinking about that smell as she'd lain in the back, bound and gagged. Thinking that it was familiar.

She could place it now. She could almost smell it. And once she remembered it, she realized who the third man had been. She knew how everything had been done to her and why. She knew, finally, what the stakes really were.

In the morning she'd probably tell somebody. Tonight, she didn't have the energy for it. So she drank instead. She closed up the computer, hid the evidence, and sat back down to drink some more. She drank until the bottle was gone, and then when she got up to find another one, stumbled against the table and upended her purse. For a minute she just stared at it as its contents skittered and rolled across the floor. She was going to have to clean it up. Later. Right now she had more important things to do.

Molly kicked everything to the side and bent back to the cabinet, which offered her a choice of four more full bottles. She chose vodka and proceeded to half finish that one, too, because what she'd found on that computer disk was the last thing she'd ever wanted to see.

She sat alone in her empty house and she drank.

They came for her an hour later.

✦ Chapter 20 ✦

BY THE TIME MAGNUM started growling, Molly was sitting on the floor in the family room staring at the Picasso. She should get up, she thought vaguely. Magnum was probably telling her he needed to go out.

Well, hell, she thought. Let yourself out, you silly mutt.

So, Pablo, she silently addressed the painting her parents had disliked so much. *You know a lot about fury and grief, huh? Wait till you see the painting I'm gonna do after all this is over.*

Magnum growled again, more urgently. Molly managed to turn her head in that direction, because suddenly she remembered that she'd forgotten to set the alarm again, and the press was still hunting for a quote. But she didn't see a reporter, and she didn't see Magnum. She saw two men standing in the doorway from the family room into the kitchen. One tall and big, the other medium and big. Wearing ski masks.

She laughed. "Oh, for God's sake. Get a real job."

"Get up," one said in a snarl.

Molly laughed even harder. "Honey, I'm as up as I'm gonna get."

Actually, she'd passed euphoria a long time ago and was swinging over the top of this particular Ferris wheel ride straight for depression. Like she needed any help.

She shouldn't do this, she thought, a lot too late. Not during summer. She never drank during the summer.

"I said get up."

Molly took another sip of her vodka and went back to considering the jagged edges of that screaming woman on the wall. "So," she said. "You from the hospital or from the pharmaceutical company?"

That seemed to stump her gentlemen callers. They didn't seem to want to come in, and they refused to go out. They just hulked in the doorway, cutting off the light from the kitchen.

"I'm real sorry you said that," the one said.

Molly nodded. "I know you are."

"It means you know everything."

"Oh, it does that."

"I'm not going to tell you again," the big one said. "Get up."

"And I'm not going to tell *you* again," she answered. "I can't. A quick look at the dead soldiers in the room will offer motive."

"We'll kill you right here if you don't get on your fuckin' feet!"

Molly did manage to swing her head around. "And ruin a perfectly good Picasso? How thoughtless. Tell him to come here."

Another pause in the conversation. Another silent communication between the two. It occurred to Molly that these guys reminded her a lot of the FBI guys, and that she'd never really seen them all in a room at the same time together. Wouldn't it be a kick if the FBI were involved? Heck, she'd have a contract with Oliver Stone for sure. Maybe even the "X-Files." The government so excited by a new drug that it sent in its agents to help keep the terrible truth from the hardy heroine. Considering the scope of what she'd learned today, it wouldn't have been that great a stretch to count them in.

God, she thought. She *was* drunk. If only she were enjoying herself.

"You know who it is?" the spokesman finally asked.

"I do."

"He only wants to talk to you."

Molly didn't even bother to justify that bit of trash with an answer. She just sat there.

Then Magnum started growling again.

"We're taking care of it," the one guy said over his shoulder.

"No you're not," the voice answered, obviously through the screen door to the backyard. "You were supposed to be in and out."

"Something you should know about much too well, Lance," Molly said.

There was a pause, and then a resounding, "Shit!"

Actually, she hadn't needed to hear his voice to recognize him. His scent had carried in on the wind. Eau de chicken soup. Quite an unforgettable smell in any circumstances. A surefire way to blow a stealthy approach.

"Come on in," Molly invited.

He must have taken her up on the offer, because suddenly there was a shuffling at the door and the scent wafted stronger. Lance was sweating. Molly knew that because Lance was always particularly pungent when he sweated. "Why didn't you pay attention to them the first time?" he demanded in a fury.

Molly noticed that his hair was wet and that one of his buttons had come loose. Not exactly the most terrifying image a hostage had ever beheld.

Molly ignored him, too.

"I don't think you understand, Molly," he insisted, stepping farther in, his voice a hiss of urgent conspiracy. "They want to kill you."

"I don't think *you* understand, Lance," Molly answered equably. "I don't care."

And that, finally, was the truth. After twenty years of struggling against the tide, she'd given up. 'Nam had won. Summer had won. All the sharp-eyed predators who had conspired to make her job so difficult and her life such a struggle, had won. She just didn't care anymore. She'd tried one too many times and had one too many lessons in how things were really run.

"I promise," he said. "You'll be safe if you just come along."

"And you'll respect me in the morning," she answered with a nod. "I know."

If she thought about it, this would be the easiest way. Kind of a reversal of the suicide-by-police scenario where people threatened a SWAT team just so they didn't have to pull the trigger themselves. All Molly had to do was piss these guys off enough and she wouldn't have to make another decision. She could just close her eyes and finally get a little rest.

There was just one more piece of unfinished business to take care of.

"I live here alone," she said. "I figure you parked out on Euclid so nobody knows you're here, so we have lots of time. You call him up and tell him that if he wants the disk back, he's going to have to come here and get it."

The big guy walked on in and stood right over her. "All we have to do is trash your house," he warned her, tapping a big black automatic against his leg, as if that were going to swing the vote.

Molly waved away. "Be my guest. It isn't here."

"Where is it?" Lance demanded again.

Molly lifted a wobbly finger. "Ah, the question of the hour. When he comes, I'll tell him."

The big guy squatted down, settled the barrel of the gun right between Molly's eyes. "You'll tell me."

Molly wondered why she wasn't sweating herself. She should have been puking scared. "No, I won't. I'll tell him."

And then she pushed the gun aside, which seemed to make her captor even more unhappy.

Lance stepped in. "Just tell me why."

Molly was stunned to feel tears in her eyes. "Because I want him to face me and tell me what the hell was so important about this."

This time, it was Lance who laughed. "Yeah, that's easy for you to say. You're sitting in a house worth fuckin' millions. What the hell do you know?"

"Good point." What did she know? She sure didn't know how to read people or listen to grapevines. When she interviewed for her next job, Molly was going to pass out a questionnaire for all prospective coemployees to fill out, just so she could avoid this kind of embarrassment again.

Uh-huh.

"Tell you what," Lance offered. "You tell us where the disk is and he can bring it with him when he comes."

"I don't think so."

"We're going to ruin your house looking for it."

"Just do it quietly or you'll get caught. A lot of nosy neighbors around here."

Lance stood there a minute, pouting much like he did when he had a patient with abdominal pain to work up.

"Watch her," he snapped. Then he spun on his heel and headed out of the room. Molly went back to her vodka, and the shorter guy perched on the arm of a chair. The other one contented himself with just standing right over her so she could see his gun real close up.

"Ain't that a Picasso?" the medium one asked.

"Like it?" Molly asked, feeling more and more distanced from what was going on. "It's yours. After I'm gone, of course."

The guy was shaking his head as if he hadn't heard her. "He was one crazy son of a bitch."

It must have been the vodka. There couldn't have been another reason Molly was laughing.

"He's coming," Lance announced, walking back in the room.

The big guy grunted in disgust. "There are more fun ways of doing this."

He reached over to stroke Molly's throat with the barrel of the gun, which Molly took to mean he was anticipating every one. Still, Molly felt no terror at all. Nothing more than weariness.

For a few minutes the four of them just sat in a stony silence, the only sounds coming from the trees in the backyard and evening traffic out on Euclid. Molly decided she wanted some answers. Especially from this quasi terrorist who had never had the motivation to go as far as the driveway to see a patient. Molly just couldn't get over the idea of his being part of an elaborate cover-up.

"Did he come to you or the other way around, Lance?"

Leaning his hip against the door, Lance peered at her, as if looking for the hidden meaning. "It was kind of a mutual understanding."

"Which means he told you what to do and you did it."

"I organized it."

"What, the entire smoke screen, or just my merry part in it?"

"You. Once we found out that you were nosing around. You're like a pit bull, ya know it? Once you've got a piece of pants leg, you just don't let go."

"I'll take that as a compliment. So you were in charge of scaring me away. Where'd you find these two?" she asked. "Central casting?"

"You don't need to know."

Molly nodded and poured again. Everything seemed to make more sense that way. Too bad her hand was shaking so badly. The vodka sloshed over onto the parquet flooring. "You know you're being set up, don't you?"

God, she thought. That was straight out of an Alan Ladd movie. Next, Barbara Stanwyck would pull a gat from her garter belt or something.

"Don't be ridiculous," Lance said. "I'm about to make a fuckin' fortune on this stock. You could have too, ya know. I could have worked it. I can still work it."

"A generous offer, Lance, but I doubt I'm supposed to make it through the evening, which doesn't give me much time to realize substantial fiscal gain. Before I go, though, let me clarify a thing or two for you. Argon was looking for a fall guy, in case things got hot. Somebody to go down with the proverbial ship and leave Argon virtually unscathed. You guys are the candidates."

"How do you do that?" the littler henchman spoke up again. "You got two bottles of Stoli in you and you sound like a fuckin' English teacher."

"I talk much better when I'm drunk," Molly assured him. "I talk the best right before I pass out."

"Don't be melodramatic," Lance said. "Argon isn't setting anybody up, and nobody's gonna hurt you."

Molly smiled at him. "Of course not. Argon is perfectly happy to have me running around publicizing their little peccadillo with the hottest drug since aspirin. I talk and half the city's economy goes bust."

"Then don't talk."

"Gosh," she said, closing her eyes. "Why didn't I think of that?"

Magnum barked, and all heads turned toward the door.

"He's here already," Lance said, coming to attention. Both gunmen got to their feet.

"Molly?"

It took Molly a full five seconds to register the voice. "Oh, my God." She groaned, twitching to sudden life. "Sam."

"He's not here already," the big guy corrected his weapon. Molly was already trying to pull herself to her feet.

"Do something!" Lance insisted in a hiss.

Molly stumbled toward the kitchen. "Coming, Sam!"

She damn near threw up on the spot. Her heart had just jump-started, and her hands were sweaty. She couldn't let Sam be exposed to this. "Stay right here," she told the gunmen. "I'll get him to leave."

The big guy, the one with the terrifying voice, leveled his gun. "Do that."

"You okay?" Sam asked through the screen door when he saw her. "After today, I thought I should ask."

Molly smiled blearily at him, hoping like hell he didn't hear her heart thumping because there were men around the corner ready to hurt him if she didn't do this correctly. Her dying tonight wasn't a problem anymore. Sam was another story entirely.

"I'm drunk, Sam." She smiled again. "It seemed like the thing to do."

Sam peered at her as if she were trying to change color on him. "You want a little company?"

"I'm no company at all, Sam. Thanks, but I'm just going to stare at the TV a while and hit the sack. I'll be by in the morning for tea and bagels. Okay?"

"Did you—"

She waved him off. "Tell you tomorrow. Right now, I think I'm going to be sick."

That tended to send any sane person in the other direction. Sam hovered a minute or two longer, then trudged the other way. Molly fought an urge to call him back. To apologize to him. To thank him for everything he'd been to her.

That was when she knew that this time, she probably meant it. This time, she just didn't see a way over the hill.

So instead of walking over to pet Magnum where he was curled up by the dryer in the laundry room, she simply headed into the family room and sat back down on the floor.

"Were you serious about that sick part?" Lance asked.

Molly didn't bother to look over at him. "Dead serious. Pardon the pun. How long are we waiting?"

"Not long."

"God preserve me from amateurs."

"He'll be here soon and this will all be over."

Molly almost laughed all over again. "Just tell me one thing, Lance. What the hell is it that sets Transcend off?"

"Sets it off?"

"Oh, that's right. You probably haven't read the real transcripts. It mimics a massive manic-depressive episode, at the end of which the user seems to slam into the ground like a crashing jet. It also seems to be addictive as hell. For some people. You don't know what it reacts to?"

"Hell, no. What do I care? The final study looks

great, and the FDA is gearing up to approve, which means Grace is going to be launched into the major leagues of national drug trials. And I'm poised to get the inside scoop on all of it."

"Yeah, life couldn't be much sweeter."

Molly was just thinking that she wasn't going to last much longer when Magnum went back on alert. He was growling again, and this time he sounded oddly adult and menacing. Appropriate. Maybe she should have gotten him a long time ago. He seemed to know who the real bad guys were.

Molly closed her eyes. She heard the shuffle of footsteps at the back door; she heard Lance get up to answer it. She smelled pipe smoke and realized that the person she'd trusted most in her life had just come to kill her.

Molly actually made it back to her feet. She'd be damned if she'd face him at a disadvantage.

"I'm here," he said, his voice still so gentle and tired. "What do you want from me, Molly?"

Molly faced him then. "I want you to tell me why, Gene."

Criminals should look evil. They should look aggressive, have lantern jaws and small eyes, and smell like day-old fish. Gene Stavrakos looked like a teddy bear who'd been left out in the rain.

He stood there in her family room as if he were in church looking for answers. Huddled, rumpled, small. Molly wanted to hit him. She wanted to pummel that sweet, kind face until she didn't recognize it anymore, because he'd held her secrets in the palms of his hands so carefully for so long, and now he'd just shattered them on the floor.

"You don't understand," he said.

"Obviously not."

He took in a breath, looked away, seemed to snag

his attention on the woman on the wall. "I'm tired, Molly. I've been fighting my way upstream for over twenty years hoping it would get better. It never gets better. Budgets get cut, and managed care doesn't recognize psychiatric conditions. The newest generations of drugs are taking the patients away at the internist level, and the government is throwing chronic patients out on the street. I can't practice my craft."

"So you sell it out?"

"So I find a way to get major grant money for the hospital, a retirement account for me, and some recognition as a researcher."

Molly nodded. "I know. I saw the letter. When were you going to tell Bart Banerjee that you were going to steal his research?"

"Not steal it," he insisted in tones of perfect rationalization. "I'm going to be the medical spokesman for the product. I have a higher profile name than Bart, which Argon needed. I research for them after this, and Bart gets the empty chair at the college." Gene, so healthy-looking only a few days ago, was blanched the color of paper. "I don't have a choice anymore, Molly."

Molly nodded. She walked out of the family room without a word, all four men following behind her, and she headed for the Tang Dynasty vase in the front hallway. It was there, at the bottom of the vase, that she'd hidden the disk. She said nothing more, just handed it over to Gene.

Reaching into his pocket, Gene produced a magnet. A couple of passes over the disk, and whatever had been stored there was history.

"What was it?" Molly asked, watching passively. "It never says here. What is the trigger that sets off Transcend?"

Gene actually smiled. "Testosterone."

Molly gaped. "You're kidding."

"Do you know what they called the lunch group before it became the Shitkicker's Club?"

It all became so absurdly clear. "The Testosterone Club, because trial lawyers have an excessive amount in their systems."

Gene nodded. "If it had just been that, we would never have had a problem. We could have restricted it. After all, in the drug trials, Transcend did perform spectacularly. But it seems that one of the reasons people become more decisive and aggressive on Transcend is that it somehow increases testosterone levels. So it starts working really well, and then after an extended period . . ."

"Whammo."

"Whammo."

Molly shook her head. "No wonder Argon is terrified."

She just got that same, sweet, tired smile.

"Who else?" she asked. "Who else is involved from the hospital?"

"Oh, nobody. Not deliberately. Not more than they would be for any other drug trial."

"What about Tim McGuire?"

"The alderman?" he asked. "Well, that's a funny thing. He came to the people at Argon and helped convince them to make use of Pearl's indiscretion to keep the attention away from the drug. He knew about it from Mary Margaret Ryan."

"Peg," Molly said automatically. "Her name was Peg."

Peg, who had called Tim McGuire ineffectual. So ineffectual that he'd taken full advantage of an opportunity like Pearl's death to put a power squeeze on the enemy whose job he wanted, all the while putting several major local powers in his pocket.

Molly couldn't handle any more. She had the most horrible feeling that if she asked many more questions, she'd find out that it had been Sam who'd sneaked around emptying out all those computers.

Molly was sure there was something else she needed to know. More of the conspiracy theory to unravel. She'd lost her impetus, though. She knew that the time for polite conversation was just about over. Especially when Gene reached into his pocket and pulled out six bottles of pills.

"There should be plenty here," he said, handing them to the one masked man.

"No," Molly said, stepping up to him. "You do it."

Gene started away from her as if she'd asked him to rape her. "What?"

"You want me dead, you face me. You do it. Don't give it to somebody else so that later you can say that you didn't really know what was going on. I *want* you to know."

"No, Molly. I won't do that."

"Then you're not just a thief, Gene. You're a coward."

"Yes, Molly. I'm a coward."

Gene turned away, and out of nowhere, Molly came to terrible life. The old 'Nam rage swamped her, and she launched herself at him. Nails and teeth and shrieks.

"I trusted you, you son of a bitch!" she yelled, pushing him back toward the kitchen.

Gene never lifted a hand to defend himself. The big guy yanked Molly off him like a jacket.

"I'm sorry," Gene said, and the awful thing was, Molly believed he meant it.

She made another try for him. Gene sidestepped her like a boxer and let the big guy take care of business. The big guy punched Molly in the face.

Molly went down like a rock. Somewhere through

the fog of alcohol, she knew she was going to hurt like hell in a minute. She was going to puke all over her kitchen floor, which she thought might be under her left cheek. She was still trying to watch Gene, who had deliberately turned away from her to walk out the back door.

"This is what medicine is about?" she demanded, trying so hard to see. Her head was reeling and her heart thundered with scalding fury. Gene was leaving her with a guy who didn't just like to kill women, he liked to hurt women. "Gene!"

"You're gonna make this hard, aren't you?" the big gunman said over her head.

Molly tasted blood in her mouth and spat it at him. "You bet your ass I am."

Not because she thought it would change the outcome. Not that she cared anymore whether it did. But she couldn't abide the idea of simply letting Gene give her to somebody else so she could be quietly disposed of. She was going to have to leave her mark any way she could. She was going to try like hell to pay Gene back for doing this.

The gunman pulled her up by her hair. "Good," he whispered in her ear. "I like it that way."

Magnum never barked. The first time Molly knew she had another visitor in this endless night of surprises was the sound of a laconic voice and the smell of Lagerfeld cologne.

"Oh, shit, Saint Molly. You know this kind of thing is against my religion."

Molly bucked against the big guy. "Get the hell out of here, Frank!"

She saw him then. Standing there, just inside the back door in jeans and T-shirt and tennis shoes. Grinning over at Gene as if the two of them shared a great private joke. "She's wild about me."

And then, he simply swung.

Gene went down even harder than Molly had. Lance screamed like a pig and the guy who held Molly raised the hand with the gun in it.

"Frank!" Molly yelled, literally lifting herself off the ground and slamming into her assailant. "Duck!"

Molly connected. Frank ducked. The shot went wide. The one from the other gunman, though, didn't.

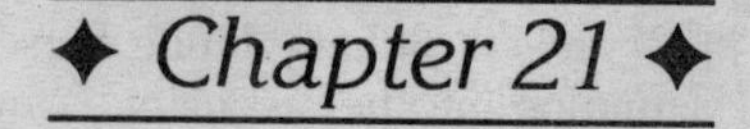

Chapter 21

MOLLY SAW THE BULLET hit Frank high in the chest. He grunted and slammed back against the cabinets. Molly heard a terrible howling sound and realized it was coming from her own throat. They'd killed him. They'd killed Frank, when he'd just come to try and proposition her. When he'd seen what was going on and stayed to help.

They killed him, and that changed everything.

Molly forgot her assailant had a gun. She just remembered that he had eyes and testicles and tender knees. She punched and jabbed and slammed as hard as she could. She heard his surprised oaths as she connected, and heard the scuffling on the floor beyond. She heard his partner yelling for him to move so he could get a clear shot.

Molly knew she was going to lose. The guy was just too big for her. When he got over the surprise, he was going to pummel her to death. It didn't matter.

"Move, J.T., move!" that high voice shrilled.

Lance was slamming out the screen door like his hair was on fire. Gene staggered to his feet and looked down at Frank. Somehow Molly could see them, even as she focused on those cold eyes beneath that knit cap. Even as she bit and kicked and scratched to get that mask off and the stupid charade over with.

"This is against my better judgment," she heard on a rasp.

Frank's rasp.

Frank wasn't dead.

Gene was trying to follow Lance out the door. If he did, there would be no way Frank would survive. No way Gene would allow it, especially since he wouldn't be there to see it happen.

"Gene, he's hurt!" Molly screamed. "Help him!"

The minute she lost her focus, her assailant brought the gun down against the side of her head.

Molly toppled sideways into the kitchen table, sending the whole thing clattering to the floor. She landed and heard the big guy gasping and cursing as he followed.

"It's not your shot," he was saying to his partner. "It's mine."

Molly couldn't move. She couldn't breathe or see. She knew that fifteen minutes ago, she'd been waiting for this moment to happen. That she should just shut her eyes and look forward to oblivion.

She couldn't let Frank get himself killed.

She heard her assailant coming and rolled into him.

A bullet crashed into the cabinets inches from her head. She heard a guttural curse and felt the guy struggle for balance, like a sawed tree about to go. Molly reached straight up for a handful of testicle and yanked with everything she had. She heard not just one scream, but two.

"My eyes, my eyes, what did you do?"

It was the little guy. Shrieking like he was on fire and hopping around. Molly didn't pay attention. She was trying to scrabble away from the big guy with the gun, and kept slipping over the stuff she'd lost from her purse. Combs, brushes, checkbooks, pens. Comb, brush, checkbook, pen, stun gun.

Stun gun.

Jesus, she thought, twisting around for it even as the big guy finally made up his mind and went after her again. Wrapping her hand around the gun and flipping off the safety, Molly did her best to roll free.

He anticipated her this time. He got her by the hair and pulled. It was Molly's turn to shriek. She came completely off the ground when he pulled. She found herself damn near eye to eye with him for the briefest of seconds, and saw that she'd finally succeeded. The mask was off. The man who was trying to kill her had a face damn near as ugly as Magnum's. But she didn't know him. Oddly enough, it relieved her.

He was raising his other hand, the one with the gun in it. He was going to hit her harder this time, and she wasn't going to get another chance. When his hand came up, she wedged hers straight up the center of his chest. Jammed it against his neck. Hit the trigger.

The stun gun buzzed like a mechanical wasp in full rage. Molly's assailant jumped as if he'd been hit with a defibrillator. Stiffened. His eyes rolled, and he went down like a sequoia. Pulling herself free just in time, Molly grabbed the edge of the counter to keep herself upright. Then she bent to retrieve the gun.

The other gunman was hopping around over by the family room, trying to keep hold of his gun as he clutched at his eyes and shrilled. When Molly looked to see why, she saw that Frank, instead of being dead, was slumped against the cabinets, her can of pepper spray in his hand, his chest glistening and dark with blood. Gene had disappeared.

"Goddamn it, Frank," she muttered, suddenly

shaking and terrified as she stumbled over to yank the gun away from the second attacker. "What was that all about?"

"You really do bring out the worst in me, Saint Molly," Frank challenged with a wry grin, even though that grin was playing across an ashen mouth. He was pale and sweaty and bleeding. "Do you realize I made it all the way through 'Nam without so much as a rug burn? A couple of weeks with you, and I'm lying in a pool of my own blood. I don't think I want to make a habit of this."

"Me, either," she admitted, tossing guns in her top cabinet and then reaching for a kitchen towel. When she bent to shove it hard against the bright red stain on Frank's chest, he winced dramatically.

"I do appreciate your providing the defense equipment," he admitted on a gasp. "I fell right on the damn thing."

"The pepper spray?" she asked, grabbing the phone. "I'm glad it works. I've never used it before."

"You couldn't have a gun, like other macho heroines?"

Molly couldn't help it. She grinned at him, even as she was busy dialing 911 and applying pressure to his chest and trying to breathe past a panic that had never in her career plagued her at the sight of blood. "See what trouble a gun can get you in? Stun guns are much more civilized."

He was fading. Molly could see it in his eyes, hear it in the funny grunting little breaths he was beginning to take.

"This is nine-one-one," the pleasant, efficient voice answered. "What is your emergency?"

"Send the police and paramedics to my house," Molly instructed, then gave the address. "I've had an armed break-in. The gunman shot a man in the chest.

Tell the paramedics it's a code three. I also have two suspects here. I'm not sure how long I can control them."

"Will you stay on the line, ma'am?"

"Sure," she said, then dropped the phone. Alongside her, the big guy began to stir. Molly picked up her stun gun and hit him again. The little guy saw that and simply sat down on the floor in the family room.

"Enjoy the Picasso," Molly suggested, her focus completely on Frank.

"Yes, ma'am."

"They got . . . the disk," Frank said, looking vague. "I saw it . . . sorry."

"No, they didn't," Molly allowed in her best unconcerned voice even as she prayed for Frank to just shut up and hold on. "I downloaded the whole thing into the hospital mainframe before I left work today. Then I left a note on Sasha's computer about where to find it if she had to."

Frank's eyes betrayed his surprise as they tracked her way.

Molly saw the trouble he had focusing and pressed harder. "I figured it would be safe as long as I wanted it to be. I labeled it Kosher Menus for Passover. Besides," she said offhandedly, "Peg left a paper trail, just in case. I know where it is."

Frank tried to laugh and didn't quite make it. "I'm gonna . . . have to rethink . . . my . . . opinions of you, Saint . . . Molly."

"Try Miss Molly," she suggested, trying her best to get him comfortable. "As in, good golly."

His nod was damn near imperceptible. "Good golly . . . it is."

And then she lost him.

• • •

What a novel idea, Molly thought as she surveyed the pandemonium in her backyard. A Labor Day picnic. Well, not exactly Labor Day. That had been eight days ago. But nobody from a hospital trauma center could hope to get off on the last summer holiday of the season, so the First Official End of Summer Brain-Fry and Hooha had been scheduled for the second Wednesday following Labor Day, kind of like Easter following the equinox. The Grace rite of passage celebrating the fact that summer can only last so long.

So far it looked to be the beginning of a decent tradition. The yard was packed with people of all ages, with most of the men clustered around the barbecue grill Molly had borrowed from Sam, and most of the women examining Molly's garden. Reggae pulsed from James's boom box, and Magnum barked like a dog in heaven as he chased all the kids around.

The kids were secretly Molly's favorite part. They filled her yard with dissonant music and bright colors and sly eyes, threatening her fish and trampling her summer flower beds in an effort to keep the ball away from her dog, who was growing at a frightening rate. Irish setter, the vet had pronounced upon seeing him. Also bull terrier, husky, and not a little mastiff. A big, ugly puppy that would grow into a bigger, uglier dog. Still, a dog that barked when Molly needed and played all other times. A dog who had spent his puppyhood waiting for kids to torment.

"They're beautiful, my Sara and Josh, *nu*?" Sam demanded from the lawn chair next to Molly's.

Molly lifted a beer for a sip. "And smart, too, Sam."

Sam nodded. "Sara is the mirror of my Myra."

"How is she?"

"She sends her best. We got her a brand-new television, you know."

Molly knew. In the end, Sam had been wilier than any of them. He'd sold his stock in Argon, just as he'd said. Then he'd sold short and made a brand new fortune when the stock plummeted a week later.

"You give her a kiss for me when you see her, Sam."

At the far corner of the yard, Kevin and his son were pitching horseshoes with Lorenzo and Rhett. Winnie was arguing politics with one of the trauma surgeons, and Sam's daughter was instructing Betty Wheaton in the proper way to fly fish. A good gathering indeed. Something Molly had waited far too long to do. Something she should have thought of years ago to defray the stresses of summer. A person could get through almost anything if it meant a celebration at the end.

It wasn't all happy. Not everybody had come out unscathed. Not everybody had come out alive. But Molly had, and decided, sitting here on a day when the humidity had broken and the sky was the clean, crisp blue of early autumn, that she was glad.

"So, have the prosecutors decided how they're handling it yet?" Sasha asked, standing just to the side with her own beer in hand.

"They're still splitting everything up among agencies."

"I imagine the piece on '60 Minutes' helped get things jump-started."

Molly grinned and sipped. "I nominated Winnie for the outraged physician performance of the year."

Sasha snorted. "She was only outraged because she didn't figure out what was going on first."

Molly considered her boss. "She had other things on her plate."

In the end, the truth about Pearl's note had stayed with Kevin and Molly. Molly saw no reason to crucify a brilliant and desperately needed medical examiner for one moment of weakness. After all, Molly knew perfectly well how that felt.

"My favorite part was when they ambushed Tim McGuire in the city hall parking lot with the proof that he'd walked off with that file."

"Just a man taking advantage of a breaking situation," Molly admitted. "He figured he'd not only protect his Argon stock but his rise in politics, too. After all, he was the one who ratted on the mayor in the first place."

"Well," Molly mused evenly. "What can you expect? He is a lawyer."

"A little more respect for the profession that saved your life," came the voice of contradiction.

Molly peered over the tops of her sunglasses at him. "Excuse me?" she retorted. "Who saved whom?"

Frank grinned for her, and Molly found herself grinning back. "I've dedicated the rest of my life to serving her," he told Sasha with that sly light that even got a smile out of Sasha.

"You're going to get her judgment overturned on the malpractice thing?" Sasha asked, still not believing it.

"Not me," he protested, hand to still healing chest. "It would ruin my reputation. I did, however, furnish a few motions a competent lawyer would have made on her behalf. A piece of evidence or two he should have gotten introduced in court."

Sasha gave Molly a grudging nod. "He doesn't seem so bad."

It was Molly's turn to snort. "He's just paying me back for ruining my kitchen floor and making me stick my hand into his chest."

"She did the CPR," Sam offered. "I saw it myself."

Frank leaned a little closer so that Molly could smell that damn Lagerfeld again. His eyes were sparkling with invitation, and there was just no question about what it was he was proposing. "I might have been dead, but I wasn't oblivious," he told Sasha with salacious relish. "She gave me the kiss of life. You just don't get over a thing like that."

Sasha hooted in disgust. "You kissed a *lawyer?"* she protested.

Molly stretched out in her chair and sipped her beer. "I wore protection."

Frank eased himself down onto the last empty lawn chair with a grimace. "Ungrateful wretch."

He'd just made it into a comfortable position when Abigail showed up and climbed into his lap. Settling her plump hand against her father's cheek, the little girl smiled silently up at Molly. It had been Molly who had held her while her daddy had been sick. Molly had held all three kids, crying with them, letting them yell. She'd even given them her mother's cookbooks the night after Frank had gone into cardiac arrest for the second time. Poor Magnum had gotten to the point where he saw those things and ran.

"Are you sure you didn't invest with Lance?" Molly asked Frank one last time.

Frank sighed. Ab carefully rested her head against her daddy's chest so he could rearrange her slipping hair ribbons. "I'm not going to tell you again, Miss Molly. Your doctor is a not very bright coconspirator who decided that that tale of woe would tarnish your good faith in the only real white knight in this whole scenario."

"Shows you how stupid he was," Sasha offered dryly. "He figured he had to tarnish the reputation of a lawyer."

"I'm not going to take much more of this lawyer stuff," Frank protested.

"Of course you will," Sam said. "As long as you think it will get you somewhere. *Nu?*"

And so, life went on. The two gunmen were in jail. Lance was out on bond, the drug company was preparing its defense, and Transcend was in the process of being reevaluated. Joey was back in his cave, and Frank was back in his practice, although he wasn't with Marsdale anymore. He was going to set up by himself so he could make all his own decisions about whom to protect and whom not to. Molly was due back on duty next evening in the ER, and the night after that in the ME's office.

There had been one more suicide that summer. Gene had been found in his garage with the car running. Molly hurt hard when she thought about it. All that promise, all that dedication, gone to waste. That special, sweet gift buried beneath an avalanche of disinterest and manipulation. Gene had saved her life too many times to count. Molly wished she could have returned the favor. She knew, though, that he'd made that decision a long time before the night he'd closed the door and turned on the engine.

Her friends were safe, though. She had children in her yard and people she thought maybe she could call if she had problems. It didn't, finally, get much better than this.

"Young man!"

"You're kidding!"

All the heads lifted from the chair backs to see what the commotion was about. Molly saw Winnie glaring, hands on hips, at her son, who was grinning like a Cheshire Cat. Alongside, Vic was holding something in his hands and swearing.

"What's the matter?" Kevin demanded.

"He figured it out!" Vic said, sounding highly insulted.

"What?"

"The question mark. He figured out the question mark!"

Everybody moved. When they reached the little group by the back fence, it was to find Vic staring at the deflated balloon in his hand as if it had personally bitten him.

"Well?" Molly asked.

He looked up, truly hurt. "Watch."

Evidently Winnie's son had already drawn the question mark on the side of the balloon, one of those long, skinny kinds clowns made dogs out of. Vic put the balloon to his mouth and began to blow. The balloon began to expand. The question mark changed configuration, and suddenly everyone began to laugh.

"Well, doesn't that about say it all?" somebody demanded.

Molly couldn't have put it better. When the balloon was blown up, the question mark turned into an exclamation point.

HarperPaperbacks *By Mail*

READ THE BESTSELLERS THAT EVERYONE'S RAVING ABOUT!

HEAT

by Stuart Woods

Jesse Warden has been unjustly convicted and imprisoned for a crime he didn't commit. To gain his freedom, Jesse makes a deal with the government to infiltrate a dangerous and reclusive religious cult, but in the process feels control of his own life slipping away.

DOWNTOWN

by Anne Rivers Siddons

A tender, joyous, and powerful story of the end of innocence at a time when traditional values are in question and the air is full of possibility.

EVERYTHING TO GAIN

by Barbara Taylor Bradford

Life seems almost perfect until an exceptionally cruel act of random violence tears apart the fabric of one woman's happiness. This is about a remarkable woman who, by virtue of her own strength and courage, has everything to gain.

TWELVE RED HERRINGS

by Jeffrey Archer

An inventive new collection of a dozen short stories—each with a twist. Cleverly styled, with richly drawn characters and ingeniously plotted story lines, each of the twelve pieces ends with a delightfully unexpected turn of events.

SACRED CLOWNS

by Tony Hillerman

Officer Chee attempts to solve two modern murders by deciphering the sacred clowns' ancient message to the people of Tano pueblo in this *New York Times* bestseller.